ACT ONE

Written by Aleš Kot
Drawn by Danijel Žeželj
Colored by Jordie Bellaire
Lettered by Aditya Bidikar
Design by Tom Muller
Production by Ryan Brewer

CHAPTER ONE:

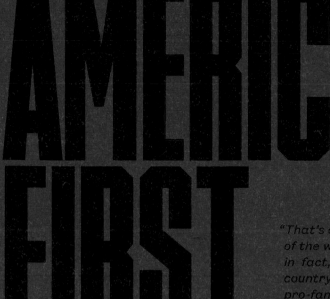

AMERICA FIRST

"That's one of the unintended consequences of the women's liberation movement – that, in fact, the women that would lead this country would be feminine, they would be pro-family, they would have husbands, they would love their children. They wouldn't be a bunch of dykes."
—**Steve Bannon**

The community is sick
(Please believe)
And the community is blind
(In labor and hope)
Yell
(And joy)

And it's colder than Poland
('Cause like a little boy)
And the sun is not shining
(I have destroyed)
Here
(Hope and joy)

And we're tangled in the shit
(And lately I dream about)
Of each other's ruined
(Angels with molotovs)
Affairs

"Could've Moved Mountains"
—**A Silver Mt. Zion**

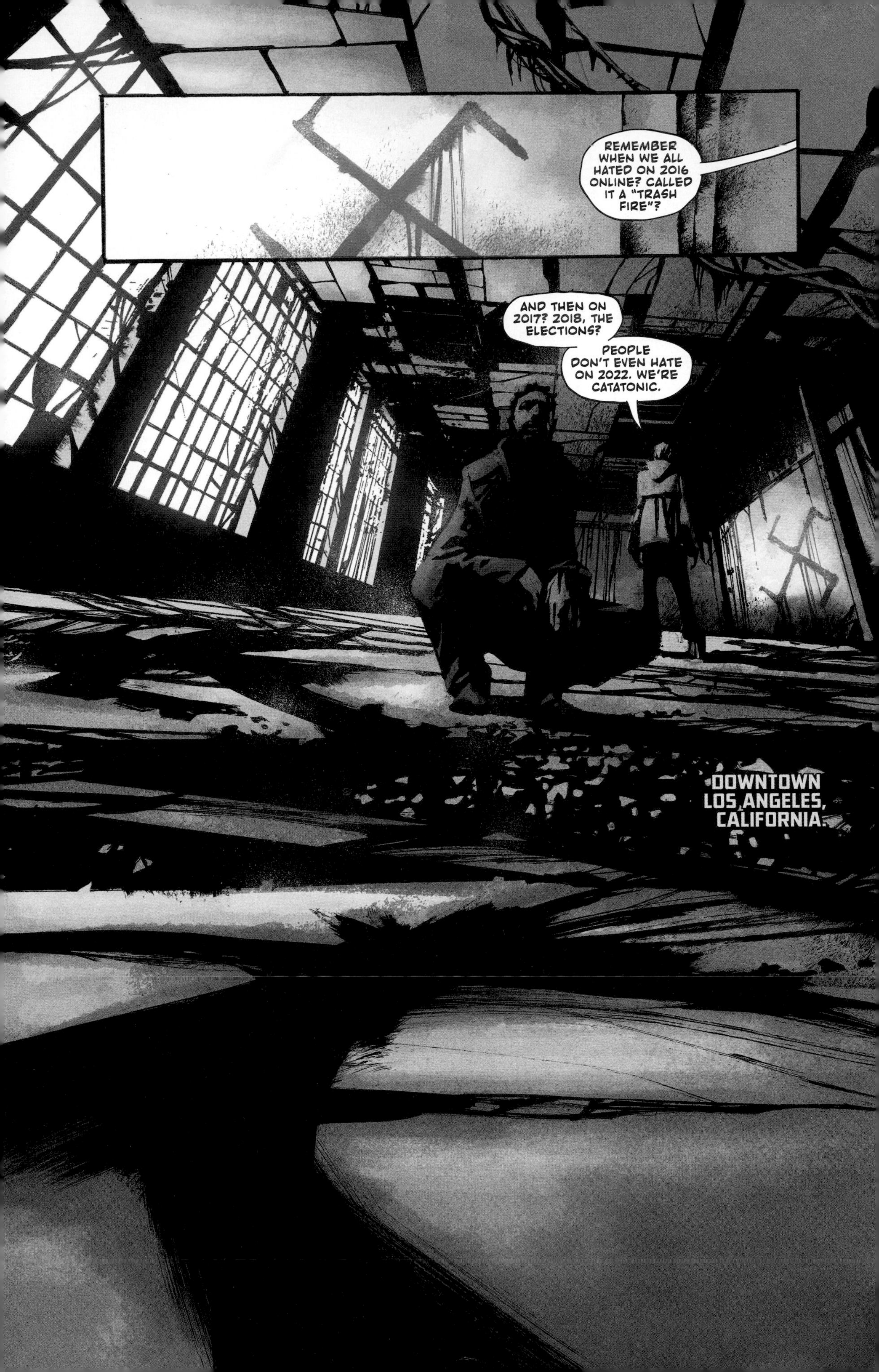
REMEMBER WHEN WE ALL HATED ON 2016 ONLINE? CALLED IT A "TRASH FIRE"?
AND THEN ON 2017? 2018, THE ELECTIONS?
PEOPLE DON'T EVEN HATE ON 2022. WE'RE CATATONIC.
DOWNTOWN LOS ANGELES, CALIFORNIA.

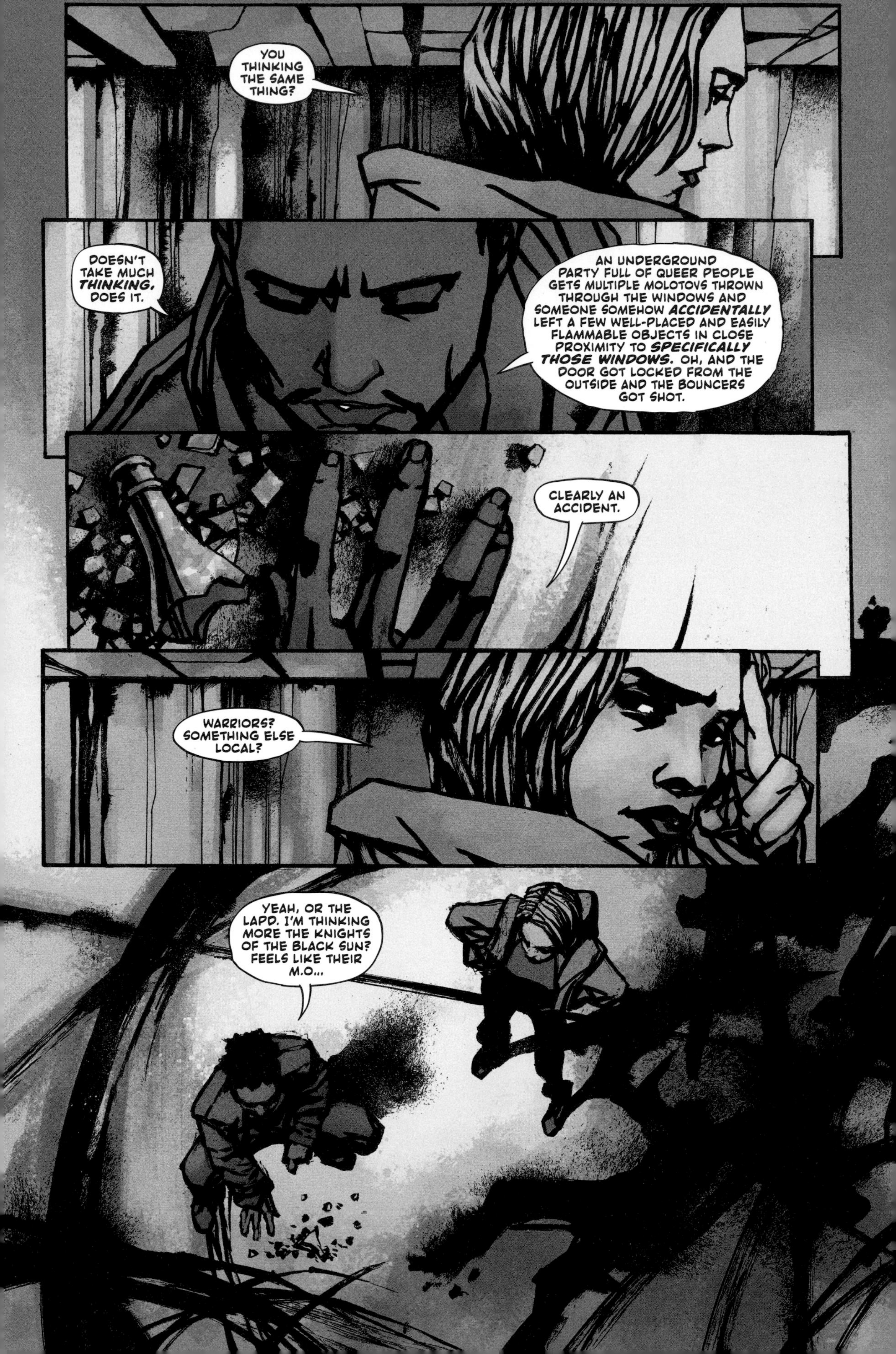
YOU THINKING THE SAME THING?
DOESN'T TAKE MUCH *THINKING*, DOES IT.
AN UNDERGROUND PARTY FULL OF QUEER PEOPLE GETS MULTIPLE MOLOTOVS THROWN THROUGH THE WINDOWS AND SOMEONE SOMEHOW *ACCIDENTALLY* LEFT A FEW WELL-PLACED AND EASILY FLAMMABLE OBJECTS IN CLOSE PROXIMITY TO *SPECIFICALLY THOSE WINDOWS.* OH, AND THE DOOR GOT LOCKED FROM THE OUTSIDE AND THE BOUNCERS GOT SHOT.
CLEARLY AN ACCIDENT.
WARRIORS? SOMETHING ELSE LOCAL?
YEAH, OR THE LAPD. I'M THINKING MORE THE KNIGHTS OF THE BLACK SUN? FEELS LIKE THEIR M.O...

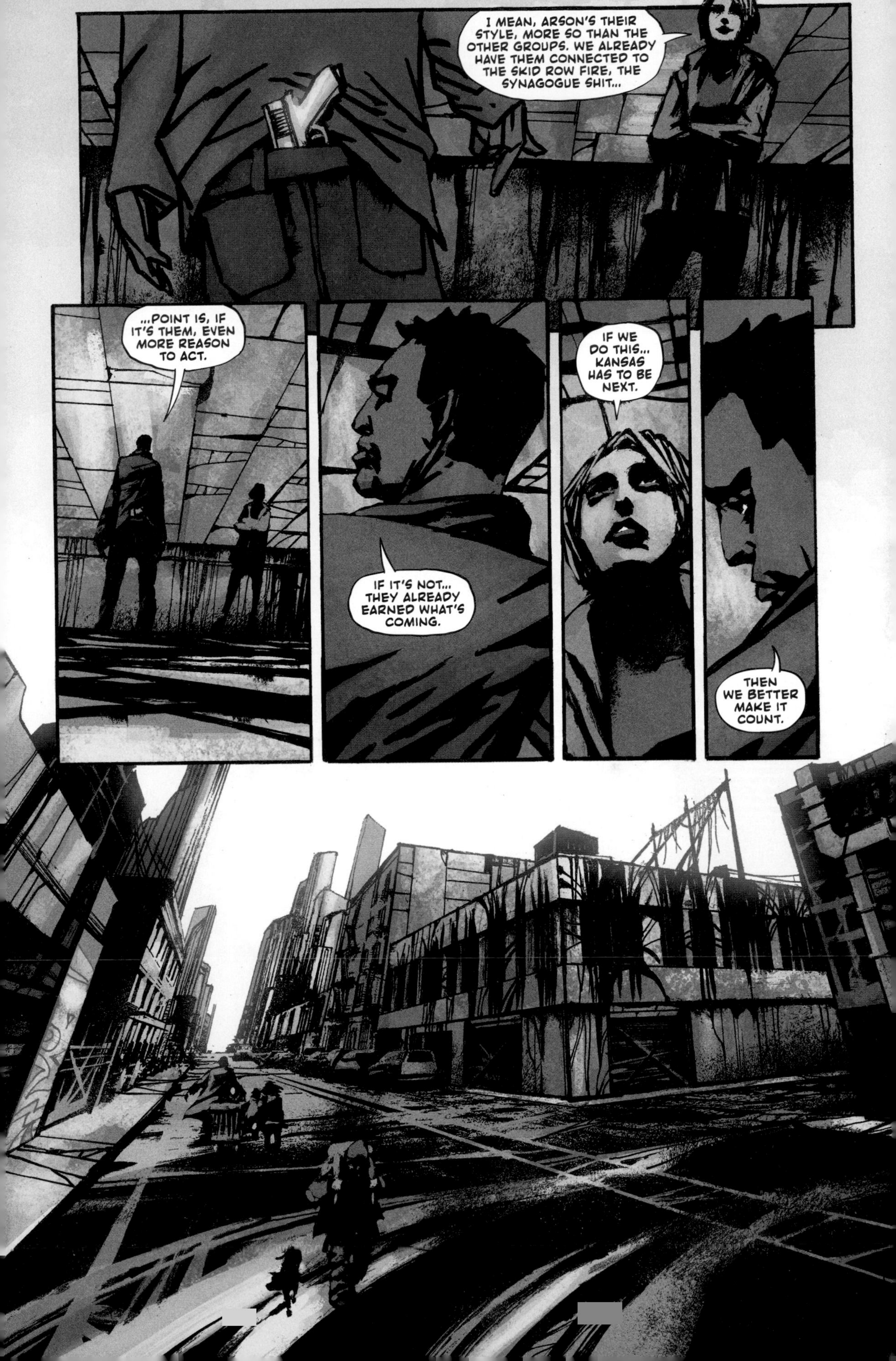
I MEAN, ARSON'S THEIR STYLE, MORE SO THAN THE OTHER GROUPS. WE ALREADY HAVE THEM CONNECTED TO THE SKID ROW FIRE, THE SYNAGOGUE SHIT...
...POINT IS, IF IT'S THEM, EVEN MORE REASON TO ACT.
IF IT'S NOT... THEY ALREADY EARNED WHAT'S COMING.
IF WE DO THIS... KANSAS HAS TO BE NEXT.
THEN WE BETTER MAKE IT COUNT.

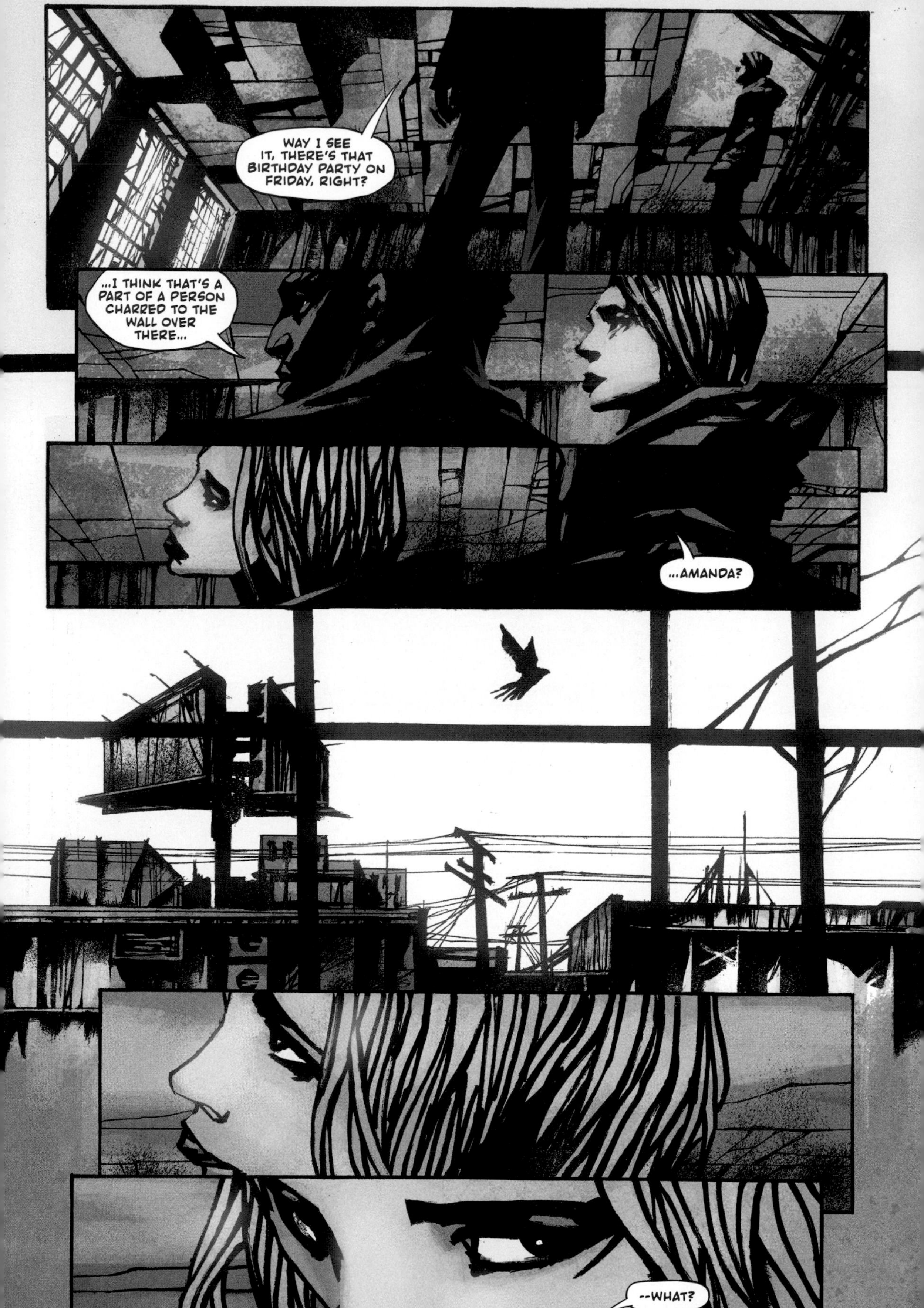
WAY I SEE IT, THERE'S THAT BIRTHDAY PARTY ON FRIDAY, RIGHT?
...I THINK THAT'S A PART OF A PERSON CHARRED TO THE WALL OVER THERE...
...AMANDA?
--WHAT?

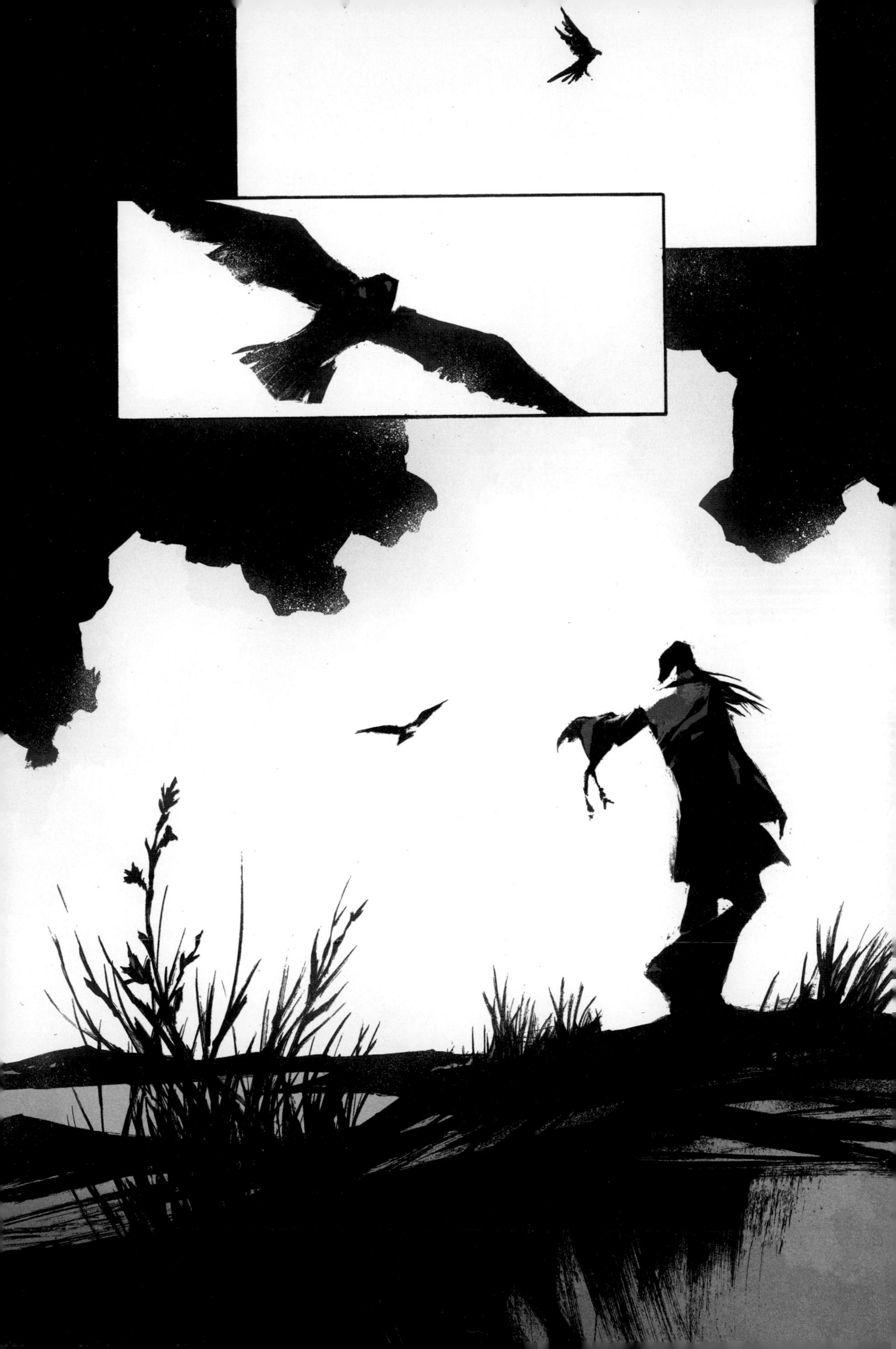

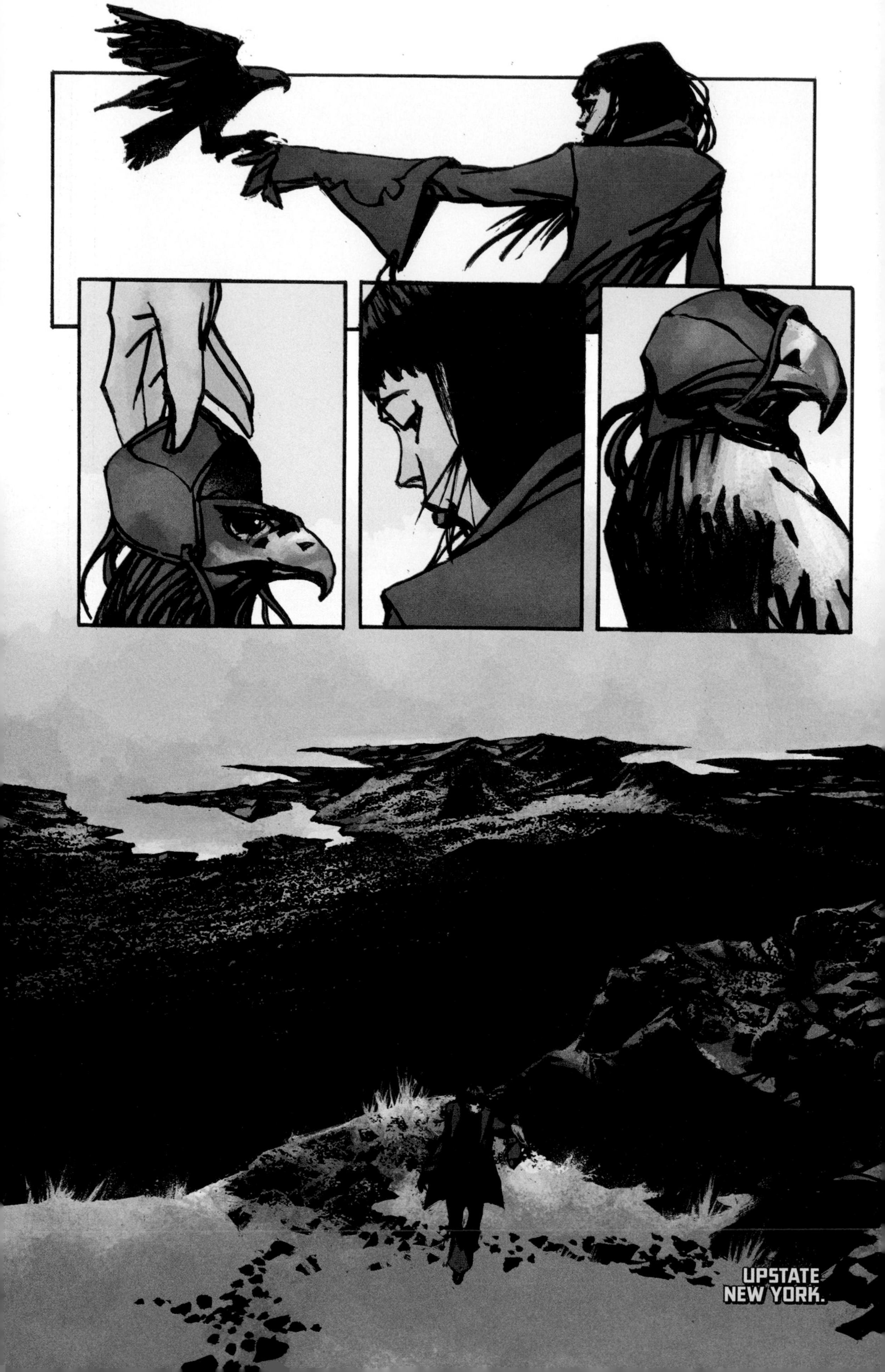
UPSTATE
NEW YORK.

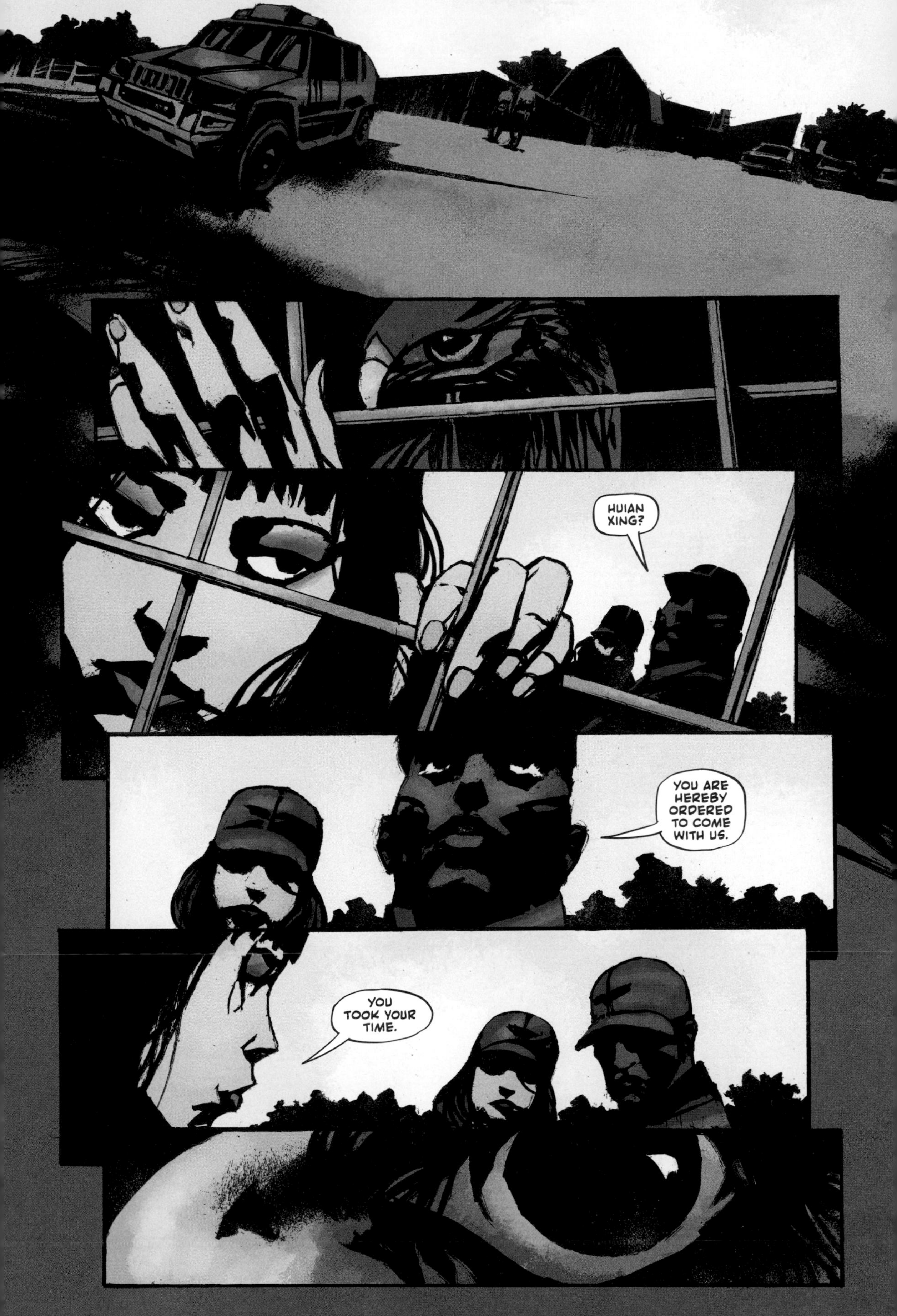
HUIAN XING?
YOU ARE HEREBY ORDERED TO COME WITH US.
YOU TOOK YOUR TIME.

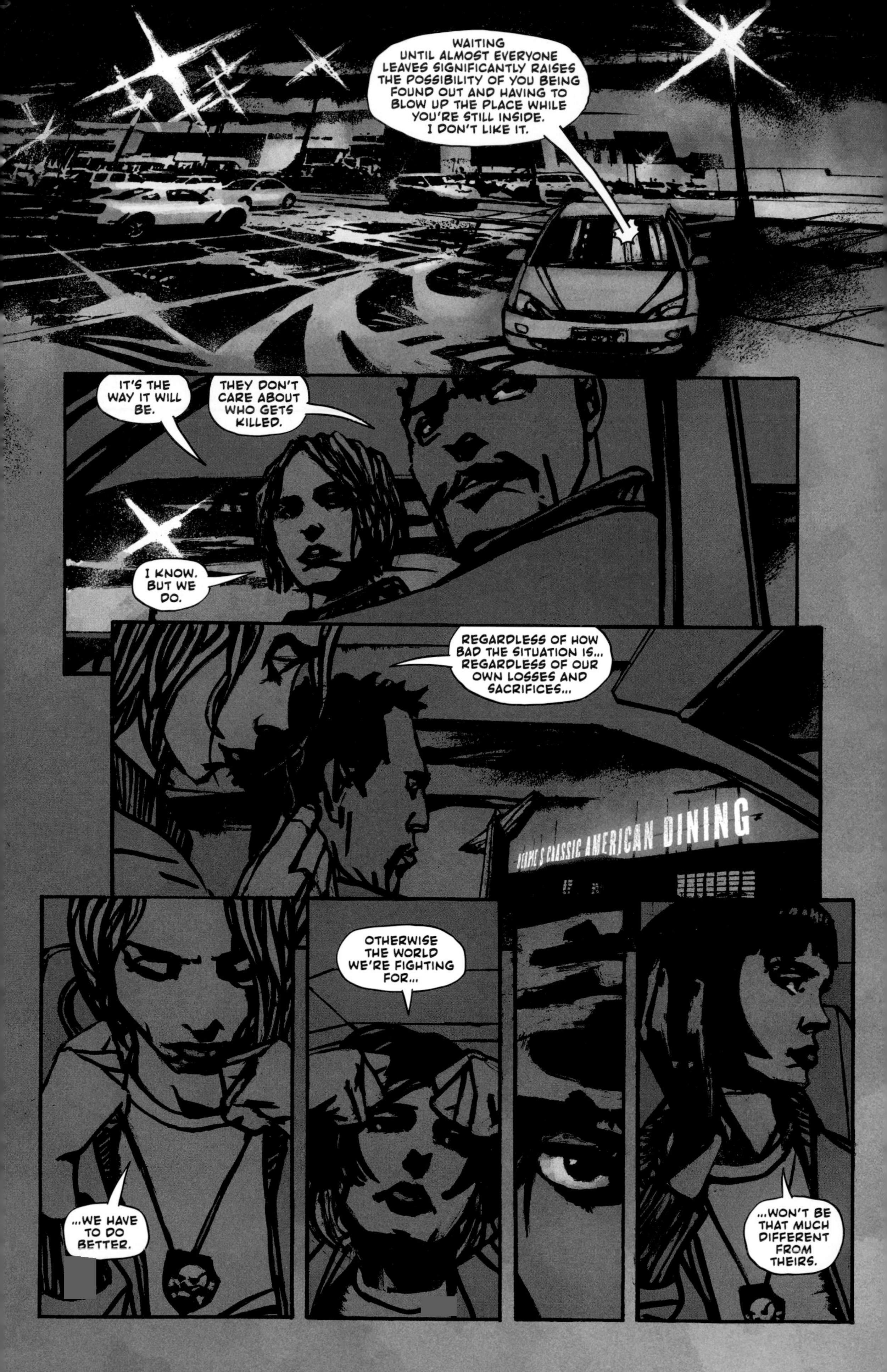
WAITING UNTIL ALMOST EVERYONE LEAVES SIGNIFICANTLY RAISES THE POSSIBILITY OF YOU BEING FOUND OUT AND HAVING TO BLOW UP THE PLACE WHILE YOU'RE STILL INSIDE. I DON'T LIKE IT.
IT'S THE WAY IT WILL BE.
THEY DON'T CARE ABOUT WHO GETS KILLED.
I KNOW. BUT WE DO.
REGARDLESS OF HOW BAD THE SITUATION IS... REGARDLESS OF OUR OWN LOSSES AND SACRIFICES...
CLASSIC AMERICAN DINING
...WE HAVE TO DO BETTER.
OTHERWISE THE WORLD WE'RE FIGHTING FOR...
...WON'T BE THAT MUCH DIFFERENT FROM THEIRS.

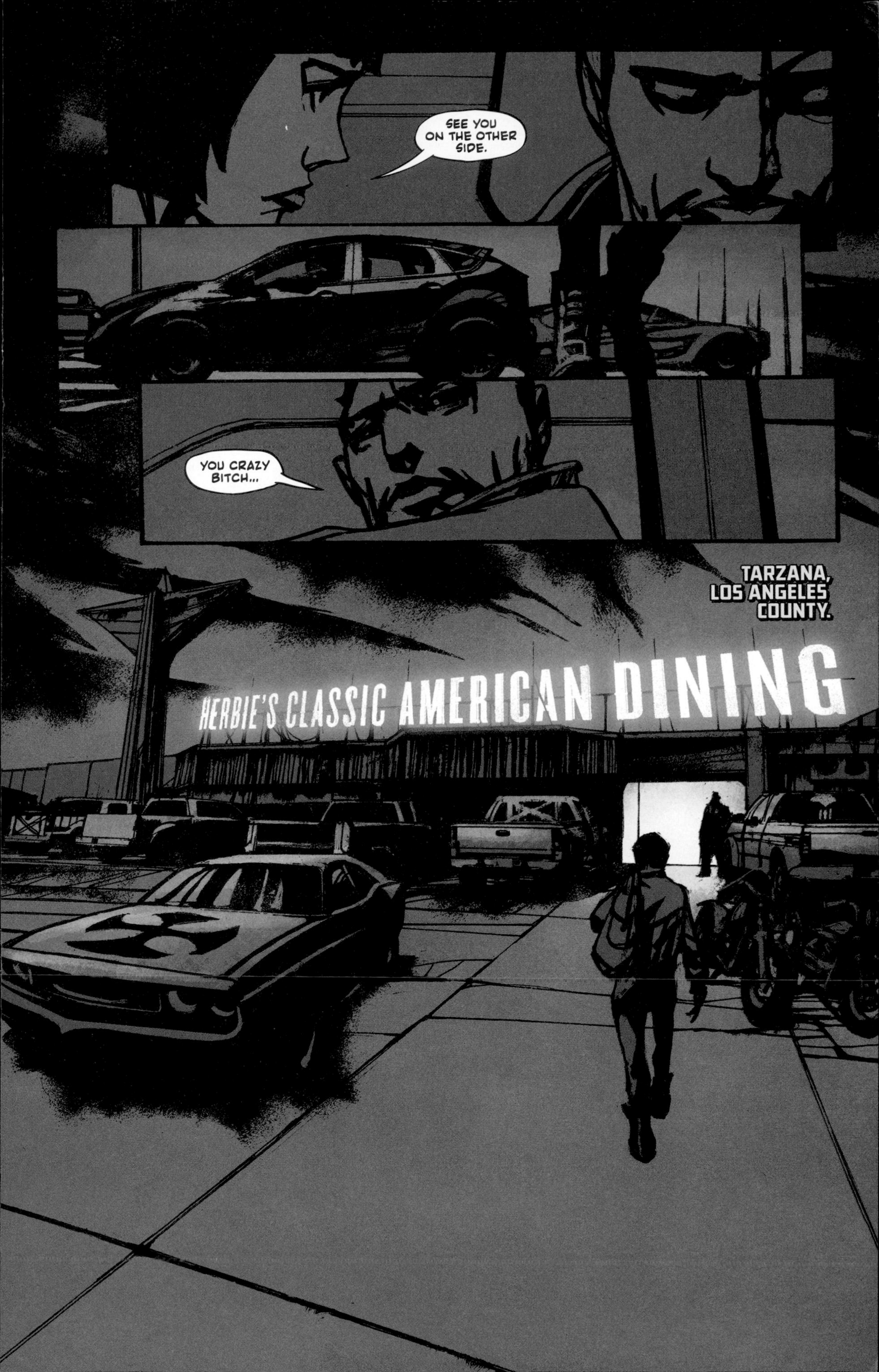
SEE YOU ON THE OTHER SIDE.
YOU CRAZY BITCH...
TARZANA, LOS ANGELES COUNTY.
HERBIE'S CLASSIC AMERICAN DINING

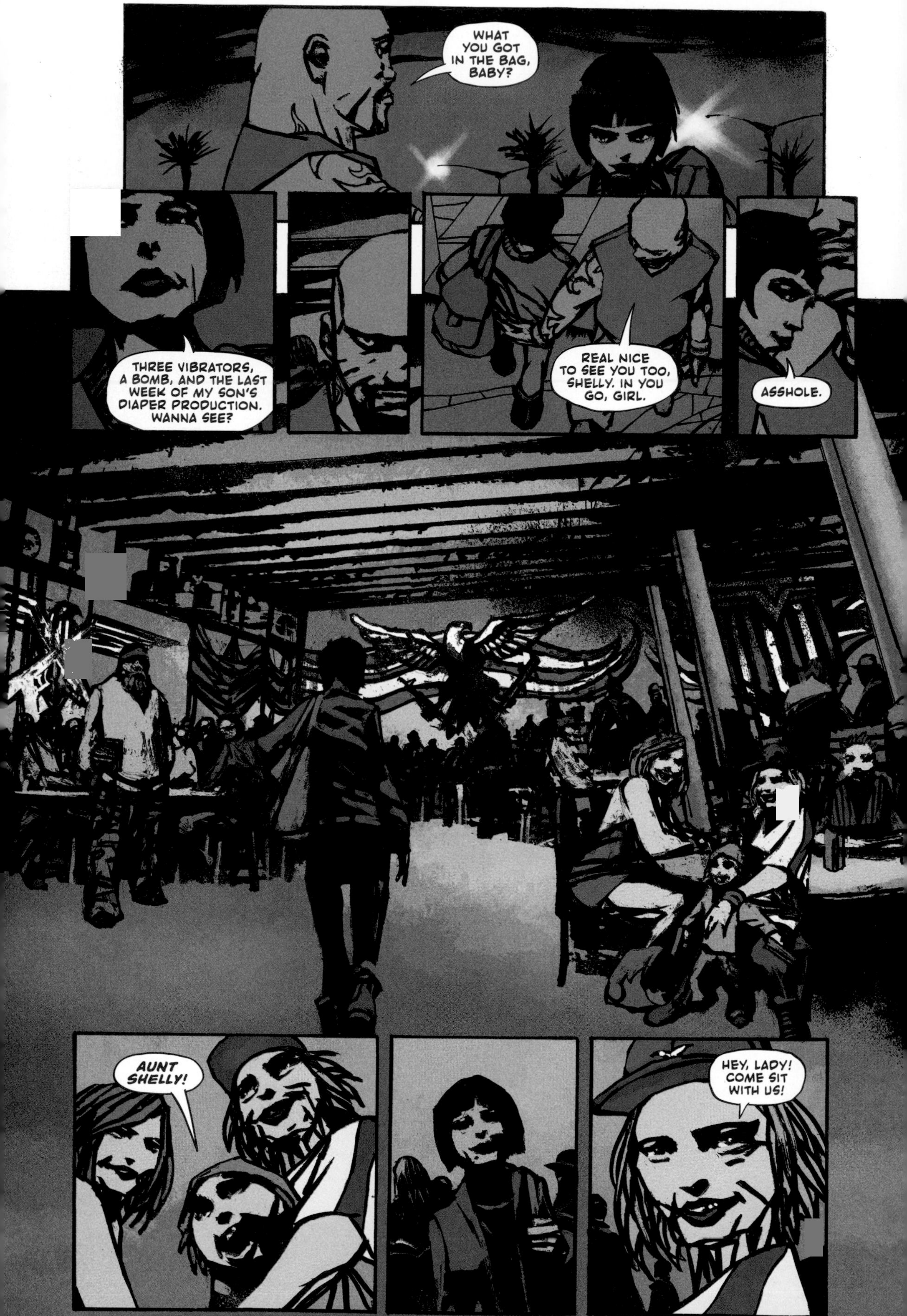
WHAT YOU GOT IN THE BAG, BABY?
THREE VIBRATORS, A BOMB, AND THE LAST WEEK OF MY SON'S DIAPER PRODUCTION. WANNA SEE?
REAL NICE TO SEE YOU TOO, SHELLY. IN YOU GO, GIRL.
ASSHOLE.
AUNT SHELLY!
HEY, LADY! COME SIT WITH US!

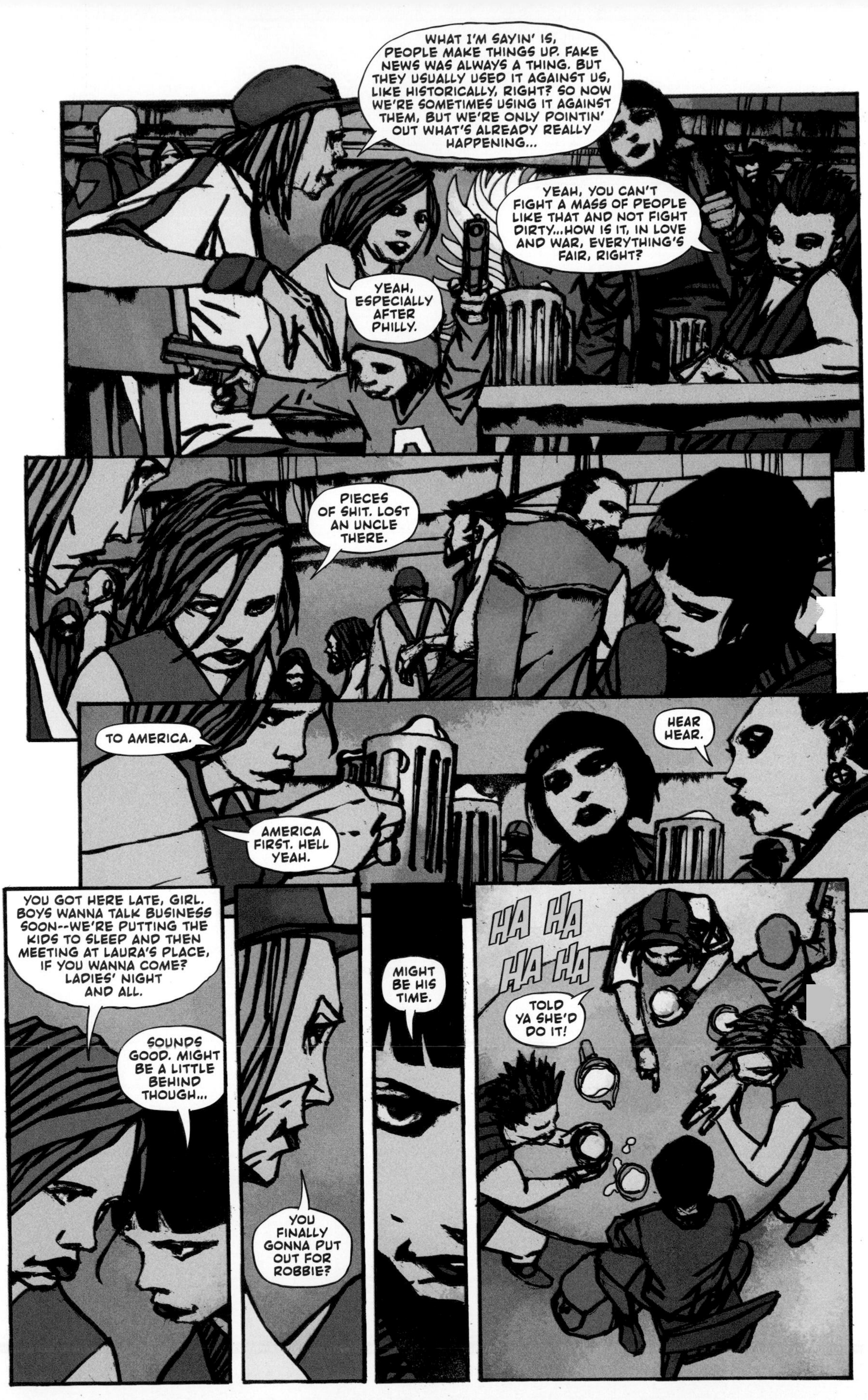
WHAT I'M SAYIN' IS, PEOPLE MAKE THINGS UP. FAKE NEWS WAS ALWAYS A THING. BUT THEY USUALLY USED IT AGAINST US, LIKE HISTORICALLY, RIGHT? SO NOW WE'RE SOMETIMES USING IT AGAINST THEM, BUT WE'RE ONLY POINTIN' OUT WHAT'S ALREADY REALLY HAPPENING...
YEAH, YOU CAN'T FIGHT A MASS OF PEOPLE LIKE THAT AND NOT FIGHT DIRTY...HOW IS IT, IN LOVE AND WAR, EVERYTHING'S FAIR, RIGHT?
YEAH, ESPECIALLY AFTER PHILLY.
PIECES OF SHIT. LOST AN UNCLE THERE.
TO AMERICA.
HEAR HEAR.
AMERICA FIRST. HELL YEAH.
YOU GOT HERE LATE, GIRL. BOYS WANNA TALK BUSINESS SOON--WE'RE PUTTING THE KIDS TO SLEEP AND THEN MEETING AT LAURA'S PLACE, IF YOU WANNA COME? LADIES' NIGHT AND ALL.
SOUNDS GOOD. MIGHT BE A LITTLE BEHIND THOUGH...
YOU FINALLY GONNA PUT OUT FOR ROBBIE?
MIGHT BE HIS TIME.
HA HA HA HA
TOLD YA SHE'D DO IT!

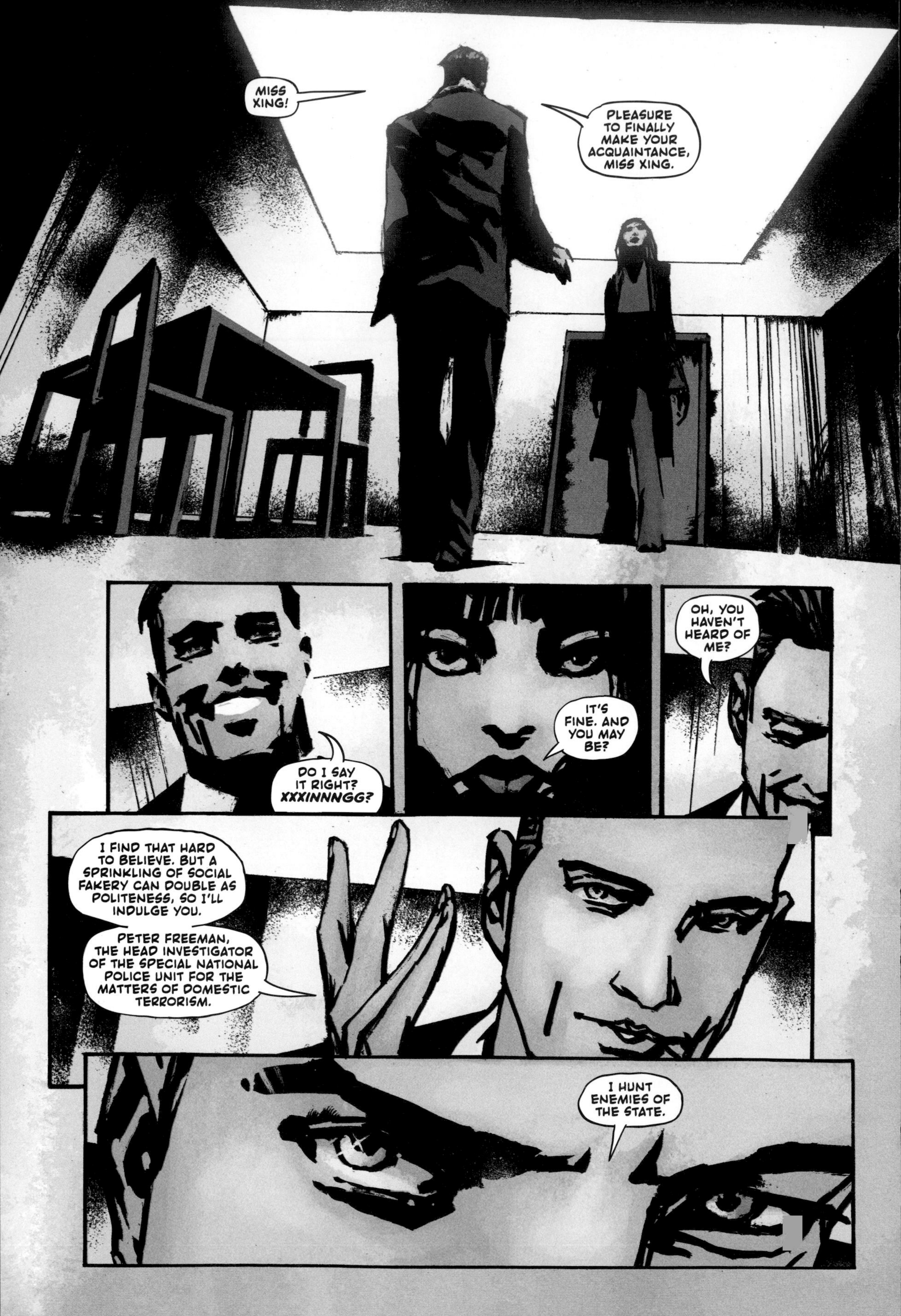
MISS XING!
PLEASURE TO FINALLY MAKE YOUR ACQUAINTANCE, MISS XING.
DO I SAY IT RIGHT? XXXINNNGG?
IT'S FINE. AND YOU MAY BE?
OH, YOU HAVEN'T HEARD OF ME?
I FIND THAT HARD TO BELIEVE. BUT A SPRINKLING OF SOCIAL FAKERY CAN DOUBLE AS POLITENESS, SO I'LL INDULGE YOU.
PETER FREEMAN, THE HEAD INVESTIGATOR OF THE SPECIAL NATIONAL POLICE UNIT FOR THE MATTERS OF DOMESTIC TERRORISM.
I HUNT ENEMIES OF THE STATE.

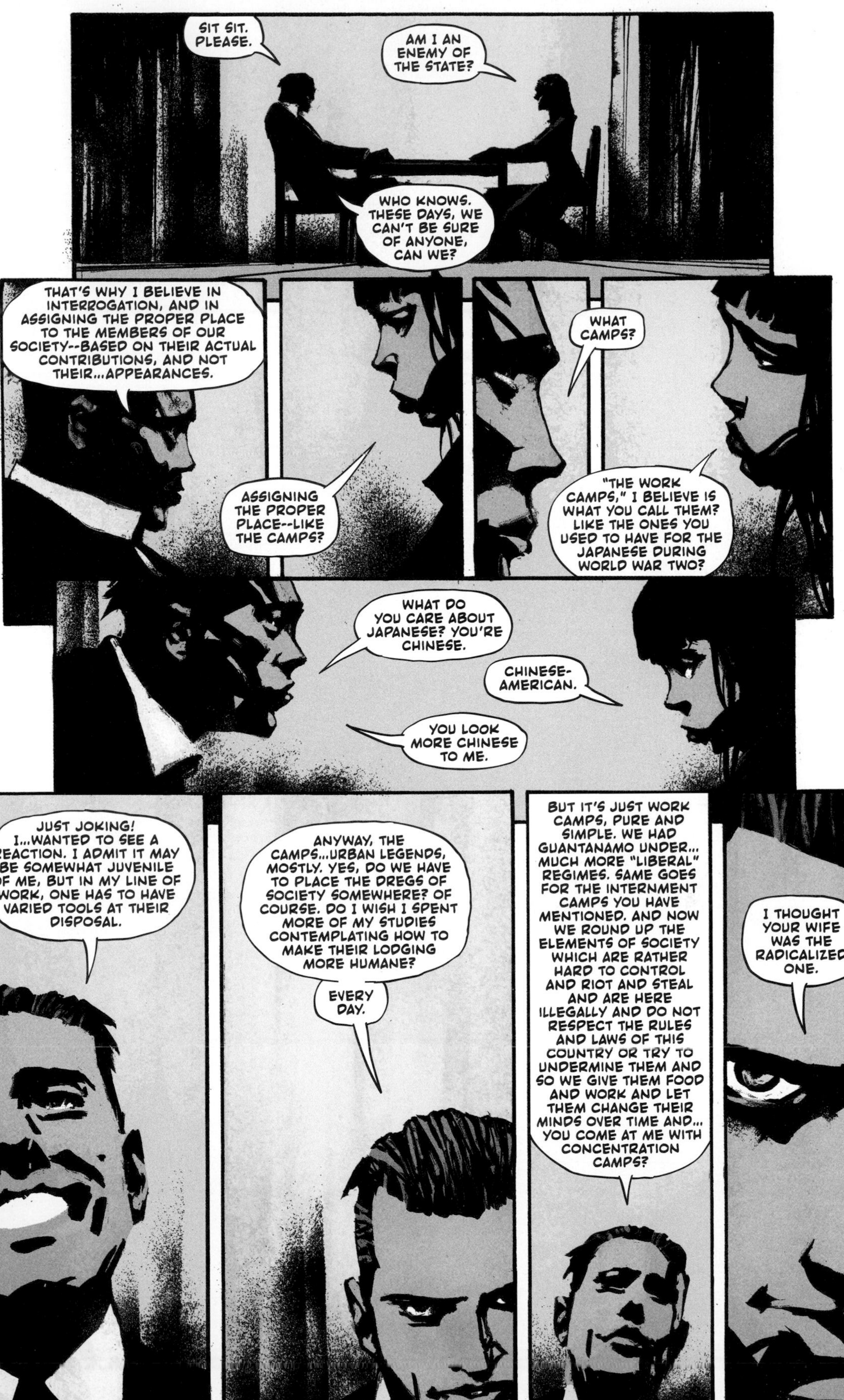
SIT SIT. PLEASE.
AM I AN ENEMY OF THE STATE?
WHO KNOWS. THESE DAYS, WE CAN'T BE SURE OF ANYONE, CAN WE?
THAT'S WHY I BELIEVE IN INTERROGATION, AND IN ASSIGNING THE PROPER PLACE TO THE MEMBERS OF OUR SOCIETY--BASED ON THEIR ACTUAL CONTRIBUTIONS, AND NOT THEIR...APPEARANCES.
ASSIGNING THE PROPER PLACE--LIKE THE CAMPS?
WHAT CAMPS?
"THE WORK CAMPS," I BELIEVE IS WHAT YOU CALL THEM? LIKE THE ONES YOU USED TO HAVE FOR THE JAPANESE DURING WORLD WAR TWO?
WHAT DO YOU CARE ABOUT JAPANESE? YOU'RE CHINESE.
CHINESE-AMERICAN.
YOU LOOK MORE CHINESE TO ME.
JUST JOKING! I...WANTED TO SEE A REACTION. I ADMIT IT MAY BE SOMEWHAT JUVENILE OF ME, BUT IN MY LINE OF WORK, ONE HAS TO HAVE VARIED TOOLS AT THEIR DISPOSAL.
ANYWAY, THE CAMPS...URBAN LEGENDS, MOSTLY. YES, DO WE HAVE TO PLACE THE DREGS OF SOCIETY SOMEWHERE? OF COURSE. DO I WISH I SPENT MORE OF MY STUDIES CONTEMPLATING HOW TO MAKE THEIR LODGING MORE HUMANE?
EVERY DAY.
BUT IT'S JUST WORK CAMPS, PURE AND SIMPLE. WE HAD GUANTANAMO UNDER... MUCH MORE "LIBERAL" REGIMES. SAME GOES FOR THE INTERNMENT CAMPS YOU HAVE MENTIONED. AND NOW WE ROUND UP THE ELEMENTS OF SOCIETY WHICH ARE RATHER HARD TO CONTROL AND RIOT AND STEAL AND ARE HERE ILLEGALLY AND DO NOT RESPECT THE RULES AND LAWS OF THIS COUNTRY OR TRY TO UNDERMINE THEM AND SO WE GIVE THEM FOOD AND WORK AND LET THEM CHANGE THEIR MINDS OVER TIME AND... YOU COME AT ME WITH CONCENTRATION CAMPS?
I THOUGHT YOUR WIFE WAS THE RADICALIZED ONE.

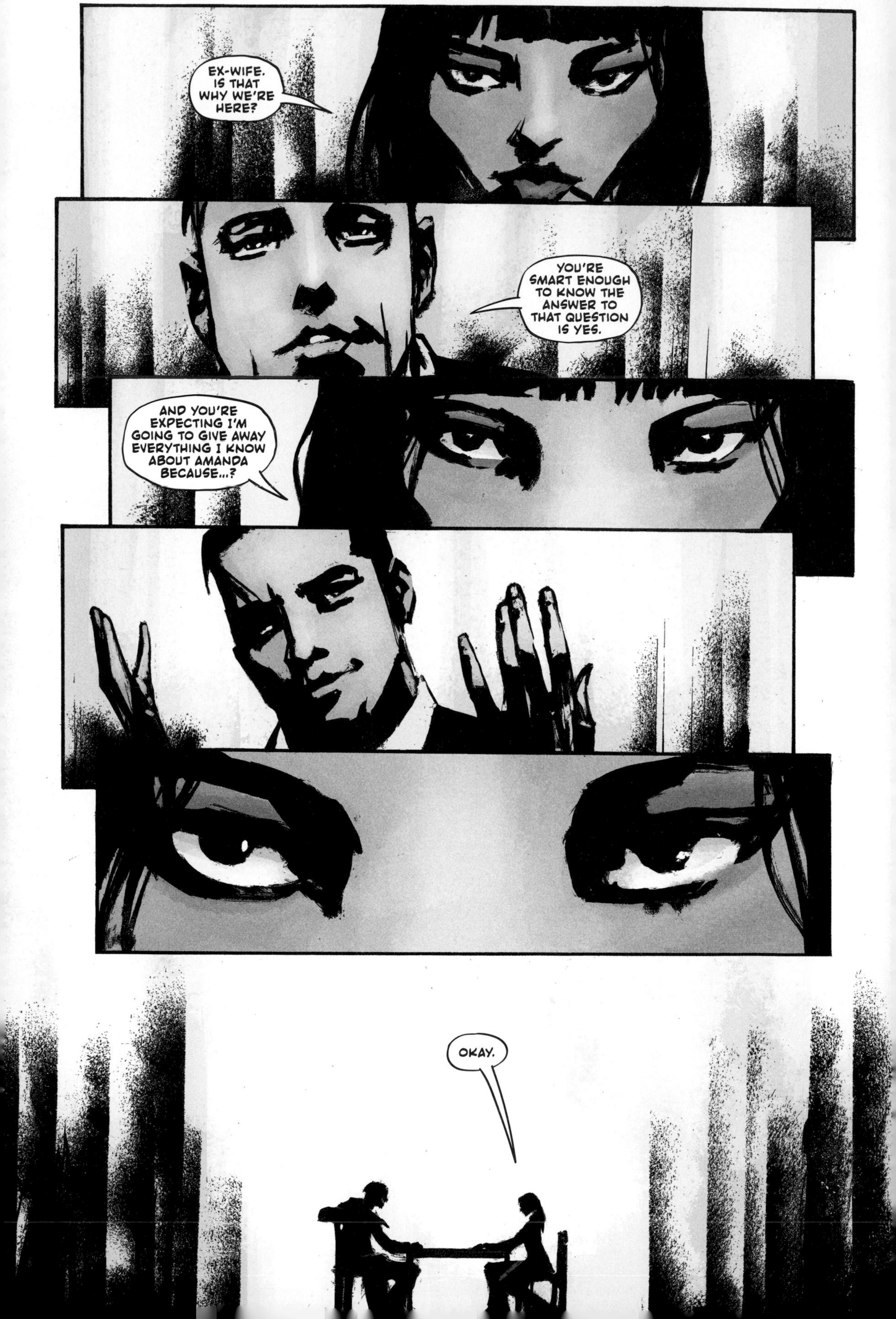
EX-WIFE. IS THAT WHY WE'RE HERE?
YOU'RE SMART ENOUGH TO KNOW THE ANSWER TO THAT QUESTION IS YES.
AND YOU'RE EXPECTING I'M GOING TO GIVE AWAY EVERYTHING I KNOW ABOUT AMANDA BECAUSE...?
OKAY.

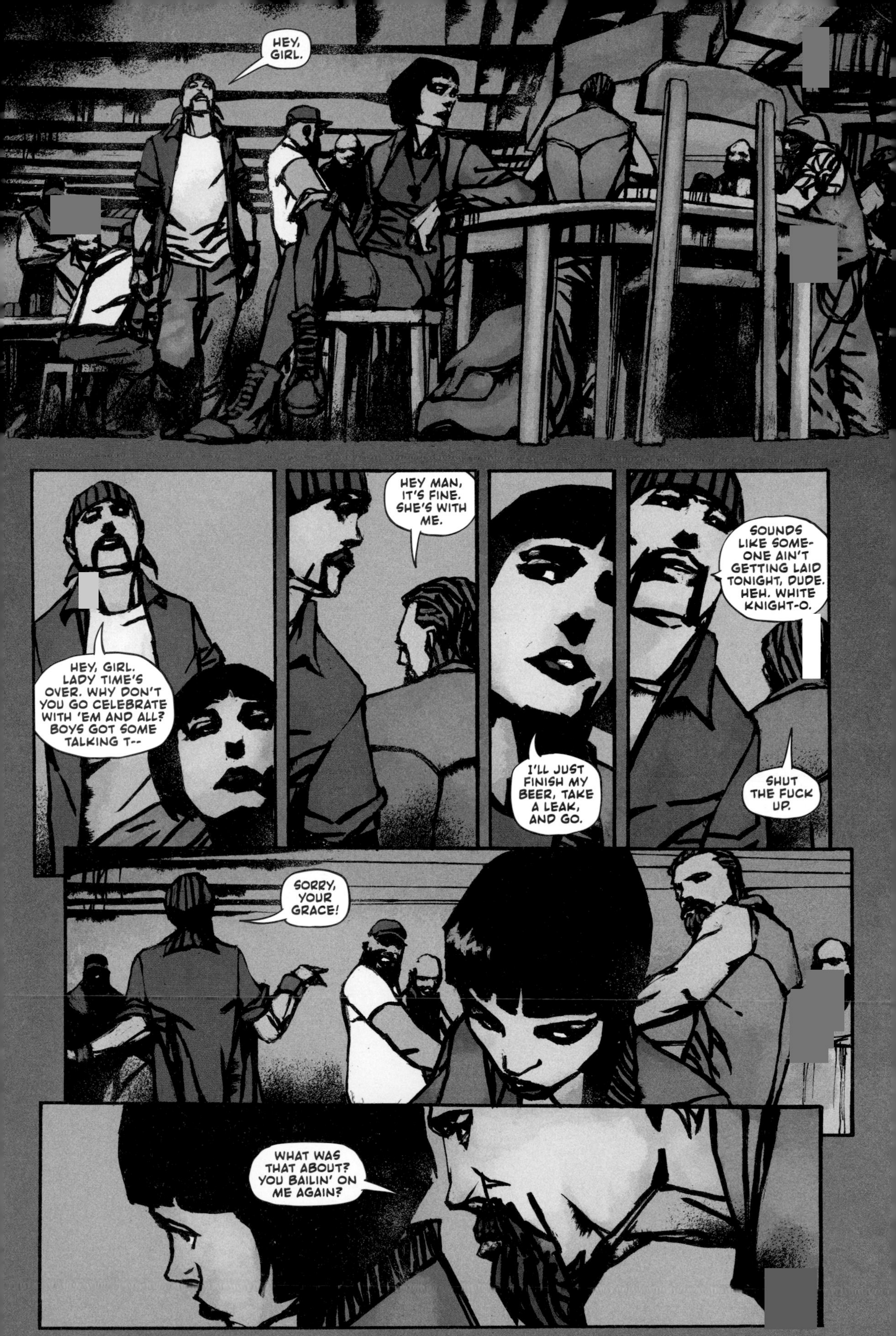
HEY, GIRL.
HEY, GIRL. LADY TIME'S OVER. WHY DON'T YOU GO CELEBRATE WITH 'EM AND ALL? BOYS GOT SOME TALKING T--
HEY MAN, IT'S FINE. SHE'S WITH ME.
I'LL JUST FINISH MY BEER, TAKE A LEAK, AND GO.
SOUNDS LIKE SOME-ONE AIN'T GETTING LAID TONIGHT, DUDE. HEH. WHITE KNIGHT-O.
SHUT THE FUCK UP.
SORRY, YOUR GRACE!
WHAT WAS THAT ABOUT? YOU BAILIN' ON ME AGAIN?

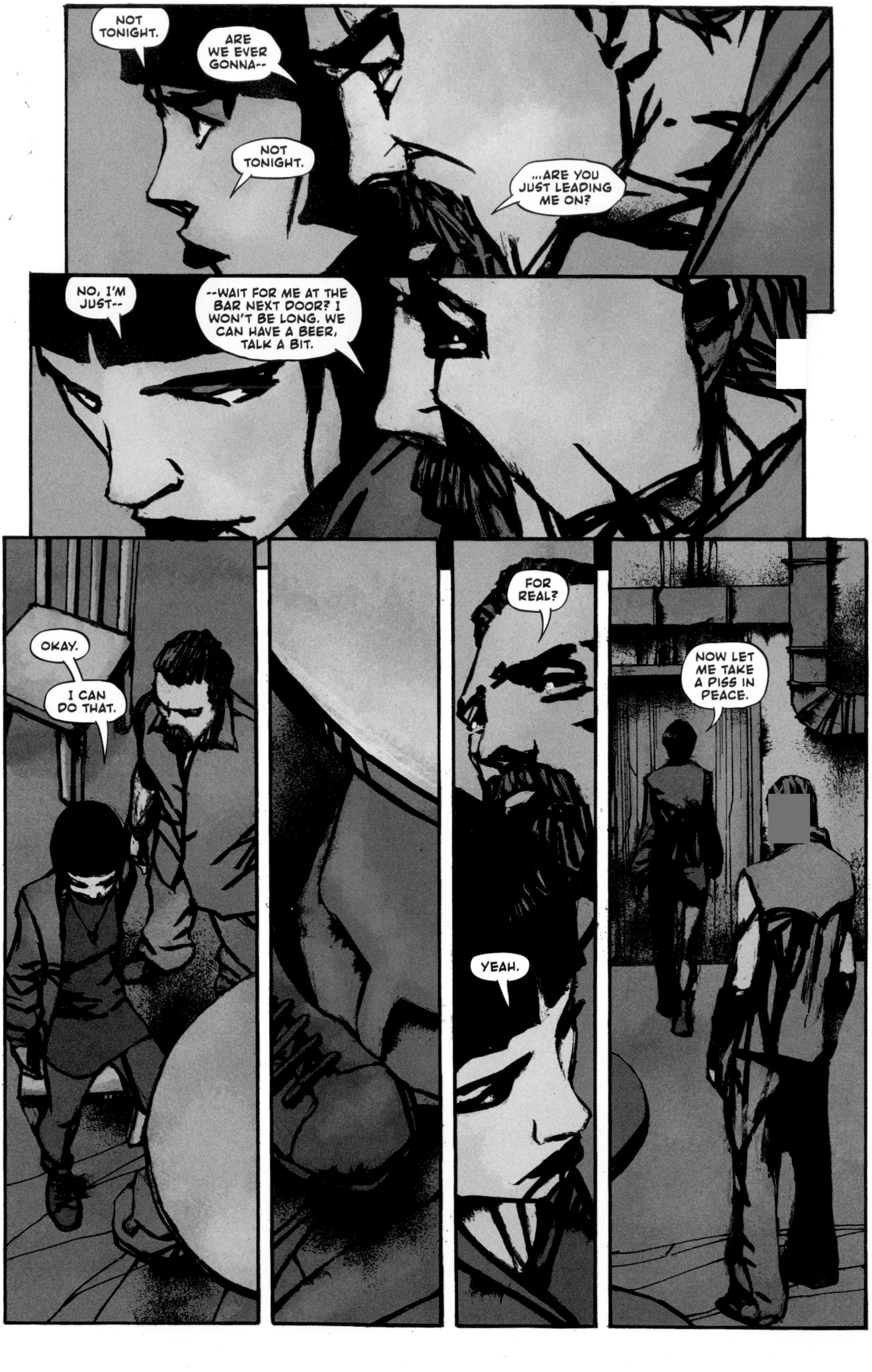
NOT TONIGHT.
ARE WE EVER GONNA--
NOT TONIGHT.
...ARE YOU JUST LEADING ME ON?
NO, I'M JUST--
--WAIT FOR ME AT THE BAR NEXT DOOR? I WON'T BE LONG. WE CAN HAVE A BEER, TALK A BIT.
OKAY.
I CAN DO THAT.
FOR REAL?
YEAH.
NOW LET ME TAKE A PISS IN PEACE.

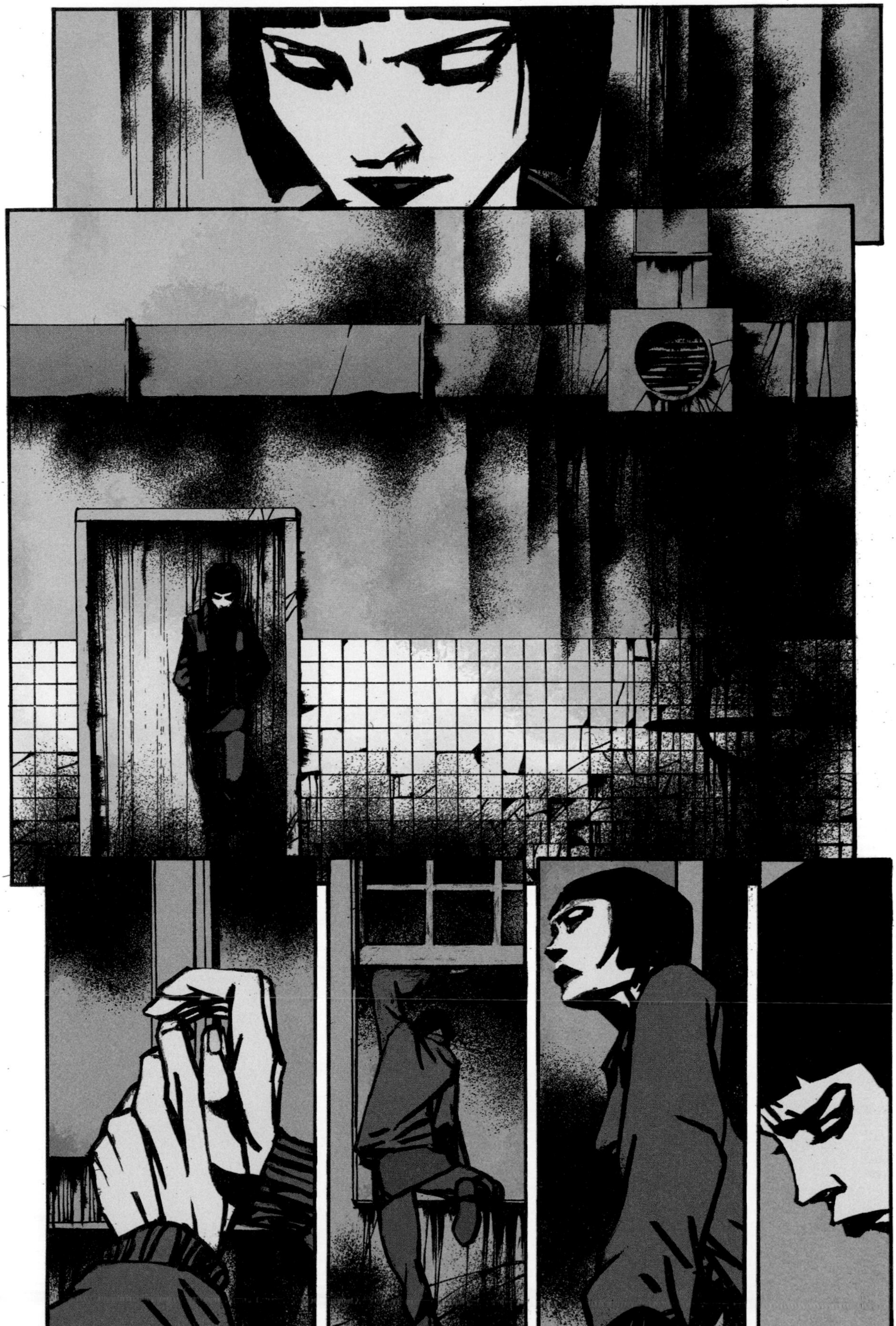

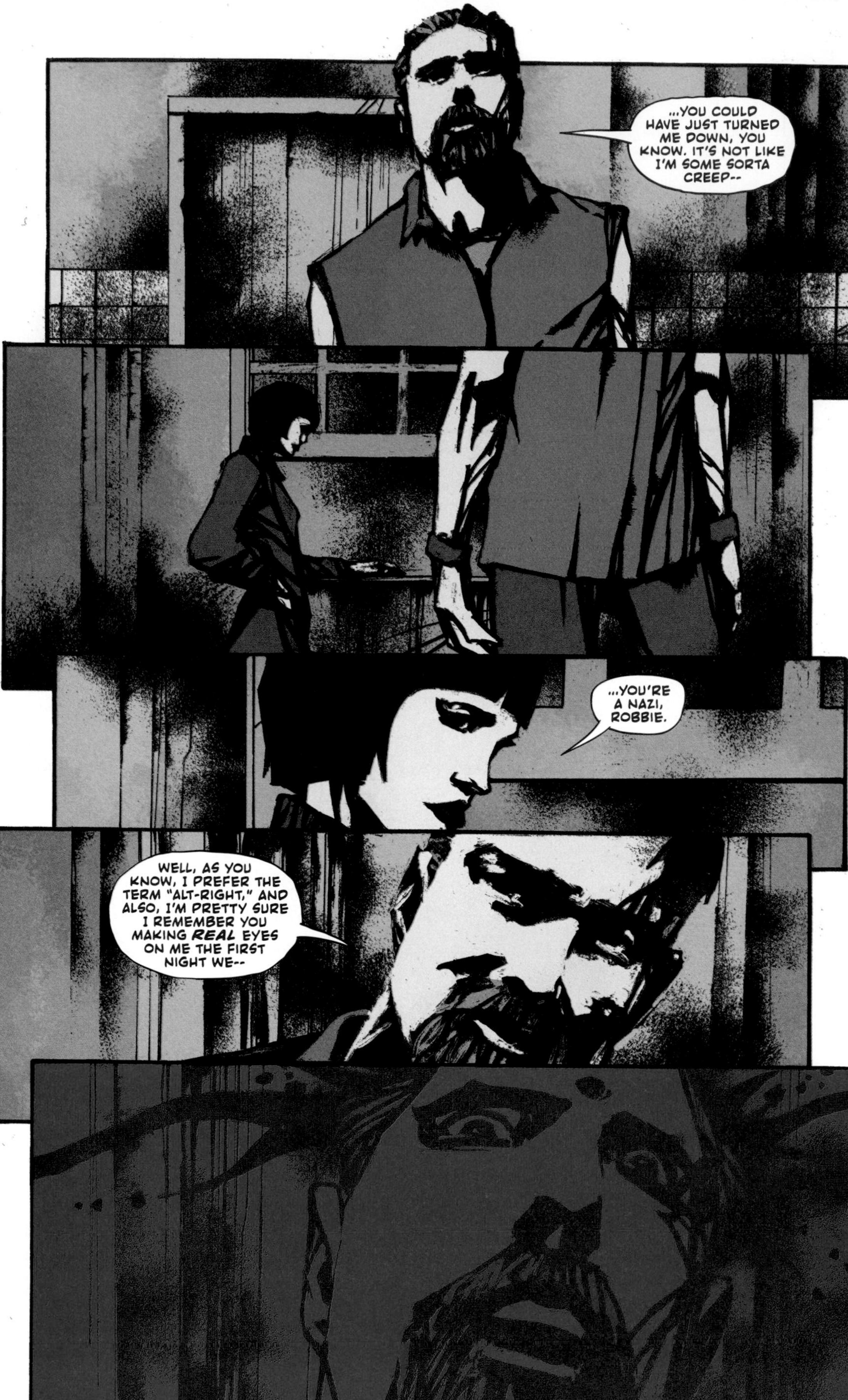
...YOU COULD HAVE JUST TURNED ME DOWN, YOU KNOW. IT'S NOT LIKE I'M SOME SORTA CREEP--
...YOU'RE A NAZI, ROBBIE.
WELL, AS YOU KNOW, I PREFER THE TERM "ALT-RIGHT," AND ALSO, I'M PRETTY SURE I REMEMBER YOU MAKING *REAL* EYES ON ME THE FIRST NIGHT WE--

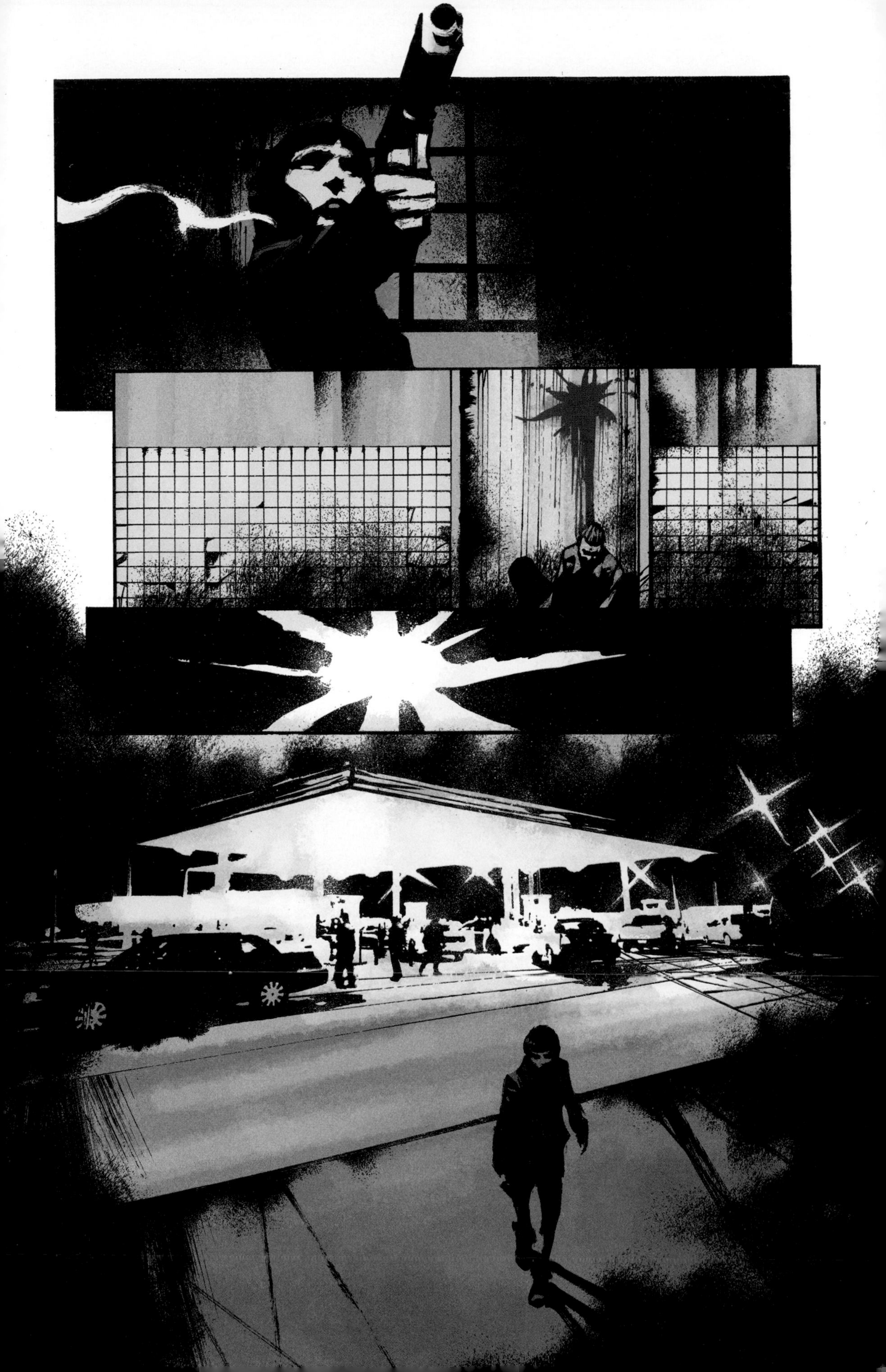

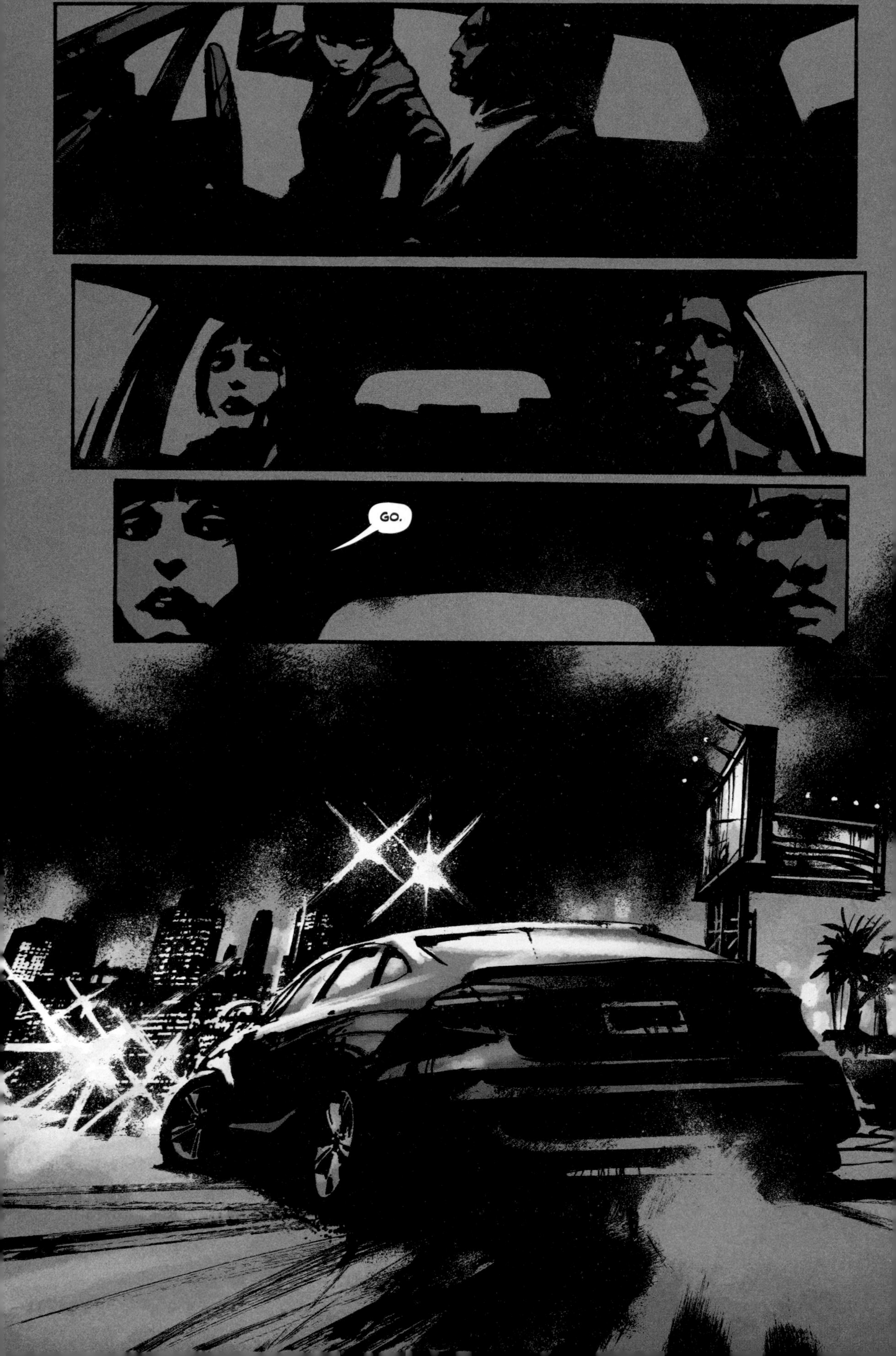
GO.

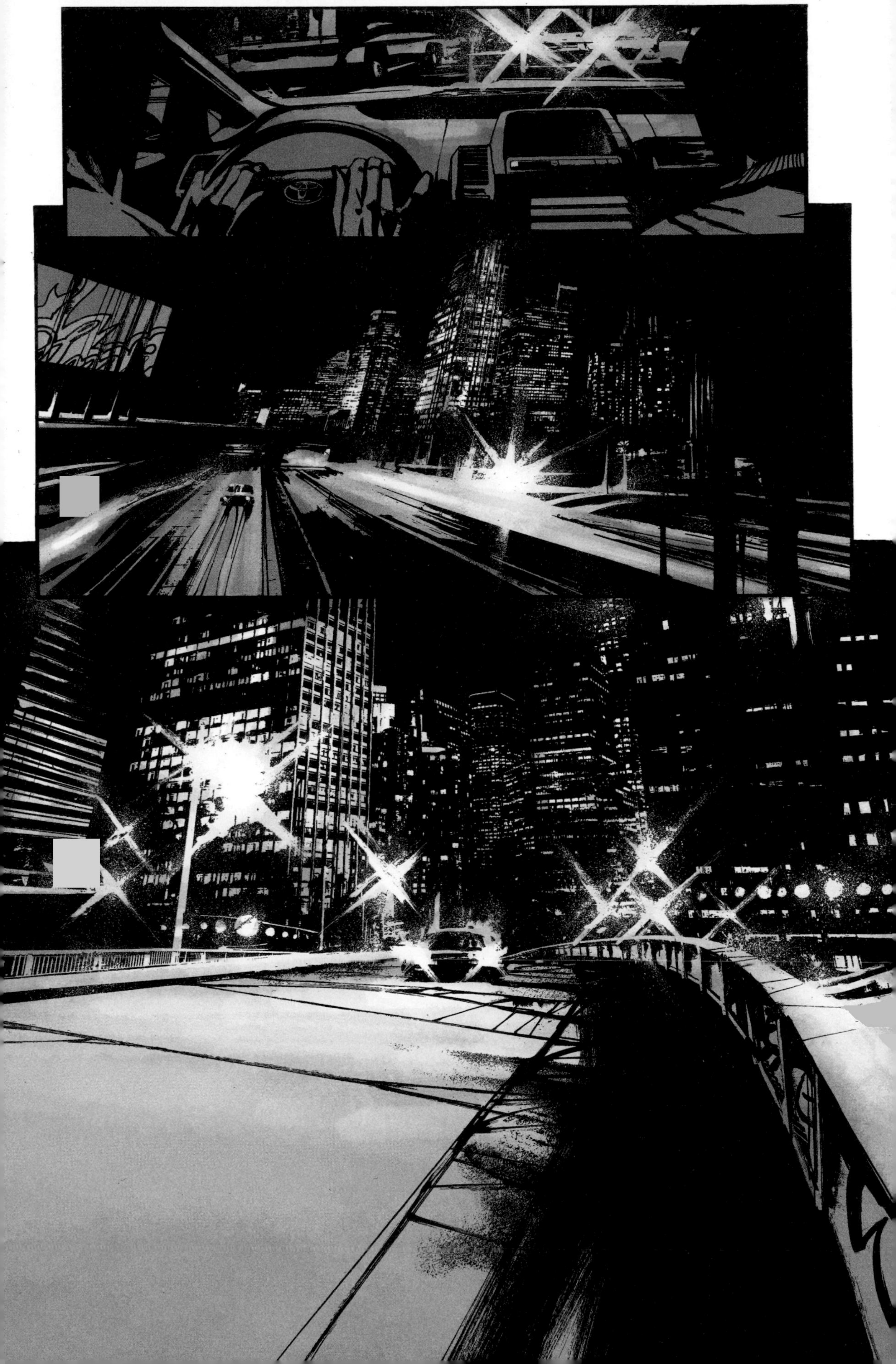

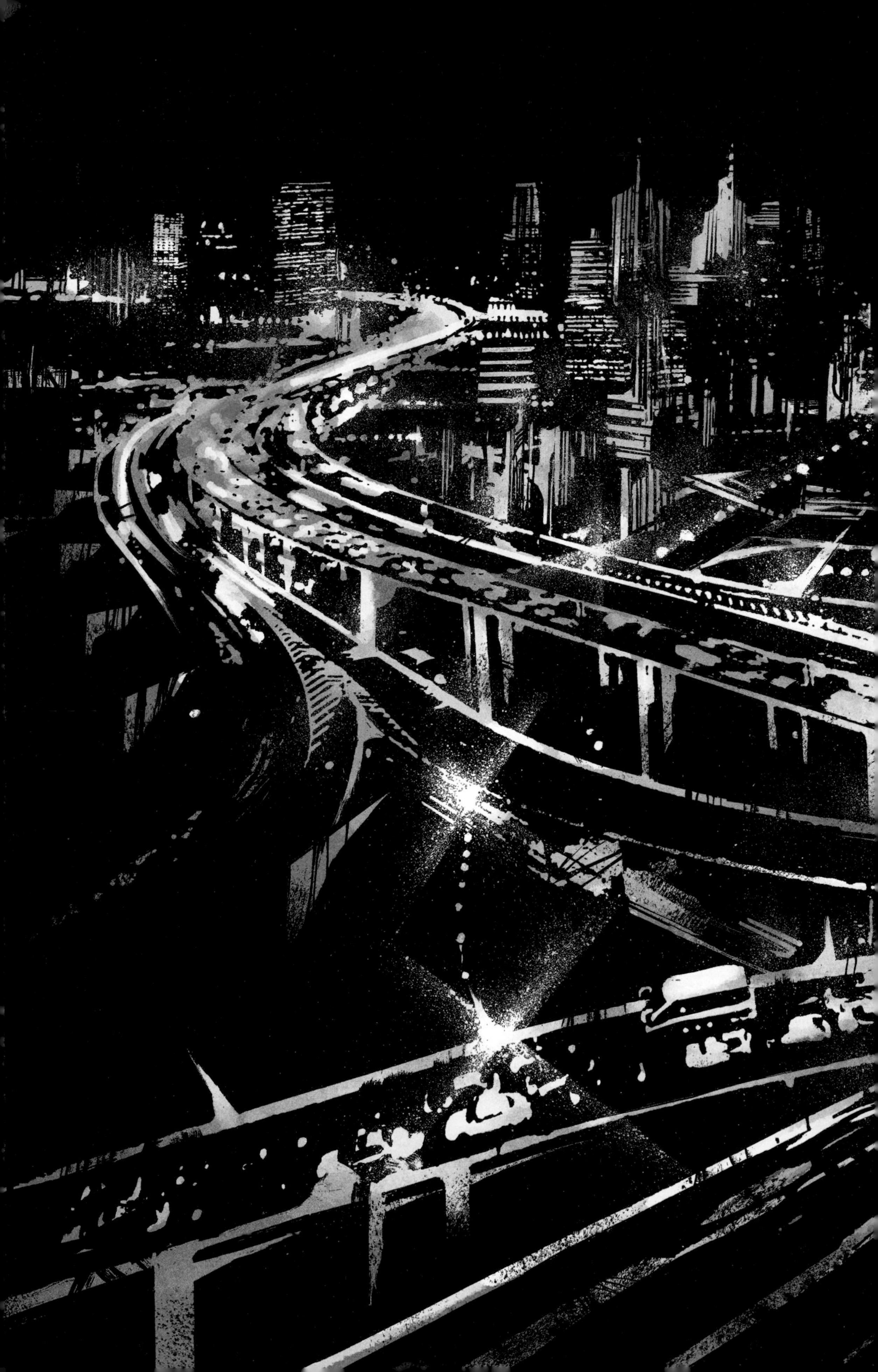

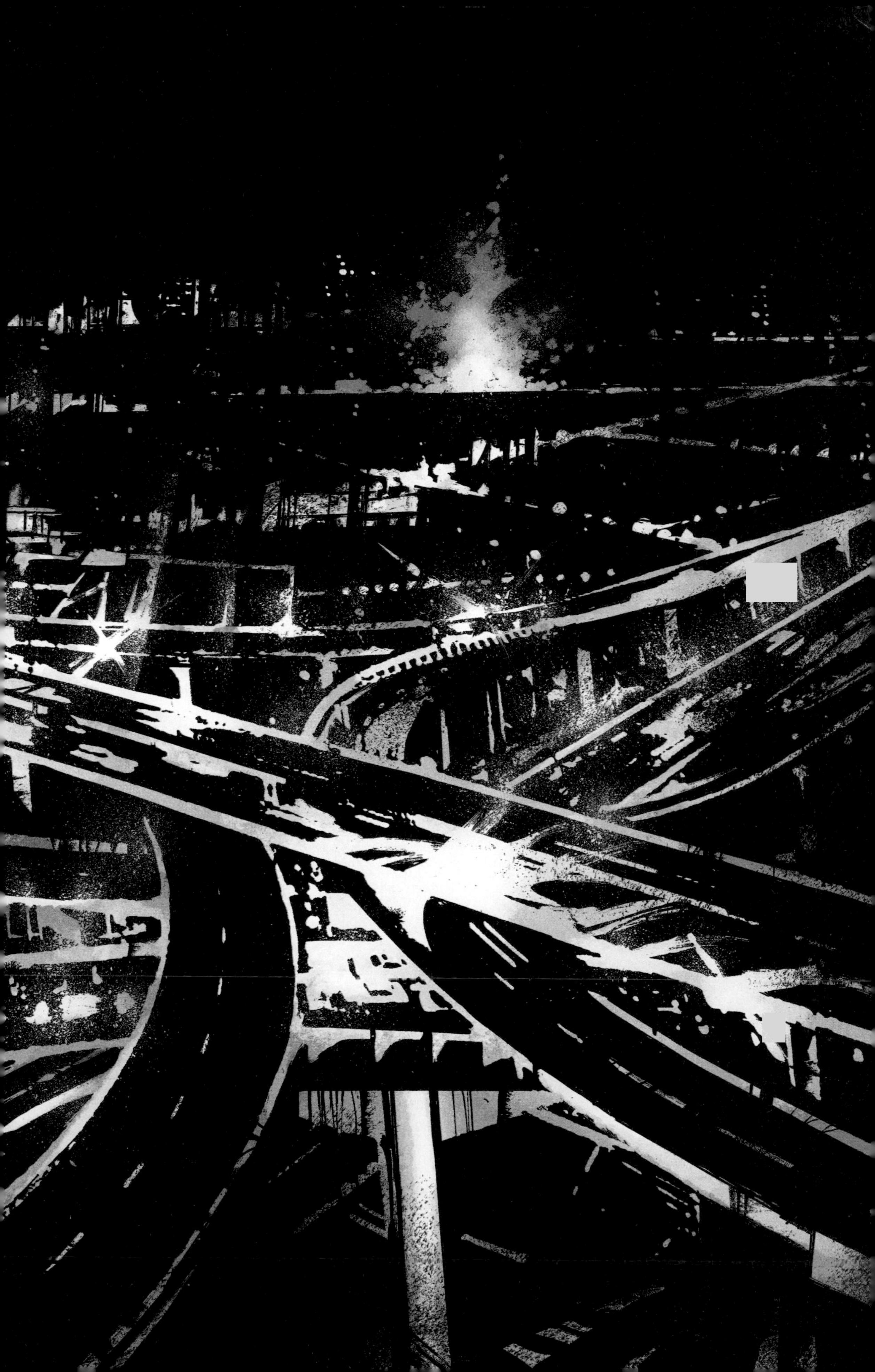

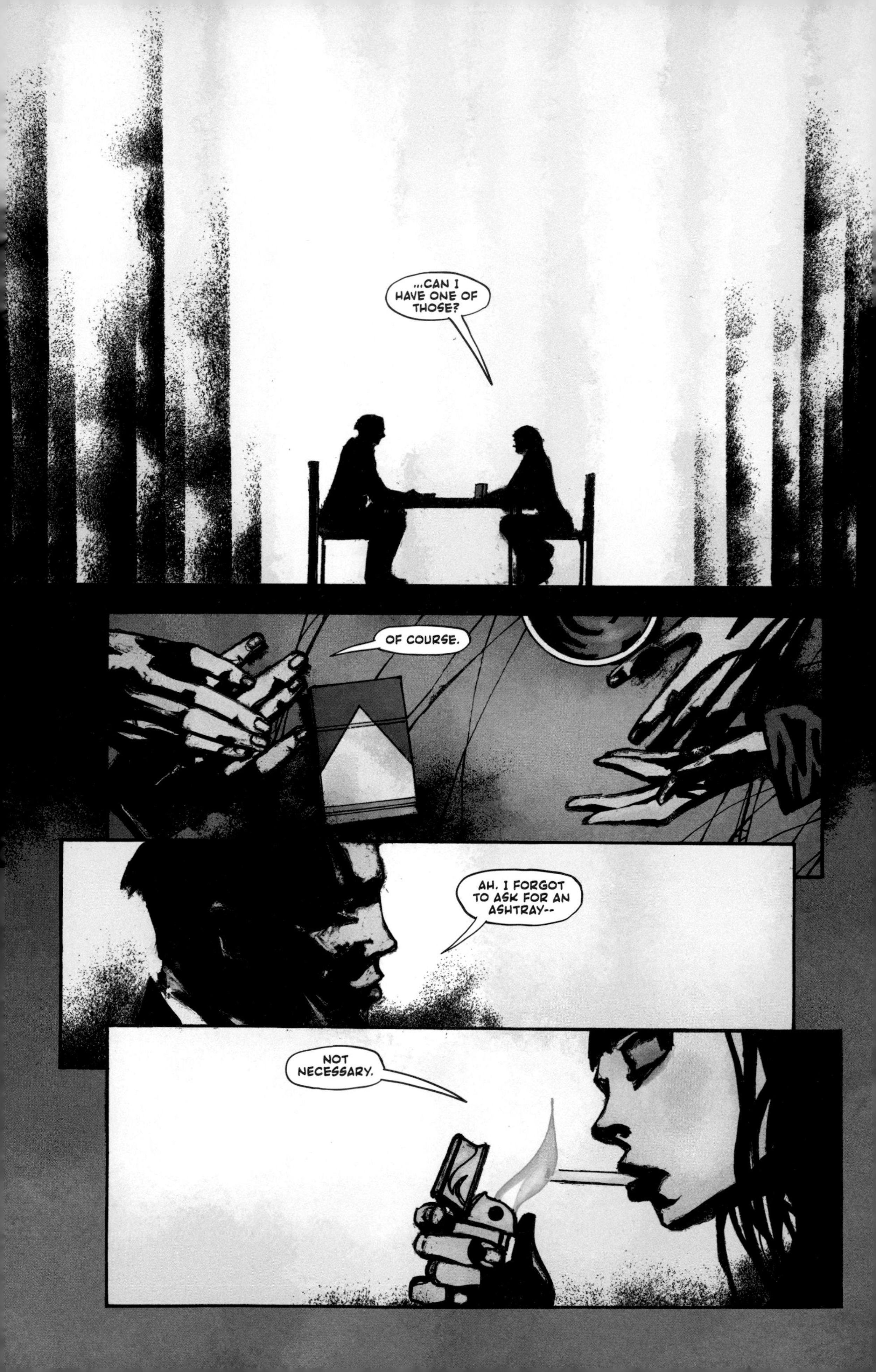
...CAN I HAVE ONE OF THOSE?
OF COURSE.
AH. I FORGOT TO ASK FOR AN ASHTRAY--
NOT NECESSARY.

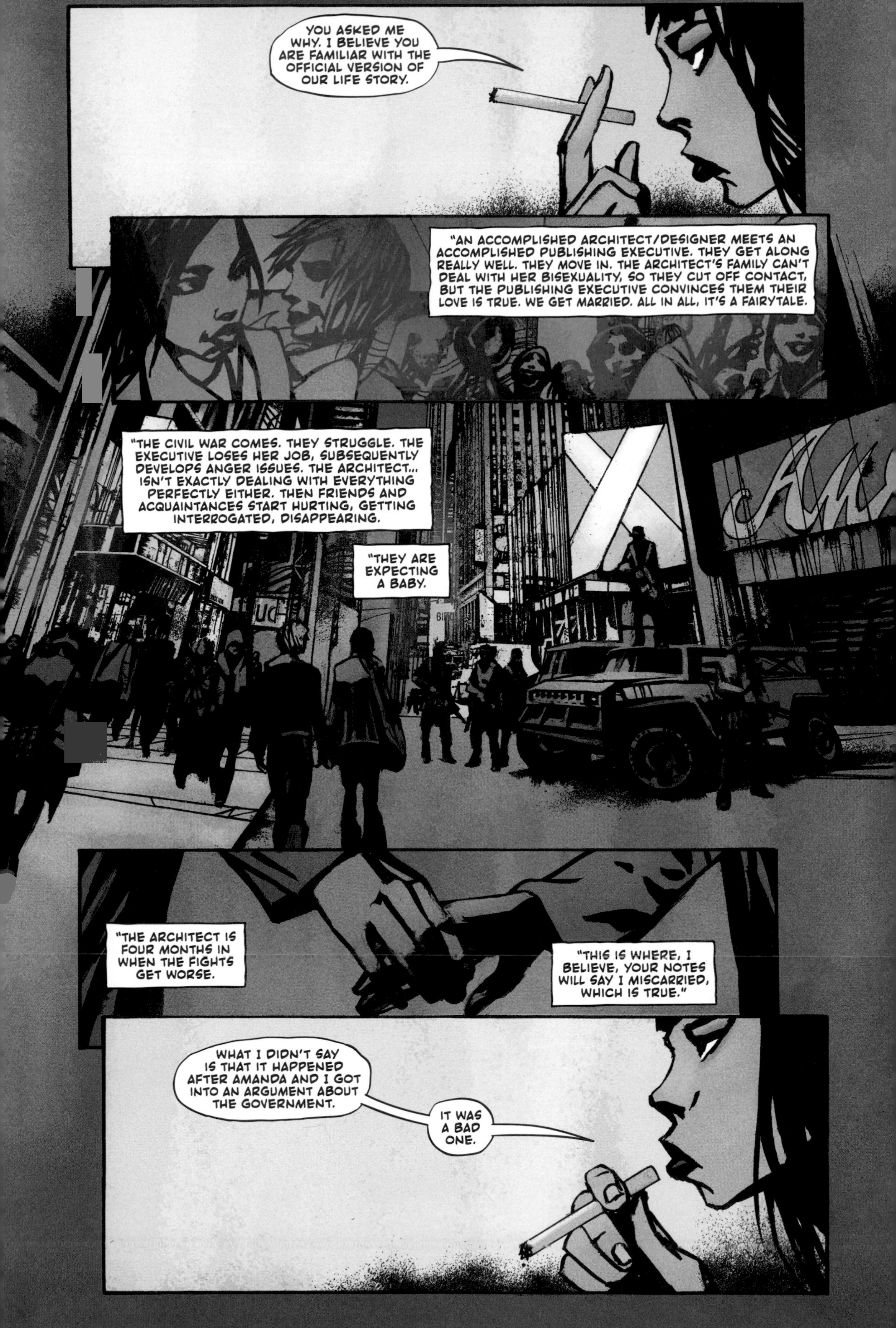
YOU ASKED ME WHY. I BELIEVE YOU ARE FAMILIAR WITH THE OFFICIAL VERSION OF OUR LIFE STORY.
"AN ACCOMPLISHED ARCHITECT/DESIGNER MEETS AN ACCOMPLISHED PUBLISHING EXECUTIVE. THEY GET ALONG REALLY WELL. THEY MOVE IN. THE ARCHITECT'S FAMILY CAN'T DEAL WITH HER BISEXUALITY, SO THEY CUT OFF CONTACT, BUT THE PUBLISHING EXECUTIVE CONVINCES THEM THEIR LOVE IS TRUE. WE GET MARRIED. ALL IN ALL, IT'S A FAIRYTALE.
"THE CIVIL WAR COMES. THEY STRUGGLE. THE EXECUTIVE LOSES HER JOB, SUBSEQUENTLY DEVELOPS ANGER ISSUES. THE ARCHITECT... ISN'T EXACTLY DEALING WITH EVERYTHING PERFECTLY EITHER. THEN FRIENDS AND ACQUAINTANCES START HURTING, GETTING INTERROGATED, DISAPPEARING.
"THEY ARE EXPECTING A BABY.
"THE ARCHITECT IS FOUR MONTHS IN WHEN THE FIGHTS GET WORSE.
"THIS IS WHERE, I BELIEVE, YOUR NOTES WILL SAY I MISCARRIED, WHICH IS TRUE."
WHAT I DIDN'T SAY IS THAT IT HAPPENED AFTER AMANDA AND I GOT INTO AN ARGUMENT ABOUT THE GOVERNMENT.
IT WAS A BAD ONE.

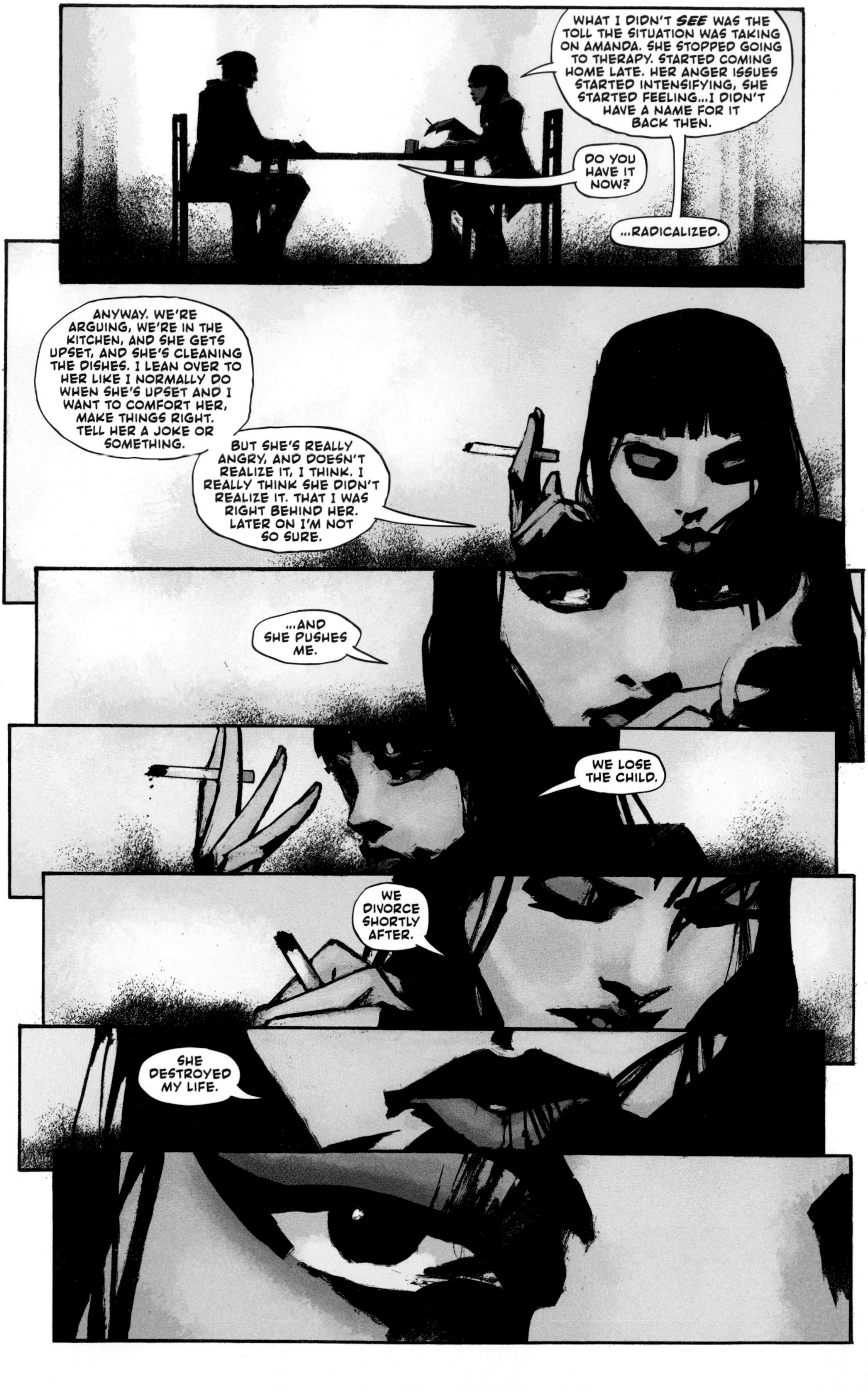
WHAT I DIDN'T SEE WAS THE TOLL THE SITUATION WAS TAKING ON AMANDA. SHE STOPPED GOING TO THERAPY. STARTED COMING HOME LATE. HER ANGER ISSUES STARTED INTENSIFYING, SHE STARTED FEELING...I DIDN'T HAVE A NAME FOR IT BACK THEN.
DO YOU HAVE IT NOW?
...RADICALIZED.
ANYWAY. WE'RE ARGUING, WE'RE IN THE KITCHEN, AND SHE GETS UPSET, AND SHE'S CLEANING THE DISHES. I LEAN OVER TO HER LIKE I NORMALLY DO WHEN SHE'S UPSET AND I WANT TO COMFORT HER, MAKE THINGS RIGHT. TELL HER A JOKE OR SOMETHING.
BUT SHE'S REALLY ANGRY, AND DOESN'T REALIZE IT, I THINK. I REALLY THINK SHE DIDN'T REALIZE IT. THAT I WAS RIGHT BEHIND HER. LATER ON I'M NOT SO SURE.
...AND SHE PUSHES ME.
WE LOSE THE CHILD.
WE DIVORCE SHORTLY AFTER.
SHE DESTROYED MY LIFE.

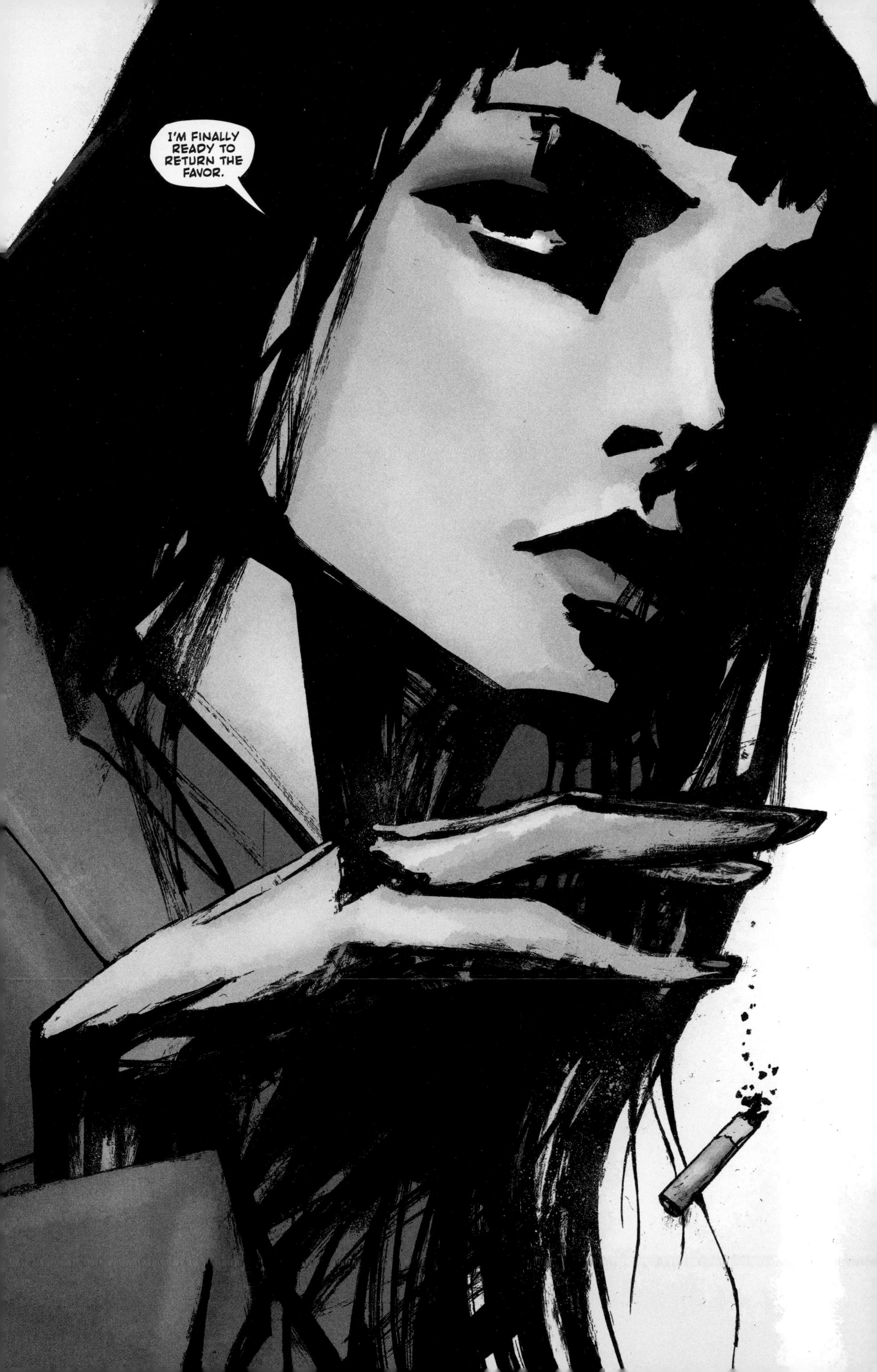
I'M FINALLY READY TO RETURN THE FAVOR.

CHAPTER TWO:

ALTERNATIVE FACTS

I am an architect / They call me a butcher

"Faster"
—Manic Street Preachers

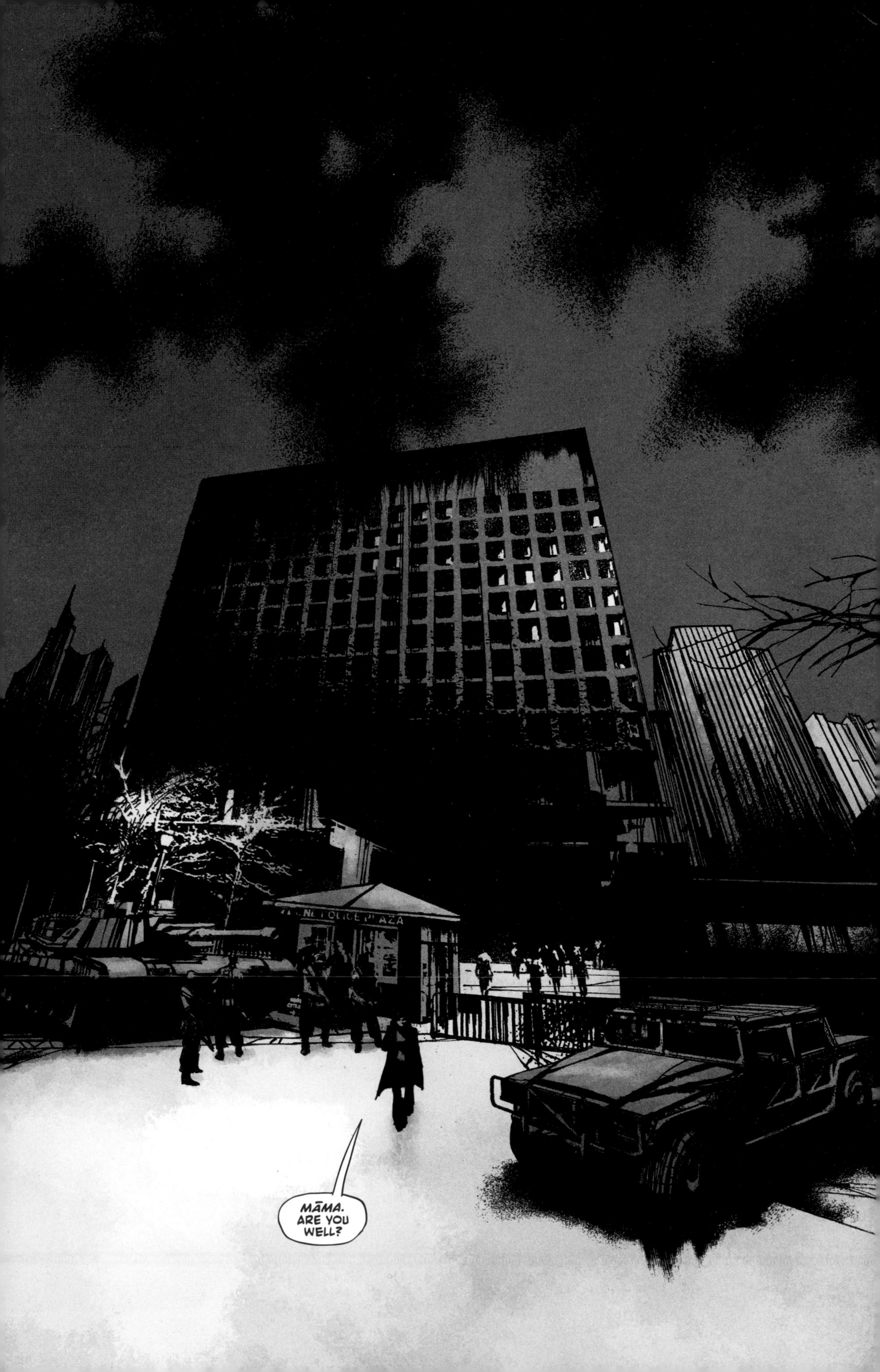
MĀMA. ARE YOU WELL?

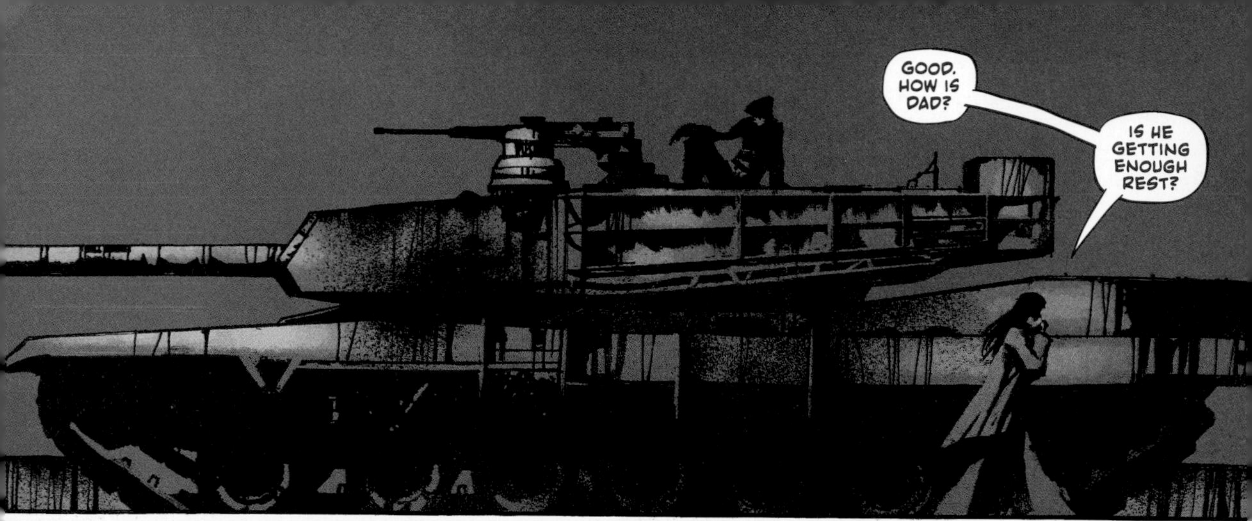
GOOD. HOW IS DAD?
IS HE GETTING ENOUGH REST?
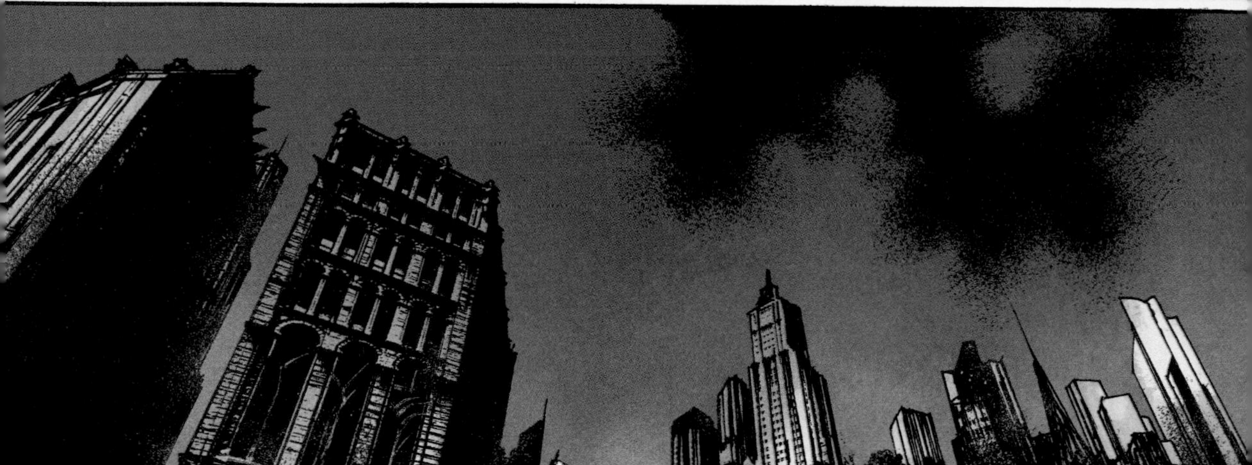
GOOD. I'M... OH, NO. I'M OUTSIDE. FOR A WALK.
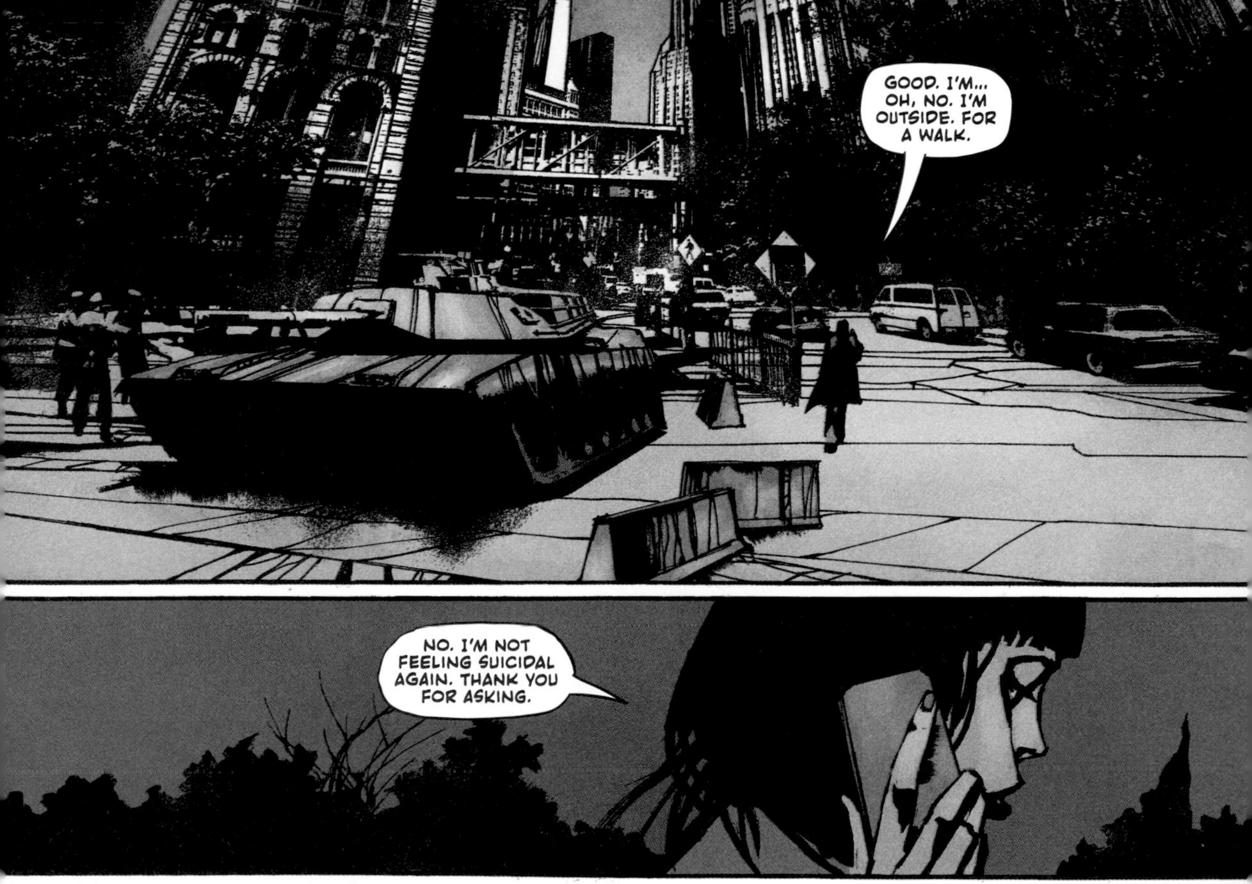
NO. I'M NOT FEELING SUICIDAL AGAIN. THANK YOU FOR ASKING.

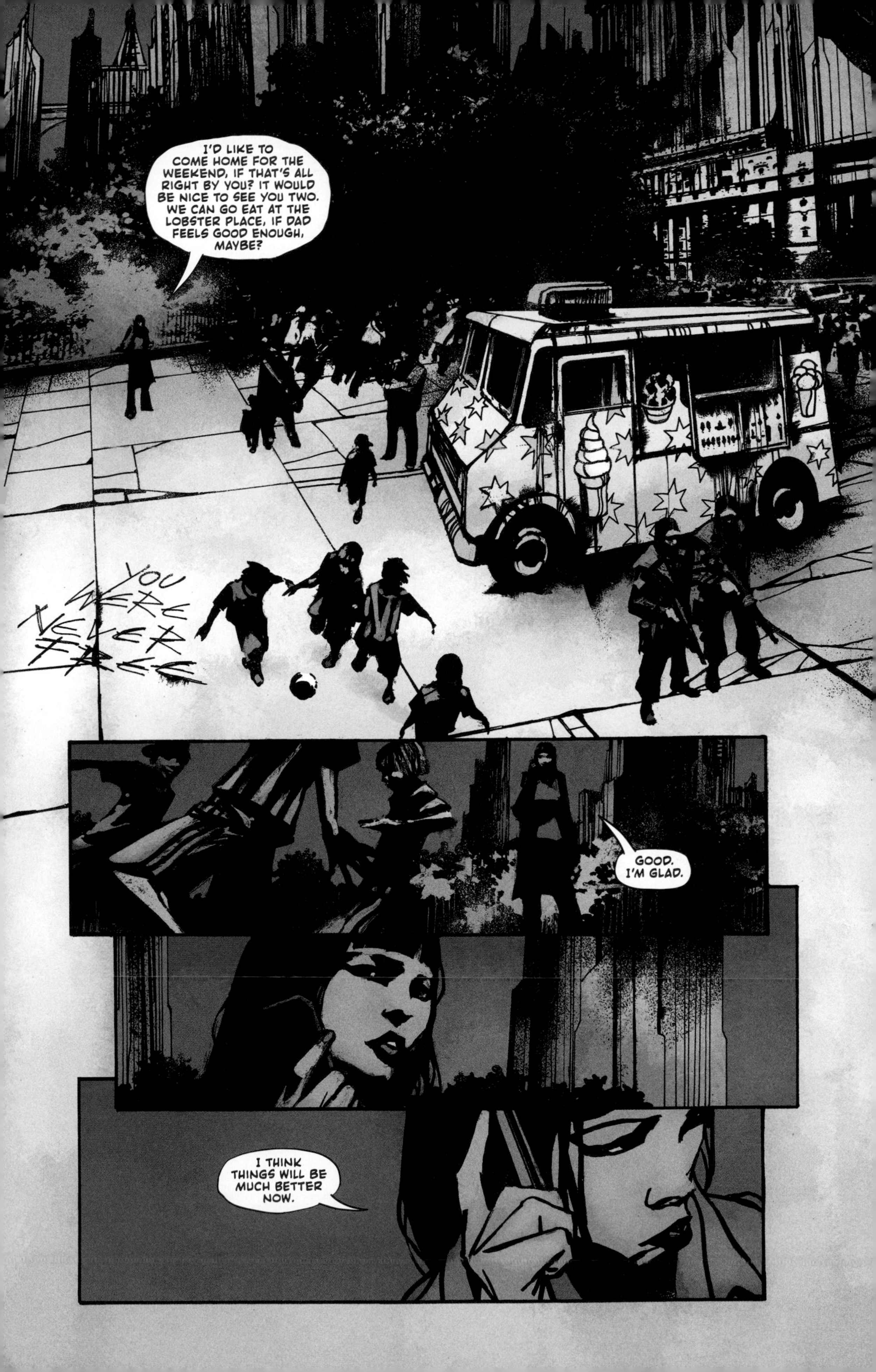
I'D LIKE TO COME HOME FOR THE WEEKEND, IF THAT'S ALL RIGHT BY YOU? IT WOULD BE NICE TO SEE YOU TWO. WE CAN GO EAT AT THE LOBSTER PLACE, IF DAD FEELS GOOD ENOUGH, MAYBE?
YOU WERE NEVER FREE
GOOD. I'M GLAD.
I THINK THINGS WILL BE MUCH BETTER NOW.

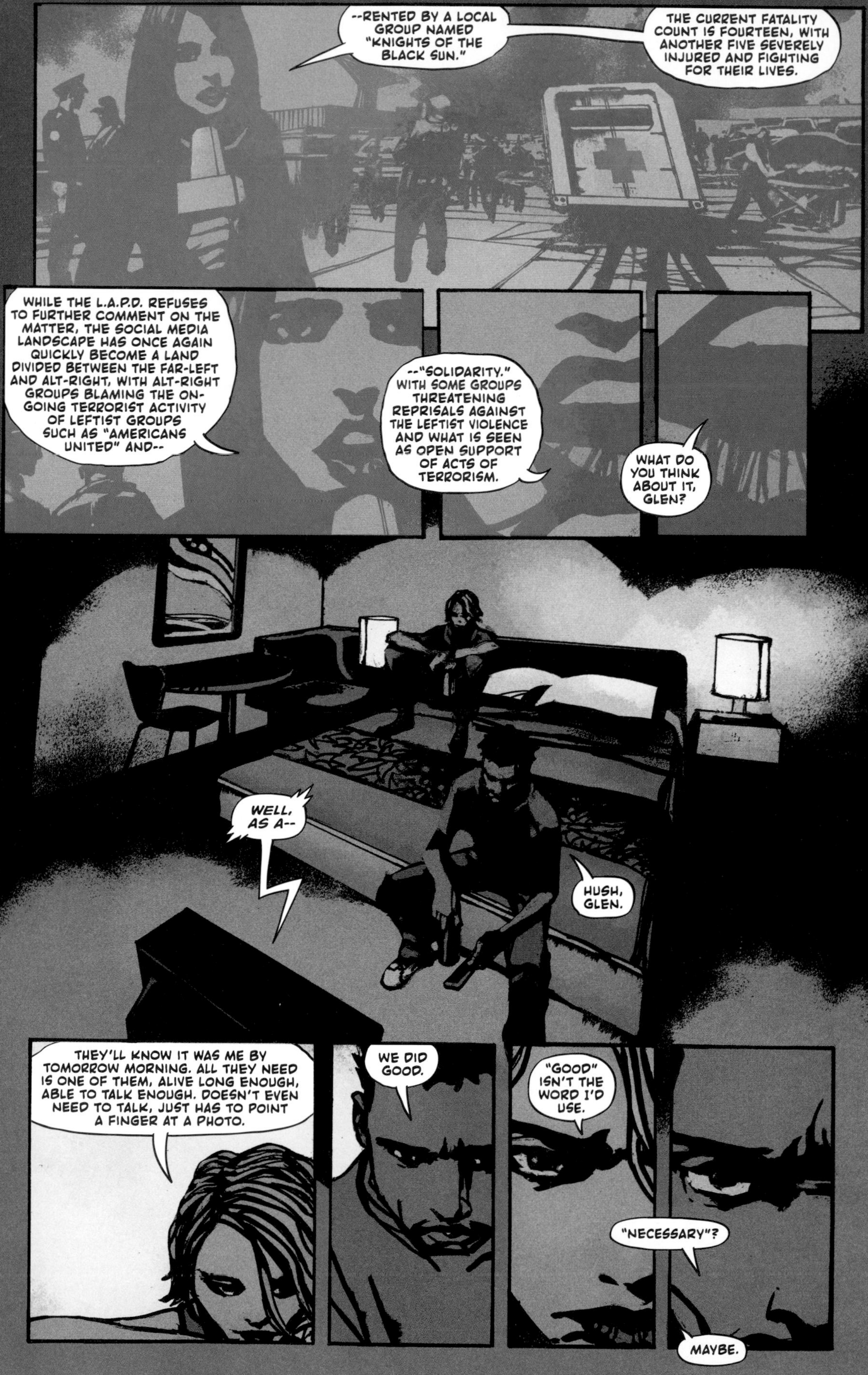
--RENTED BY A LOCAL GROUP NAMED "KNIGHTS OF THE BLACK SUN."
THE CURRENT FATALITY COUNT IS FOURTEEN, WITH ANOTHER FIVE SEVERELY INJURED AND FIGHTING FOR THEIR LIVES.
WHILE THE L.A.P.D. REFUSES TO FURTHER COMMENT ON THE MATTER, THE SOCIAL MEDIA LANDSCAPE HAS ONCE AGAIN QUICKLY BECOME A LAND DIVIDED BETWEEN THE FAR-LEFT AND ALT-RIGHT, WITH ALT-RIGHT GROUPS BLAMING THE ON-GOING TERRORIST ACTIVITY OF LEFTIST GROUPS SUCH AS "AMERICANS UNITED" AND--
--"SOLIDARITY." WITH SOME GROUPS THREATENING REPRISALS AGAINST THE LEFTIST VIOLENCE AND WHAT IS SEEN AS OPEN SUPPORT OF ACTS OF TERRORISM.
WHAT DO YOU THINK ABOUT IT, GLEN?
WELL, AS A--
HUSH, GLEN.
THEY'LL KNOW IT WAS ME BY TOMORROW MORNING. ALL THEY NEED IS ONE OF THEM, ALIVE LONG ENOUGH, ABLE TO TALK ENOUGH. DOESN'T EVEN NEED TO TALK, JUST HAS TO POINT A FINGER AT A PHOTO.
WE DID GOOD.
"GOOD" ISN'T THE WORD I'D USE.
"NECESSARY"?
MAYBE.

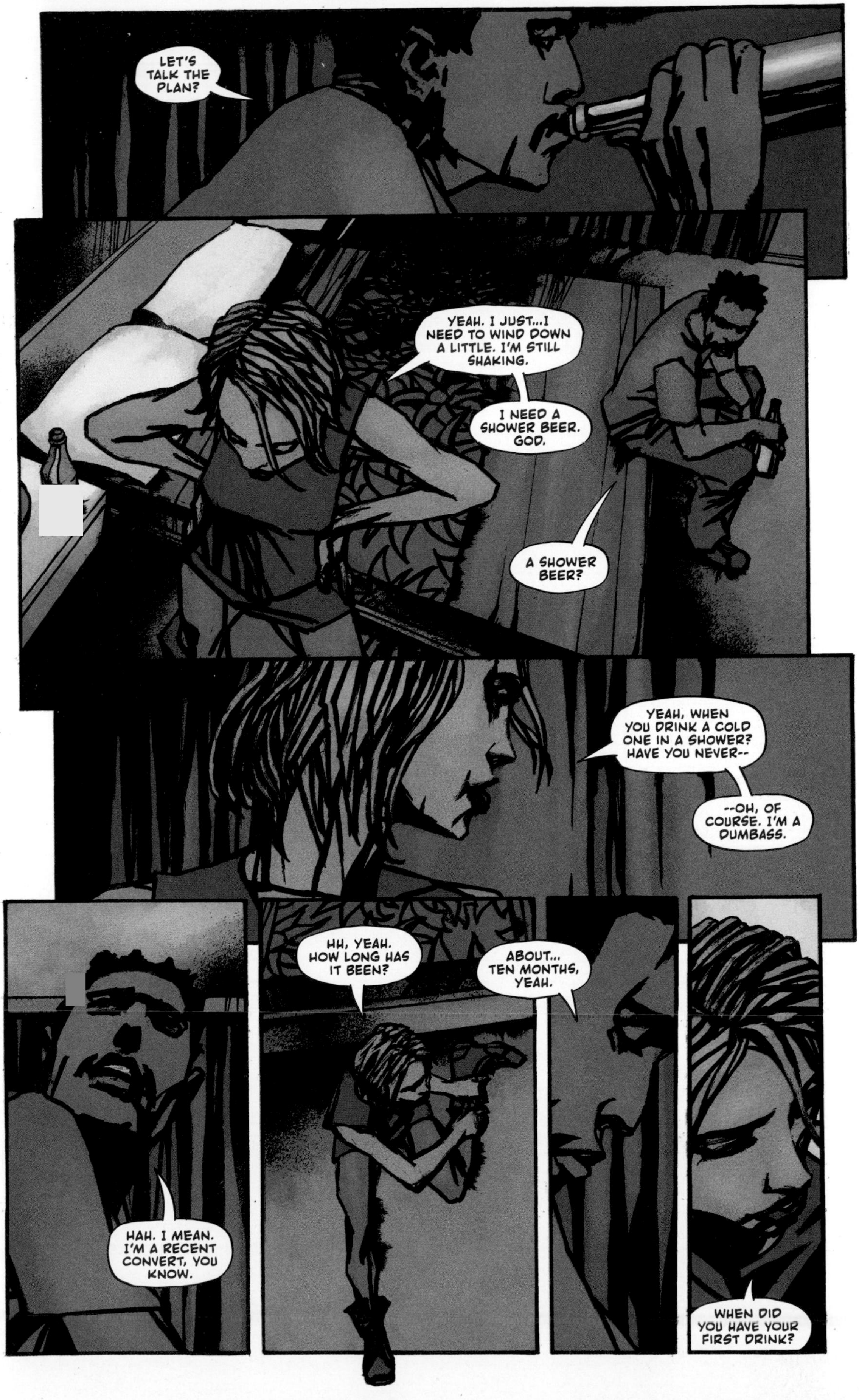
LET'S TALK THE PLAN?
YEAH. I JUST...I NEED TO WIND DOWN A LITTLE. I'M STILL SHAKING.
I NEED A SHOWER BEER. GOD.
A SHOWER BEER?
YEAH, WHEN YOU DRINK A COLD ONE IN A SHOWER? HAVE YOU NEVER--
--OH, OF COURSE. I'M A DUMBASS.
HAH. I MEAN. I'M A RECENT CONVERT, YOU KNOW.
HH, YEAH. HOW LONG HAS IT BEEN?
ABOUT... TEN MONTHS, YEAH.
WHEN DID YOU HAVE YOUR FIRST DRINK?

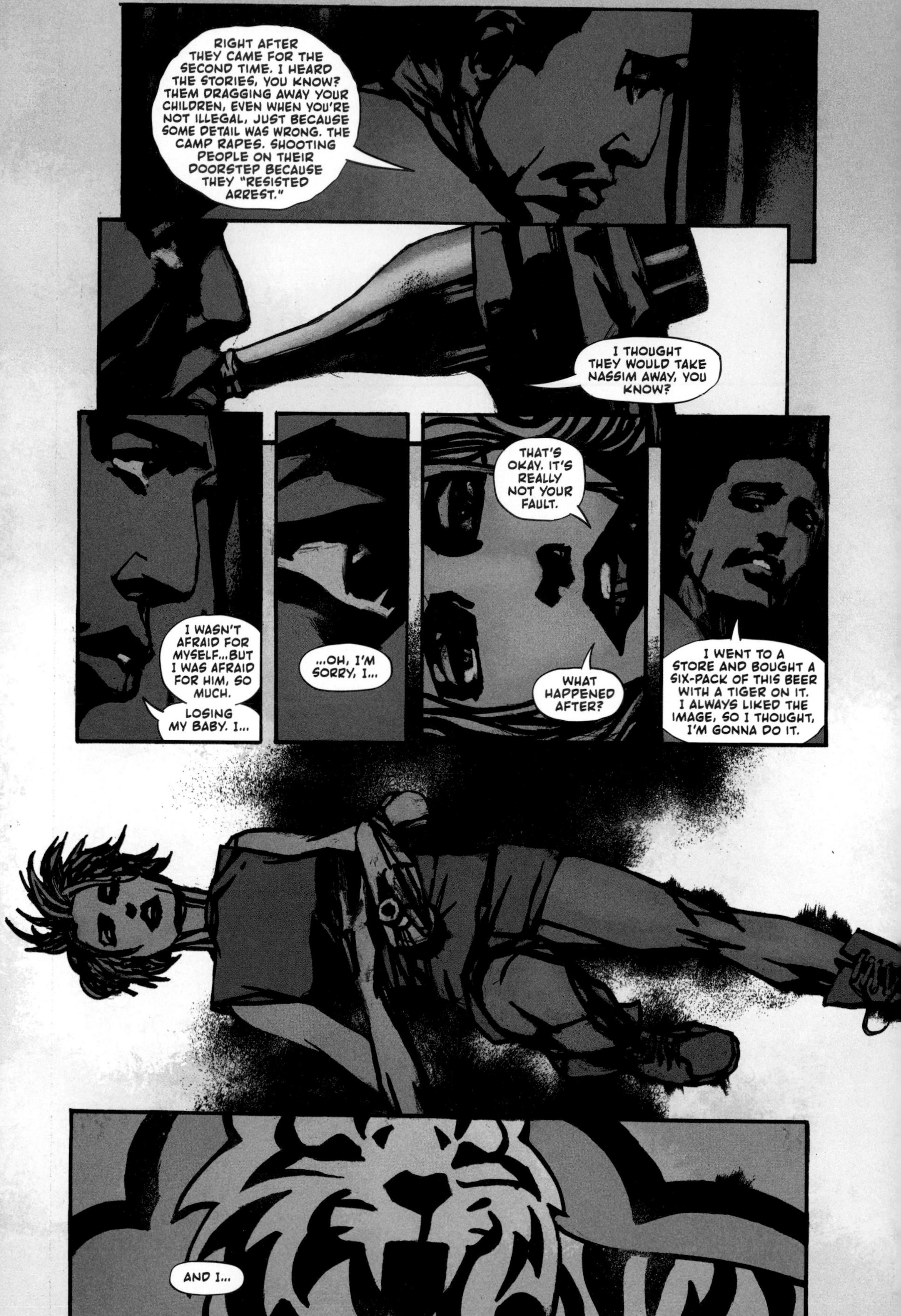
RIGHT AFTER THEY CAME FOR THE SECOND TIME. I HEARD THE STORIES, YOU KNOW? THEM DRAGGING AWAY YOUR CHILDREN, EVEN WHEN YOU'RE NOT ILLEGAL, JUST BECAUSE SOME DETAIL WAS WRONG. THE CAMP RAPES. SHOOTING PEOPLE ON THEIR DOORSTEP BECAUSE THEY "RESISTED ARREST."
I THOUGHT THEY WOULD TAKE NASSIM AWAY, YOU KNOW?
I WASN'T AFRAID FOR MYSELF...BUT I WAS AFRAID FOR HIM, SO MUCH.
LOSING MY BABY. I...
...OH, I'M SORRY, I...
THAT'S OKAY. IT'S REALLY NOT YOUR FAULT.
WHAT HAPPENED AFTER?
I WENT TO A STORE AND BOUGHT A SIX-PACK OF THIS BEER WITH A TIGER ON IT. I ALWAYS LIKED THE IMAGE, SO I THOUGHT, I'M GONNA DO IT.
AND I...

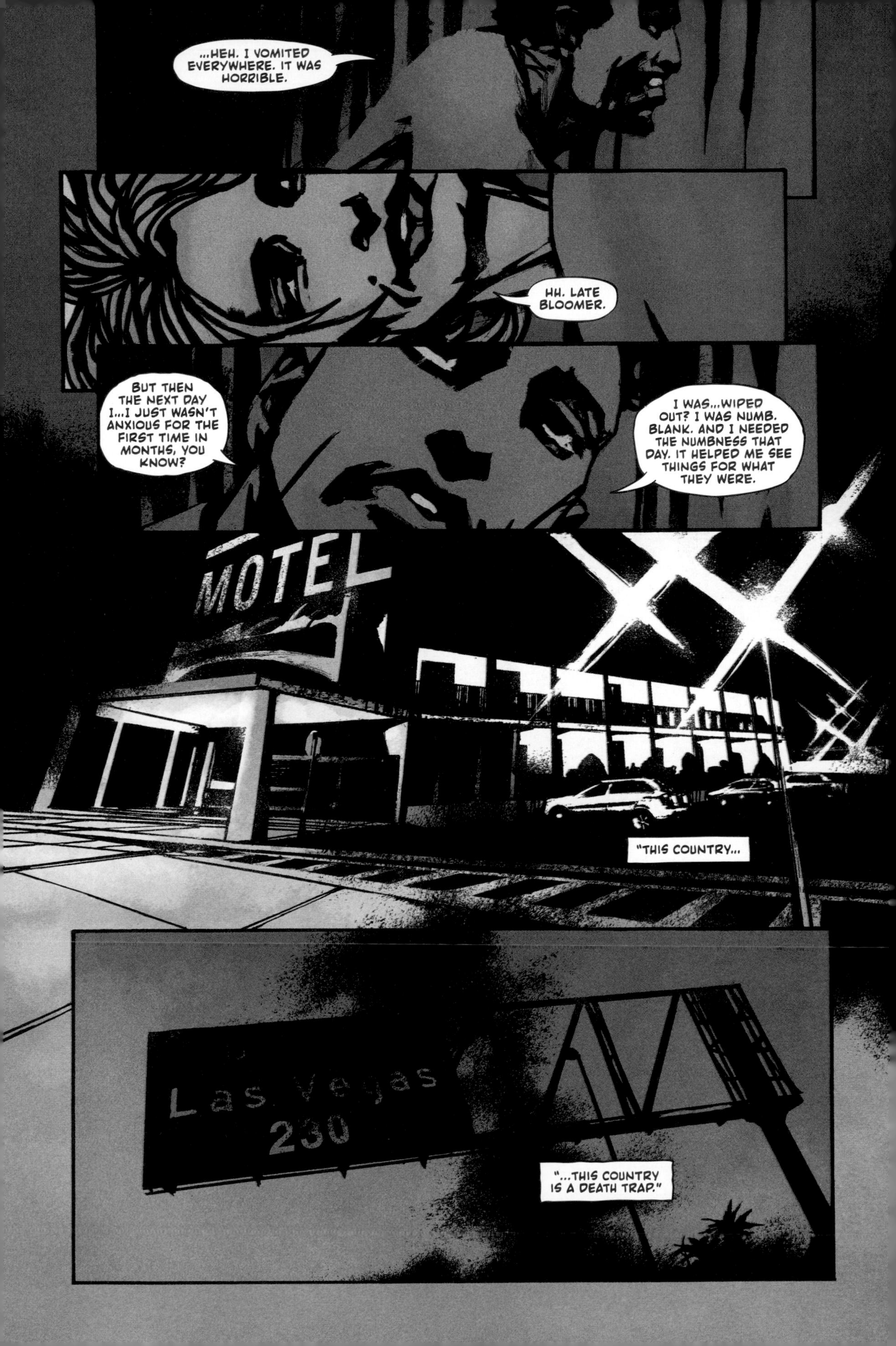
...HEH. I VOMITED EVERYWHERE. IT WAS HORRIBLE.
HH. LATE BLOOMER.
BUT THEN THE NEXT DAY I...I JUST WASN'T ANXIOUS FOR THE FIRST TIME IN MONTHS, YOU KNOW?
I WAS...WIPED OUT? I WAS NUMB. BLANK. AND I NEEDED THE NUMBNESS THAT DAY. IT HELPED ME SEE THINGS FOR WHAT THEY WERE.
MOTEL
"THIS COUNTRY...
Las Vegas
230
"...THIS COUNTRY IS A DEATH TRAP."

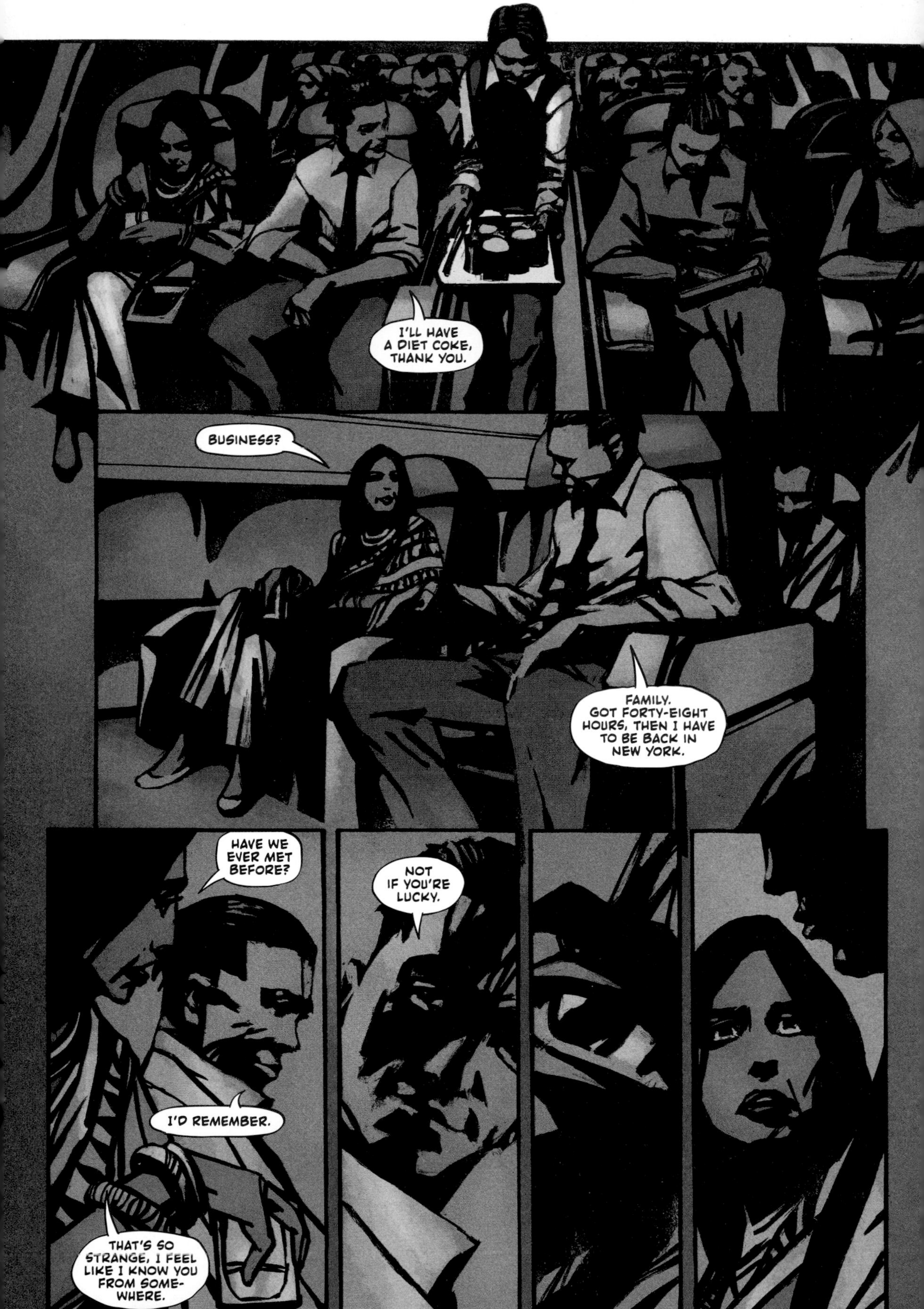
I'LL HAVE A DIET COKE, THANK YOU.
BUSINESS?
FAMILY. GOT FORTY-EIGHT HOURS, THEN I HAVE TO BE BACK IN NEW YORK.
HAVE WE EVER MET BEFORE?
I'D REMEMBER.
THAT'S SO STRANGE, I FEEL LIKE I KNOW YOU FROM SOME-WHERE.
NOT IF YOU'RE LUCKY.

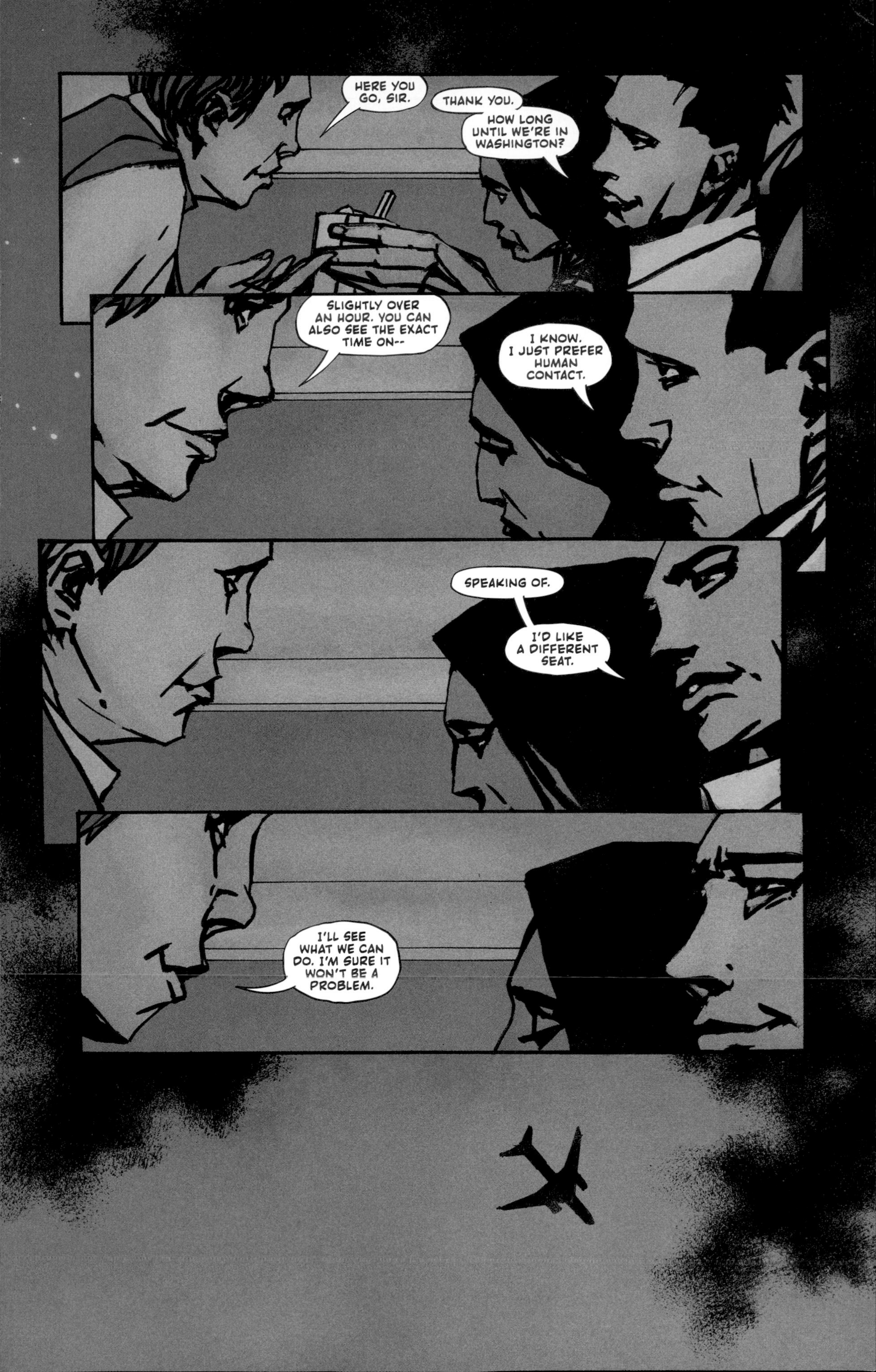
HERE YOU GO, SIR.
THANK YOU.
HOW LONG UNTIL WE'RE IN WASHINGTON?
SLIGHTLY OVER AN HOUR. YOU CAN ALSO SEE THE EXACT TIME ON--
I KNOW. I JUST PREFER HUMAN CONTACT.
SPEAKING OF.
I'D LIKE A DIFFERENT SEAT.
I'LL SEE WHAT WE CAN DO. I'M SURE IT WON'T BE A PROBLEM.

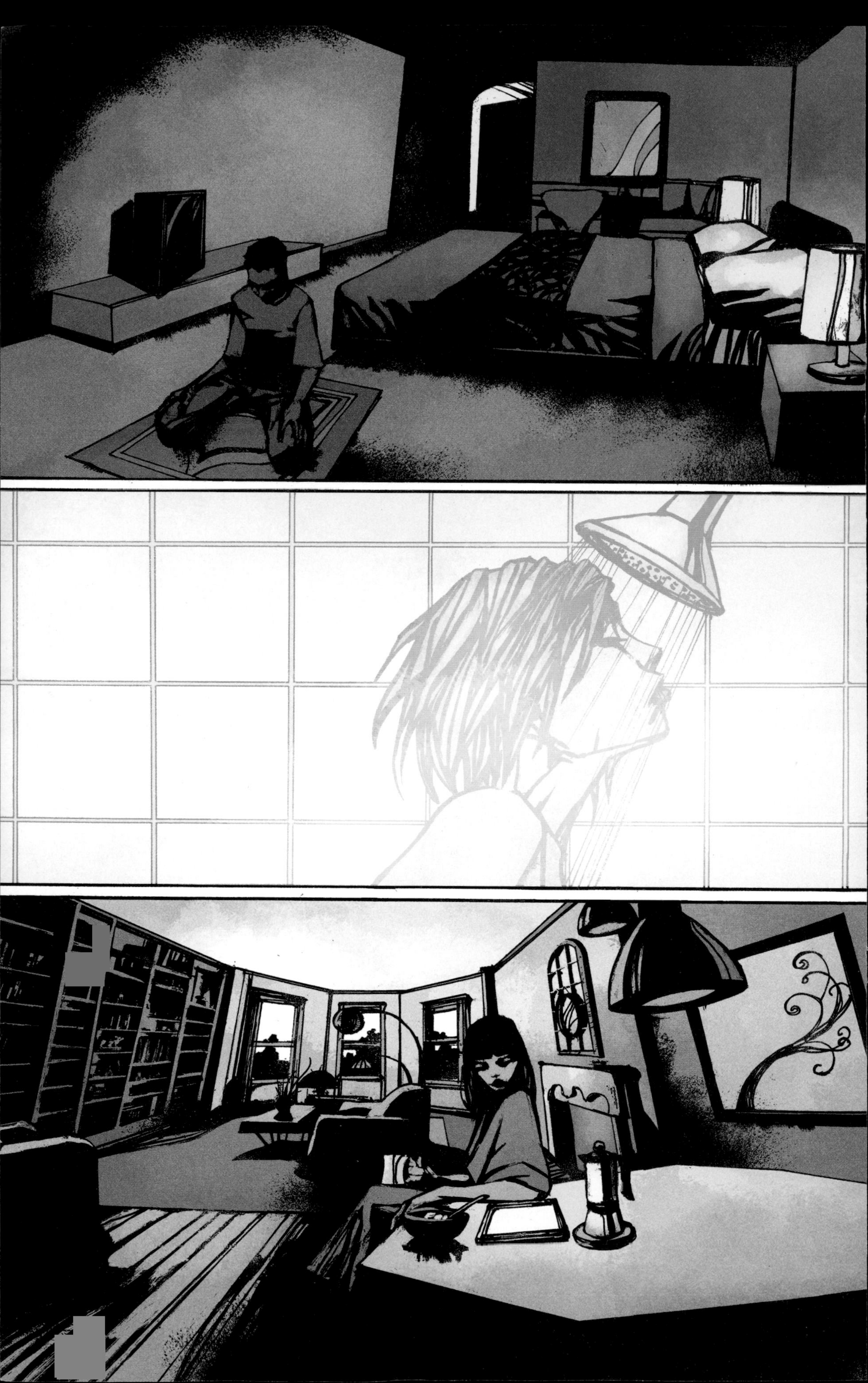

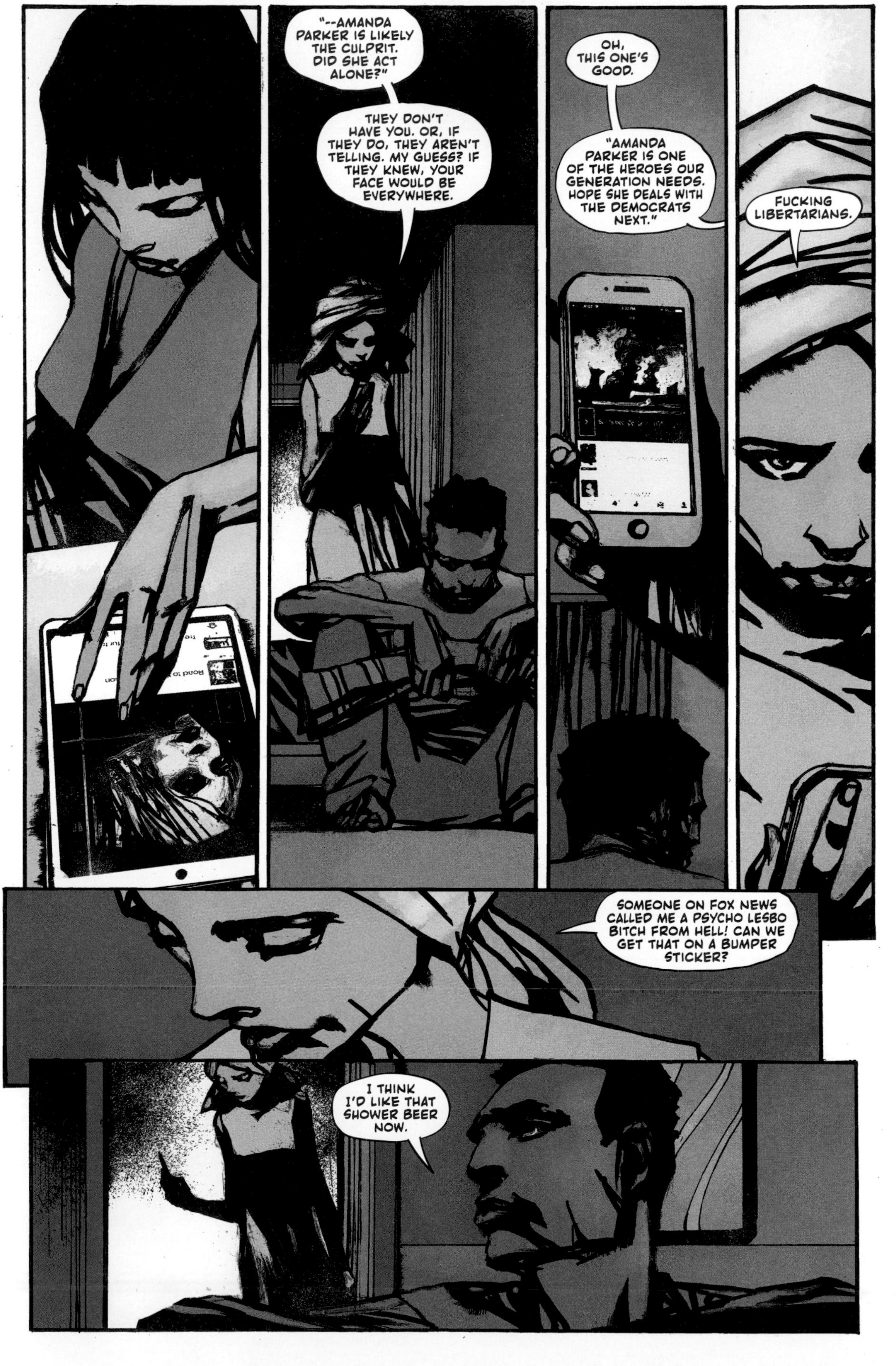
"--AMANDA PARKER IS LIKELY THE CULPRIT. DID SHE ACT ALONE?"
THEY DON'T HAVE YOU. OR, IF THEY DO, THEY AREN'T TELLING. MY GUESS? IF THEY KNEW, YOUR FACE WOULD BE EVERYWHERE.
OH, THIS ONE'S GOOD.
"AMANDA PARKER IS ONE OF THE HEROES OUR GENERATION NEEDS. HOPE SHE DEALS WITH THE DEMOCRATS NEXT."
FUCKING LIBERTARIANS.
SOMEONE ON FOX NEWS CALLED ME A PSYCHO LESBO BITCH FROM HELL! CAN WE GET THAT ON A BUMPER STICKER?
I THINK I'D LIKE THAT SHOWER BEER NOW.

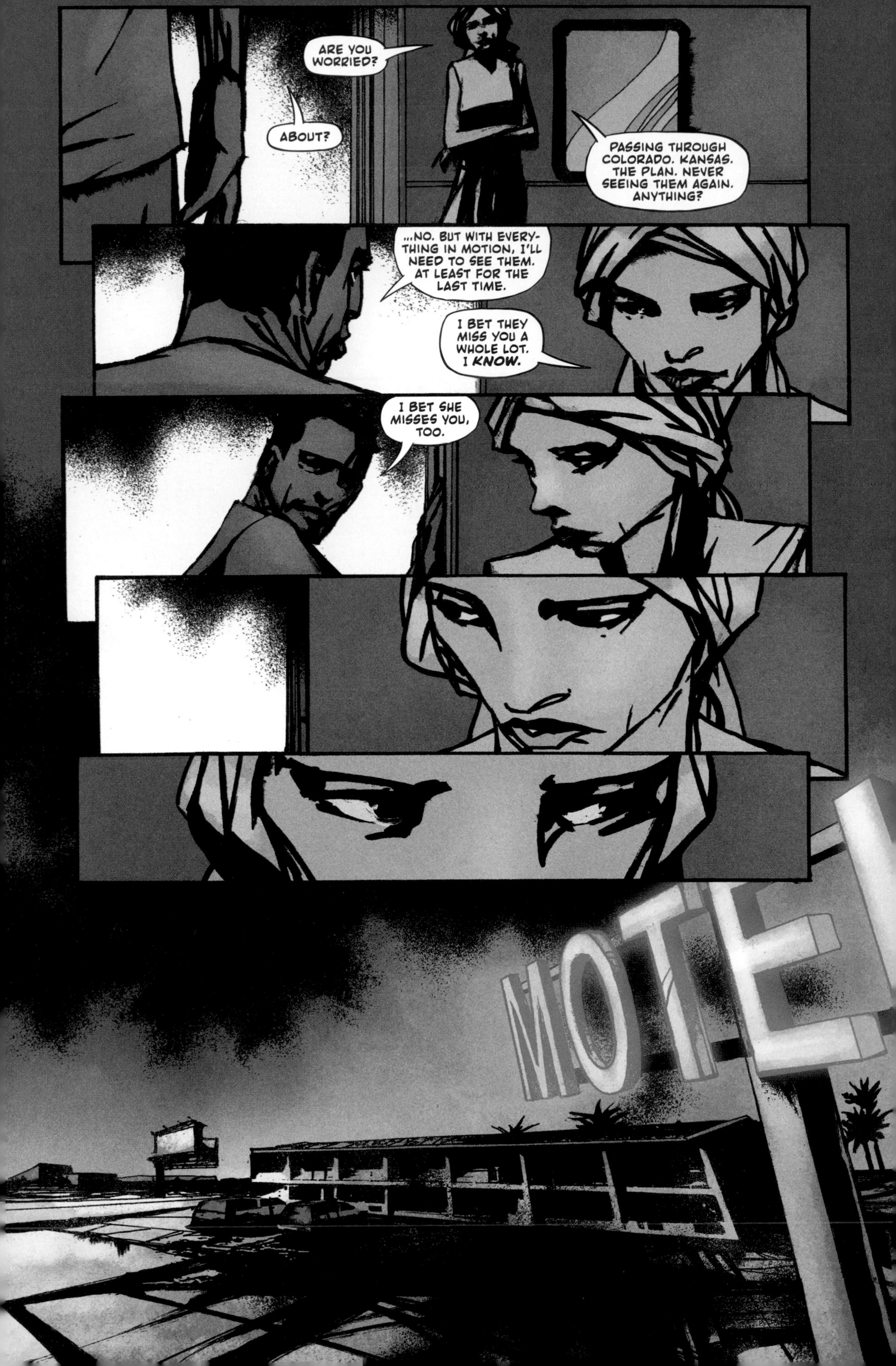
ARE YOU WORRIED?
ABOUT?
PASSING THROUGH COLORADO. KANSAS. THE PLAN. NEVER SEEING THEM AGAIN. ANYTHING?
...NO. BUT WITH EVERY-THING IN MOTION, I'LL NEED TO SEE THEM. AT LEAST FOR THE LAST TIME.
I BET THEY MISS YOU A WHOLE LOT. I ***KNOW.***
I BET SHE MISSES YOU, TOO.
MOTEL

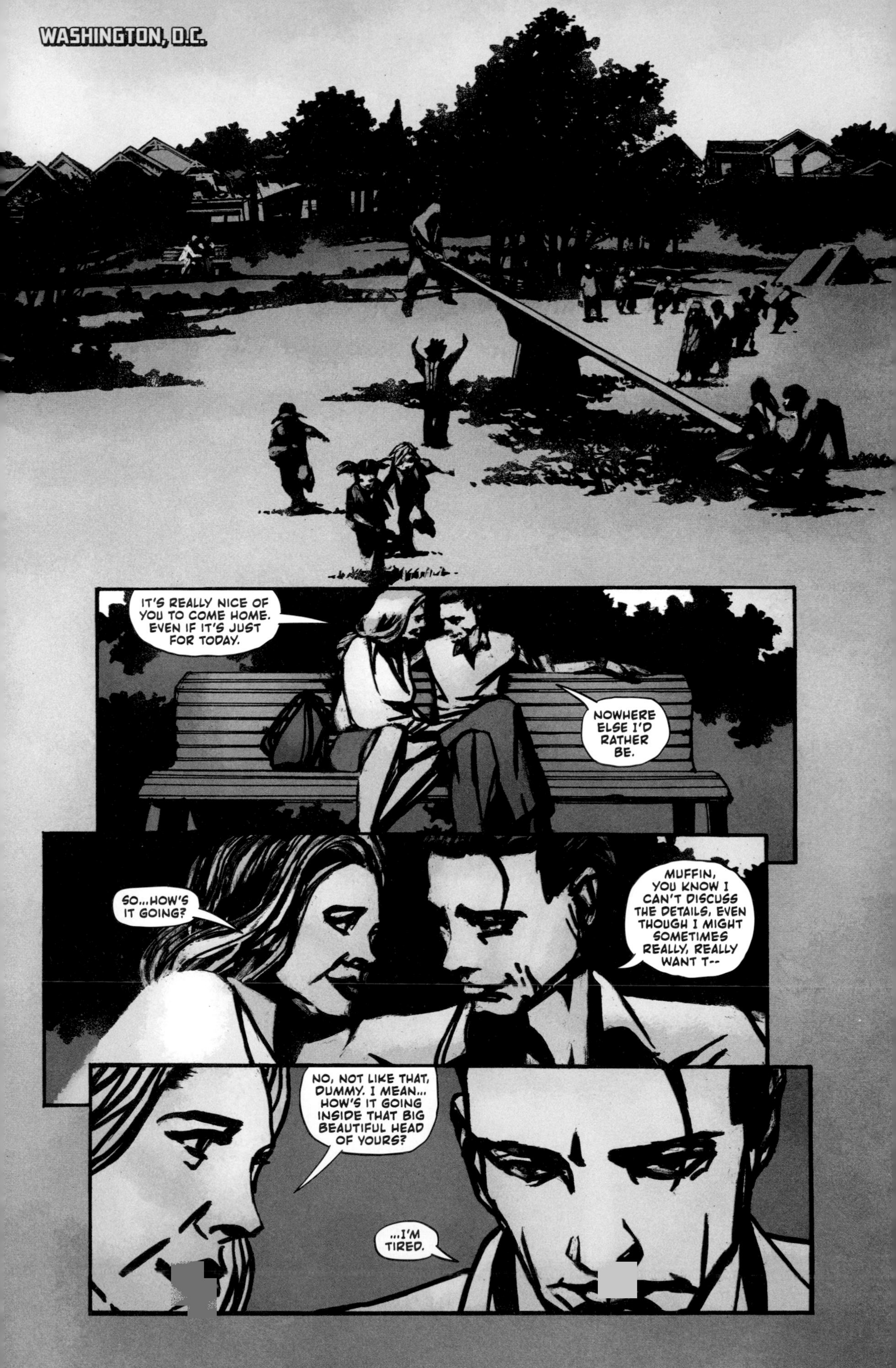
WASHINGTON, D.C.
IT'S REALLY NICE OF YOU TO COME HOME. EVEN IF IT'S JUST FOR TODAY.
NOWHERE ELSE I'D RATHER BE.
SO...HOW'S IT GOING?
MUFFIN, YOU KNOW I CAN'T DISCUSS THE DETAILS, EVEN THOUGH I MIGHT SOMETIMES REALLY, REALLY WANT T--
NO, NOT LIKE THAT, DUMMY. I MEAN... HOW'S IT GOING INSIDE THAT BIG BEAUTIFUL HEAD OF YOURS?
...I'M TIRED.

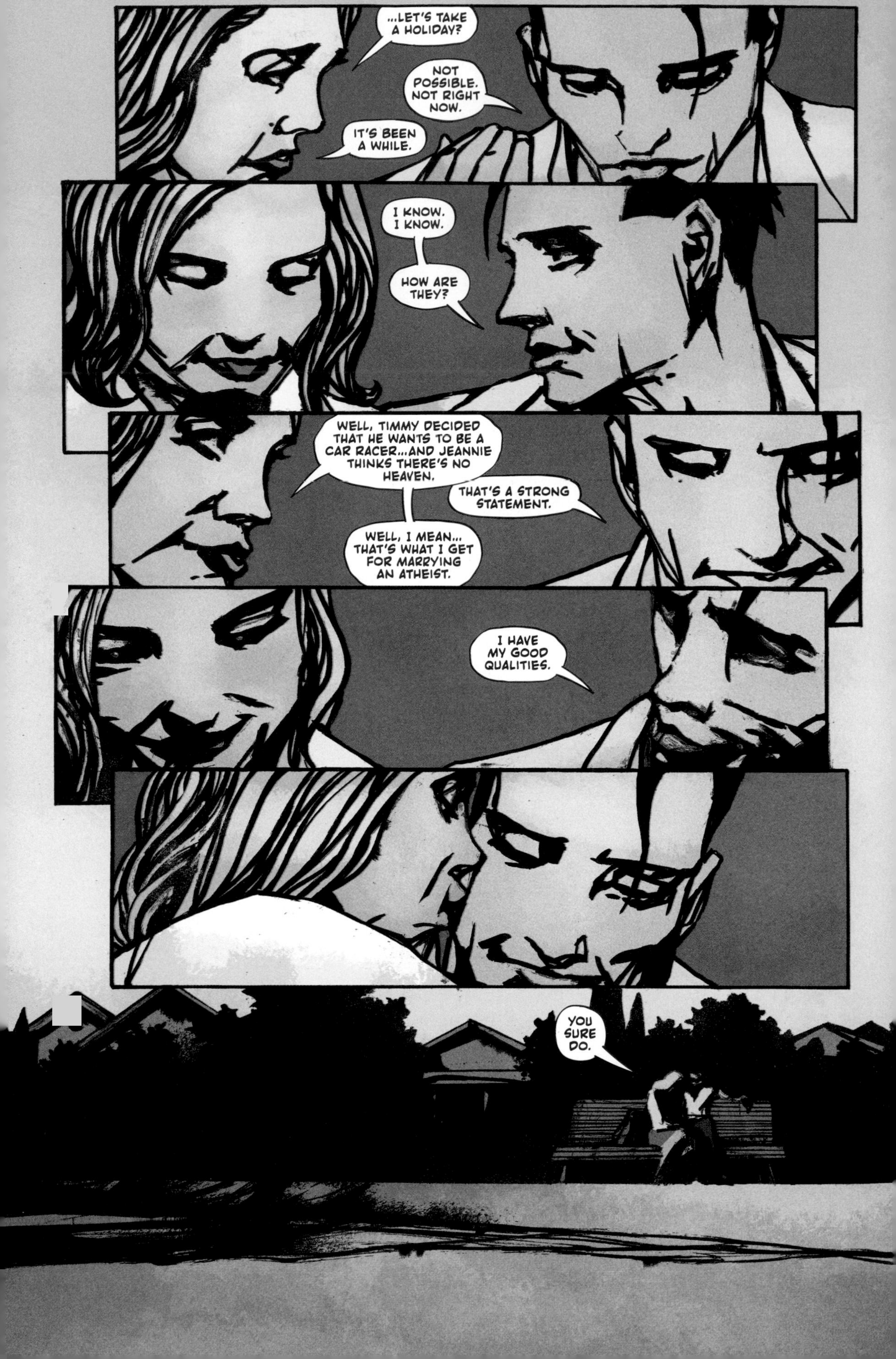
...LET'S TAKE A HOLIDAY?
NOT POSSIBLE. NOT RIGHT NOW.
IT'S BEEN A WHILE.
I KNOW. I KNOW.
HOW ARE THEY?
WELL, TIMMY DECIDED THAT HE WANTS TO BE A CAR RACER...AND JEANNIE THINKS THERE'S NO HEAVEN.
THAT'S A STRONG STATEMENT.
WELL, I MEAN... THAT'S WHAT I GET FOR MARRYING AN ATHEIST.
I HAVE MY GOOD QUALITIES.
YOU SURE DO.

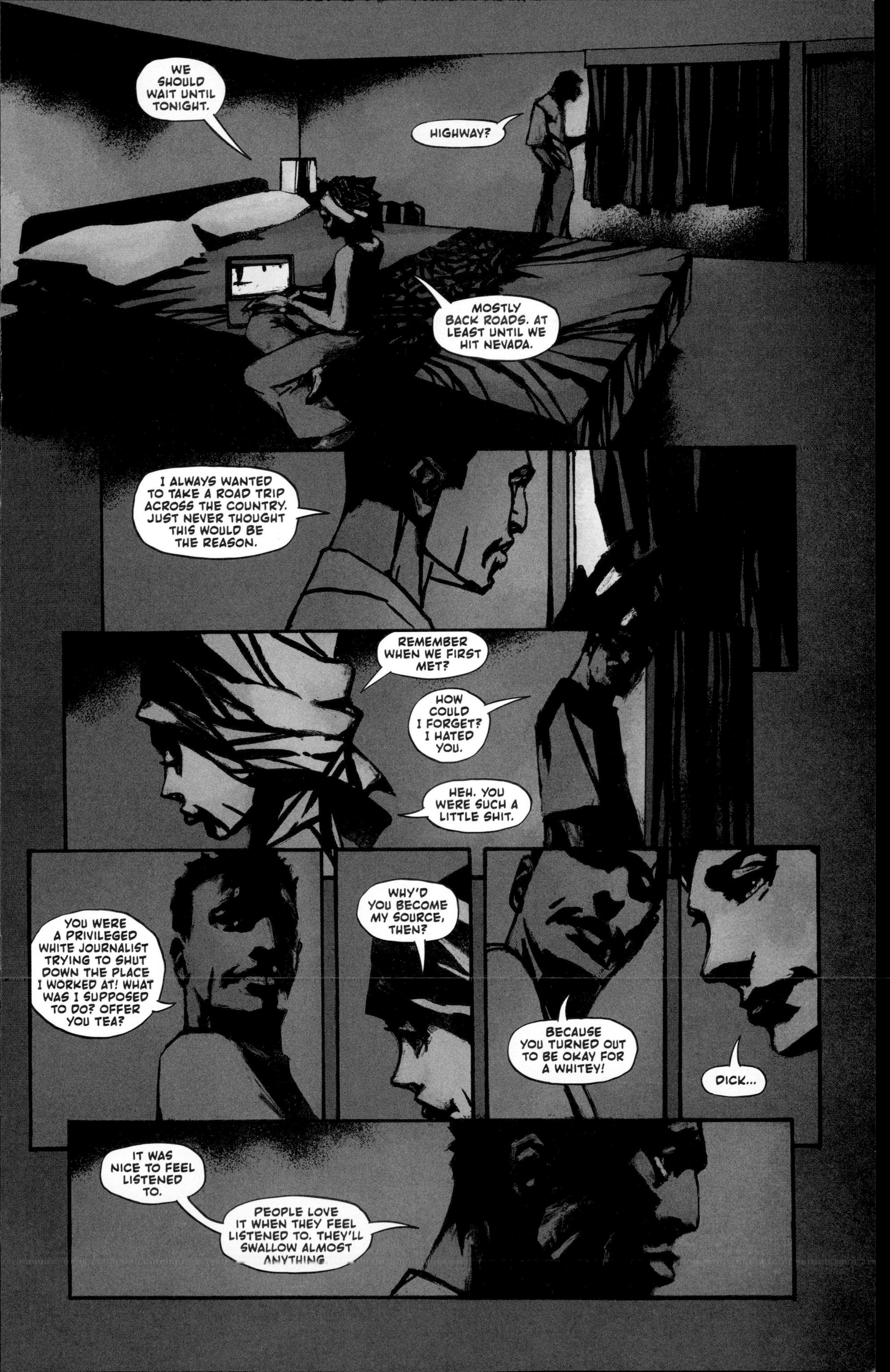
WE SHOULD WAIT UNTIL TONIGHT.
HIGHWAY?
MOSTLY BACK ROADS. AT LEAST UNTIL WE HIT NEVADA.
I ALWAYS WANTED TO TAKE A ROAD TRIP ACROSS THE COUNTRY. JUST NEVER THOUGHT THIS WOULD BE THE REASON.
REMEMBER WHEN WE FIRST MET?
HOW COULD I FORGET? I HATED YOU.
HEH. YOU WERE SUCH A LITTLE SHIT.
YOU WERE A PRIVILEGED WHITE JOURNALIST TRYING TO SHUT DOWN THE PLACE I WORKED AT! WHAT WAS I SUPPOSED TO DO? OFFER YOU TEA?
WHY'D YOU BECOME MY SOURCE, THEN?
BECAUSE YOU TURNED OUT TO BE OKAY FOR A WHITEY!
DICK...
IT WAS NICE TO FEEL LISTENED TO.
PEOPLE LOVE IT WHEN THEY FEEL LISTENED TO. THEY'LL SWALLOW ALMOST ANYTHING.

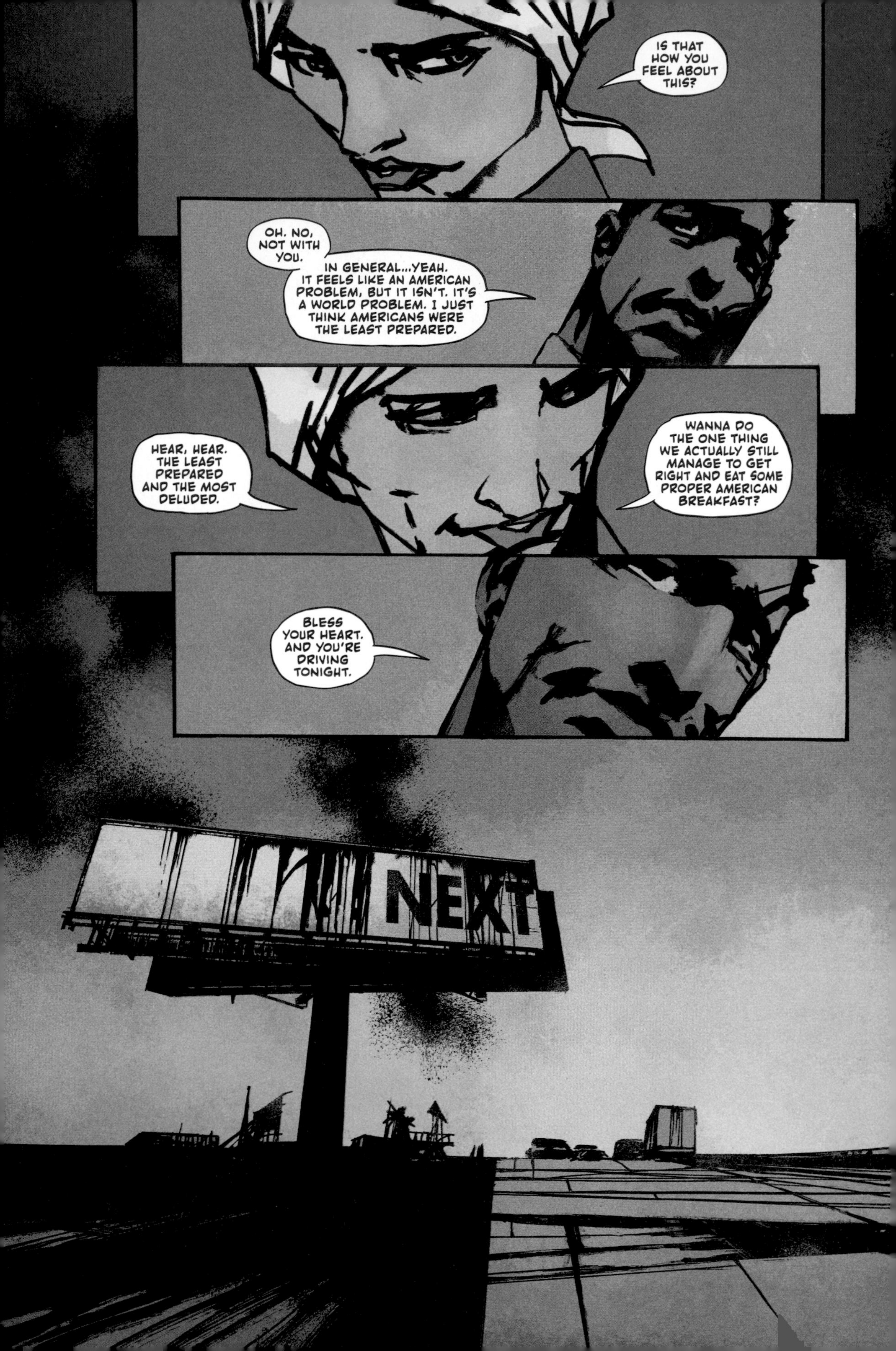

IS THAT HOW YOU FEEL ABOUT THIS?
OH. NO, NOT WITH YOU.
IN GENERAL...YEAH. IT FEELS LIKE AN AMERICAN PROBLEM, BUT IT ISN'T. IT'S A WORLD PROBLEM. I JUST THINK AMERICANS WERE THE LEAST PREPARED.
HEAR, HEAR. THE LEAST PREPARED AND THE MOST DELUDED.
WANNA DO THE ONE THING WE ACTUALLY STILL MANAGE TO GET RIGHT AND EAT SOME PROPER AMERICAN BREAKFAST?
BLESS YOUR HEART. AND YOU'RE DRIVING TONIGHT.
NEXT

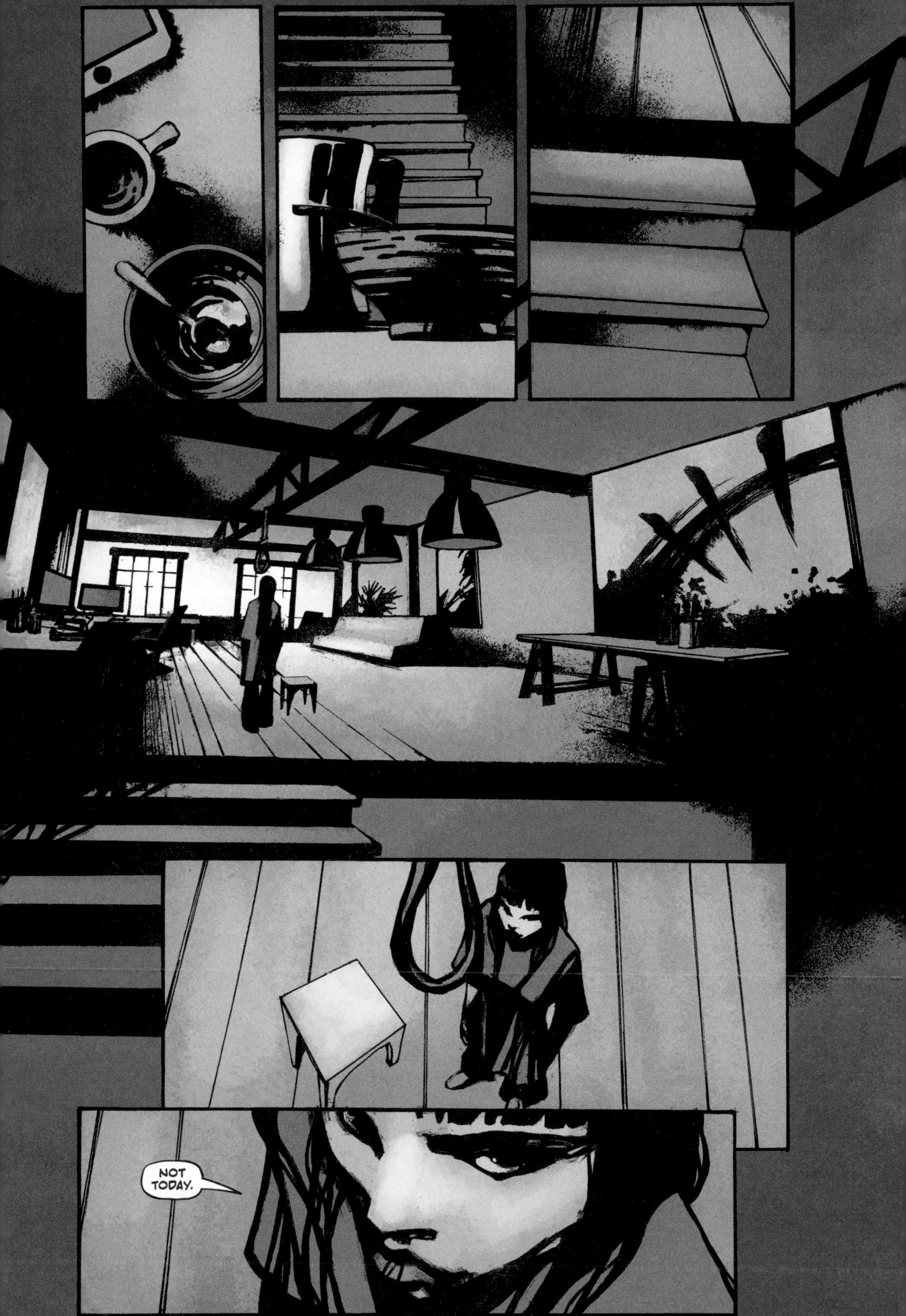
NOT TODAY.

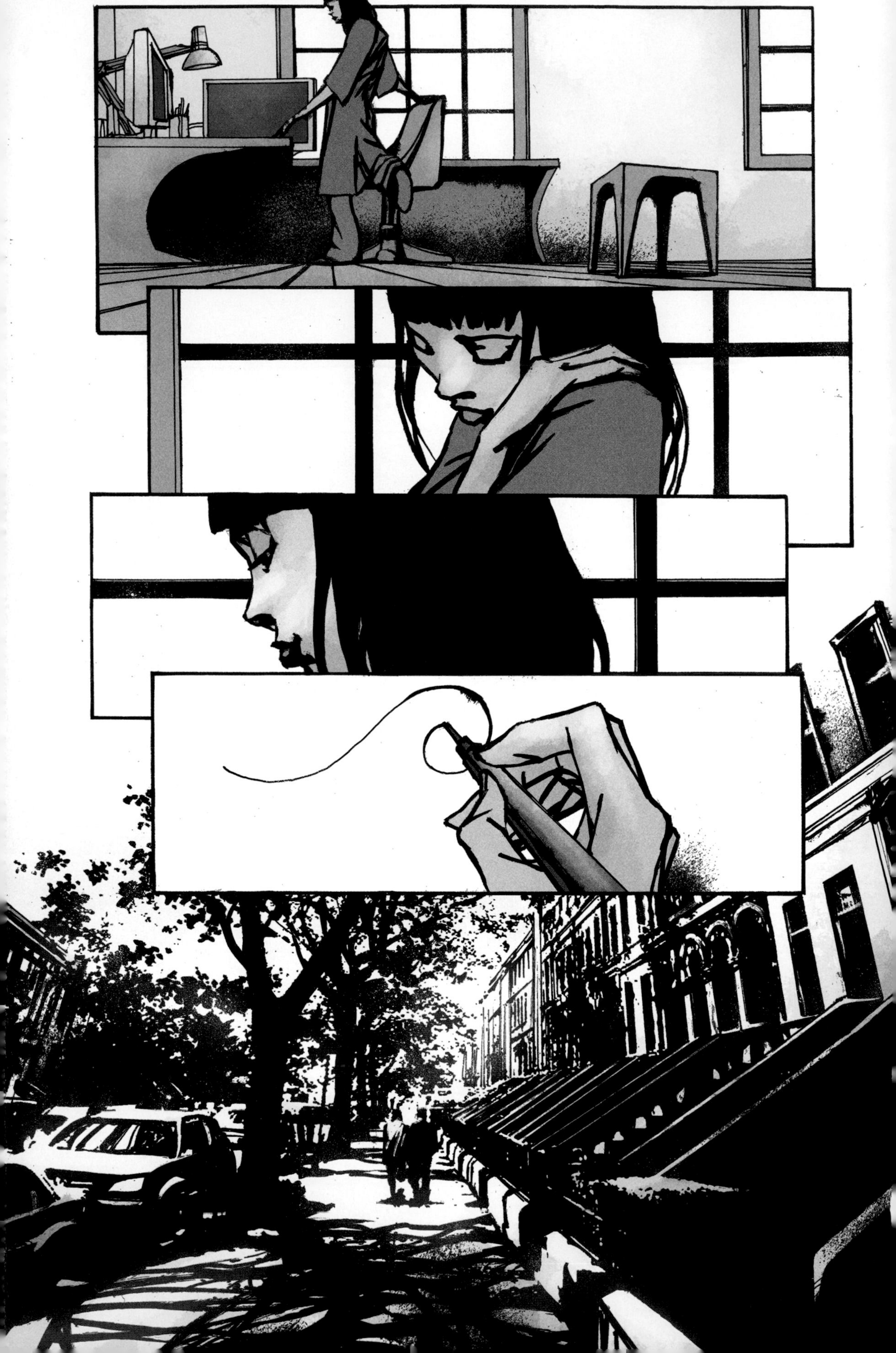

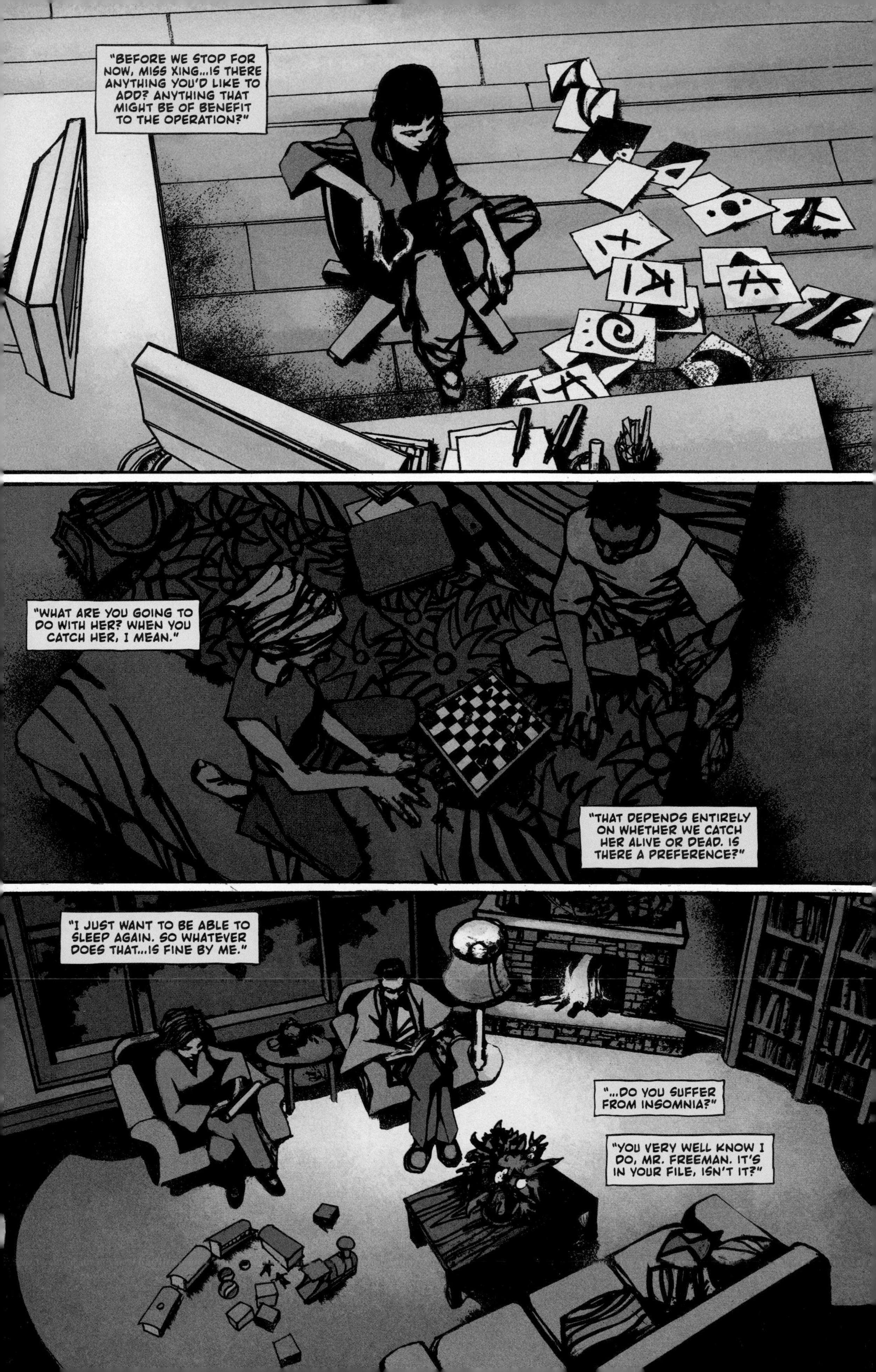
"BEFORE WE STOP FOR NOW, MISS XING...IS THERE ANYTHING YOU'D LIKE TO ADD? ANYTHING THAT MIGHT BE OF BENEFIT TO THE OPERATION?"
"WHAT ARE YOU GOING TO DO WITH HER? WHEN YOU CATCH HER, I MEAN."
"THAT DEPENDS ENTIRELY ON WHETHER WE CATCH HER ALIVE OR DEAD. IS THERE A PREFERENCE?"
"I JUST WANT TO BE ABLE TO SLEEP AGAIN. SO WHATEVER DOES THAT...IS FINE BY ME."
"...DO YOU SUFFER FROM INSOMNIA?"
"YOU VERY WELL KNOW I DO, MR. FREEMAN. IT'S IN YOUR FILE, ISN'T IT?"

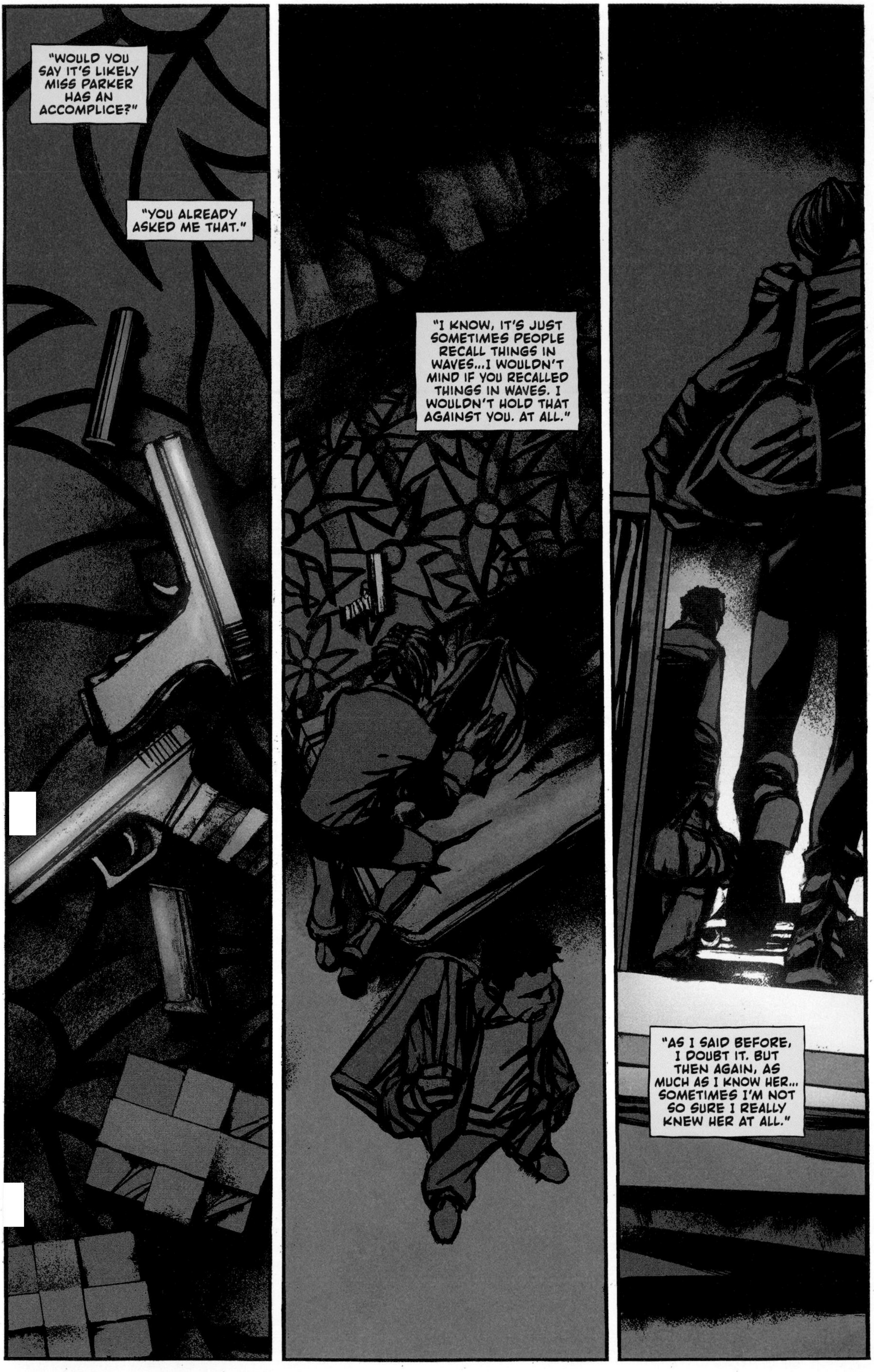
"WOULD YOU SAY IT'S LIKELY MISS PARKER HAS AN ACCOMPLICE?"
"YOU ALREADY ASKED ME THAT."
"I KNOW, IT'S JUST SOMETIMES PEOPLE RECALL THINGS IN WAVES...I WOULDN'T MIND IF YOU RECALLED THINGS IN WAVES. I WOULDN'T HOLD THAT AGAINST YOU. AT ALL."
"AS I SAID BEFORE, I DOUBT IT. BUT THEN AGAIN, AS MUCH AS I KNOW HER... SOMETIMES I'M NOT SO SURE I REALLY KNEW HER AT ALL."

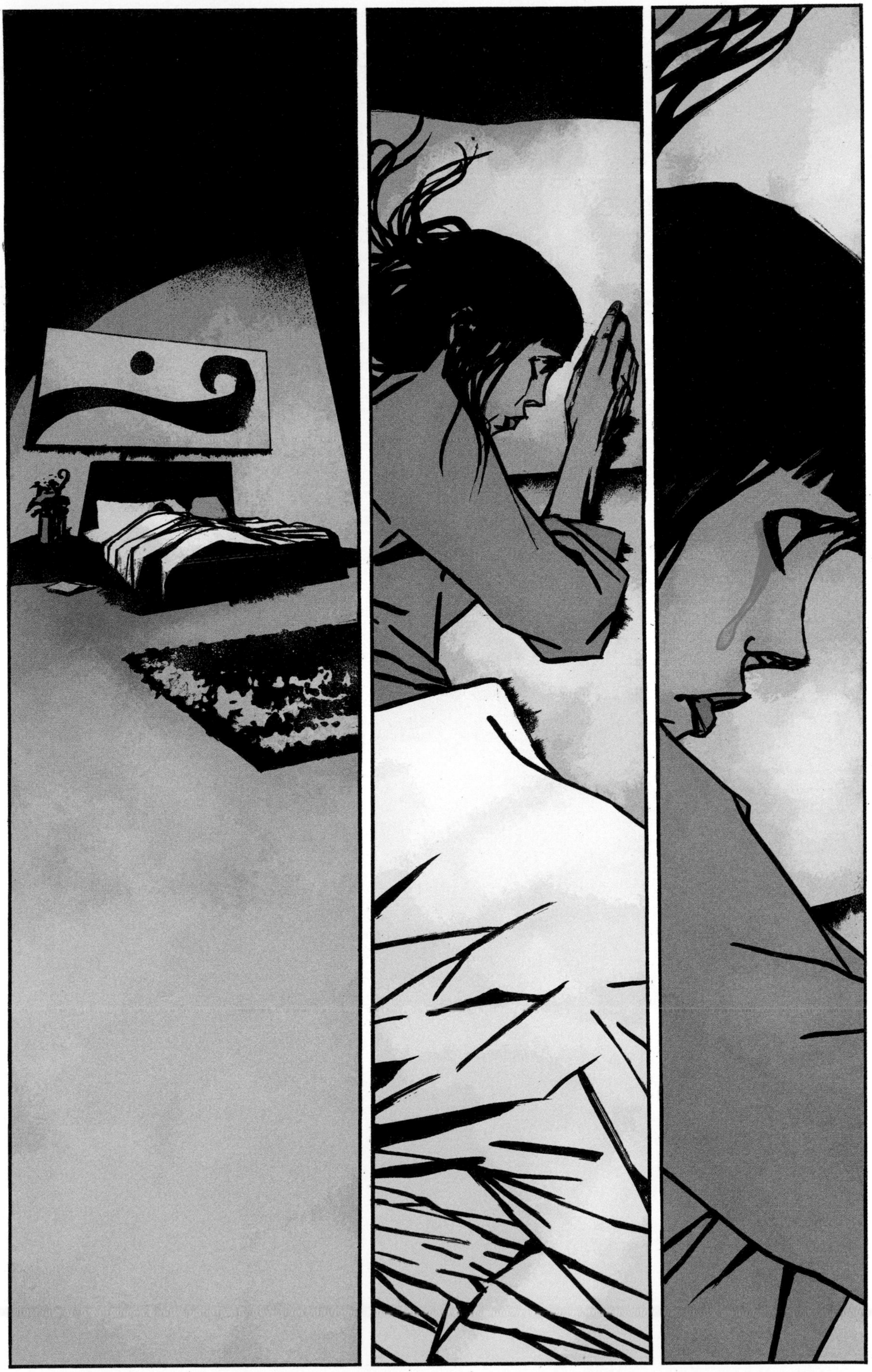

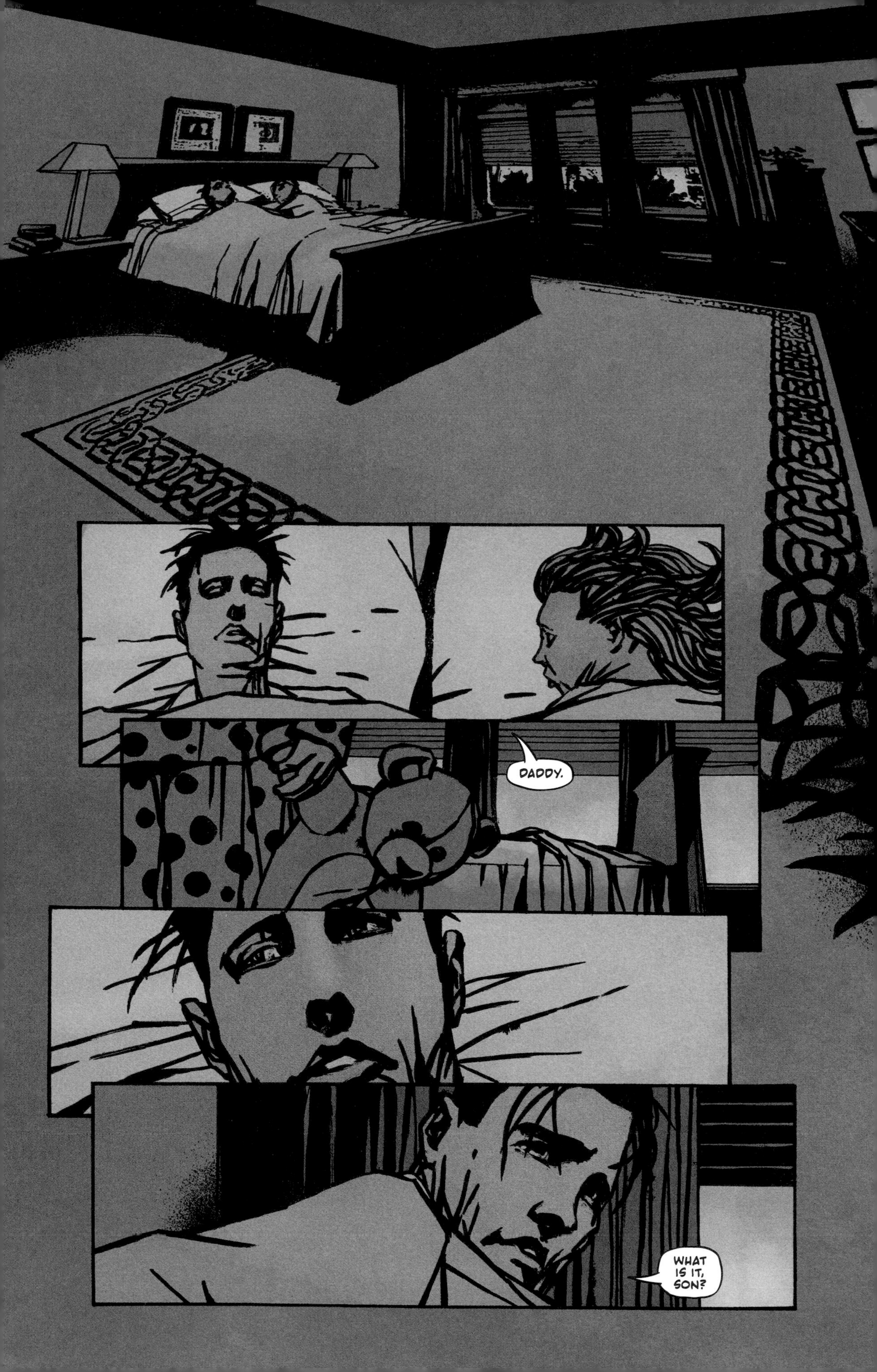
DADDY.
WHAT IS IT, SON?

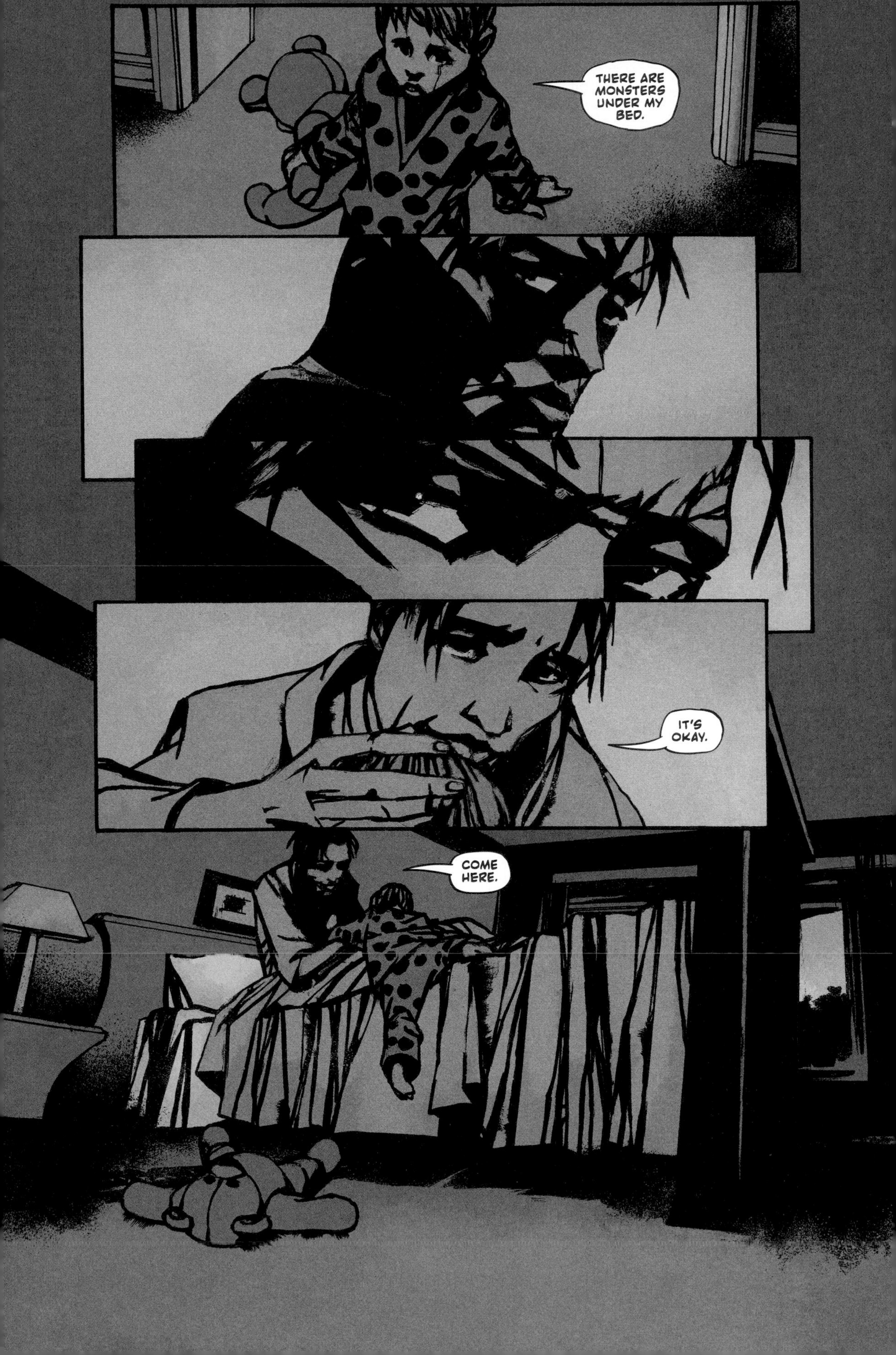
THERE ARE MONSTERS UNDER MY BED.
IT'S OKAY.
COME HERE.

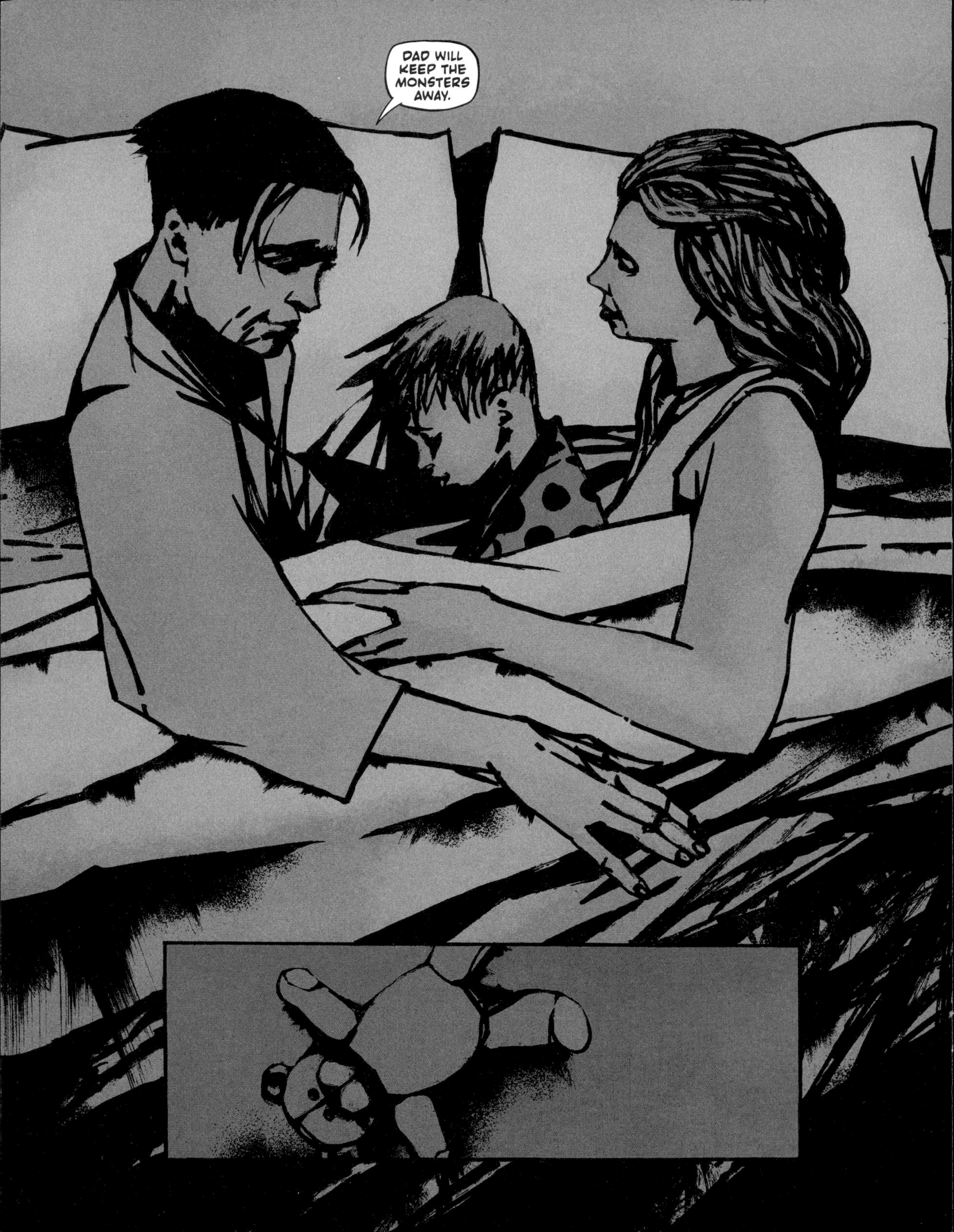
DAD WILL KEEP THE MONSTERS AWAY.

CHAPTER THREE:

THE ORDINARY VOLK

"The disappearance of a sense of responsibility is the most far-reaching consequence of submission to authority."

—Stanley Milgram

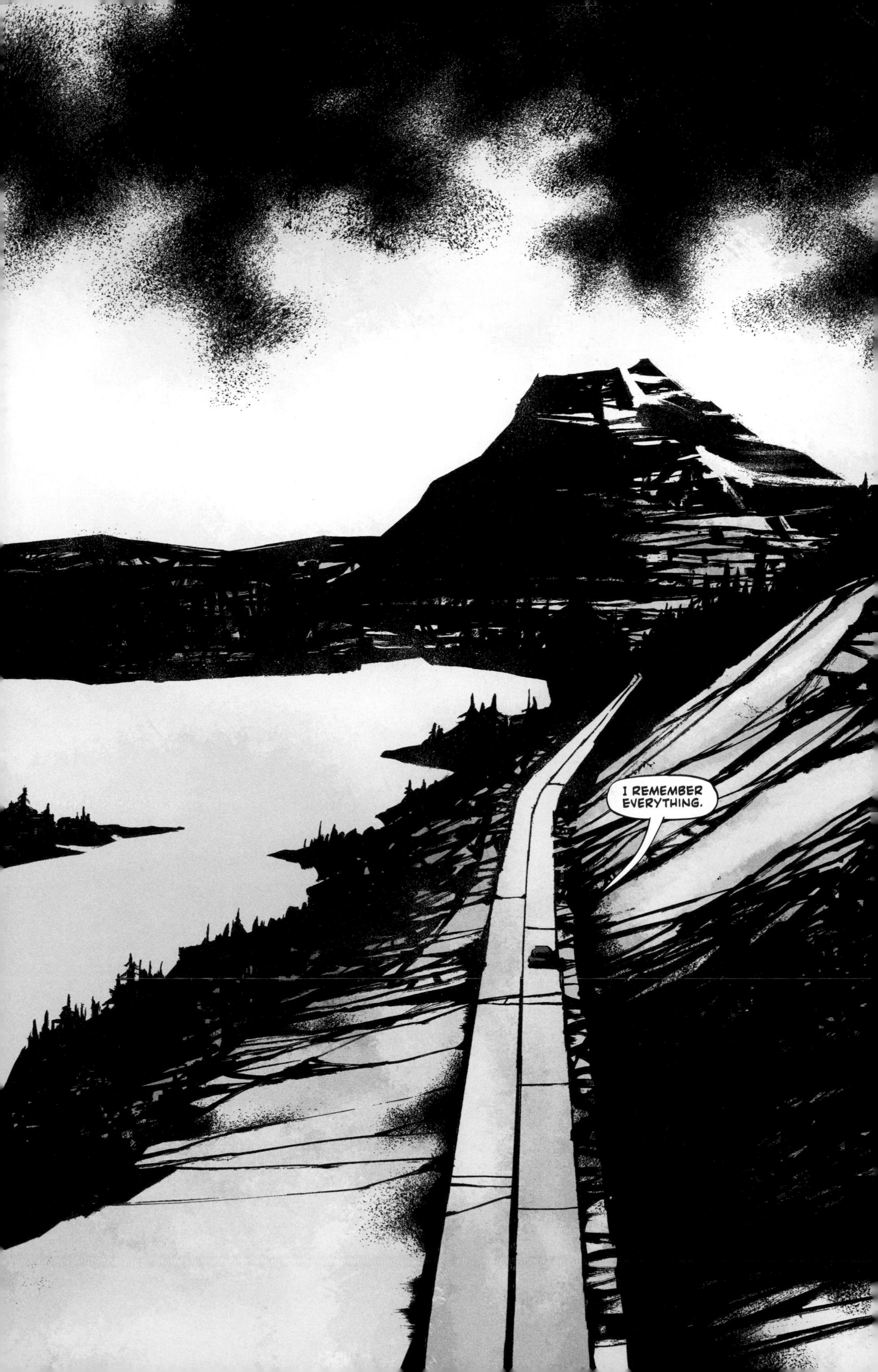
I REMEMBER EVERYTHING.

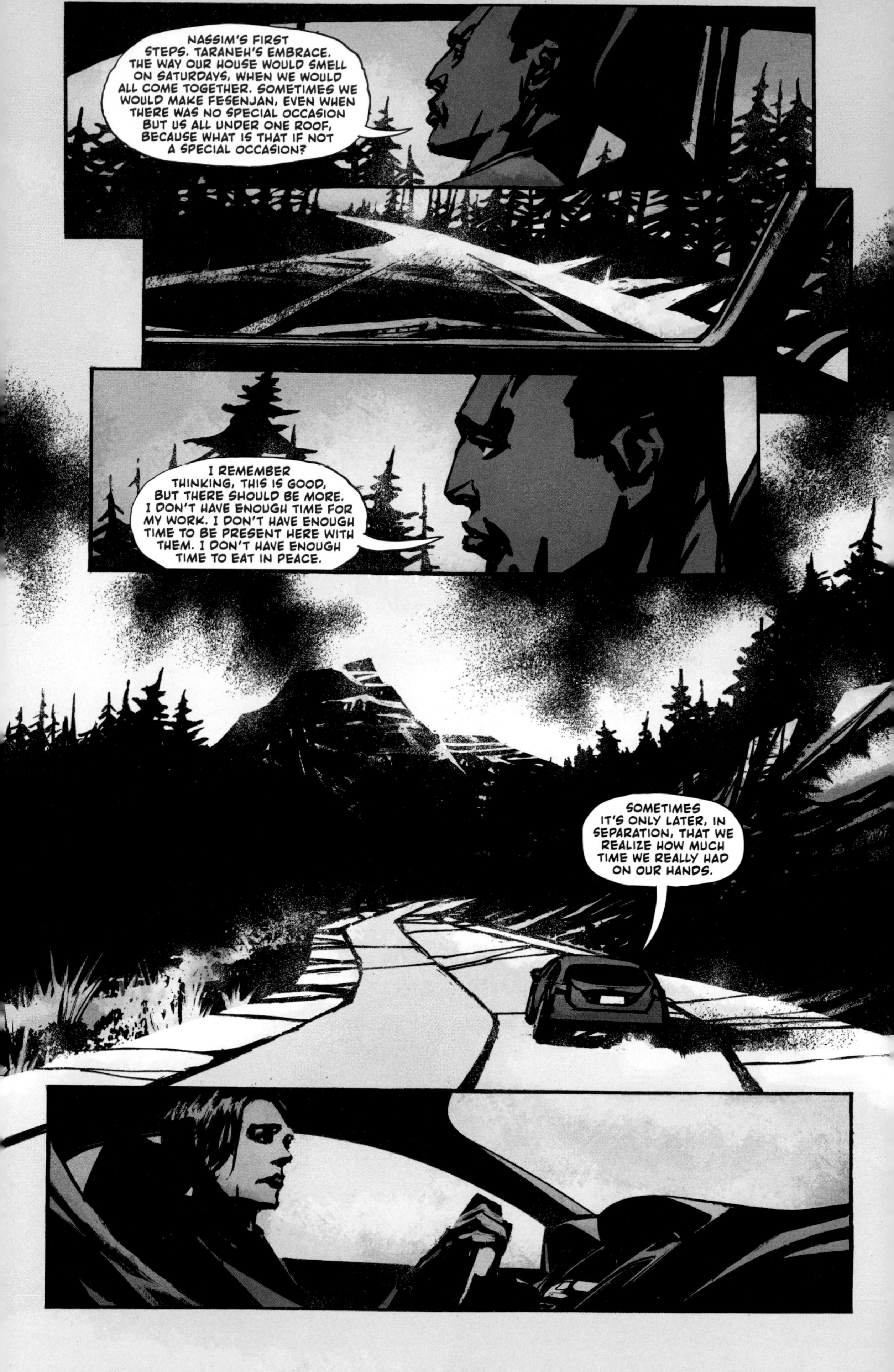
NASSIM'S FIRST STEPS. TARANEH'S EMBRACE. THE WAY OUR HOUSE WOULD SMELL ON SATURDAYS, WHEN WE WOULD ALL COME TOGETHER. SOMETIMES WE WOULD MAKE FESENJAN, EVEN WHEN THERE WAS NO SPECIAL OCCASION BUT US ALL UNDER ONE ROOF, BECAUSE WHAT IS THAT IF NOT A SPECIAL OCCASION?
I REMEMBER THINKING, THIS IS GOOD, BUT THERE SHOULD BE MORE. I DON'T HAVE ENOUGH TIME FOR MY WORK. I DON'T HAVE ENOUGH TIME TO BE PRESENT HERE WITH THEM. I DON'T HAVE ENOUGH TIME TO EAT IN PEACE.
SOMETIMES IT'S ONLY LATER, IN SEPARATION, THAT WE REALIZE HOW MUCH TIME WE REALLY HAD ON OUR HANDS.

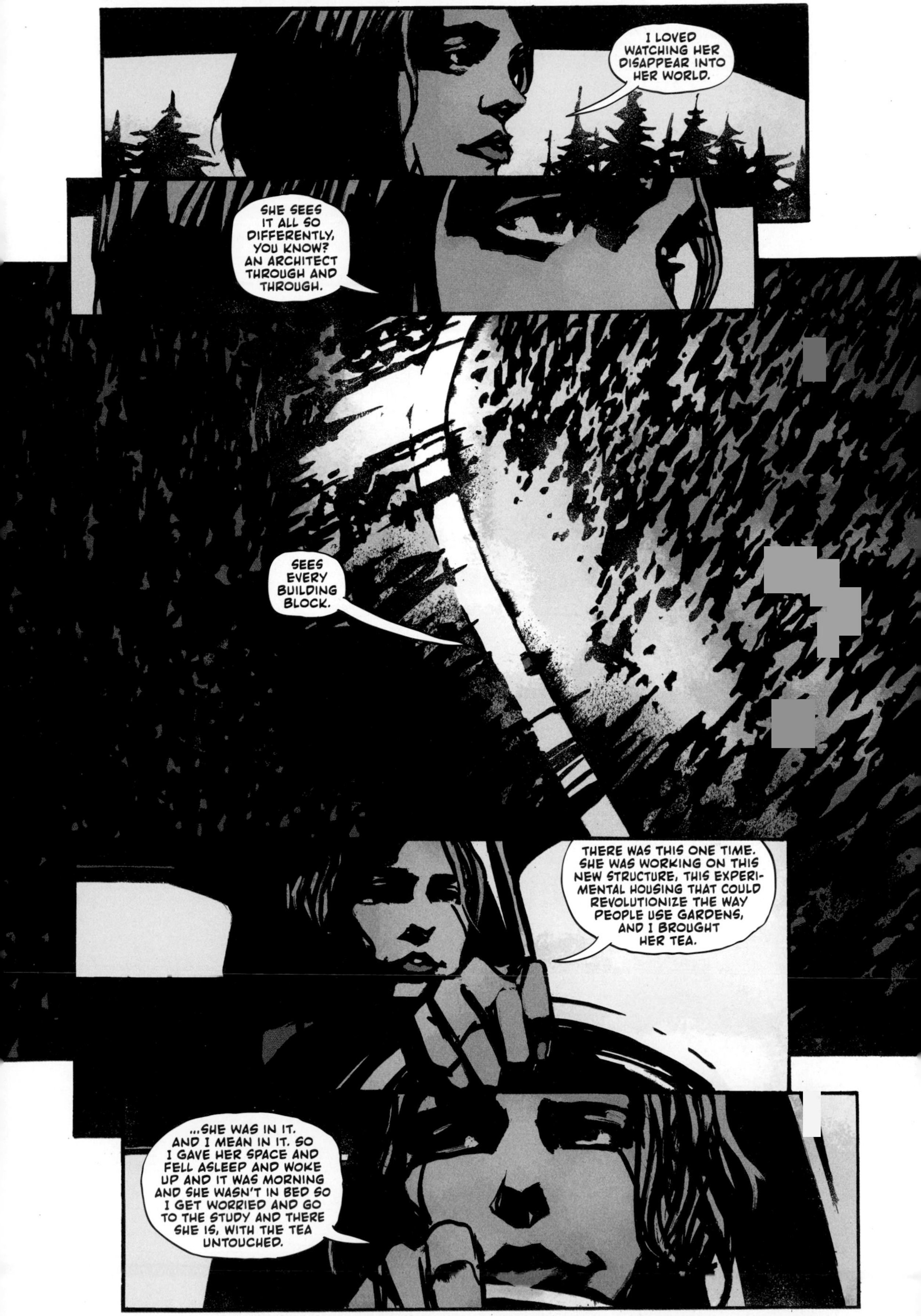
I LOVED WATCHING HER DISAPPEAR INTO HER WORLD.
SHE SEES IT ALL SO DIFFERENTLY, YOU KNOW? AN ARCHITECT THROUGH AND THROUGH.
SEES EVERY BUILDING BLOCK.
THERE WAS THIS ONE TIME. SHE WAS WORKING ON THIS NEW STRUCTURE, THIS EXPERIMENTAL HOUSING THAT COULD REVOLUTIONIZE THE WAY PEOPLE USE GARDENS, AND I BROUGHT HER TEA.
...SHE WAS IN IT. AND I MEAN IN IT. SO I GAVE HER SPACE AND FELL ASLEEP AND WOKE UP AND IT WAS MORNING AND SHE WASN'T IN BED SO I GET WORRIED AND GO TO THE STUDY AND THERE SHE IS, WITH THE TEA UNTOUCHED.

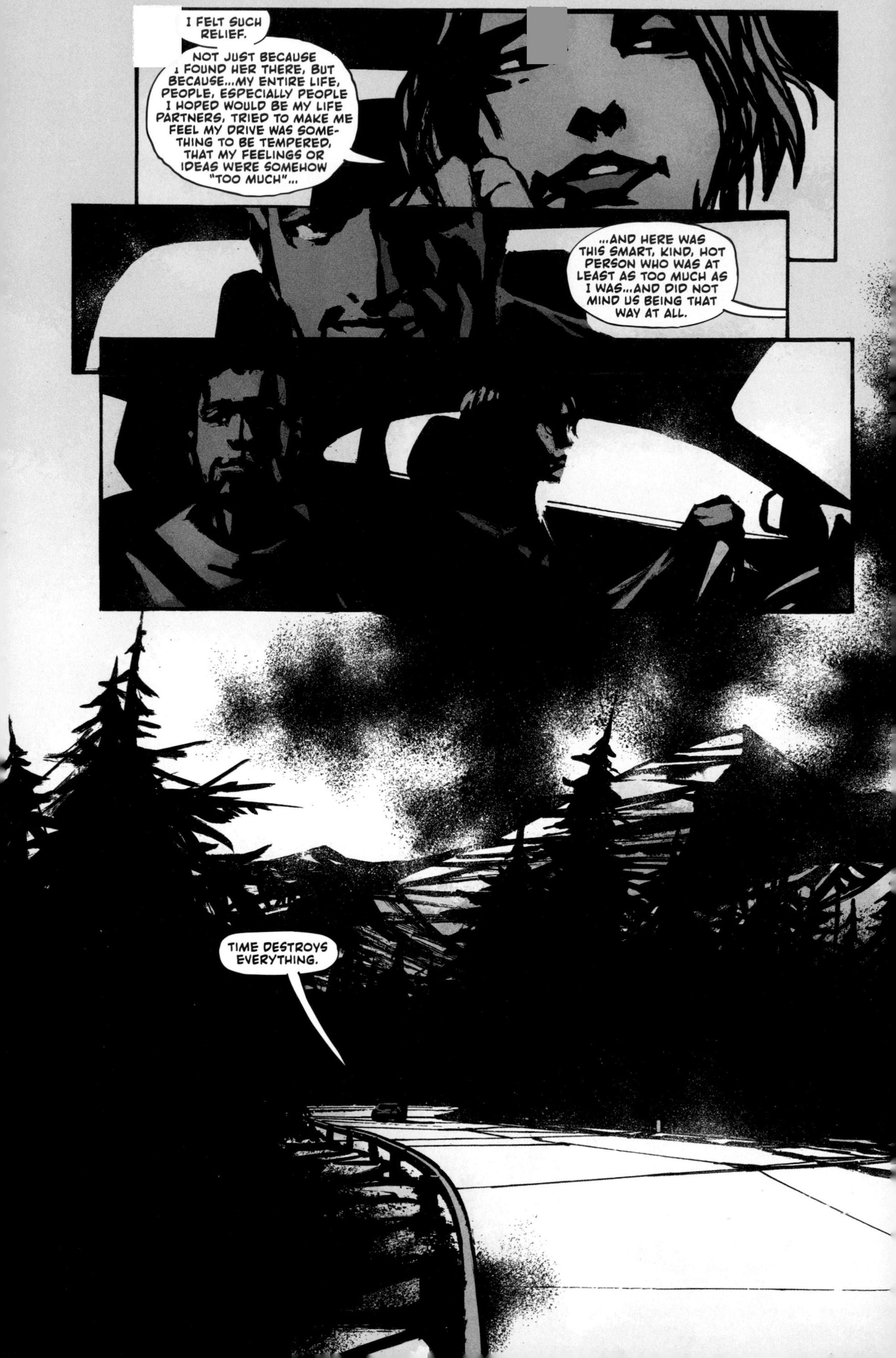
I FELT SUCH RELIEF.
NOT JUST BECAUSE I FOUND HER THERE, BUT BECAUSE...MY ENTIRE LIFE, PEOPLE, ESPECIALLY PEOPLE I HOPED WOULD BE MY LIFE PARTNERS, TRIED TO MAKE ME FEEL MY DRIVE WAS SOMETHING TO BE TEMPERED, THAT MY FEELINGS OR IDEAS WERE SOMEHOW "TOO MUCH"...
...AND HERE WAS THIS SMART, KIND, HOT PERSON WHO WAS AT LEAST AS TOO MUCH AS I WAS...AND DID NOT MIND US BEING THAT WAY AT ALL.
TIME DESTROYS EVERYTHING.

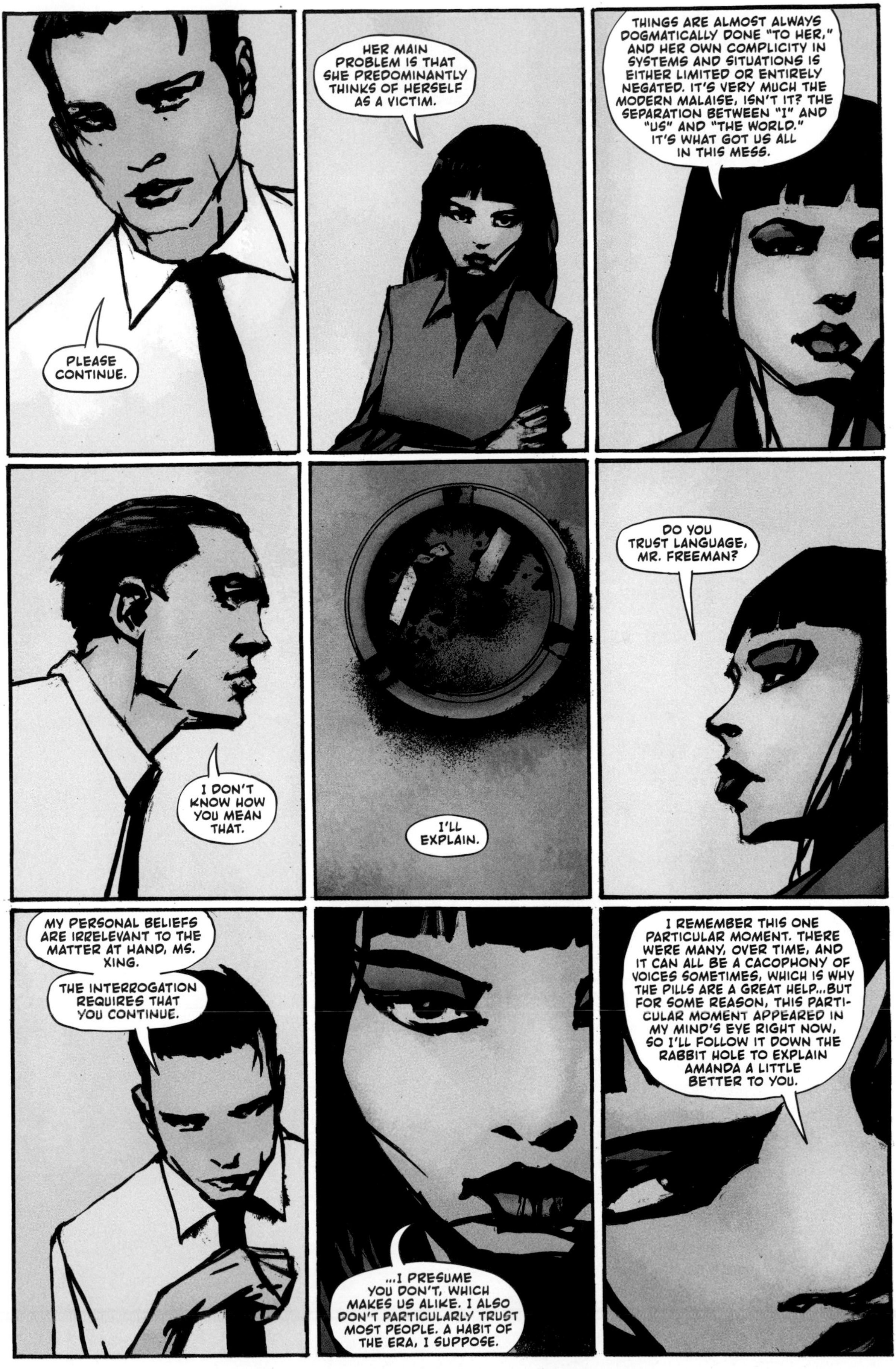
PLEASE CONTINUE.
HER MAIN PROBLEM IS THAT SHE PREDOMINANTLY THINKS OF HERSELF AS A VICTIM.
THINGS ARE ALMOST ALWAYS DOGMATICALLY DONE "TO HER," AND HER OWN COMPLICITY IN SYSTEMS AND SITUATIONS IS EITHER LIMITED OR ENTIRELY NEGATED. IT'S VERY MUCH THE MODERN MALAISE, ISN'T IT? THE SEPARATION BETWEEN "I" AND "US" AND "THE WORLD." IT'S WHAT GOT US ALL IN THIS MESS.
I DON'T KNOW HOW YOU MEAN THAT.
I'LL EXPLAIN.
DO YOU TRUST LANGUAGE, MR. FREEMAN?
MY PERSONAL BELIEFS ARE IRRELEVANT TO THE MATTER AT HAND, MS. XING.
THE INTERROGATION REQUIRES THAT YOU CONTINUE.
...I PRESUME YOU DON'T, WHICH MAKES US ALIKE. I ALSO DON'T PARTICULARLY TRUST MOST PEOPLE. A HABIT OF THE ERA, I SUPPOSE.
I REMEMBER THIS ONE PARTICULAR MOMENT. THERE WERE MANY, OVER TIME, AND IT CAN ALL BE A CACOPHONY OF VOICES SOMETIMES, WHICH IS WHY THE PILLS ARE A GREAT HELP...BUT FOR SOME REASON, THIS PARTI-CULAR MOMENT APPEARED IN MY MIND'S EYE RIGHT NOW, SO I'LL FOLLOW IT DOWN THE RABBIT HOLE TO EXPLAIN AMANDA A LITTLE BETTER TO YOU.

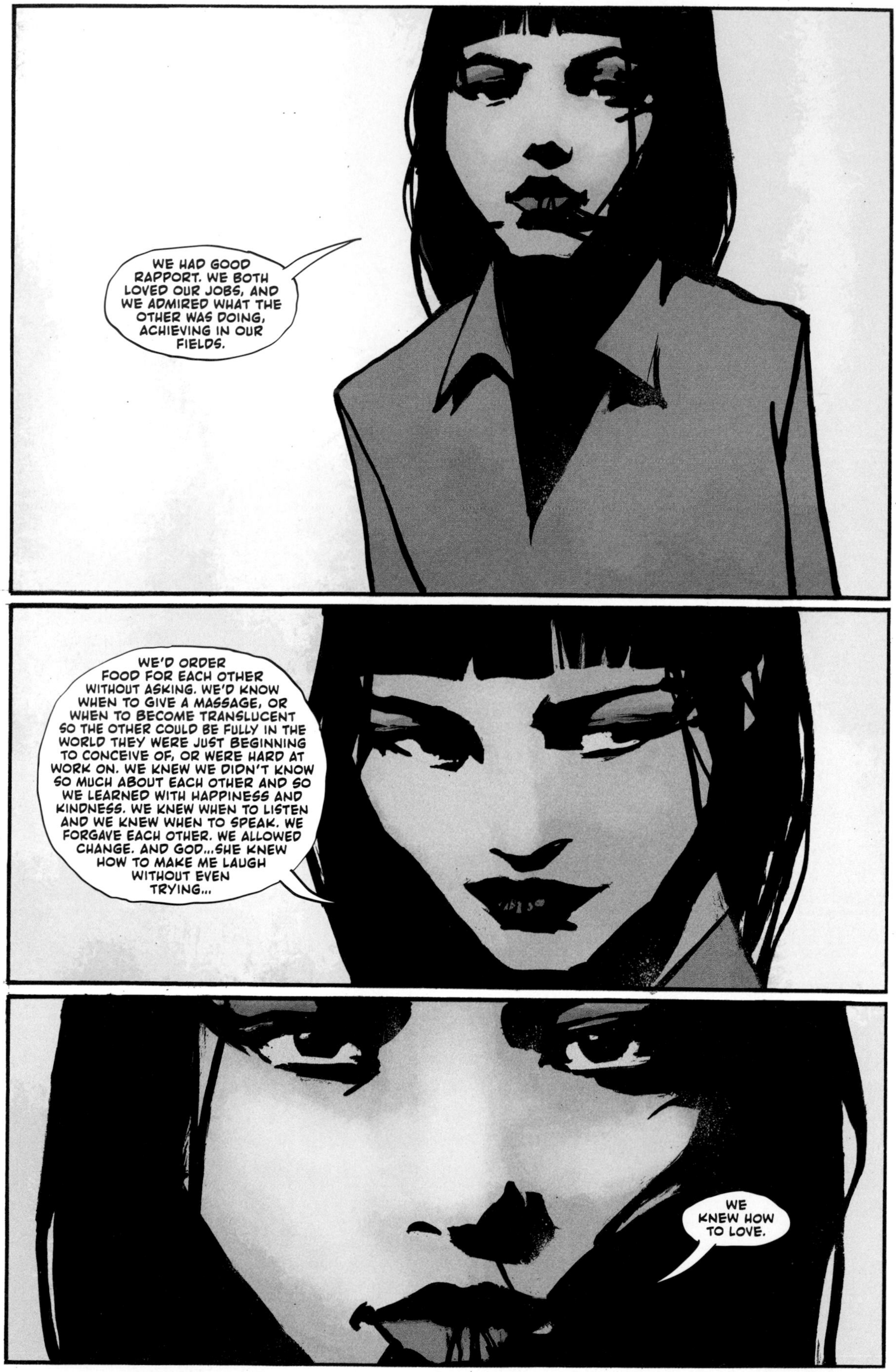
WE HAD GOOD RAPPORT. WE BOTH LOVED OUR JOBS, AND WE ADMIRED WHAT THE OTHER WAS DOING, ACHIEVING IN OUR FIELDS.
WE'D ORDER FOOD FOR EACH OTHER WITHOUT ASKING. WE'D KNOW WHEN TO GIVE A MASSAGE, OR WHEN TO BECOME TRANSLUCENT SO THE OTHER COULD BE FULLY IN THE WORLD THEY WERE JUST BEGINNING TO CONCEIVE OF, OR WERE HARD AT WORK ON. WE KNEW WE DIDN'T KNOW SO MUCH ABOUT EACH OTHER AND SO WE LEARNED WITH HAPPINESS AND KINDNESS. WE KNEW WHEN TO LISTEN AND WE KNEW WHEN TO SPEAK. WE FORGAVE EACH OTHER. WE ALLOWED CHANGE. AND GOD...SHE KNEW HOW TO MAKE ME LAUGH WITHOUT EVEN TRYING...
WE KNEW HOW TO LOVE.

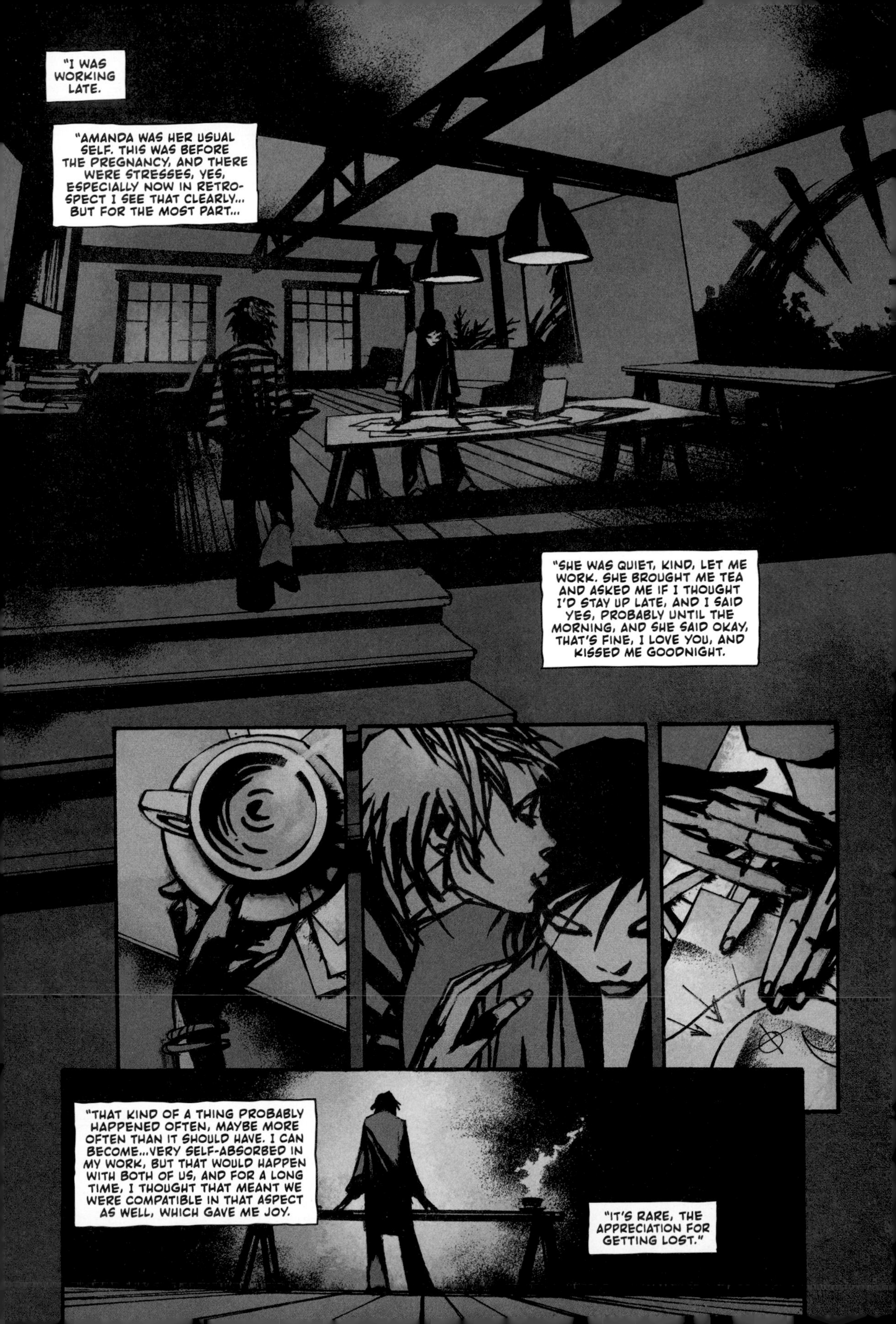
"I WAS WORKING LATE.
"AMANDA WAS HER USUAL SELF. THIS WAS BEFORE THE PREGNANCY, AND THERE WERE STRESSES, YES, ESPECIALLY NOW IN RETRO-SPECT I SEE THAT CLEARLY... BUT FOR THE MOST PART...
"SHE WAS QUIET, KIND, LET ME WORK. SHE BROUGHT ME TEA AND ASKED ME IF I THOUGHT I'D STAY UP LATE, AND I SAID YES, PROBABLY UNTIL THE MORNING, AND SHE SAID OKAY, THAT'S FINE, I LOVE YOU, AND KISSED ME GOODNIGHT.
"THAT KIND OF A THING PROBABLY HAPPENED OFTEN, MAYBE MORE OFTEN THAN IT SHOULD HAVE. I CAN BECOME...VERY SELF-ABSORBED IN MY WORK, BUT THAT WOULD HAPPEN WITH BOTH OF US, AND FOR A LONG TIME, I THOUGHT THAT MEANT WE WERE COMPATIBLE IN THAT ASPECT AS WELL, WHICH GAVE ME JOY.
"IT'S RARE, THE APPRECIATION FOR GETTING LOST."

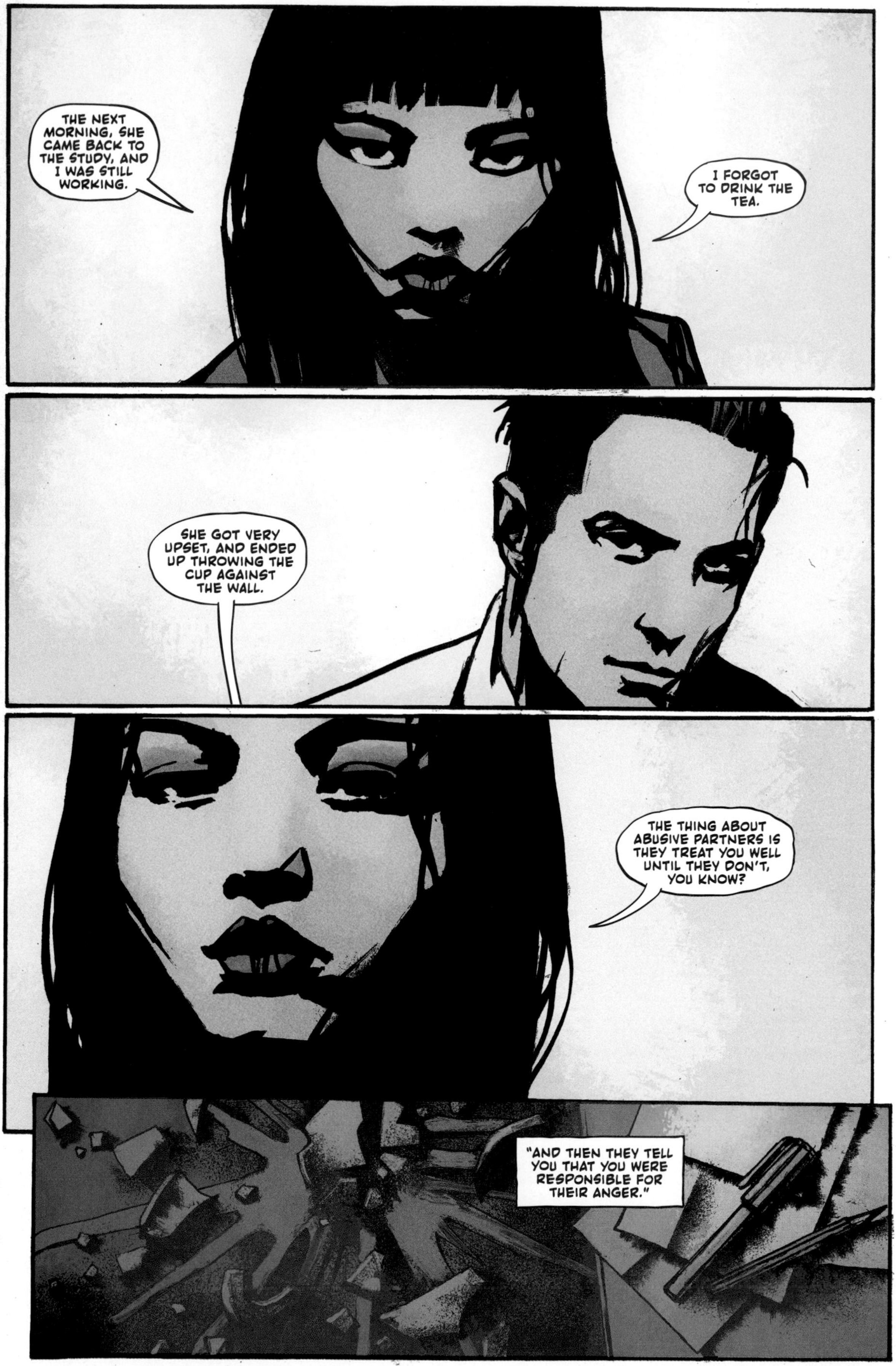
THE NEXT MORNING, SHE CAME BACK TO THE STUDY, AND I WAS STILL WORKING.
I FORGOT TO DRINK THE TEA.
SHE GOT VERY UPSET, AND ENDED UP THROWING THE CUP AGAINST THE WALL.
THE THING ABOUT ABUSIVE PARTNERS IS THEY TREAT YOU WELL UNTIL THEY DON'T, YOU KNOW?
"AND THEN THEY TELL YOU THAT YOU WERE RESPONSIBLE FOR THEIR ANGER."

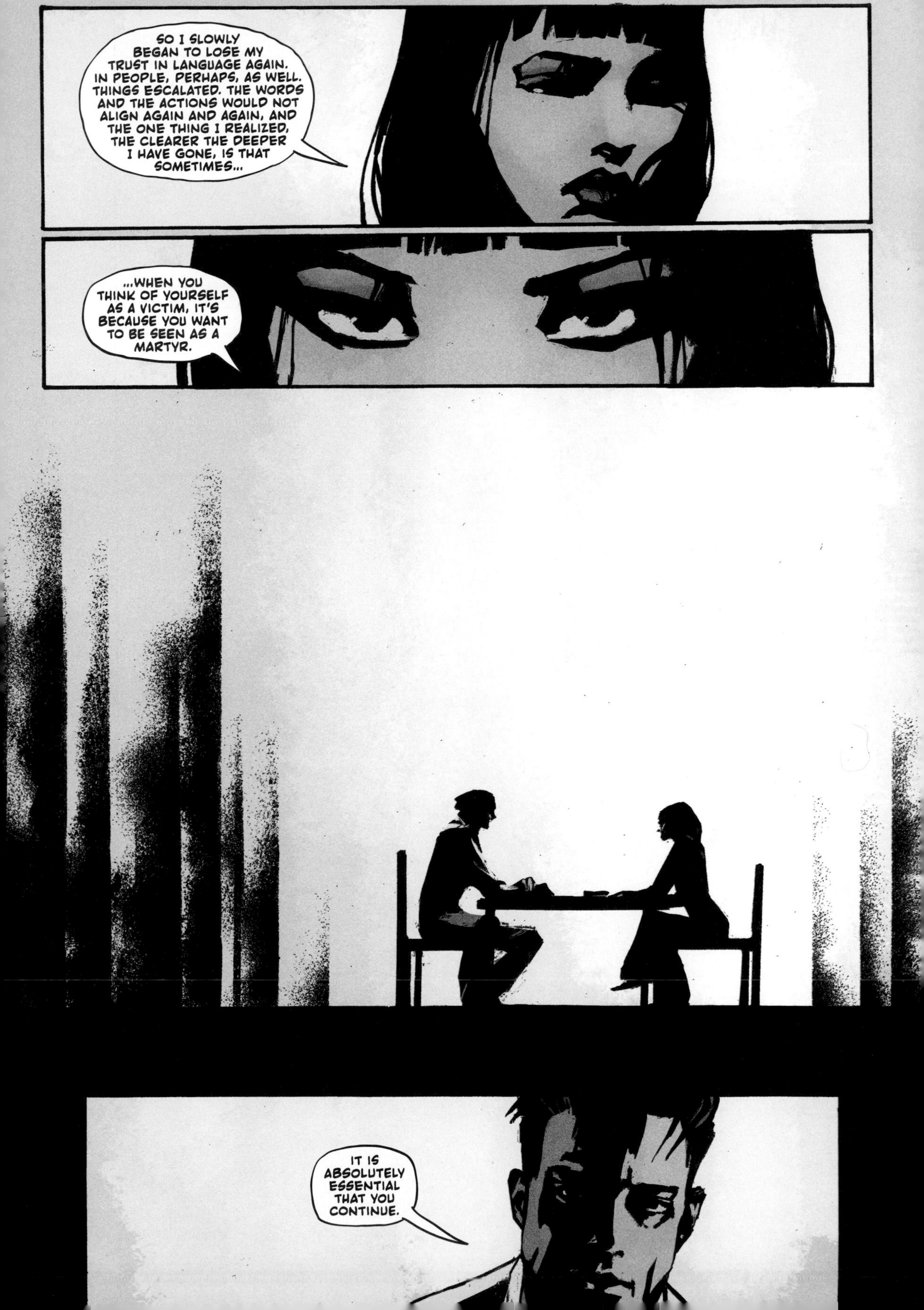
SO I SLOWLY BEGAN TO LOSE MY TRUST IN LANGUAGE AGAIN. IN PEOPLE, PERHAPS, AS WELL. THINGS ESCALATED. THE WORDS AND THE ACTIONS WOULD NOT ALIGN AGAIN AND AGAIN, AND THE ONE THING I REALIZED, THE CLEARER THE DEEPER I HAVE GONE, IS THAT SOMETIMES...
...WHEN YOU THINK OF YOURSELF AS A VICTIM, IT'S BECAUSE YOU WANT TO BE SEEN AS A MARTYR.
IT IS ABSOLUTELY ESSENTIAL THAT YOU CONTINUE.

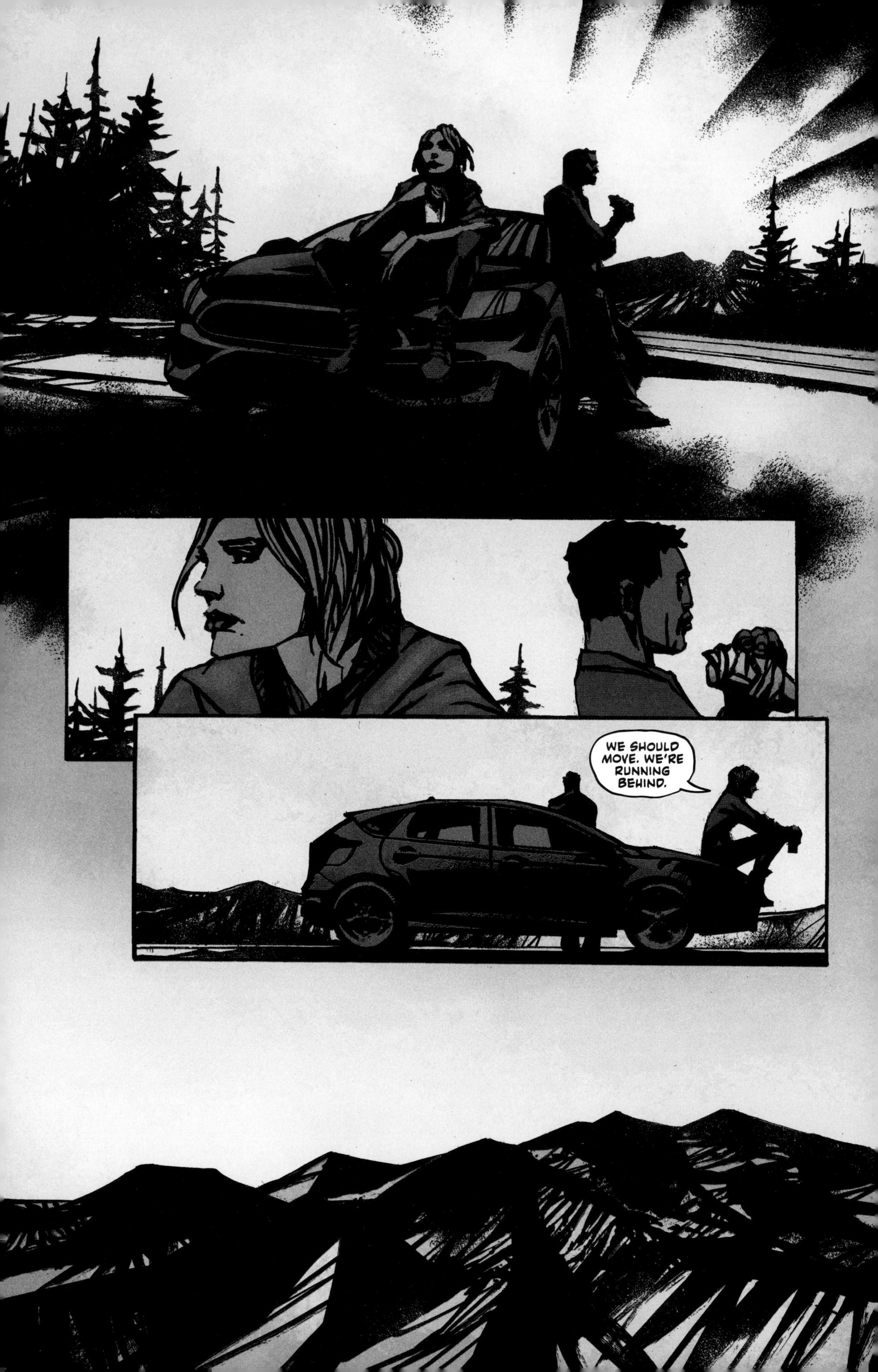
WE SHOULD MOVE. WE'RE RUNNING BEHIND.

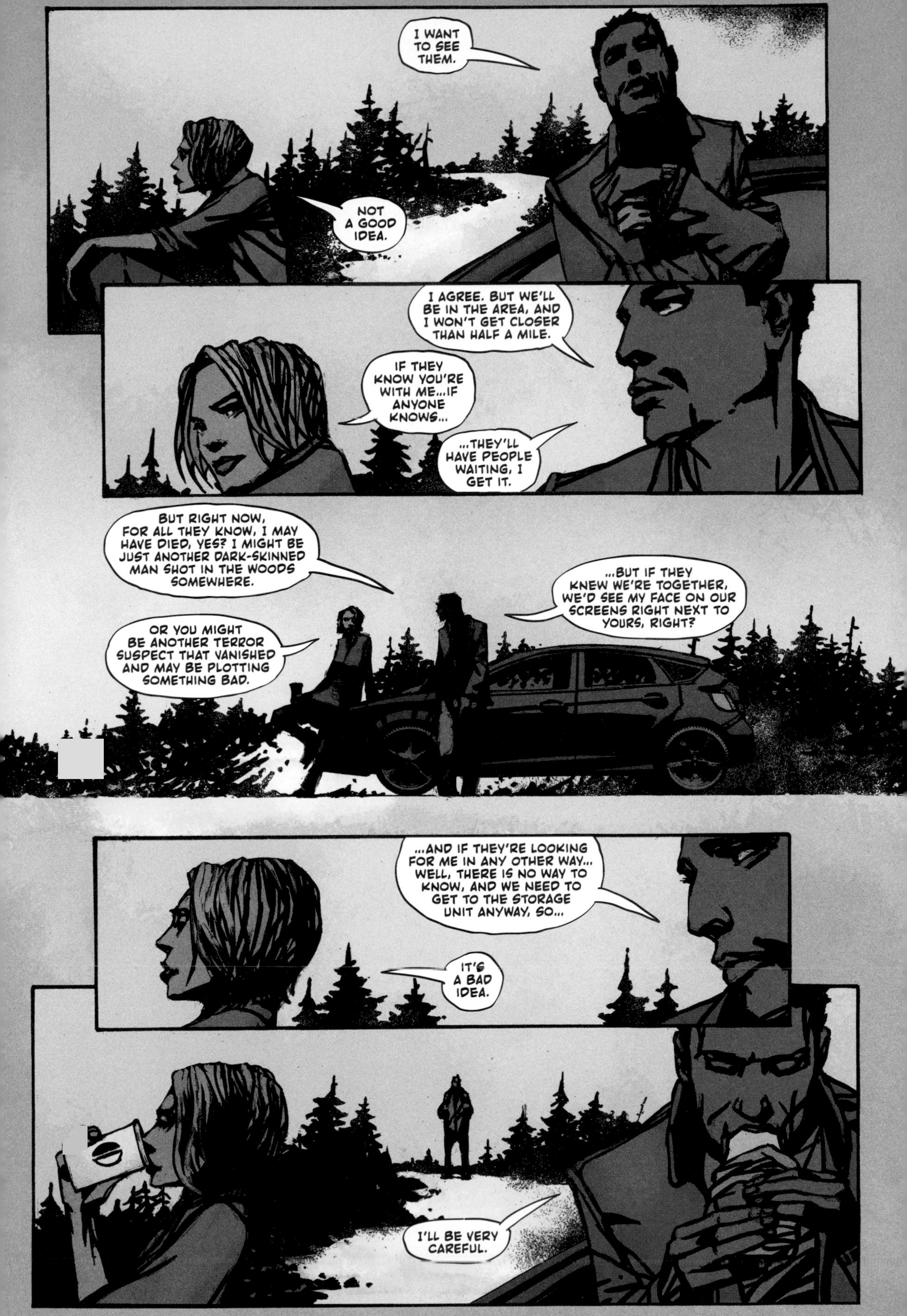
I WANT TO SEE THEM.
NOT A GOOD IDEA.
I AGREE. BUT WE'LL BE IN THE AREA, AND I WON'T GET CLOSER THAN HALF A MILE.
IF THEY KNOW YOU'RE WITH ME...IF ANYONE KNOWS...
...THEY'LL HAVE PEOPLE WAITING, I GET IT.
BUT RIGHT NOW, FOR ALL THEY KNOW, I MAY HAVE DIED, YES? I MIGHT BE JUST ANOTHER DARK-SKINNED MAN SHOT IN THE WOODS SOMEWHERE.
OR YOU MIGHT BE ANOTHER TERROR SUSPECT THAT VANISHED AND MAY BE PLOTTING SOMETHING BAD.
...BUT IF THEY KNEW WE'RE TOGETHER, WE'D SEE MY FACE ON OUR SCREENS RIGHT NEXT TO YOURS, RIGHT?
...AND IF THEY'RE LOOKING FOR ME IN ANY OTHER WAY... WELL, THERE IS NO WAY TO KNOW, AND WE NEED TO GET TO THE STORAGE UNIT ANYWAY, SO...
IT'S A BAD IDEA.
I'LL BE VERY CAREFUL.

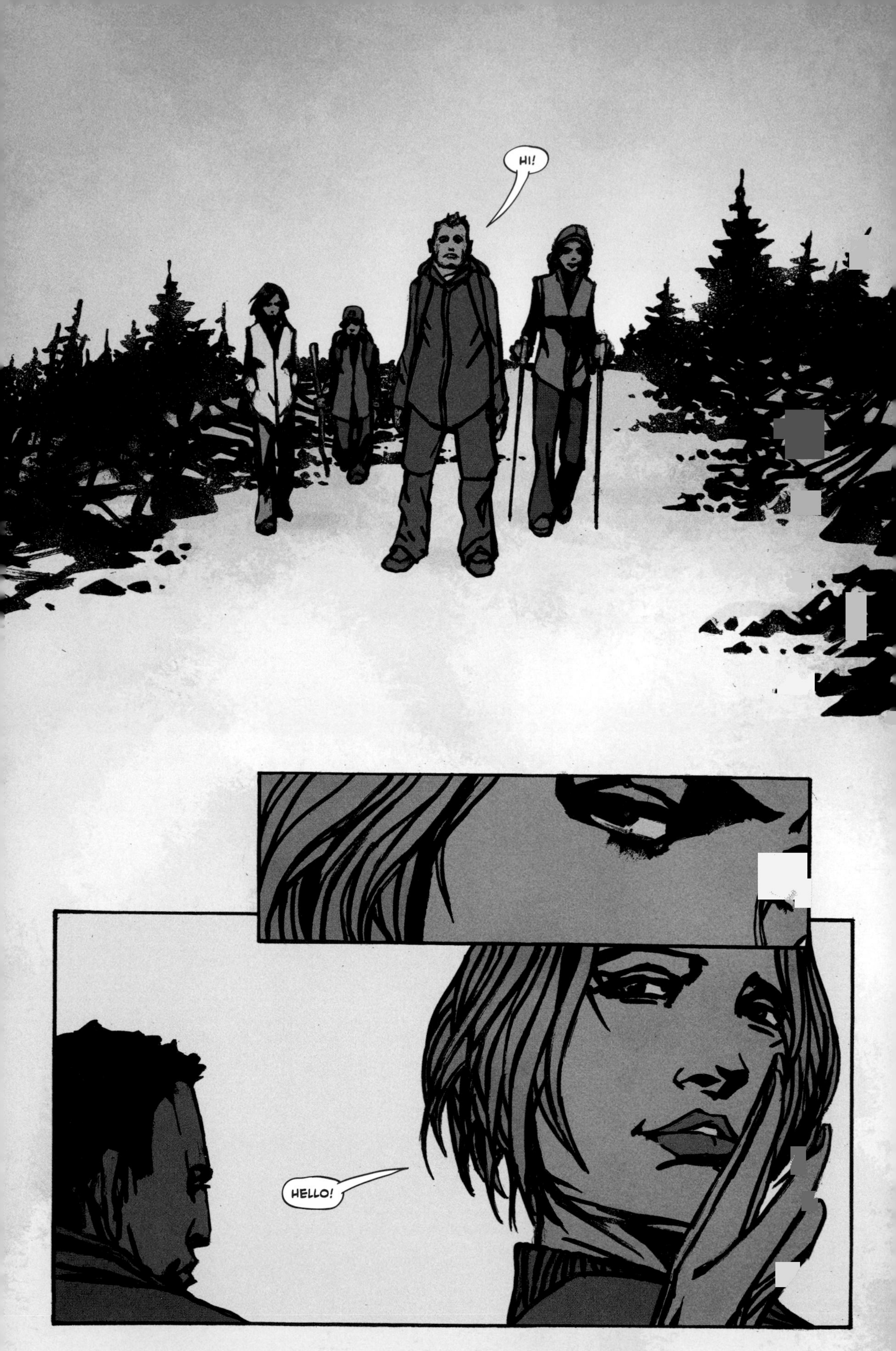
HI!
HELLO!

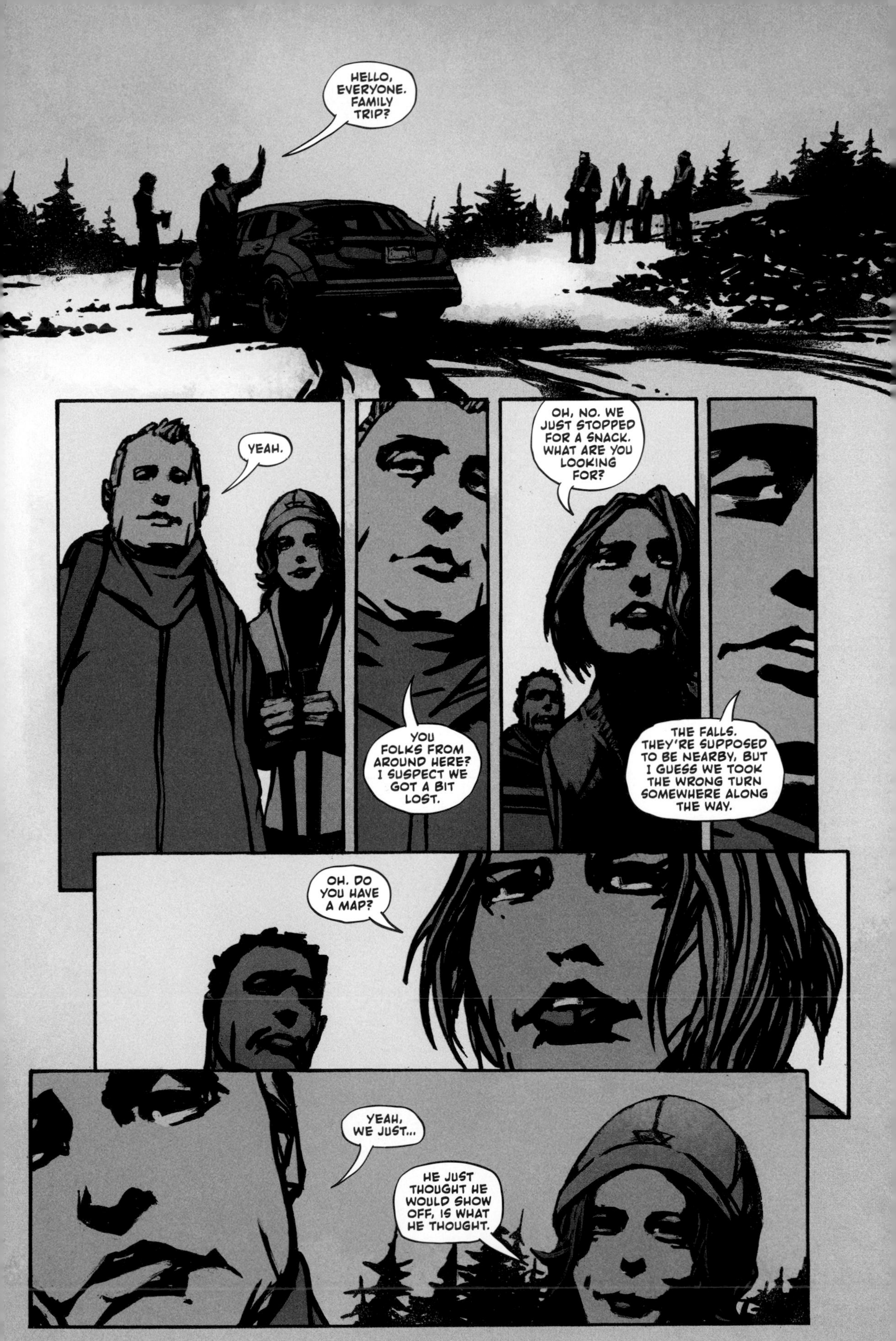
HELLO, EVERYONE. FAMILY TRIP?
YEAH.
YOU FOLKS FROM AROUND HERE? I SUSPECT WE GOT A BIT LOST.
OH, NO. WE JUST STOPPED FOR A SNACK. WHAT ARE YOU LOOKING FOR?
THE FALLS. THEY'RE SUPPOSED TO BE NEARBY, BUT I GUESS WE TOOK THE WRONG TURN SOMEWHERE ALONG THE WAY.
OH. DO YOU HAVE A MAP?
YEAH, WE JUST...
HE JUST THOUGHT HE WOULD SHOW OFF, IS WHAT HE THOUGHT.

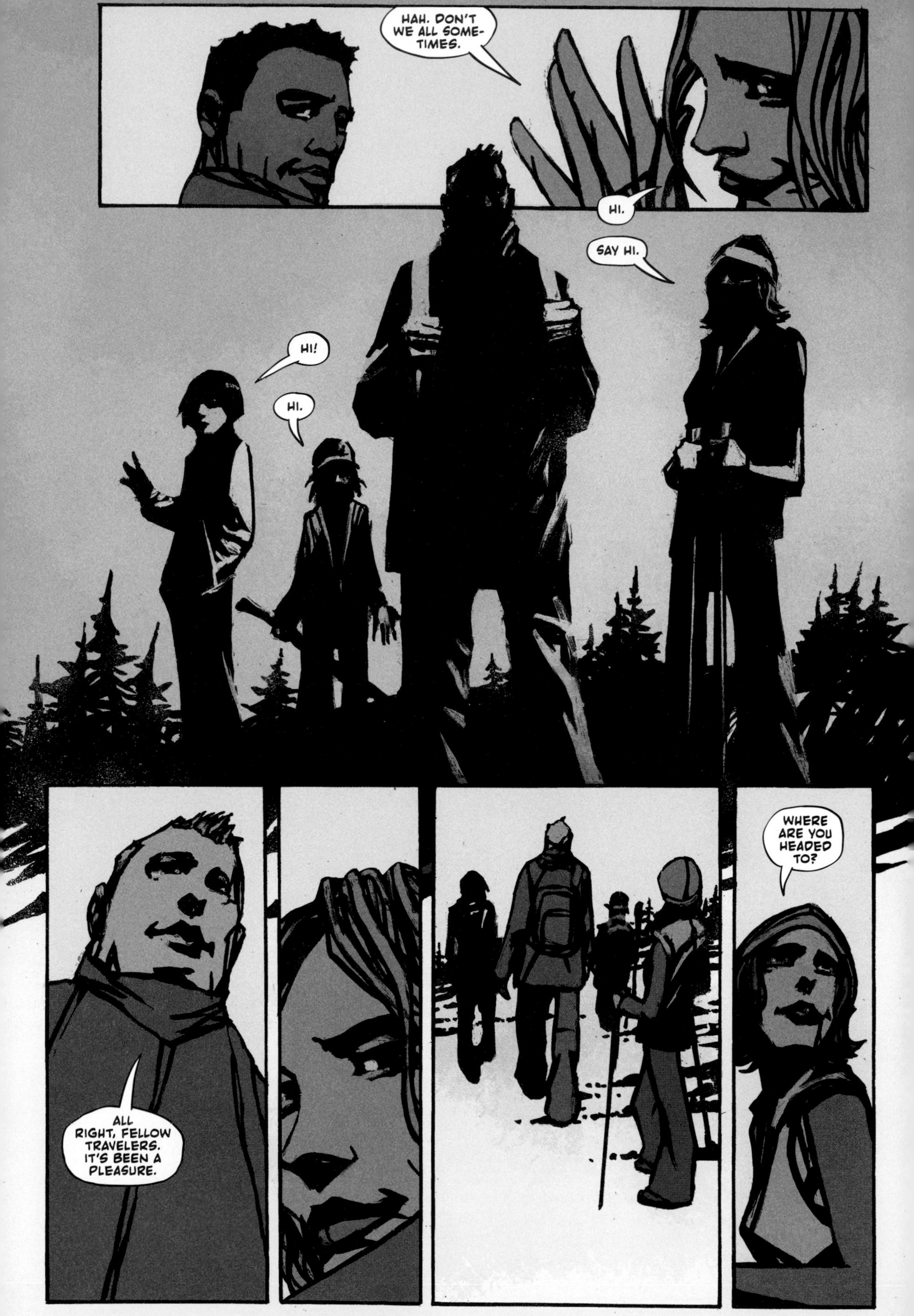
HAH. DON'T WE ALL SOME-TIMES.
HI.
SAY HI.
HI!
HI.
ALL RIGHT, FELLOW TRAVELERS. IT'S BEEN A PLEASURE.
WHERE ARE YOU HEADED TO?

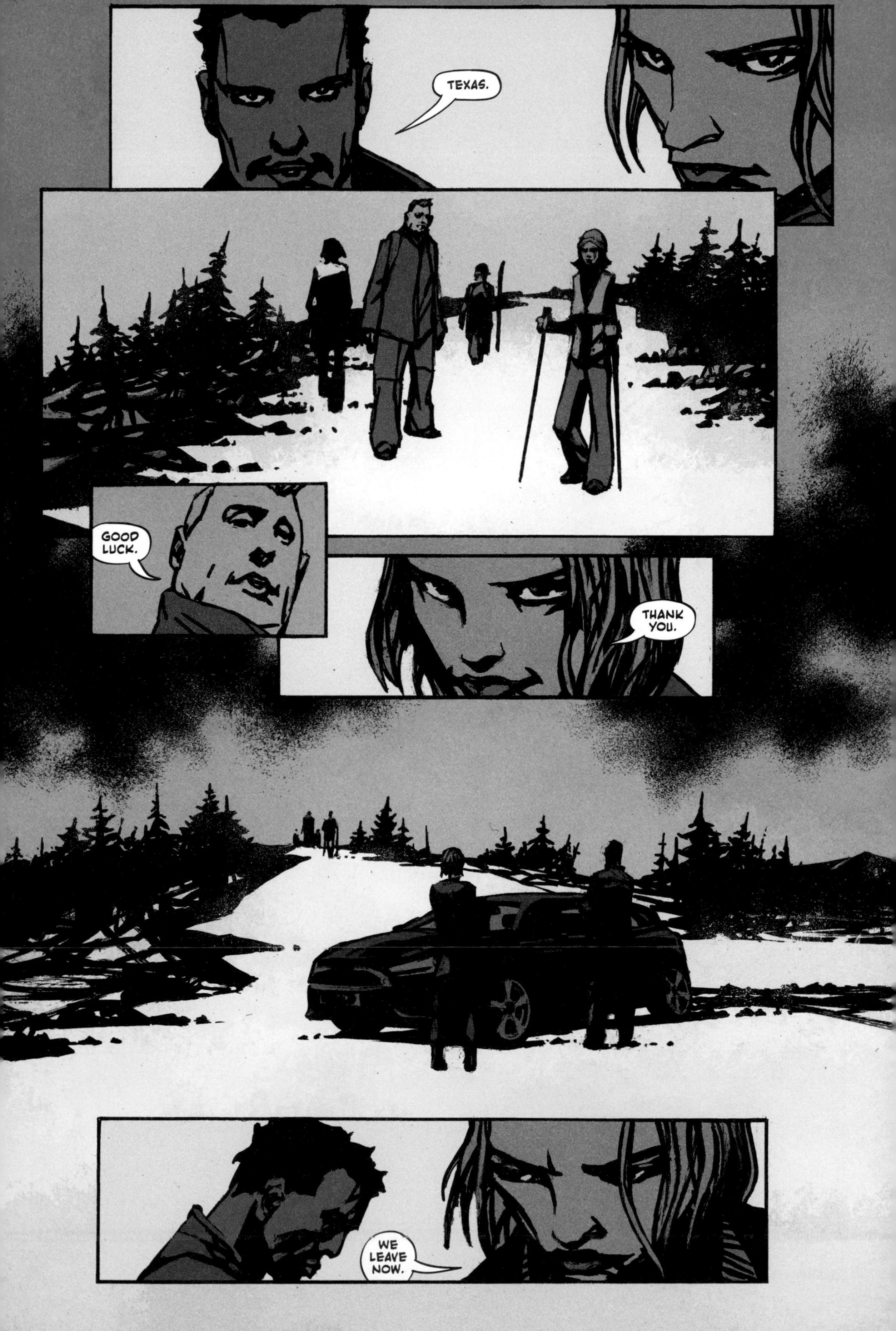
TEXAS.
GOOD LUCK.
THANK YOU.
WE LEAVE NOW.

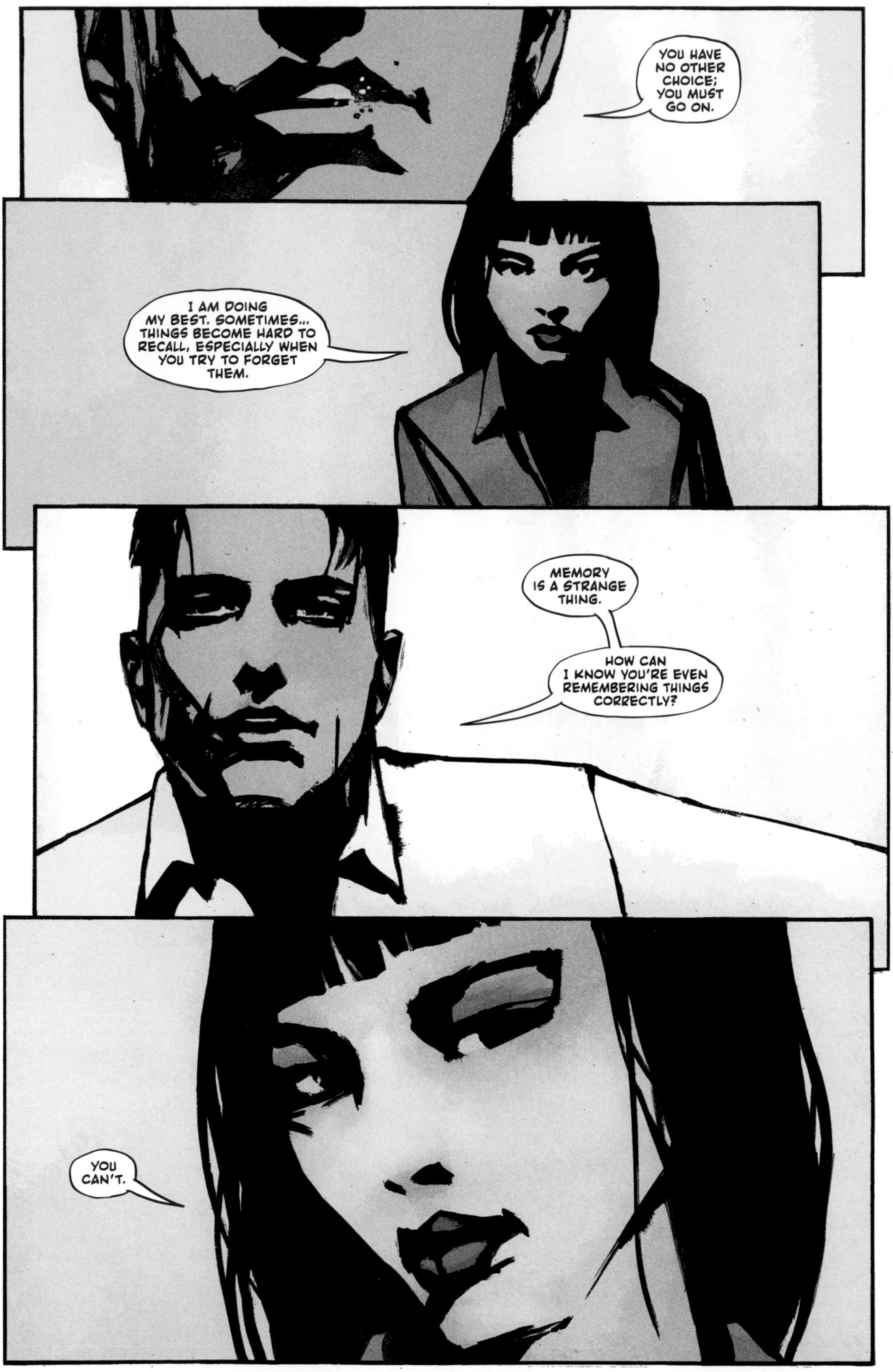
YOU HAVE NO OTHER CHOICE; YOU MUST GO ON.
I AM DOING MY BEST. SOMETIMES... THINGS BECOME HARD TO RECALL, ESPECIALLY WHEN YOU TRY TO FORGET THEM.
MEMORY IS A STRANGE THING.
HOW CAN I KNOW YOU'RE EVEN REMEMBERING THINGS CORRECTLY?
YOU CAN'T.

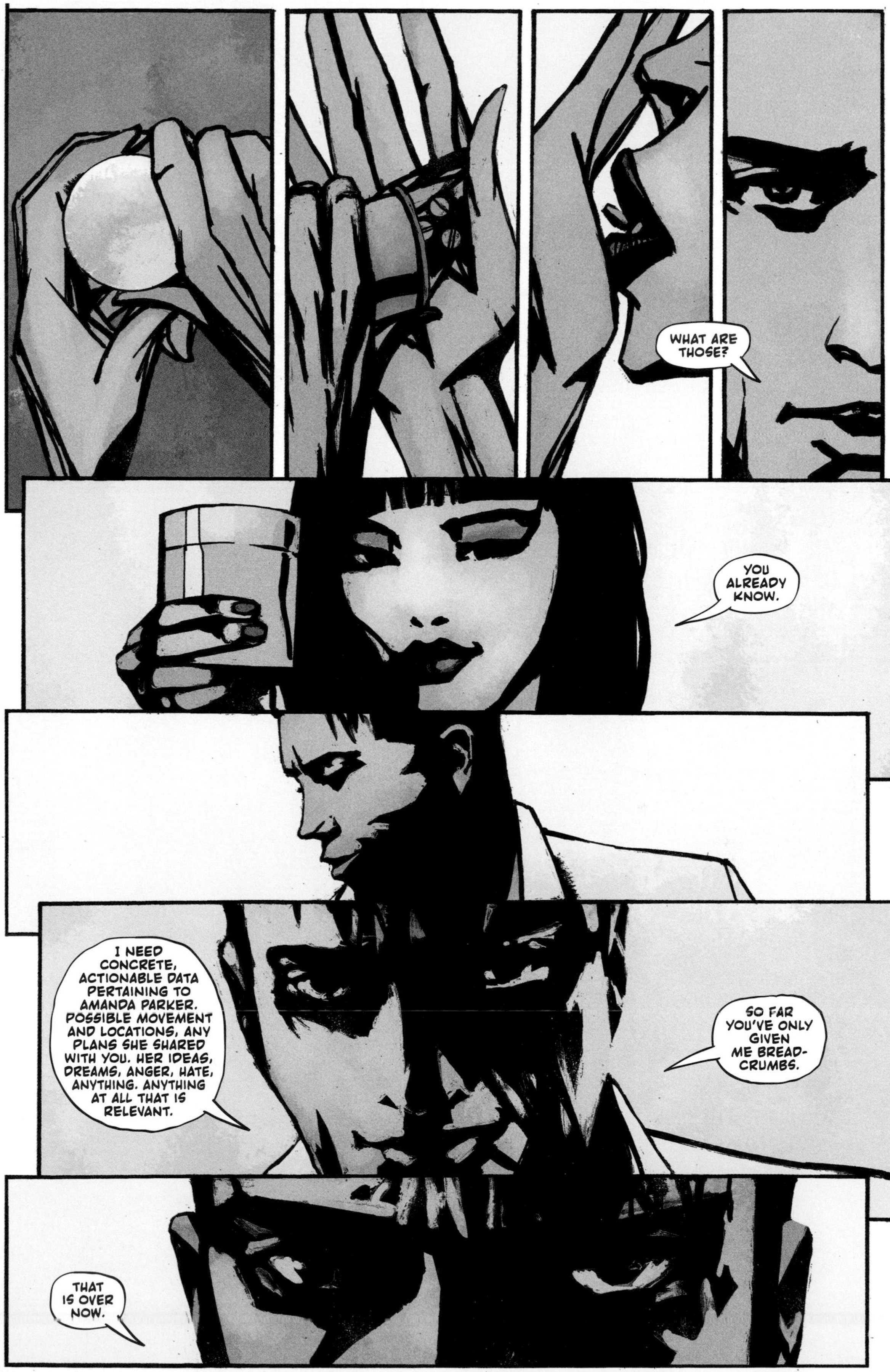
WHAT ARE THOSE?
YOU ALREADY KNOW.
I NEED CONCRETE, ACTIONABLE DATA PERTAINING TO AMANDA PARKER. POSSIBLE MOVEMENT AND LOCATIONS, ANY PLANS SHE SHARED WITH YOU. HER IDEAS, DREAMS, ANGER, HATE, ANYTHING. ANYTHING AT ALL THAT IS RELEVANT.
SO FAR YOU'VE ONLY GIVEN ME BREAD-CRUMBS.
THAT IS OVER NOW.

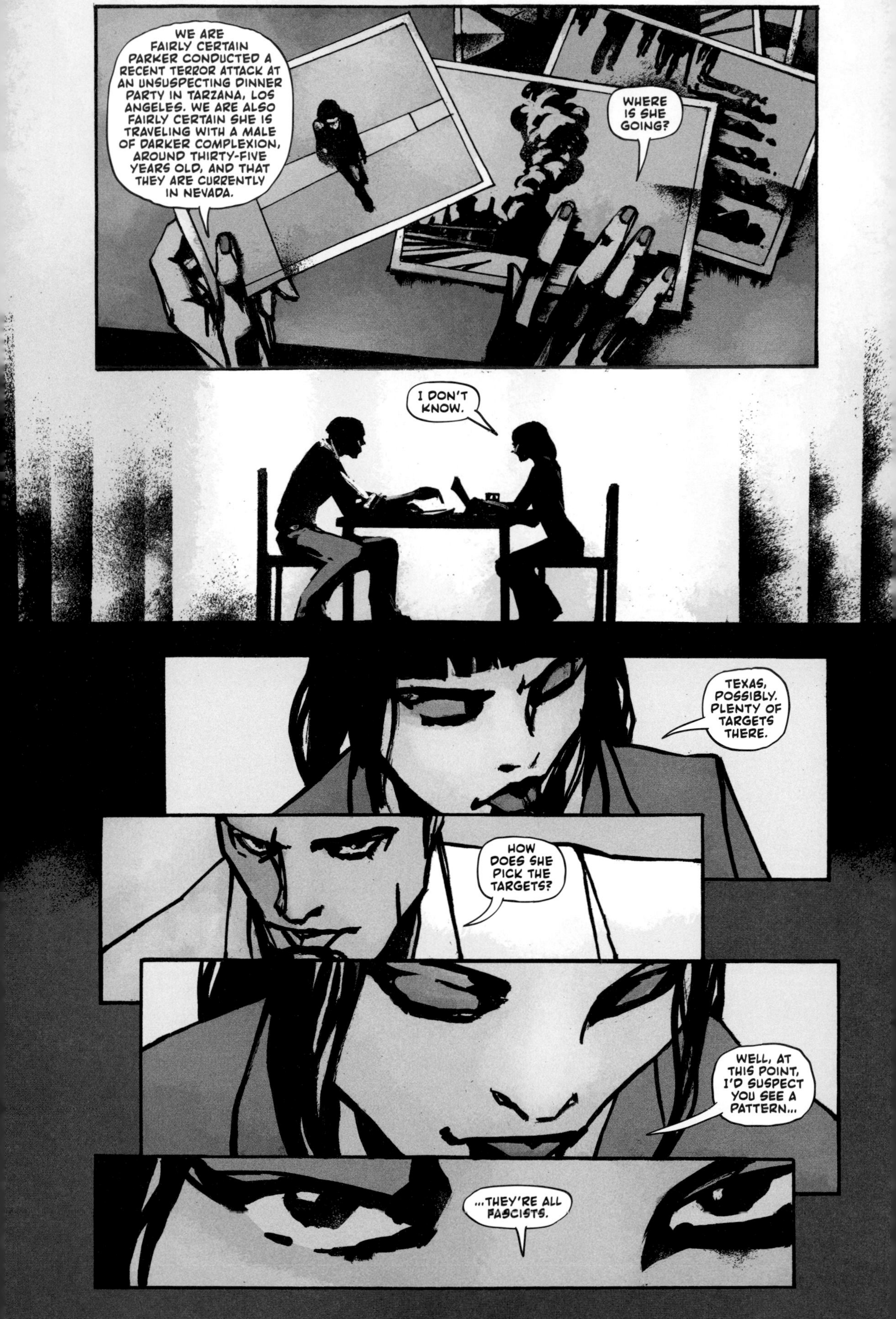
WE ARE FAIRLY CERTAIN PARKER CONDUCTED A RECENT TERROR ATTACK AT AN UNSUSPECTING DINNER PARTY IN TARZANA, LOS ANGELES. WE ARE ALSO FAIRLY CERTAIN SHE IS TRAVELING WITH A MALE OF DARKER COMPLEXION, AROUND THIRTY-FIVE YEARS OLD, AND THAT THEY ARE CURRENTLY IN NEVADA.
WHERE IS SHE GOING?
I DON'T KNOW.
TEXAS, POSSIBLY. PLENTY OF TARGETS THERE.
HOW DOES SHE PICK THE TARGETS?
WELL, AT THIS POINT, I'D SUSPECT YOU SEE A PATTERN...
...THEY'RE ALL FASCISTS.

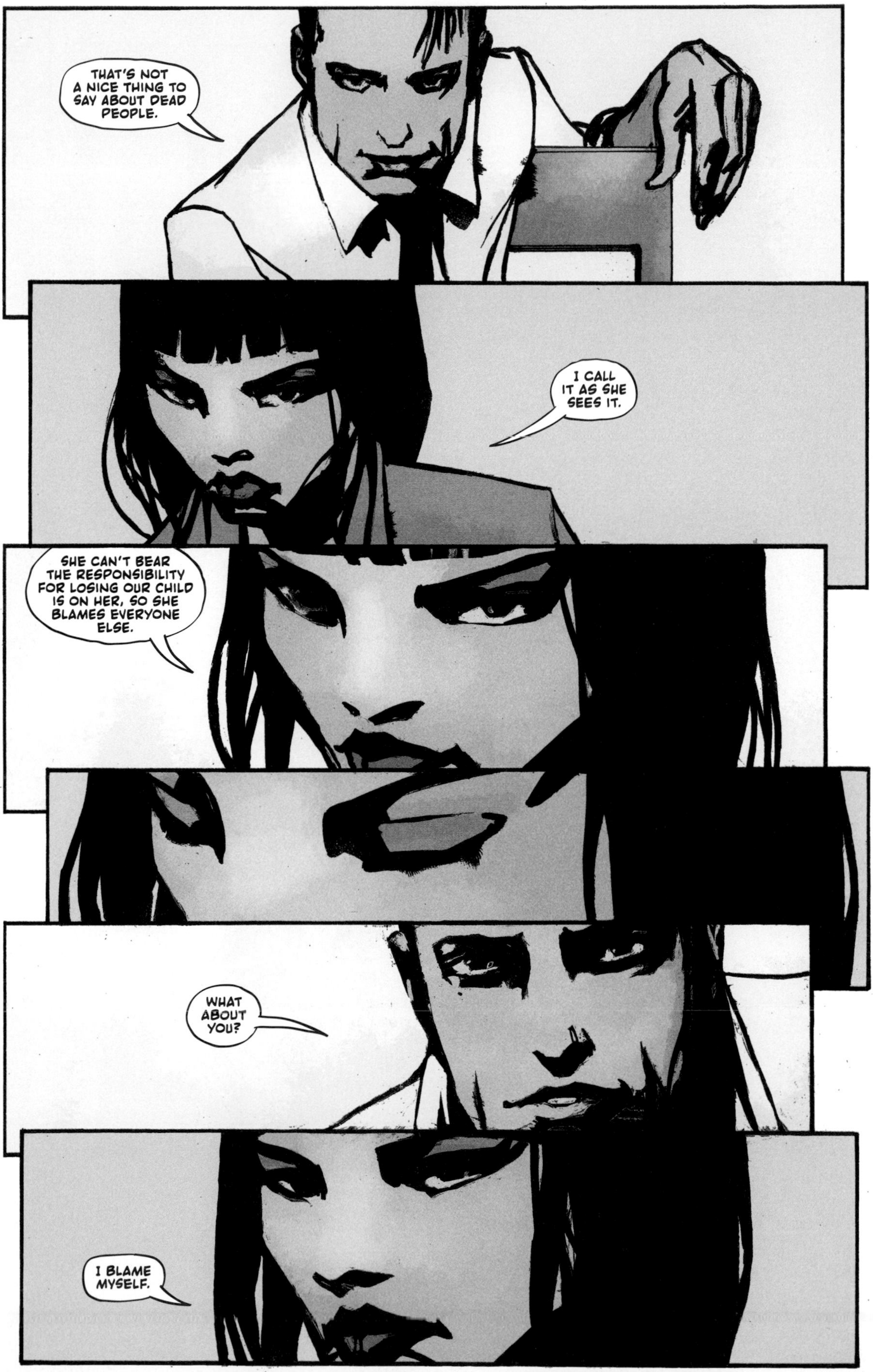
THAT'S NOT A NICE THING TO SAY ABOUT DEAD PEOPLE.
I CALL IT AS SHE SEES IT.
SHE CAN'T BEAR THE RESPONSIBILITY FOR LOSING OUR CHILD IS ON HER, SO SHE BLAMES EVERYONE ELSE.
WHAT ABOUT YOU?
I BLAME MYSELF.

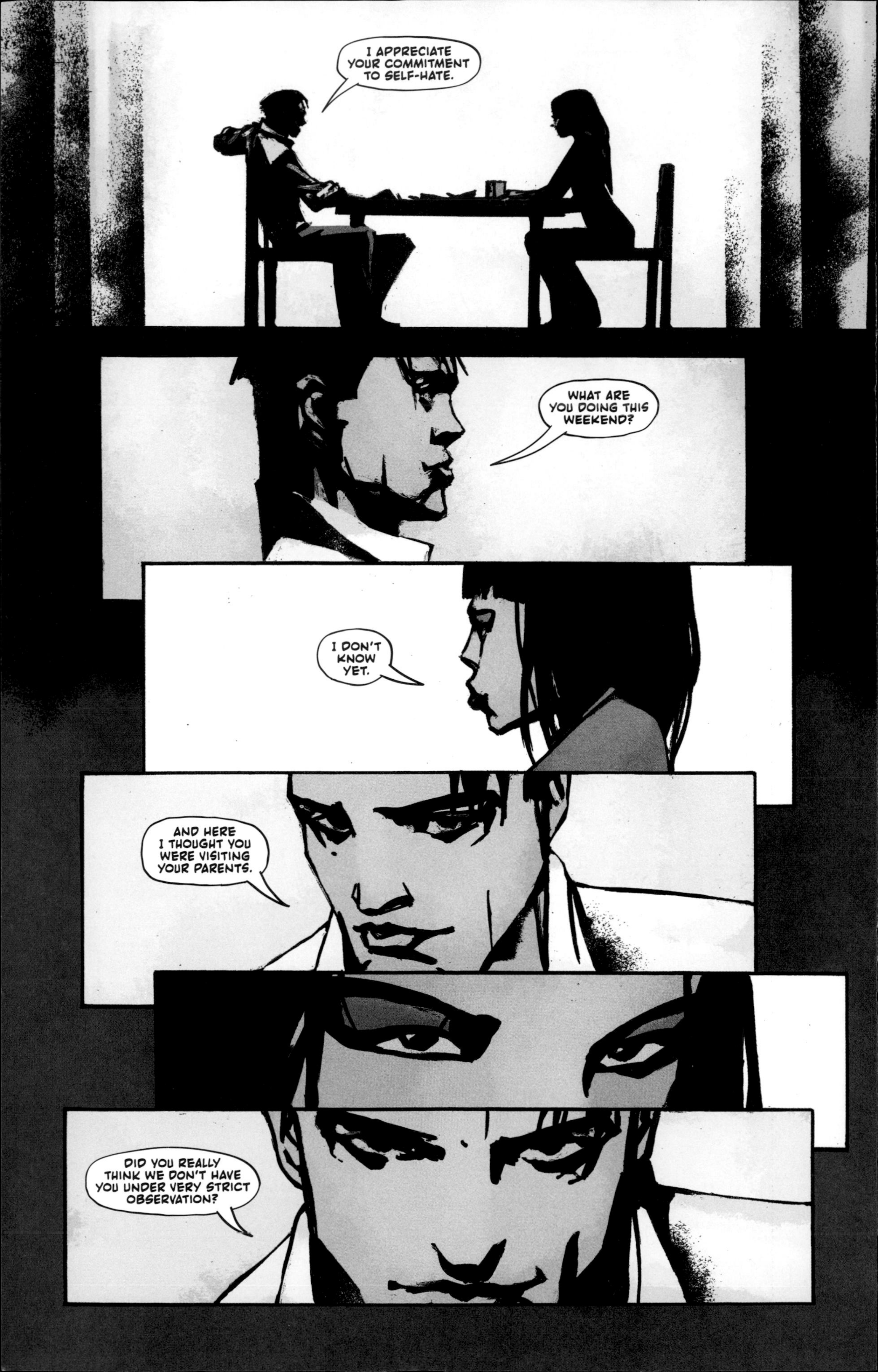
I APPRECIATE YOUR COMMITMENT TO SELF-HATE.
WHAT ARE YOU DOING THIS WEEKEND?
I DON'T KNOW YET.
AND HERE I THOUGHT YOU WERE VISITING YOUR PARENTS.
DID YOU REALLY THINK WE DON'T HAVE YOU UNDER VERY STRICT OBSERVATION?

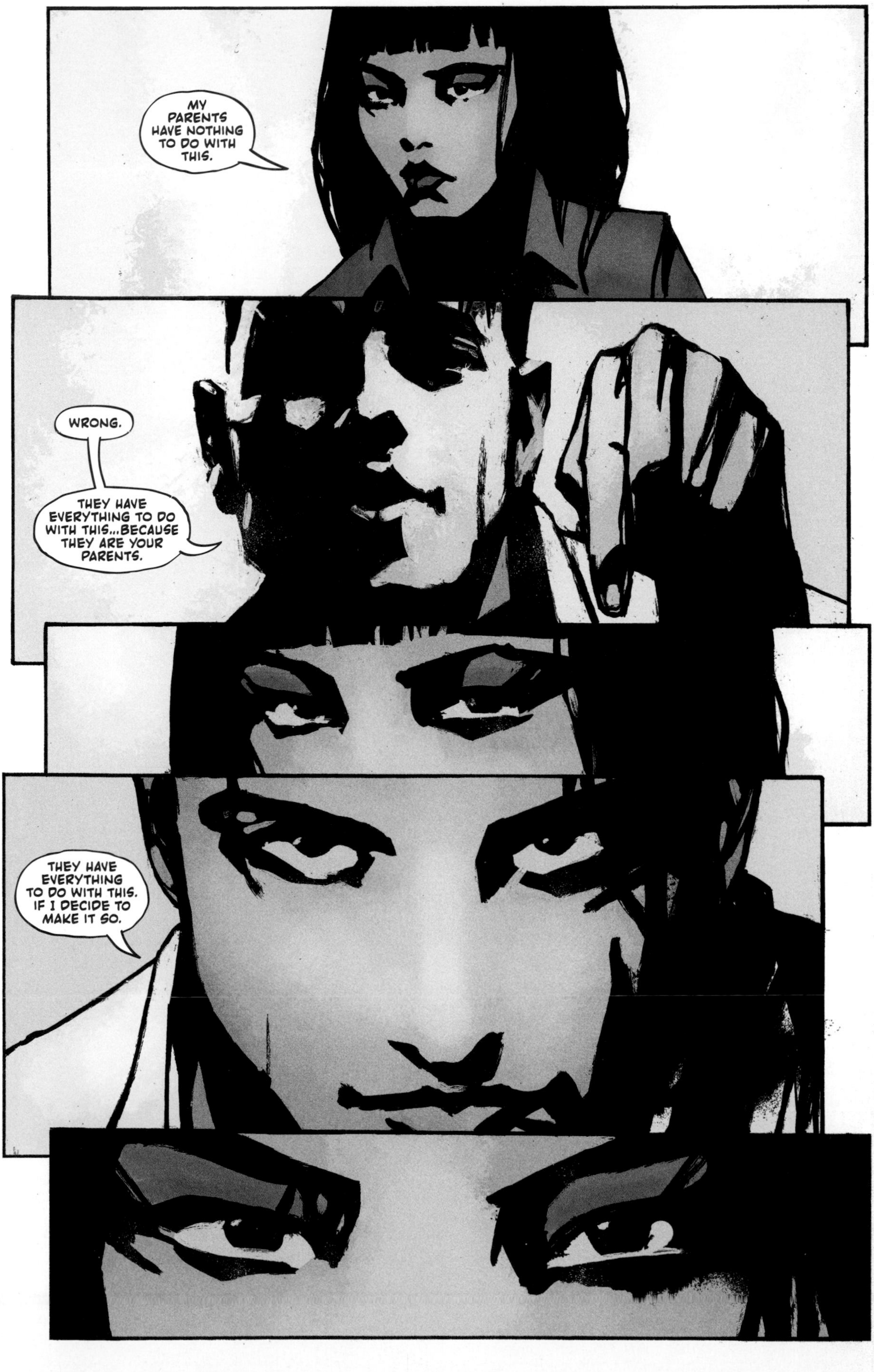
MY PARENTS HAVE NOTHING TO DO WITH THIS.
WRONG.
THEY HAVE EVERYTHING TO DO WITH THIS...BECAUSE THEY ARE YOUR PARENTS.
THEY HAVE EVERYTHING TO DO WITH THIS. IF I DECIDE TO MAKE IT SO.

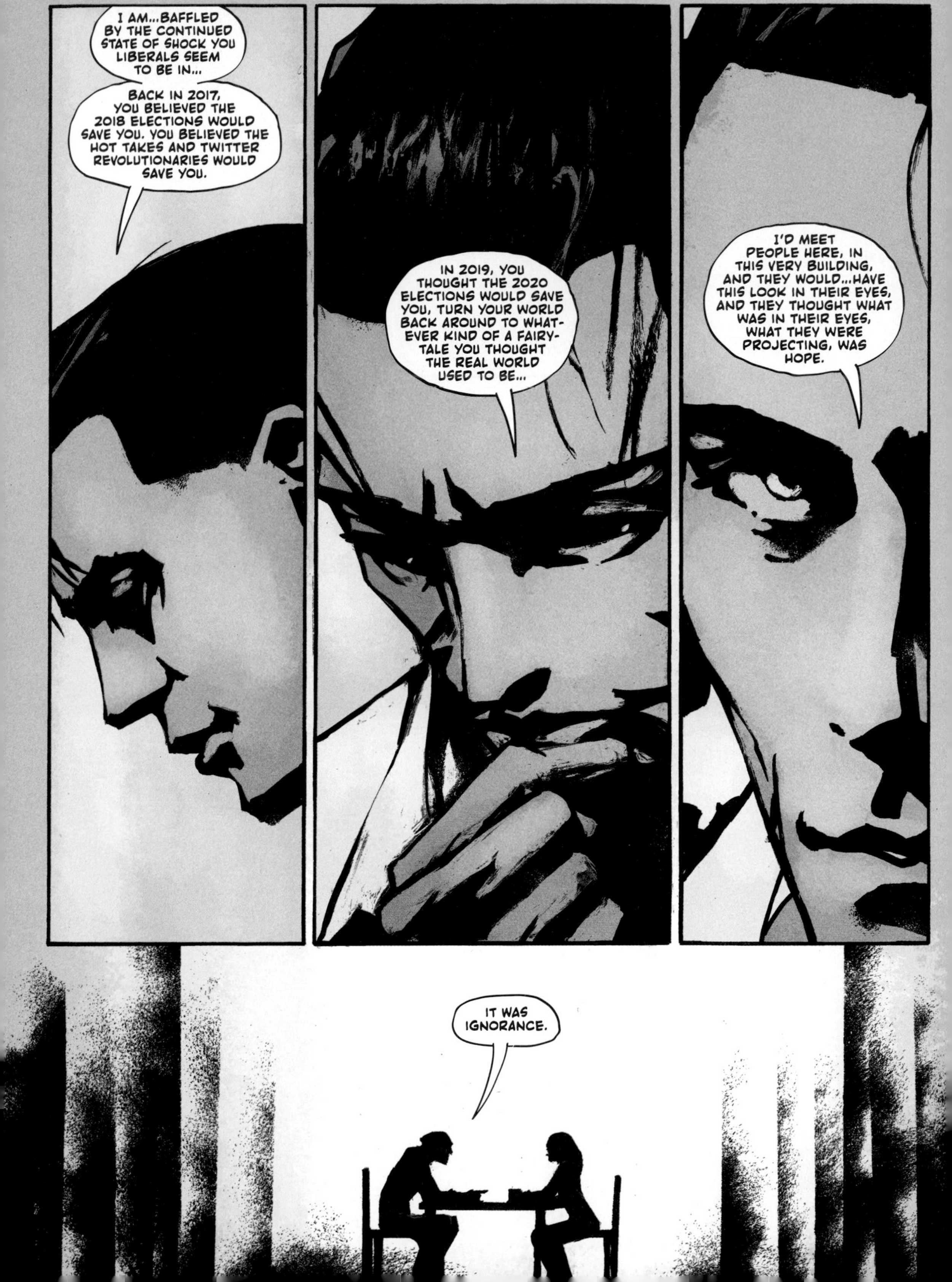

I AM...BAFFLED BY THE CONTINUED STATE OF SHOCK YOU LIBERALS SEEM TO BE IN...
BACK IN 2017, YOU BELIEVED THE 2018 ELECTIONS WOULD SAVE YOU. YOU BELIEVED THE HOT TAKES AND TWITTER REVOLUTIONARIES WOULD SAVE YOU.
IN 2019, YOU THOUGHT THE 2020 ELECTIONS WOULD SAVE YOU, TURN YOUR WORLD BACK AROUND TO WHAT-EVER KIND OF A FAIRY-TALE YOU THOUGHT THE REAL WORLD USED TO BE...
I'D MEET PEOPLE HERE, IN THIS VERY BUILDING, AND THEY WOULD...HAVE THIS LOOK IN THEIR EYES, AND THEY THOUGHT WHAT WAS IN THEIR EYES, WHAT THEY WERE PROJECTING, WAS HOPE.
IT WAS IGNORANCE.

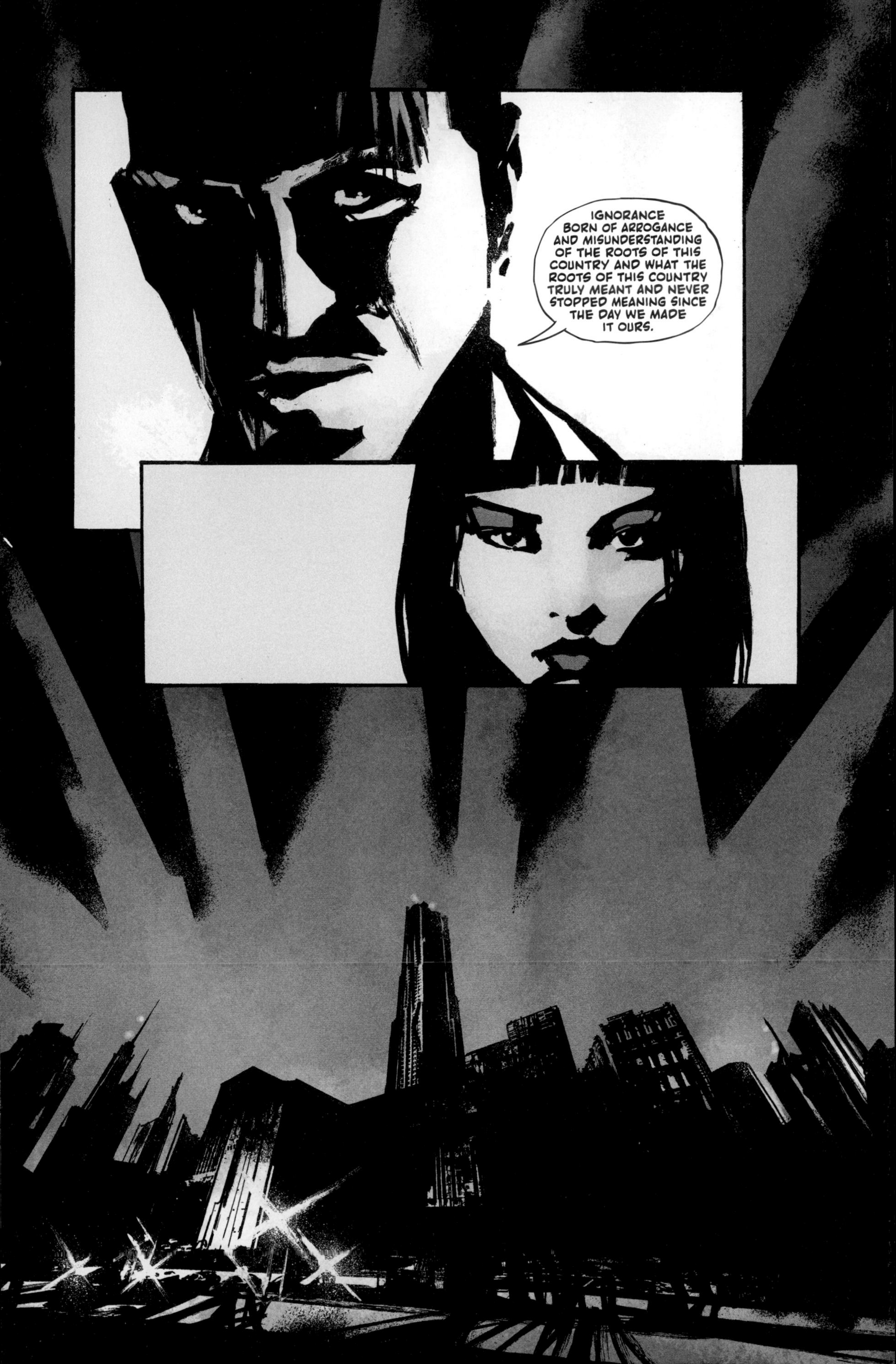
IGNORANCE BORN OF ARROGANCE AND MISUNDERSTANDING OF THE ROOTS OF THIS COUNTRY AND WHAT THE ROOTS OF THIS COUNTRY TRULY MEANT AND NEVER STOPPED MEANING SINCE THE DAY WE MADE IT OURS.

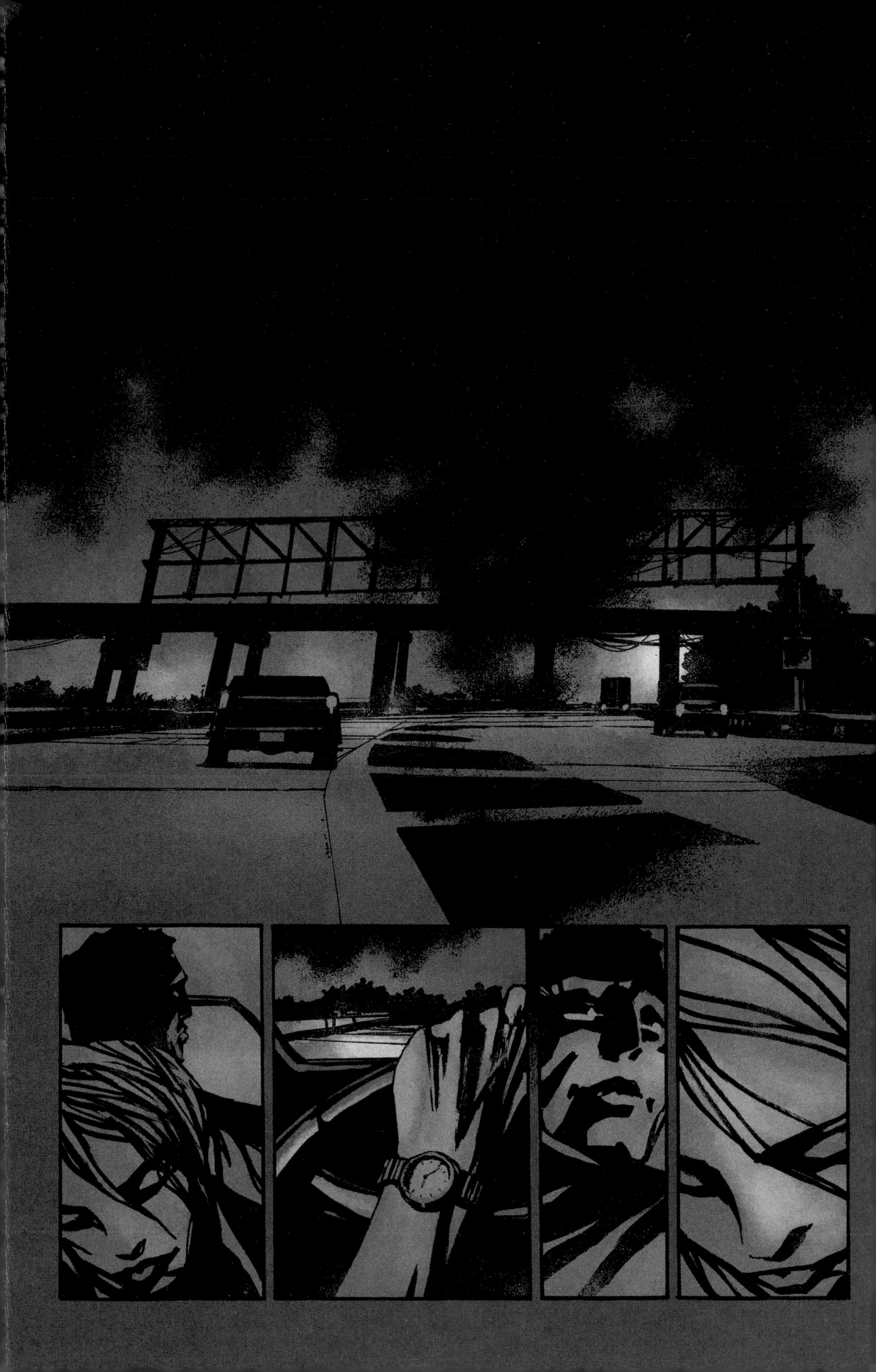

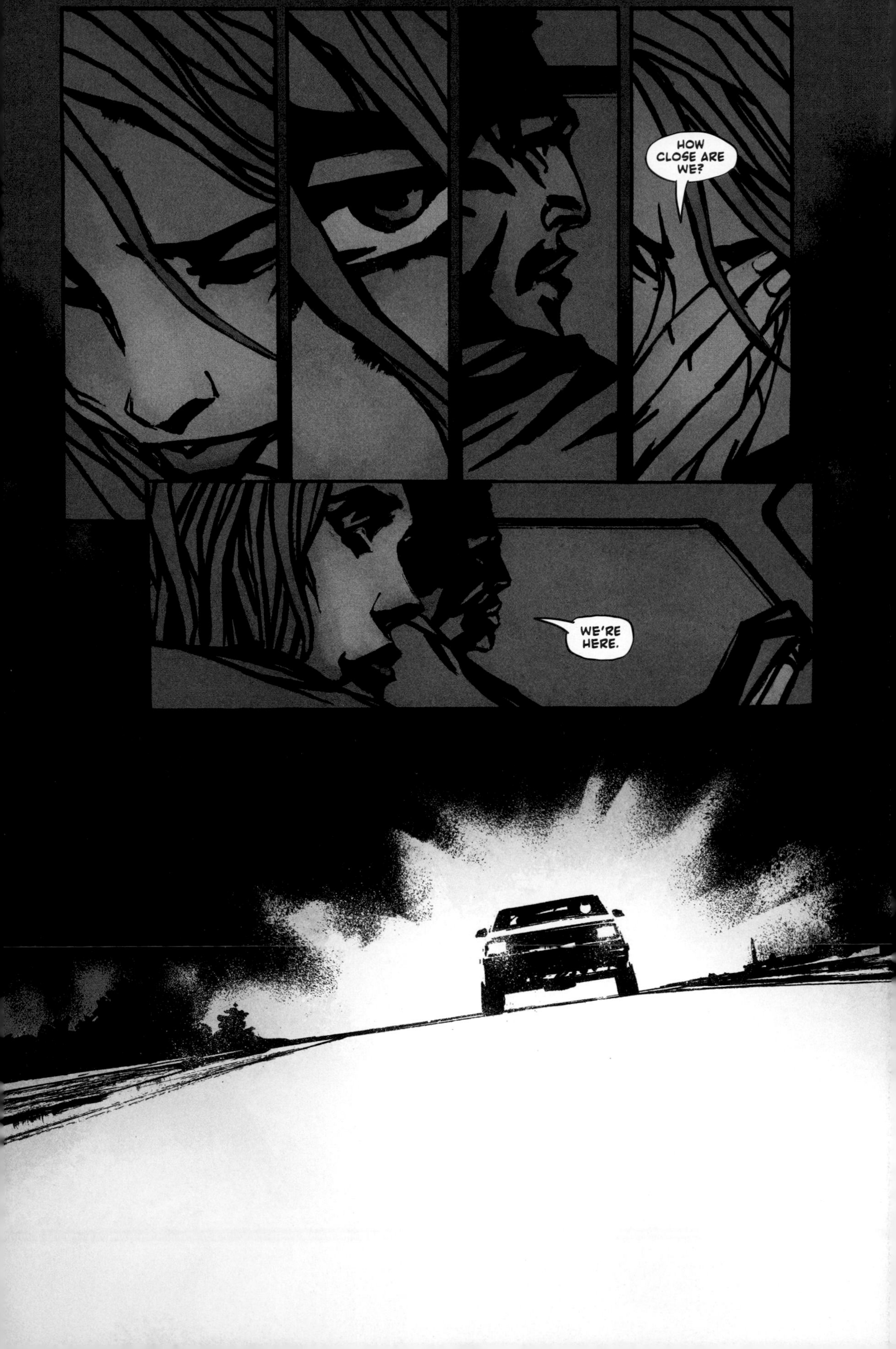
HOW CLOSE ARE WE?
WE'RE HERE.

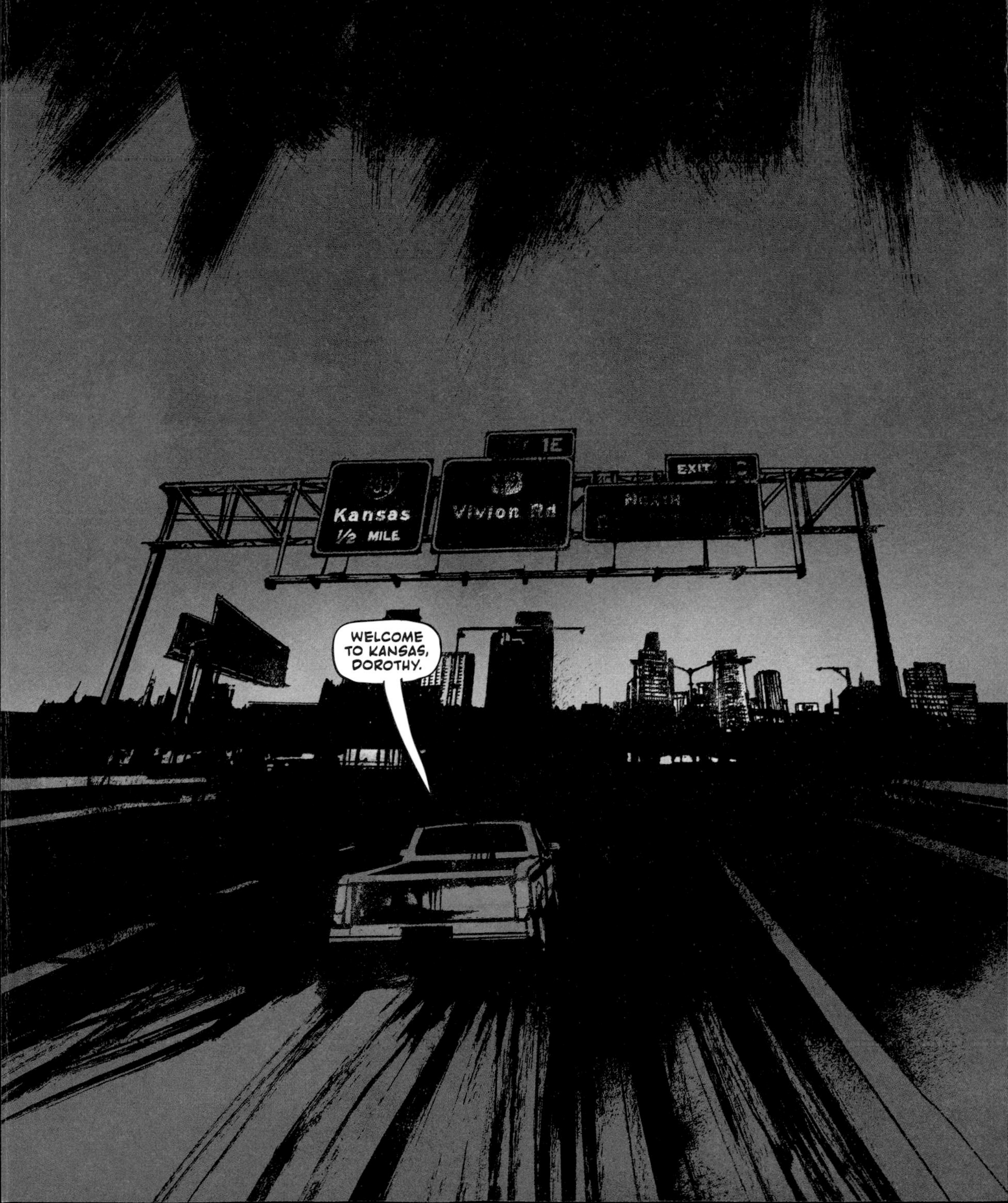

1E
EXIT
Kansas
½ MILE
Vivion Rd
WELCOME TO KANSAS, DOROTHY.

CHAPTER FOUR:

THE ADMINIS- TRATION OF FEAR

"..you think of the enemy as outside yourself, in other words a police officer, the government, the system, but that's not really the case at all, fascism is very insidious, we reproduce it all the time."

—Kathryn Bigelow

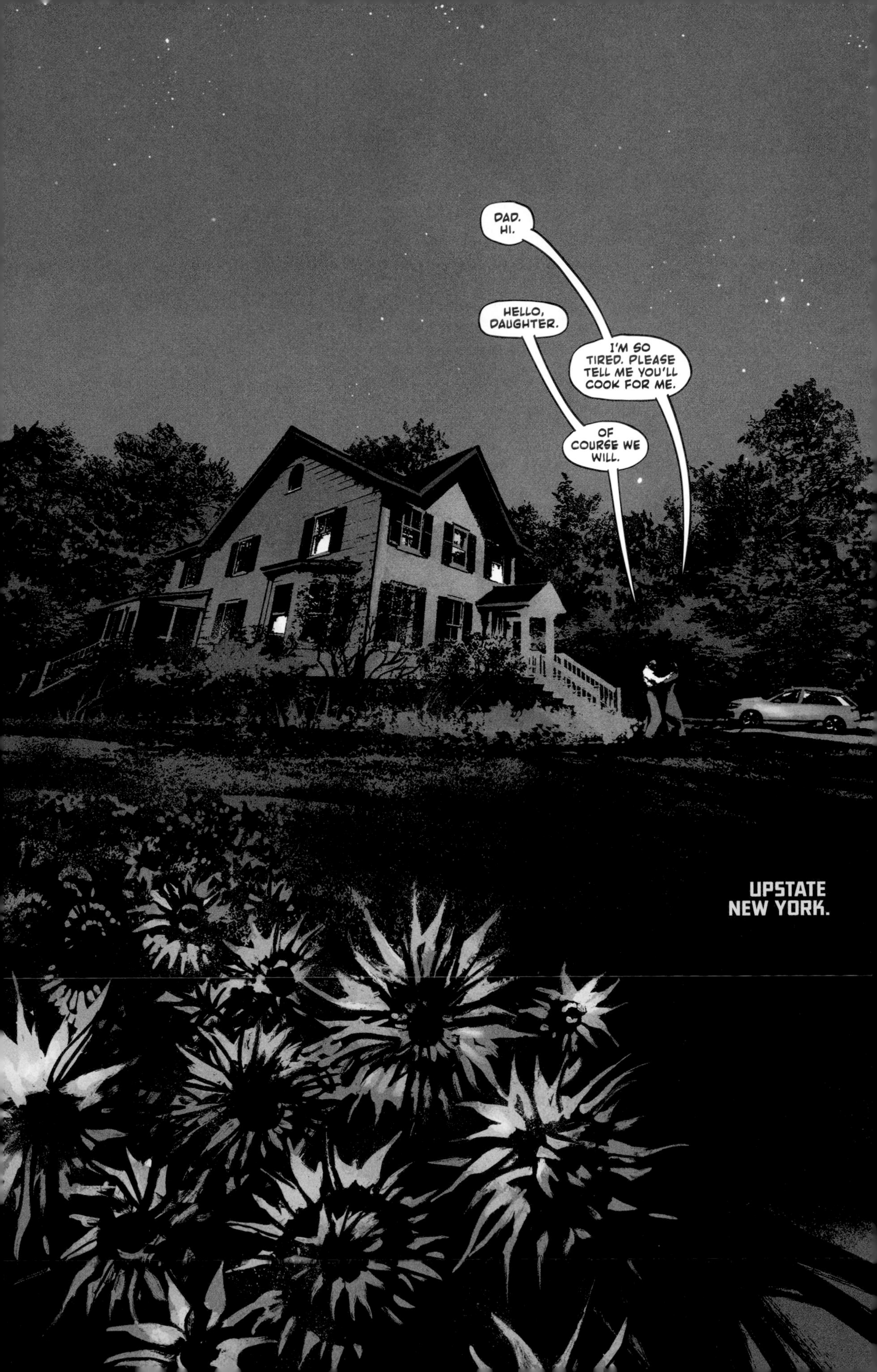
DAD.
HI.
HELLO,
DAUGHTER.
I'M SO
TIRED. PLEASE
TELL ME YOU'LL
COOK FOR ME.
OF
COURSE WE
WILL.
UPSTATE
NEW YORK.

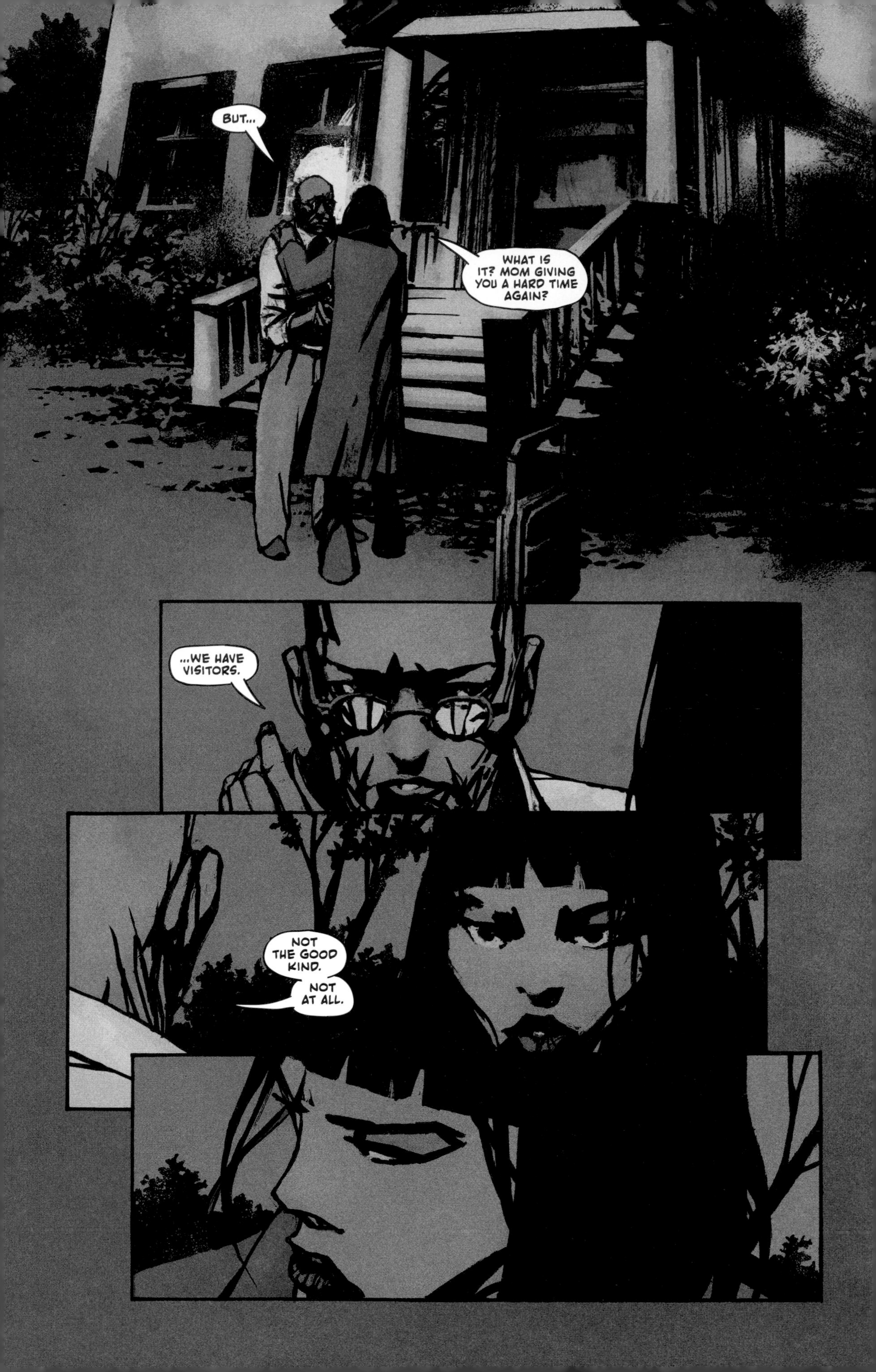
BUT...
WHAT IS IT? MOM GIVING YOU A HARD TIME AGAIN?
...WE HAVE VISITORS.
NOT THE GOOD KIND.
NOT AT ALL.

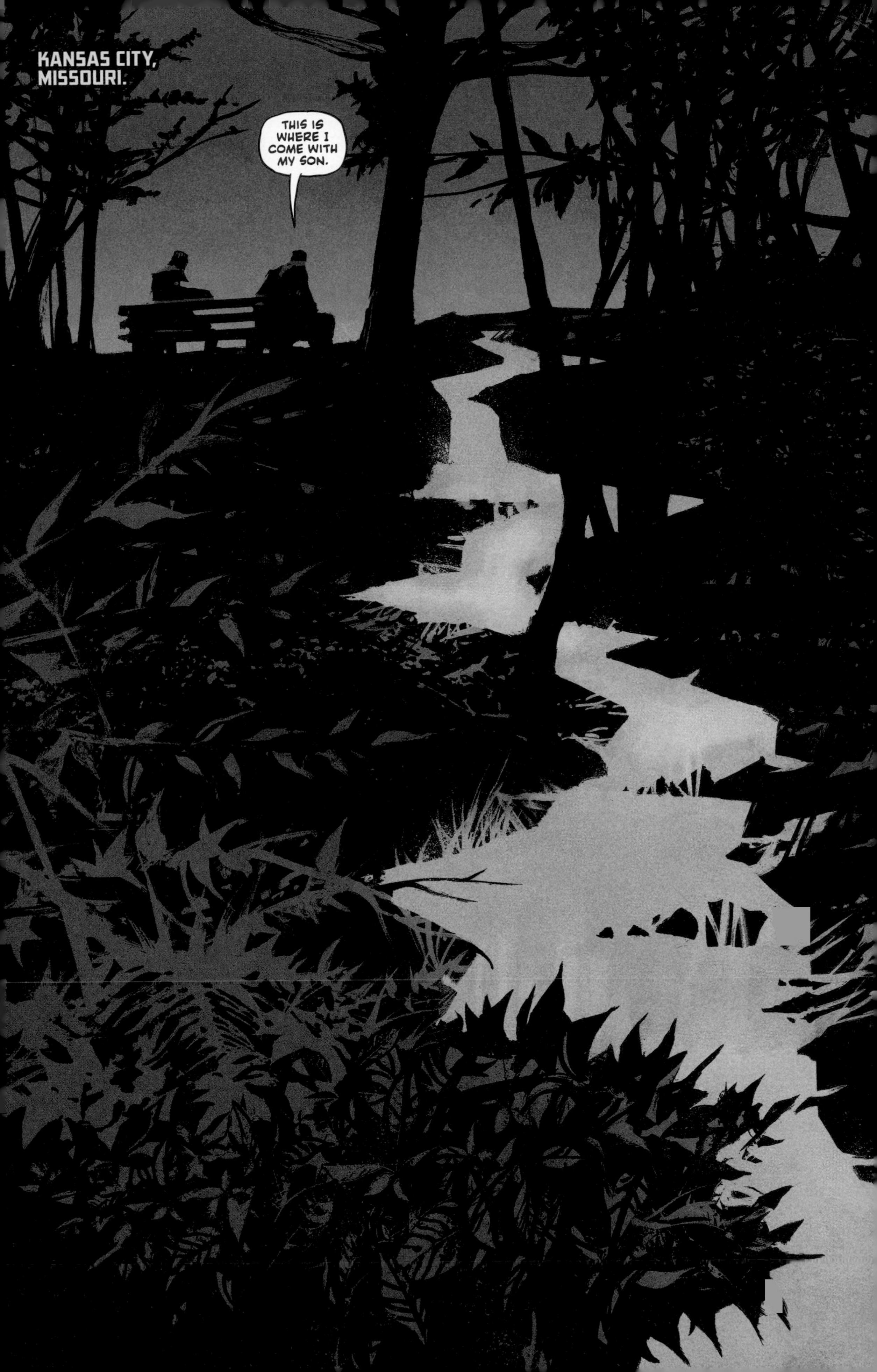
KANSAS CITY, MISSOURI.
THIS IS WHERE I COME WITH MY SON.

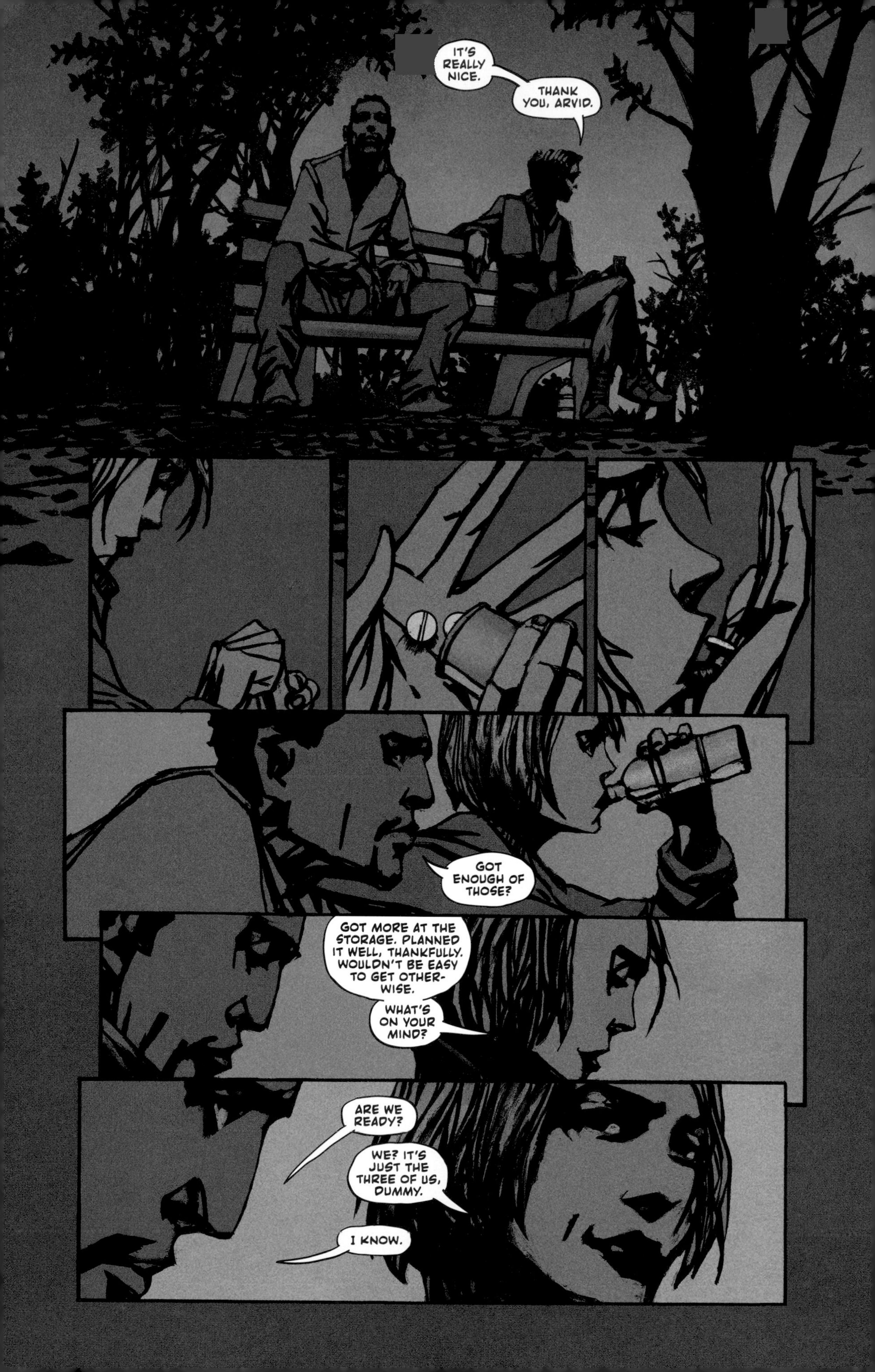
IT'S REALLY NICE.
THANK YOU, ARVID.
GOT ENOUGH OF THOSE?
GOT MORE AT THE STORAGE. PLANNED IT WELL, THANKFULLY. WOULDN'T BE EASY TO GET OTHER-WISE.
WHAT'S ON YOUR MIND?
ARE WE READY?
WE? IT'S JUST THE THREE OF US, DUMMY.
I KNOW.

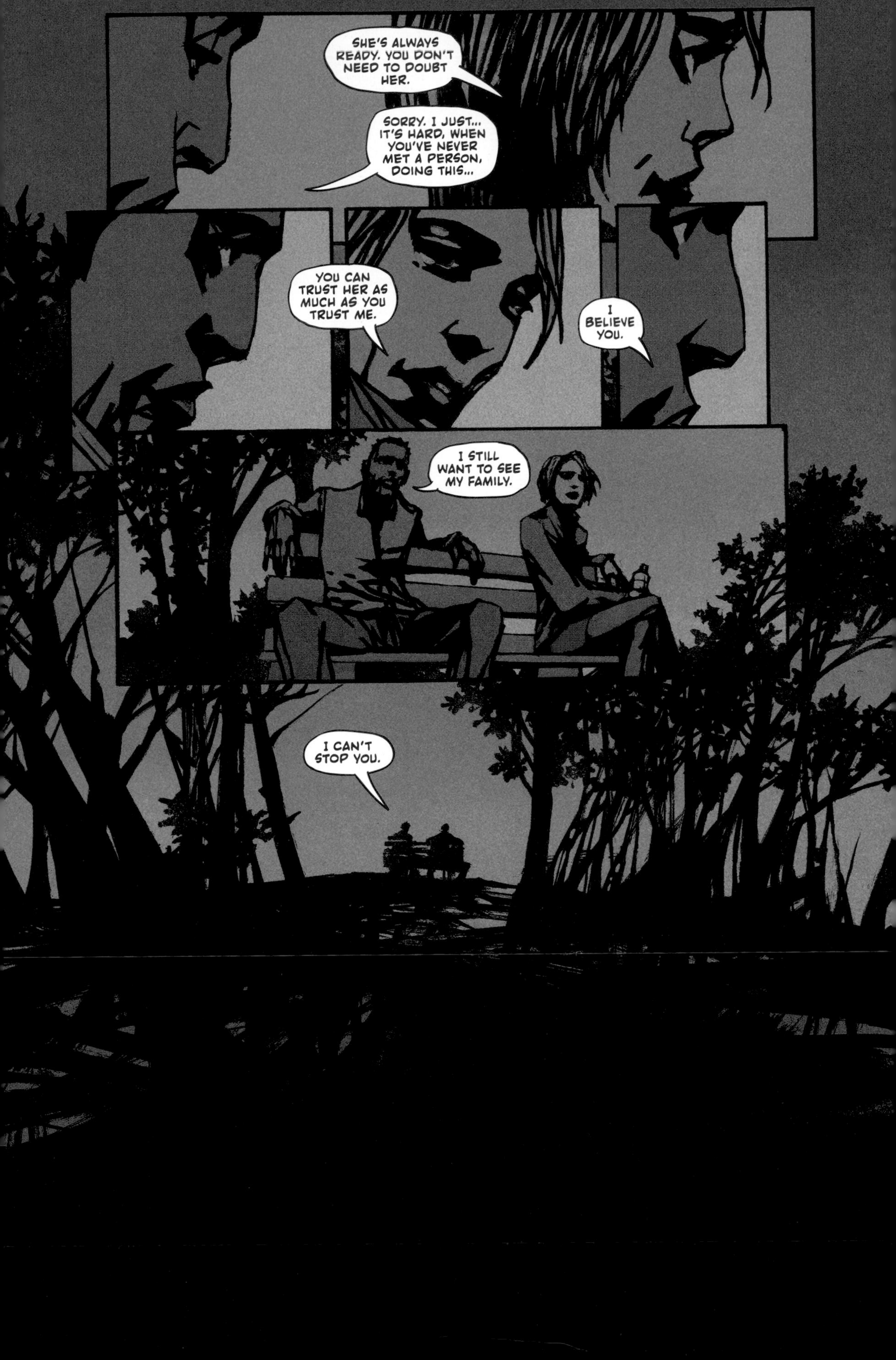
SHE'S ALWAYS READY. YOU DON'T NEED TO DOUBT HER.
SORRY. I JUST... IT'S HARD, WHEN YOU'VE NEVER MET A PERSON, DOING THIS...
YOU CAN TRUST HER AS MUCH AS YOU TRUST ME.
I BELIEVE YOU.
I STILL WANT TO SEE MY FAMILY.
I CAN'T STOP YOU.

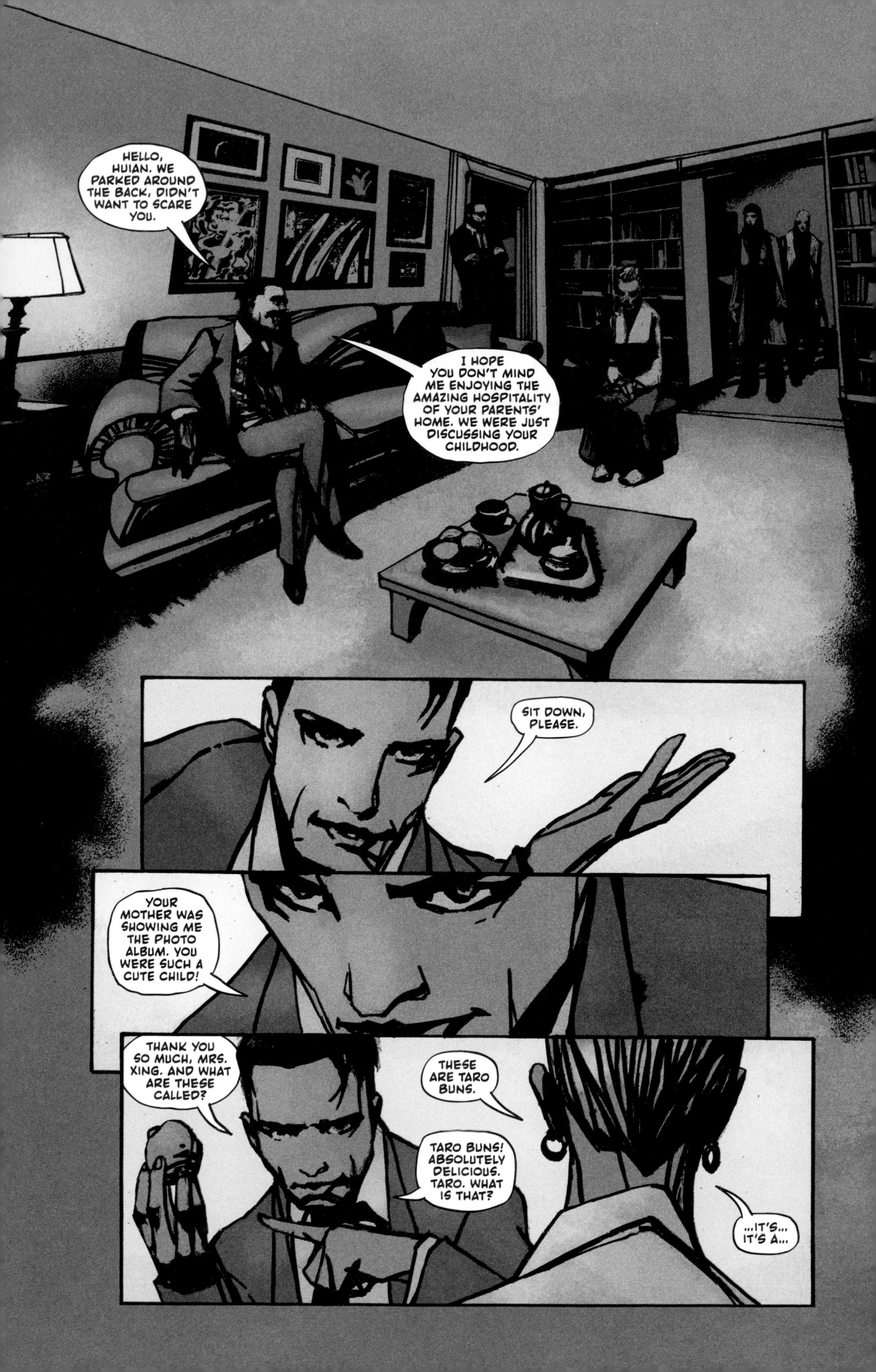
HELLO, HUIAN. WE PARKED AROUND THE BACK, DIDN'T WANT TO SCARE YOU.
I HOPE YOU DON'T MIND ME ENJOYING THE AMAZING HOSPITALITY OF YOUR PARENTS' HOME. WE WERE JUST DISCUSSING YOUR CHILDHOOD.
SIT DOWN, PLEASE.
YOUR MOTHER WAS SHOWING ME THE PHOTO ALBUM. YOU WERE SUCH A CUTE CHILD!
THANK YOU SO MUCH, MRS. XING. AND WHAT ARE THESE CALLED?
THESE ARE TARO BUNS.
TARO BUNS! ABSOLUTELY DELICIOUS. TARO. WHAT IS THAT?
...IT'S... IT'S A...

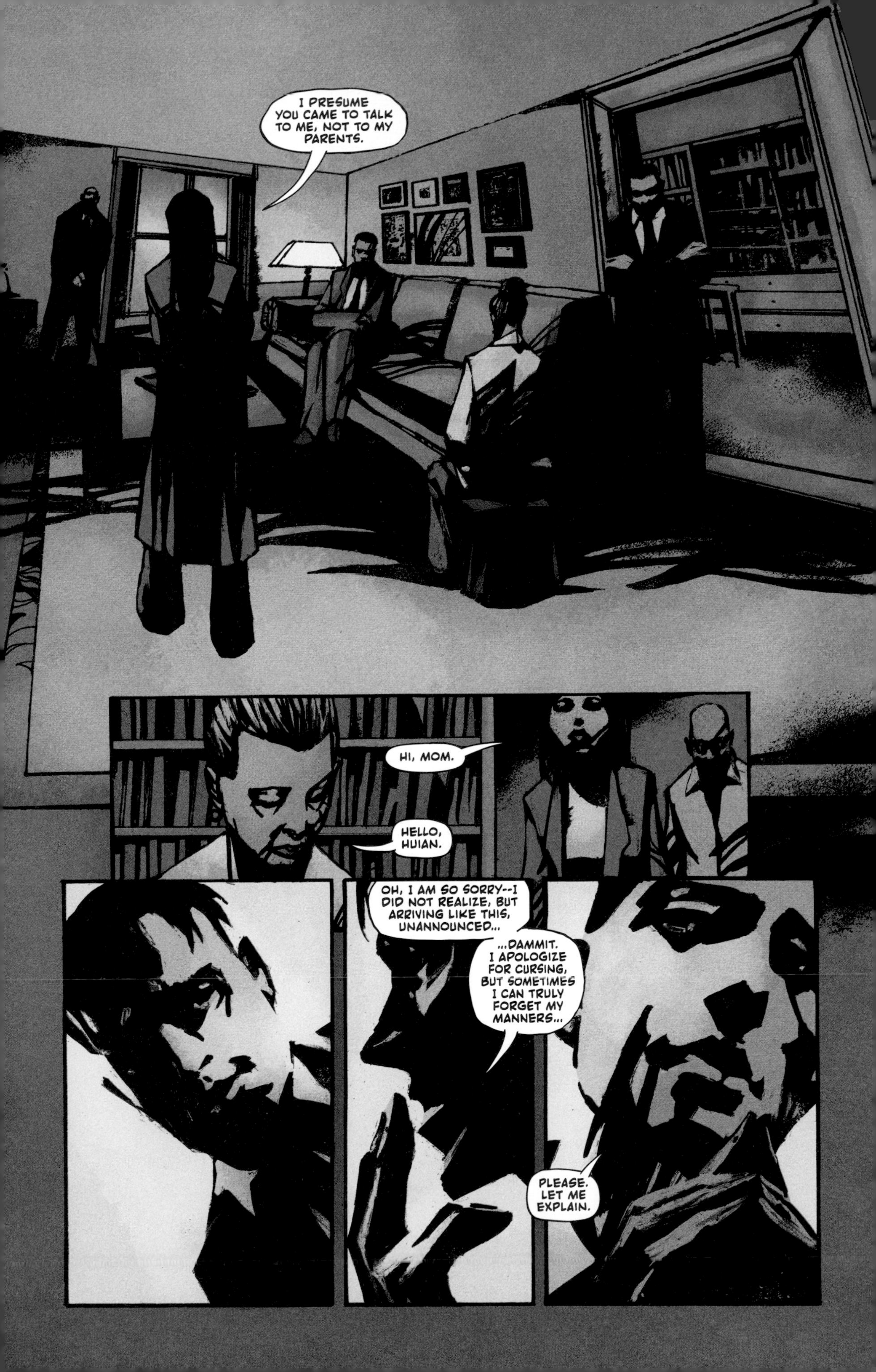
I PRESUME YOU CAME TO TALK TO ME, NOT TO MY PARENTS.
HI, MOM.
HELLO, HUIAN.
OH, I AM SO SORRY--I DID NOT REALIZE, BUT ARRIVING LIKE THIS, UNANNOUNCED...
...DAMMIT. I APOLOGIZE FOR CURSING, BUT SOMETIMES I CAN TRULY FORGET MY MANNERS...
PLEASE. LET ME EXPLAIN.

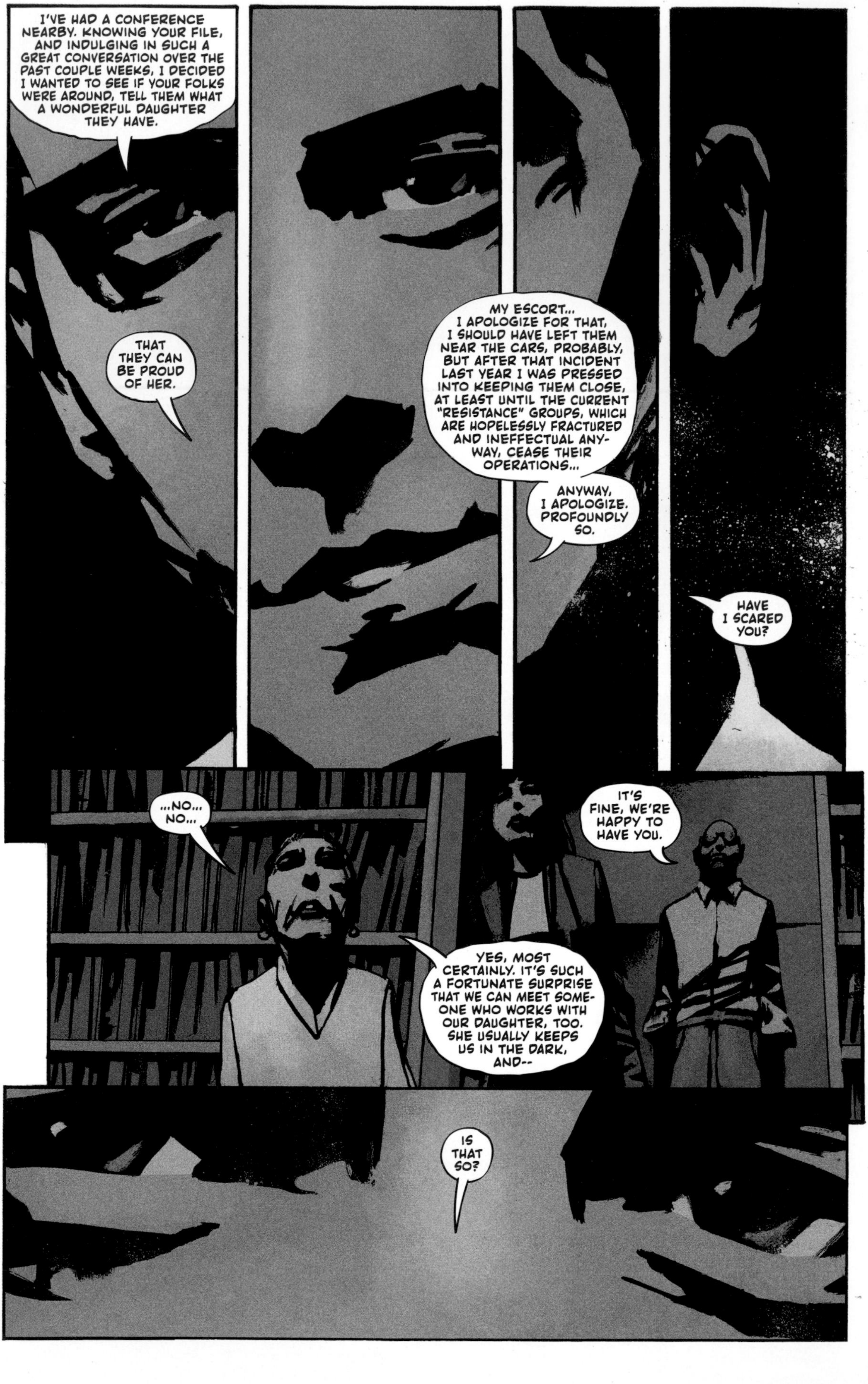
I'VE HAD A CONFERENCE NEARBY. KNOWING YOUR FILE, AND INDULGING IN SUCH A GREAT CONVERSATION OVER THE PAST COUPLE WEEKS, I DECIDED I WANTED TO SEE IF YOUR FOLKS WERE AROUND, TELL THEM WHAT A WONDERFUL DAUGHTER THEY HAVE.
THAT THEY CAN BE PROUD OF HER.
MY ESCORT... I APOLOGIZE FOR THAT, I SHOULD HAVE LEFT THEM NEAR THE CARS, PROBABLY, BUT AFTER THAT INCIDENT LAST YEAR I WAS PRESSED INTO KEEPING THEM CLOSE, AT LEAST UNTIL THE CURRENT "RESISTANCE" GROUPS, WHICH ARE HOPELESSLY FRACTURED AND INEFFECTUAL ANY-WAY, CEASE THEIR OPERATIONS...
ANYWAY, I APOLOGIZE. PROFOUNDLY SO.
HAVE I SCARED YOU?
...NO... NO...
IT'S FINE, WE'RE HAPPY TO HAVE YOU.
YES, MOST CERTAINLY. IT'S SUCH A FORTUNATE SURPRISE THAT WE CAN MEET SOME-ONE WHO WORKS WITH OUR DAUGHTER, TOO. SHE USUALLY KEEPS US IN THE DARK, AND--
IS THAT SO?

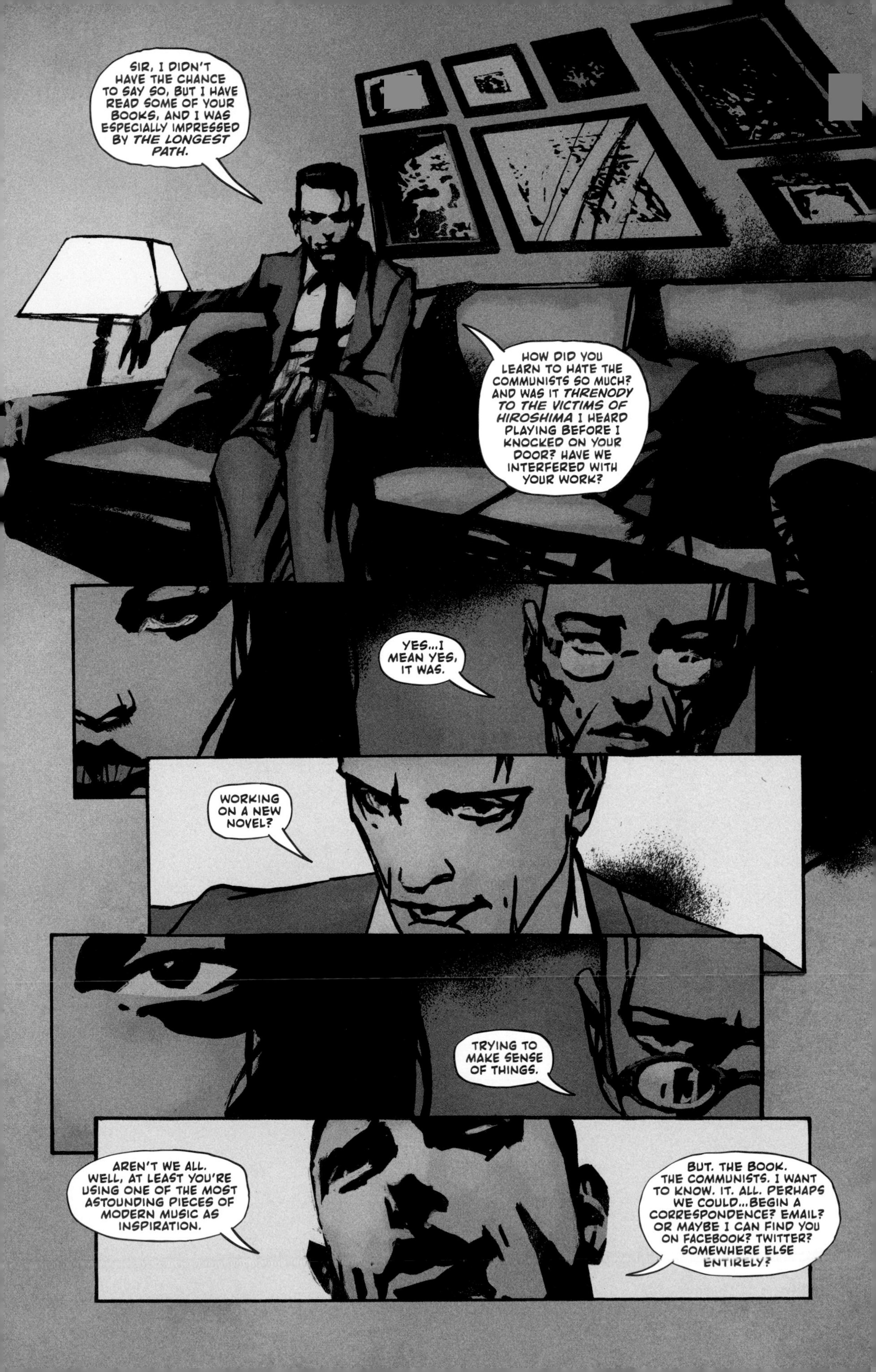
SIR, I DIDN'T HAVE THE CHANCE TO SAY SO, BUT I HAVE READ SOME OF YOUR BOOKS, AND I WAS ESPECIALLY IMPRESSED BY *THE LONGEST PATH.*
HOW DID YOU LEARN TO HATE THE COMMUNISTS SO MUCH? AND WAS IT *THRENODY TO THE VICTIMS OF HIROSHIMA* I HEARD PLAYING BEFORE I KNOCKED ON YOUR DOOR? HAVE WE INTERFERED WITH YOUR WORK?
YES...I MEAN YES, IT WAS.
WORKING ON A NEW NOVEL?
TRYING TO MAKE SENSE OF THINGS.
AREN'T WE ALL. WELL, AT LEAST YOU'RE USING ONE OF THE MOST ASTOUNDING PIECES OF MODERN MUSIC AS INSPIRATION.
BUT. THE BOOK. THE COMMUNISTS. I WANT TO KNOW. IT. ALL. PERHAPS WE COULD...BEGIN A CORRESPONDENCE? EMAIL? OR MAYBE I CAN FIND YOU ON FACEBOOK? TWITTER? SOMEWHERE ELSE ENTIRELY?

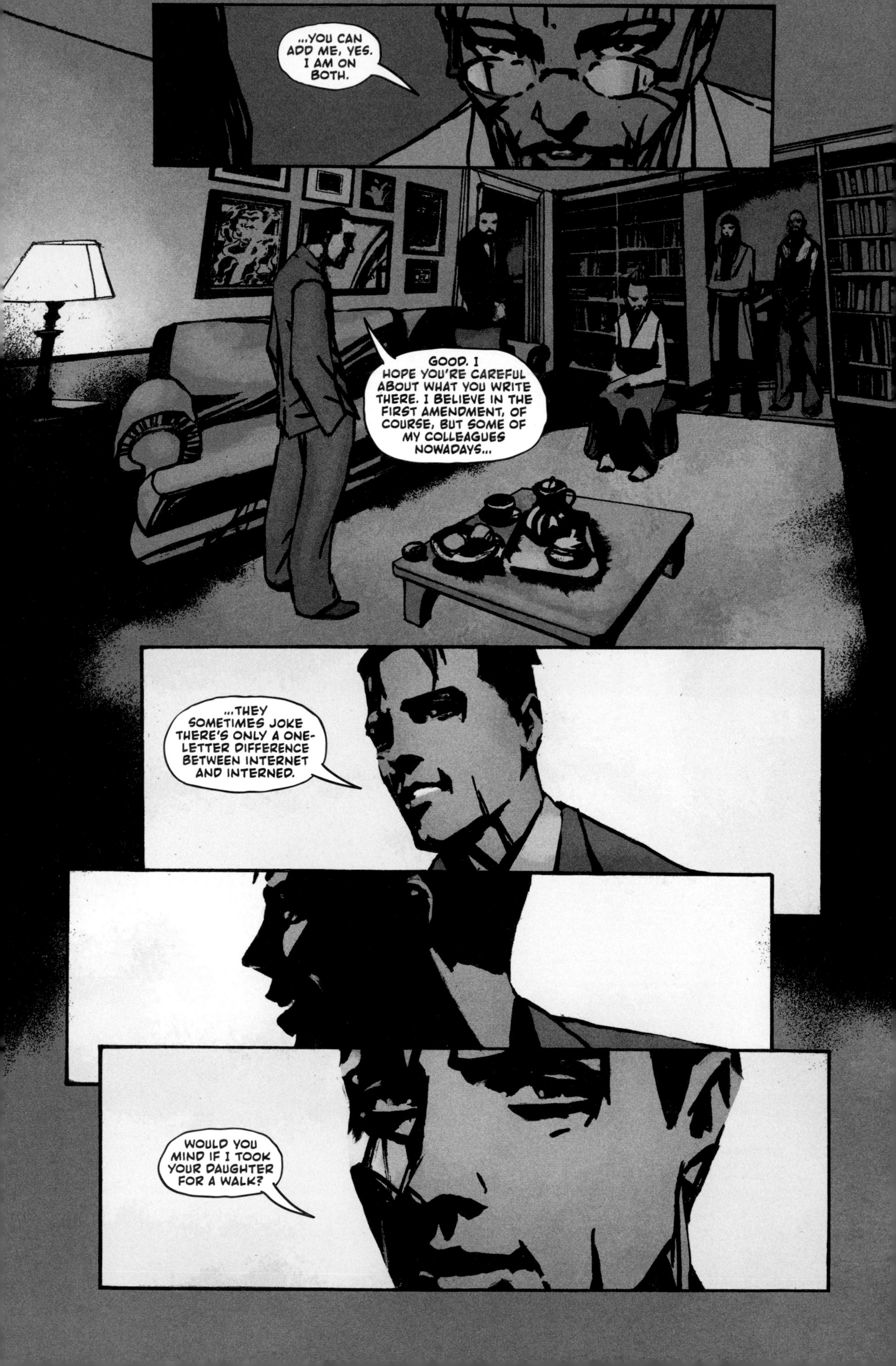
...YOU CAN ADD ME, YES. I AM ON BOTH.
GOOD. I HOPE YOU'RE CAREFUL ABOUT WHAT YOU WRITE THERE. I BELIEVE IN THE FIRST AMENDMENT, OF COURSE, BUT SOME OF MY COLLEAGUES NOWADAYS...
...THEY SOMETIMES JOKE THERE'S ONLY A ONE-LETTER DIFFERENCE BETWEEN INTERNET AND INTERNED.
WOULD YOU MIND IF I TOOK YOUR DAUGHTER FOR A WALK?

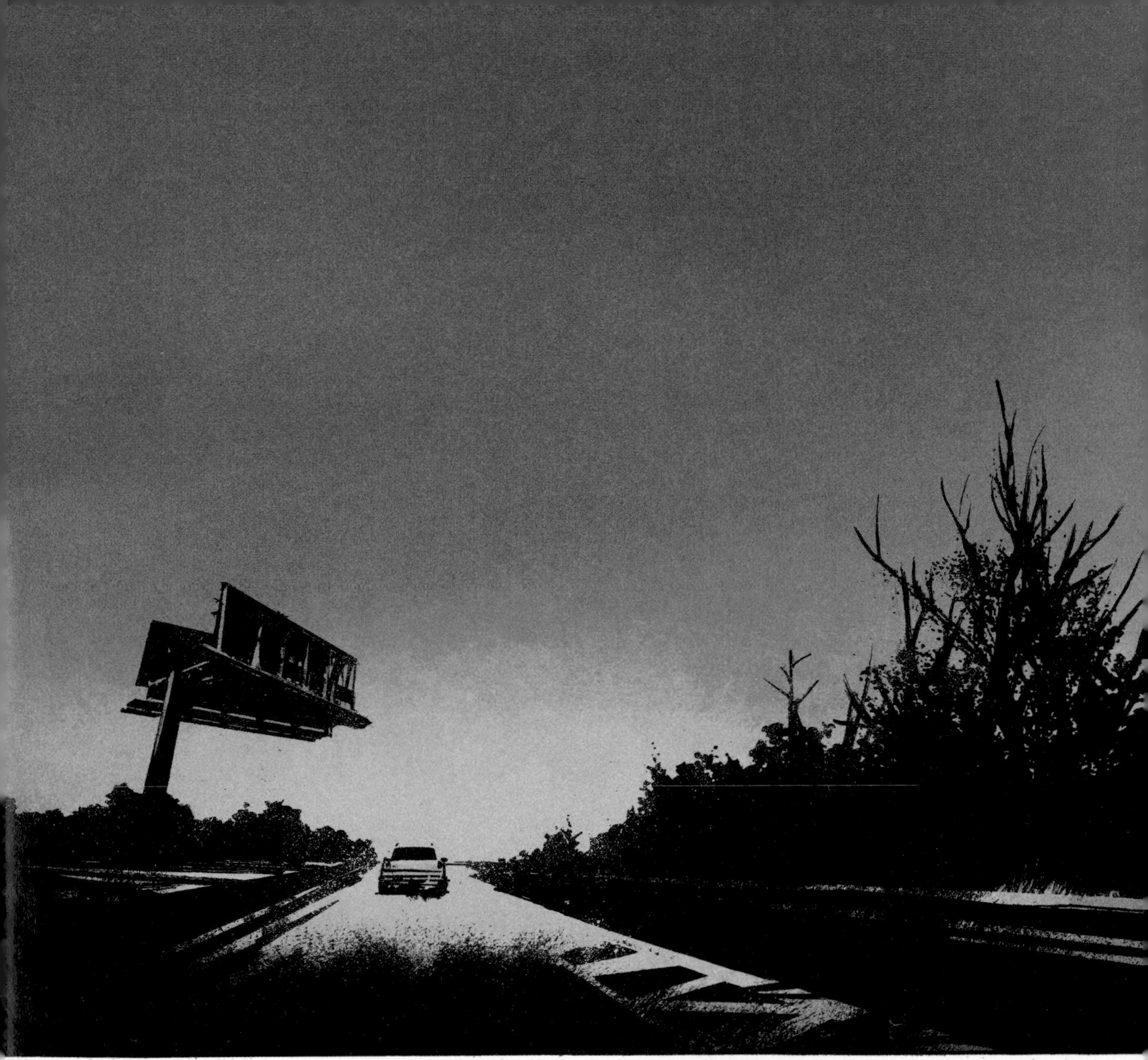

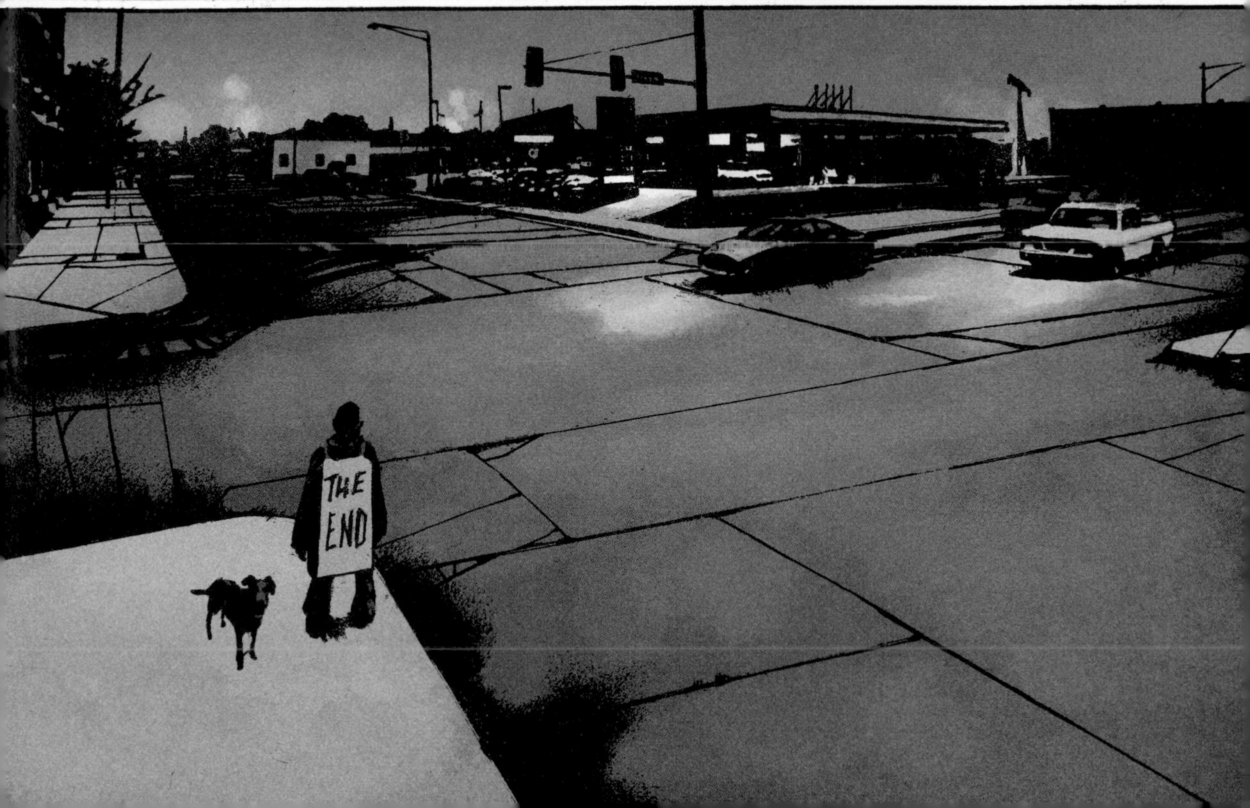
THE END

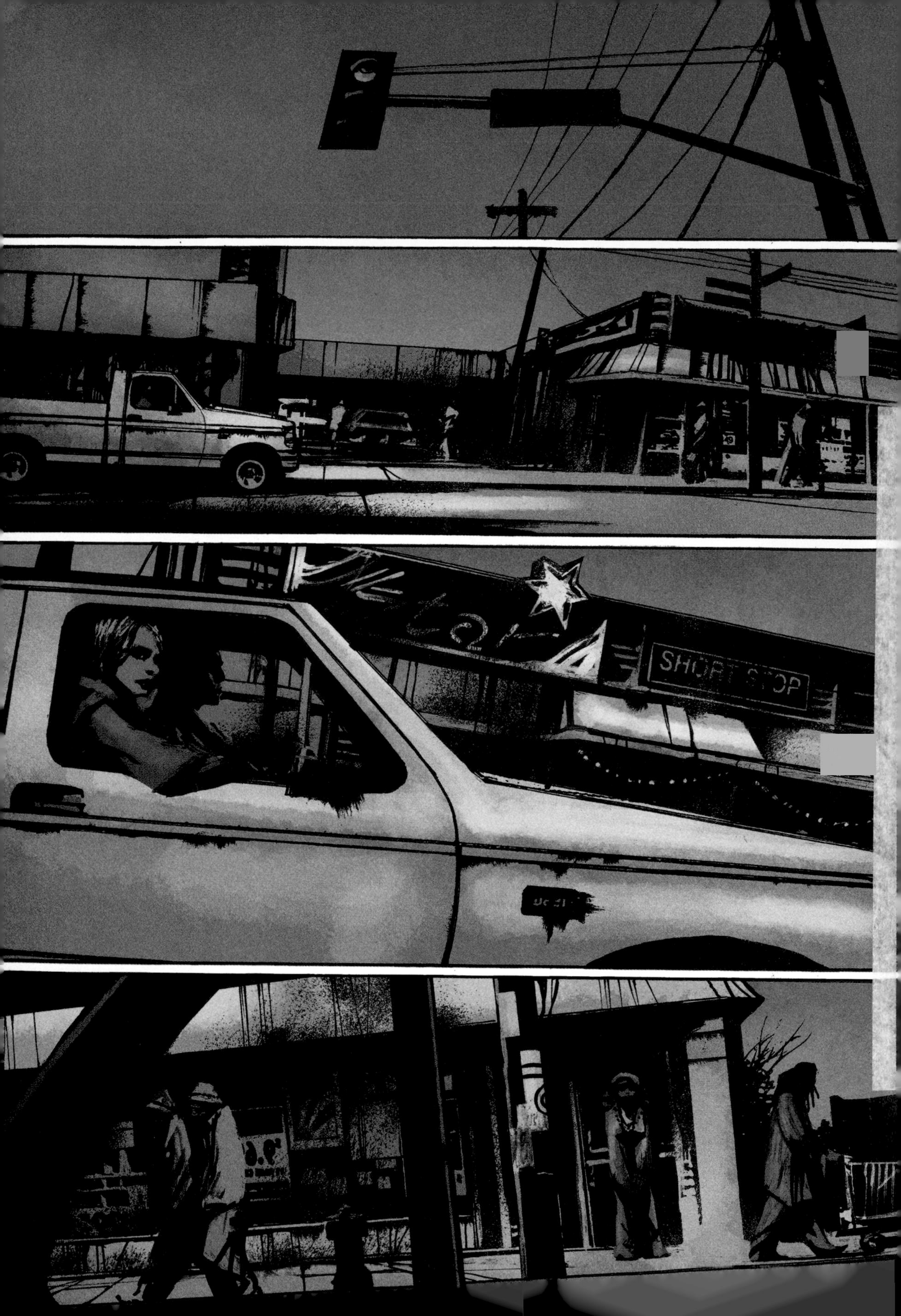
SHORT STOP

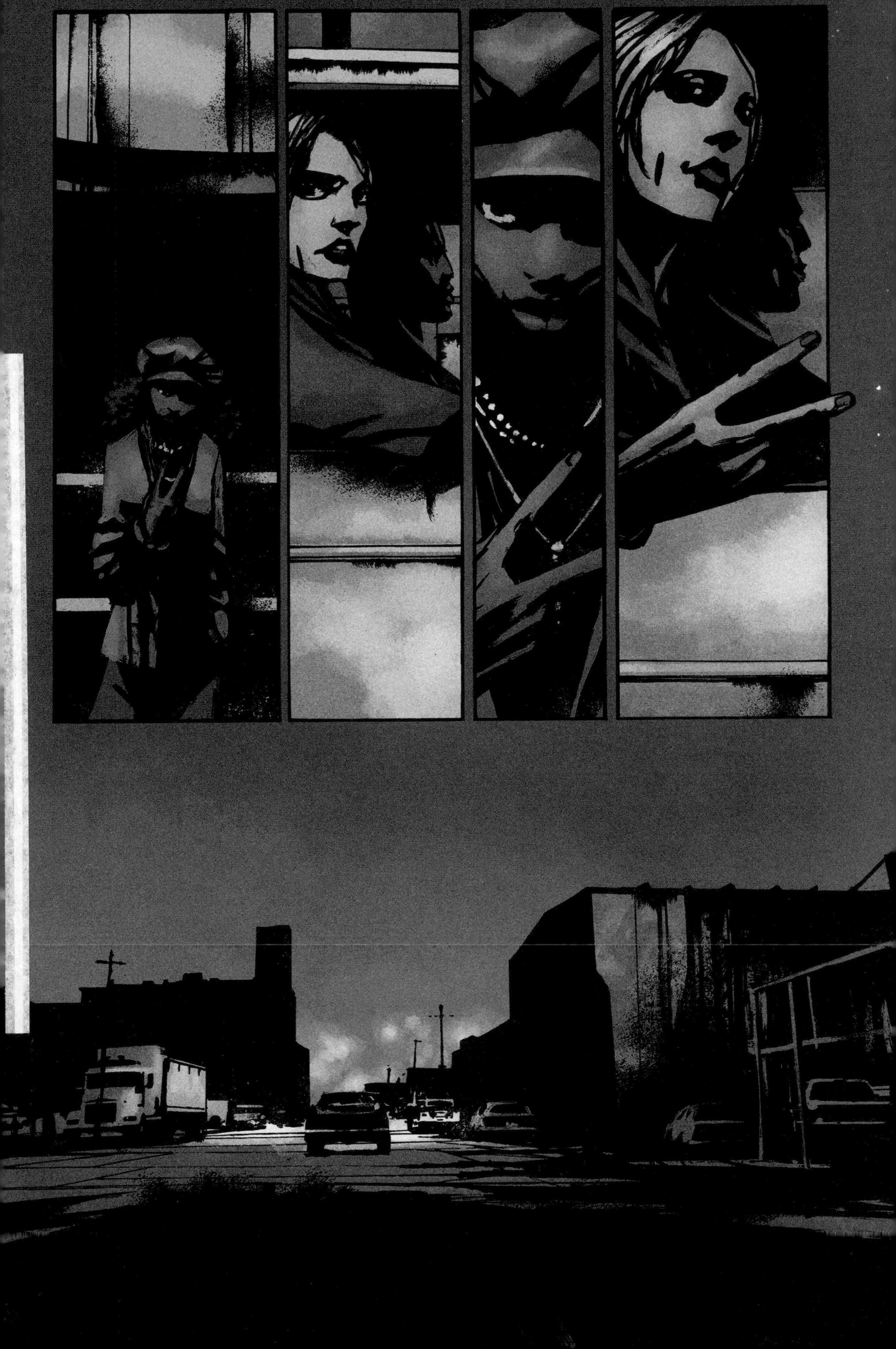

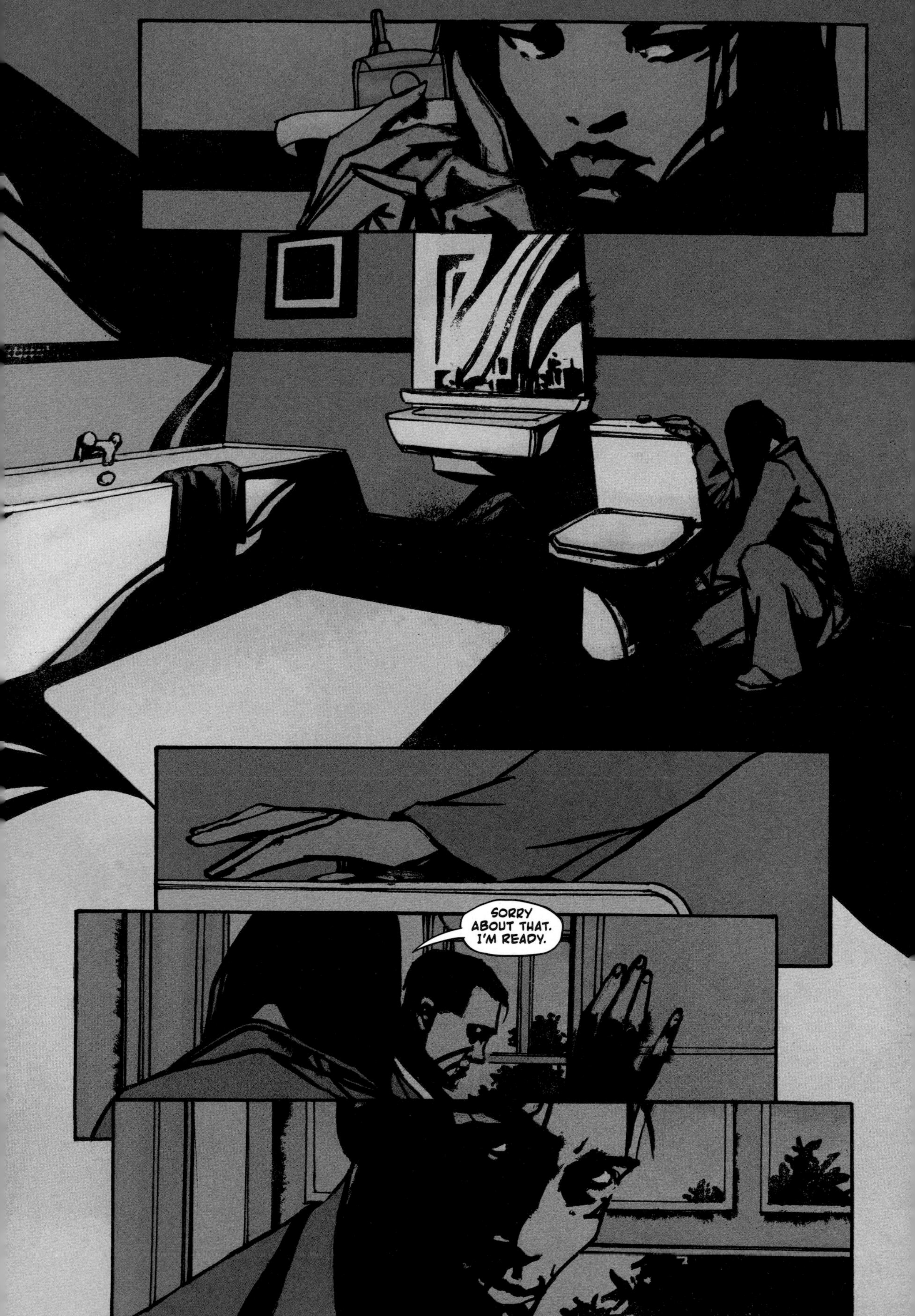
SORRY ABOUT THAT. I'M READY.

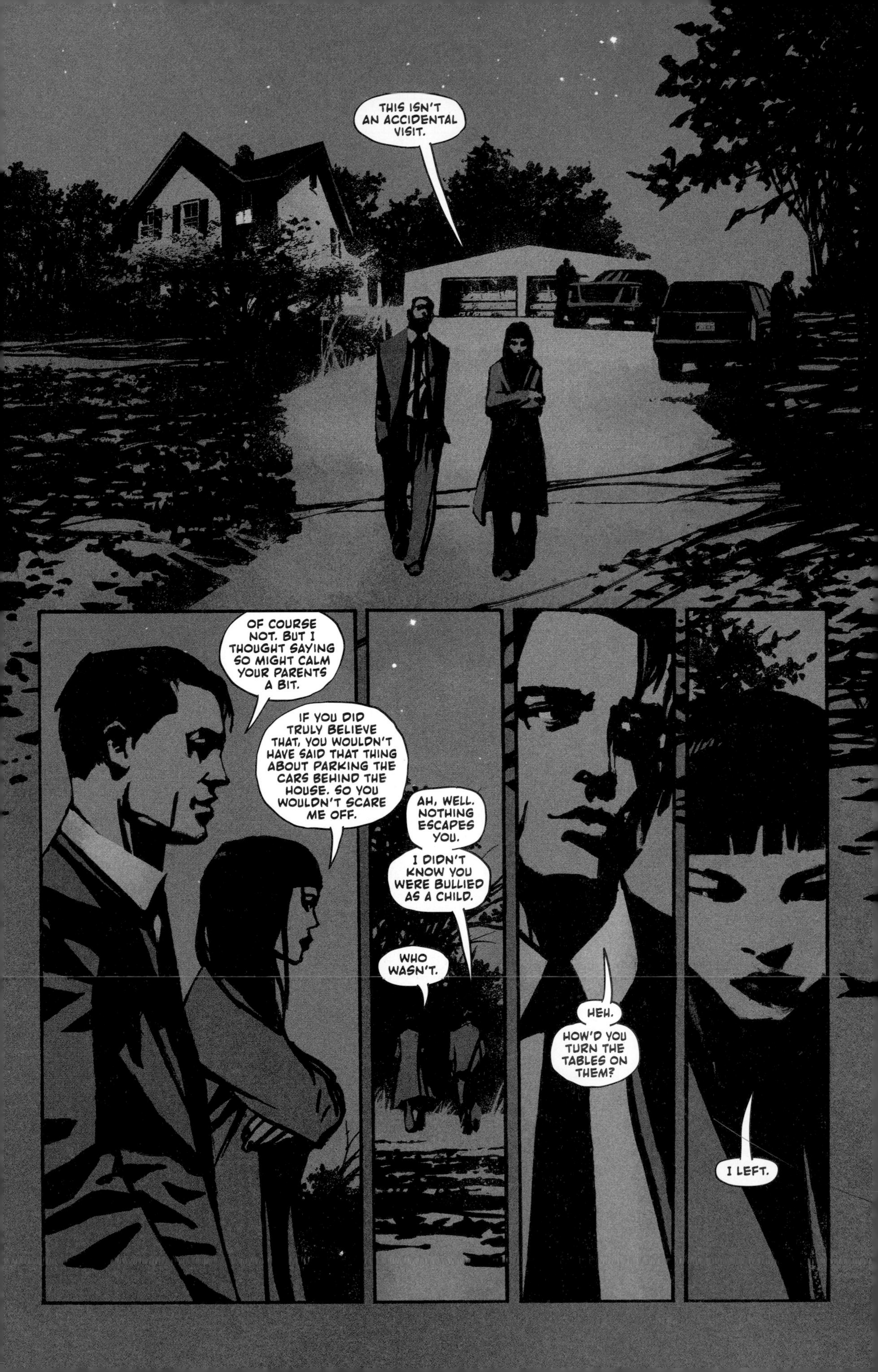
THIS ISN'T AN ACCIDENTAL VISIT.
OF COURSE NOT. BUT I THOUGHT SAYING SO MIGHT CALM YOUR PARENTS A BIT.
IF YOU DID TRULY BELIEVE THAT, YOU WOULDN'T HAVE SAID THAT THING ABOUT PARKING THE CARS BEHIND THE HOUSE. SO YOU WOULDN'T SCARE ME OFF.
AH, WELL. NOTHING ESCAPES YOU.
I DIDN'T KNOW YOU WERE BULLIED AS A CHILD.
WHO WASN'T.
HEH.
HOW'D YOU TURN THE TABLES ON THEM?
I LEFT.

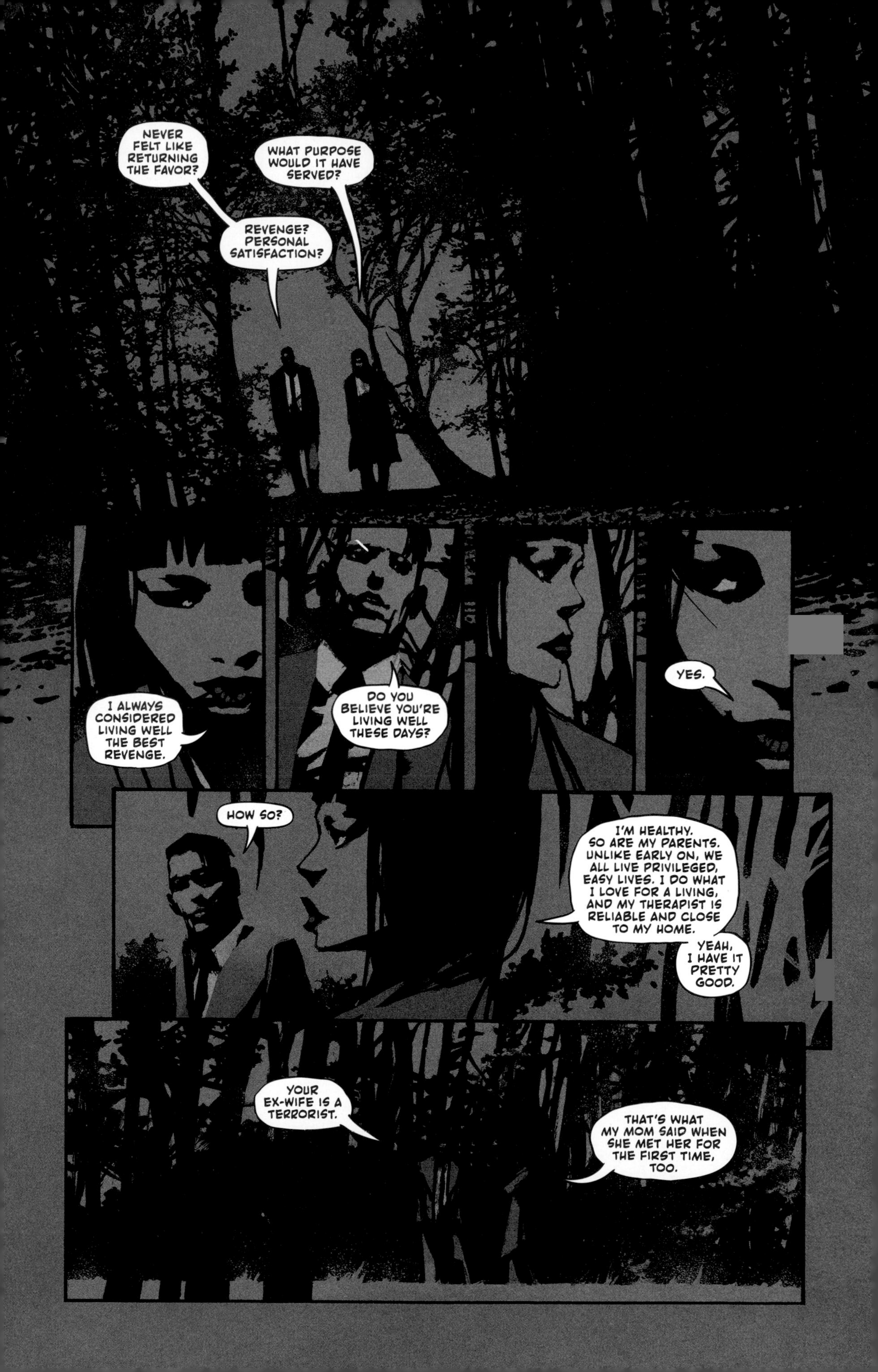
NEVER FELT LIKE RETURNING THE FAVOR?
REVENGE? PERSONAL SATISFACTION?
WHAT PURPOSE WOULD IT HAVE SERVED?
I ALWAYS CONSIDERED LIVING WELL THE BEST REVENGE.
DO YOU BELIEVE YOU'RE LIVING WELL THESE DAYS?
YES.
HOW SO?
I'M HEALTHY. SO ARE MY PARENTS. UNLIKE EARLY ON, WE ALL LIVE PRIVILEGED, EASY LIVES. I DO WHAT I LOVE FOR A LIVING, AND MY THERAPIST IS RELIABLE AND CLOSE TO MY HOME.
YEAH, I HAVE IT PRETTY GOOD.
YOUR EX-WIFE IS A TERRORIST.
THAT'S WHAT MY MOM SAID WHEN SHE MET HER FOR THE FIRST TIME, TOO.

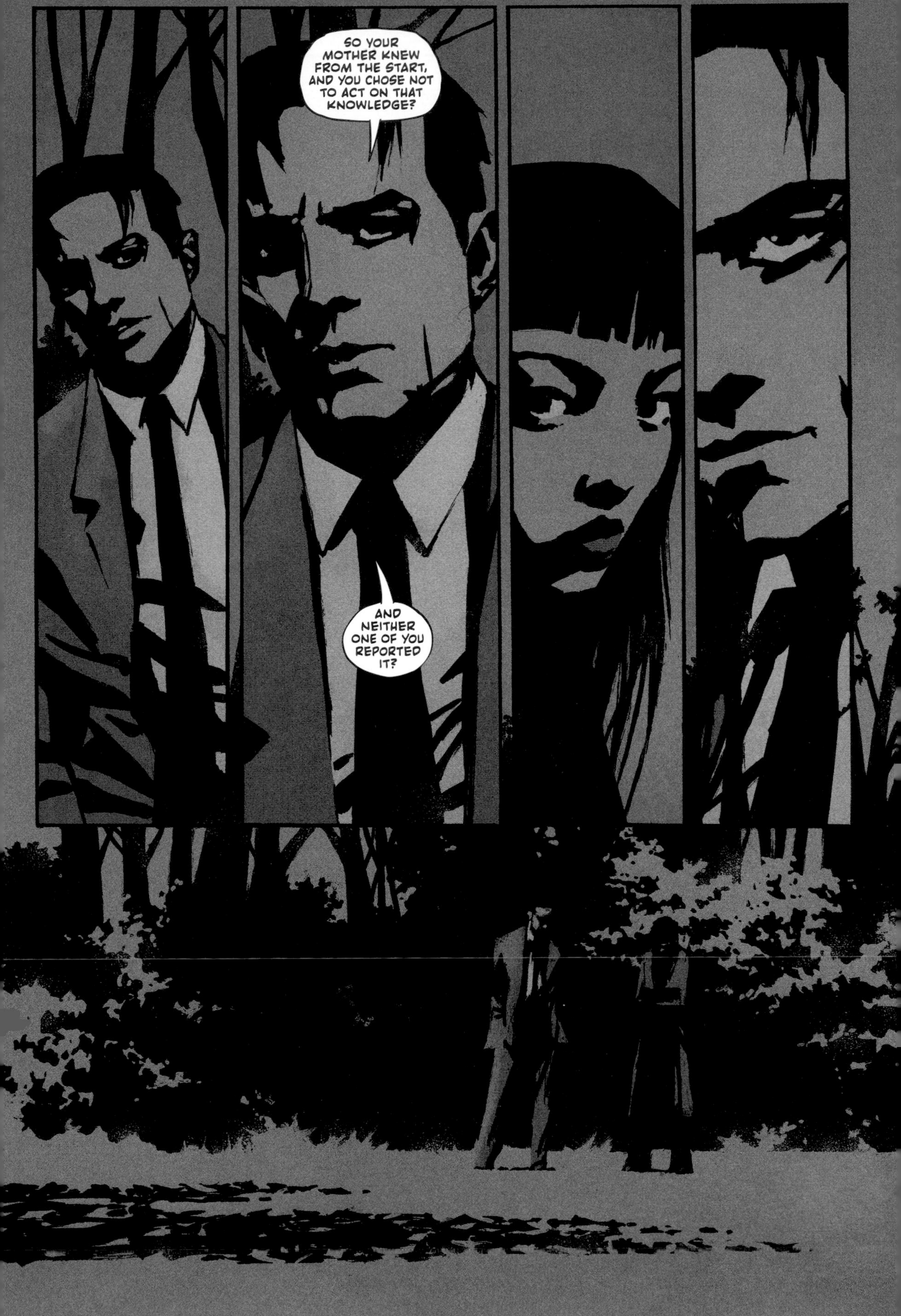
SO YOUR MOTHER KNEW FROM THE START, AND YOU CHOSE NOT TO ACT ON THAT KNOWLEDGE?
AND NEITHER ONE OF YOU REPORTED IT?

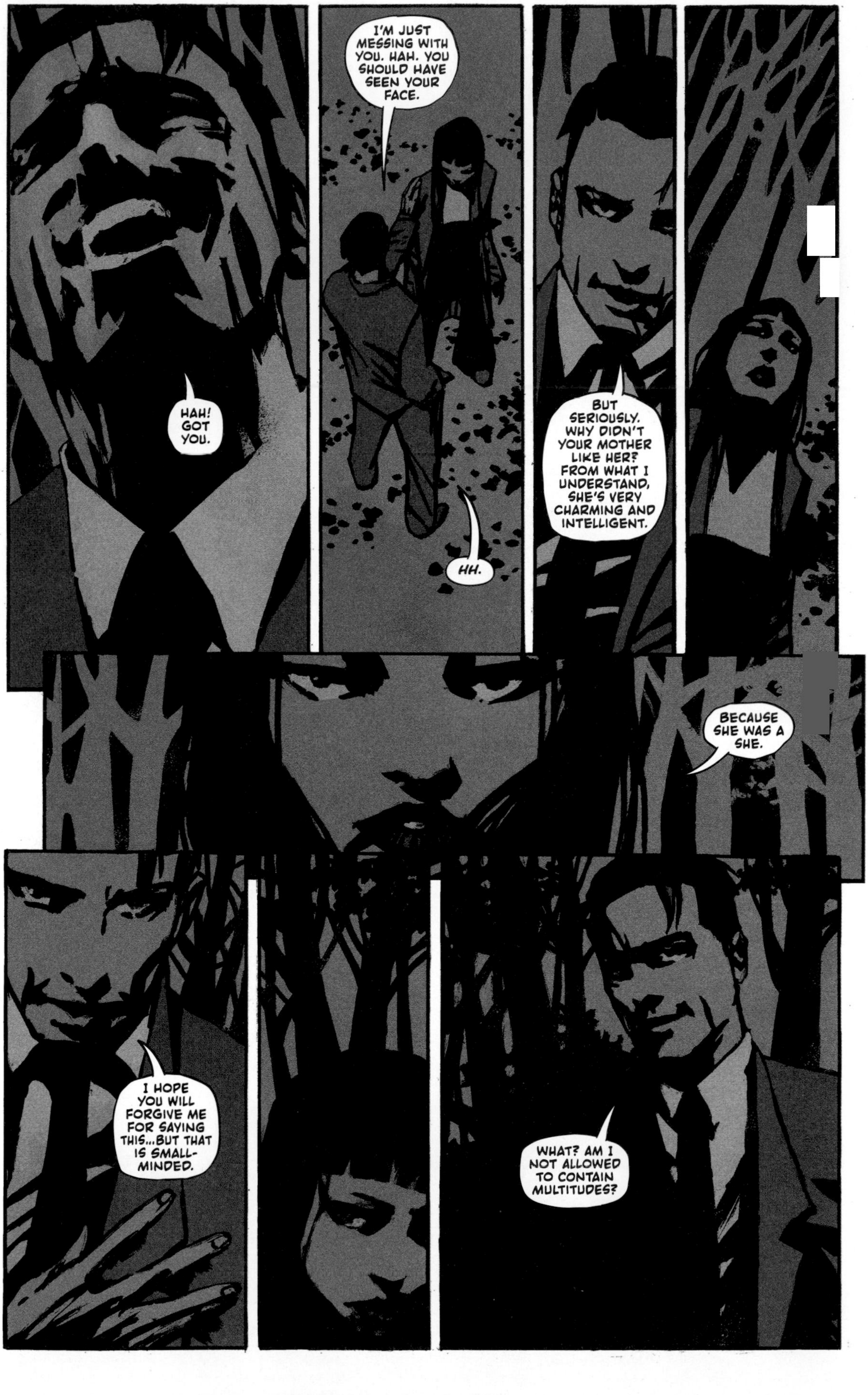
HAH! GOT YOU.
I'M JUST MESSING WITH YOU. HAH. YOU SHOULD HAVE SEEN YOUR FACE.
HH.
BUT SERIOUSLY. WHY DIDN'T YOUR MOTHER LIKE HER? FROM WHAT I UNDERSTAND, SHE'S VERY CHARMING AND INTELLIGENT.
BECAUSE SHE WAS A SHE.
I HOPE YOU WILL FORGIVE ME FOR SAYING THIS...BUT THAT IS SMALL-MINDED.
WHAT? AM I NOT ALLOWED TO CONTAIN MULTITUDES?

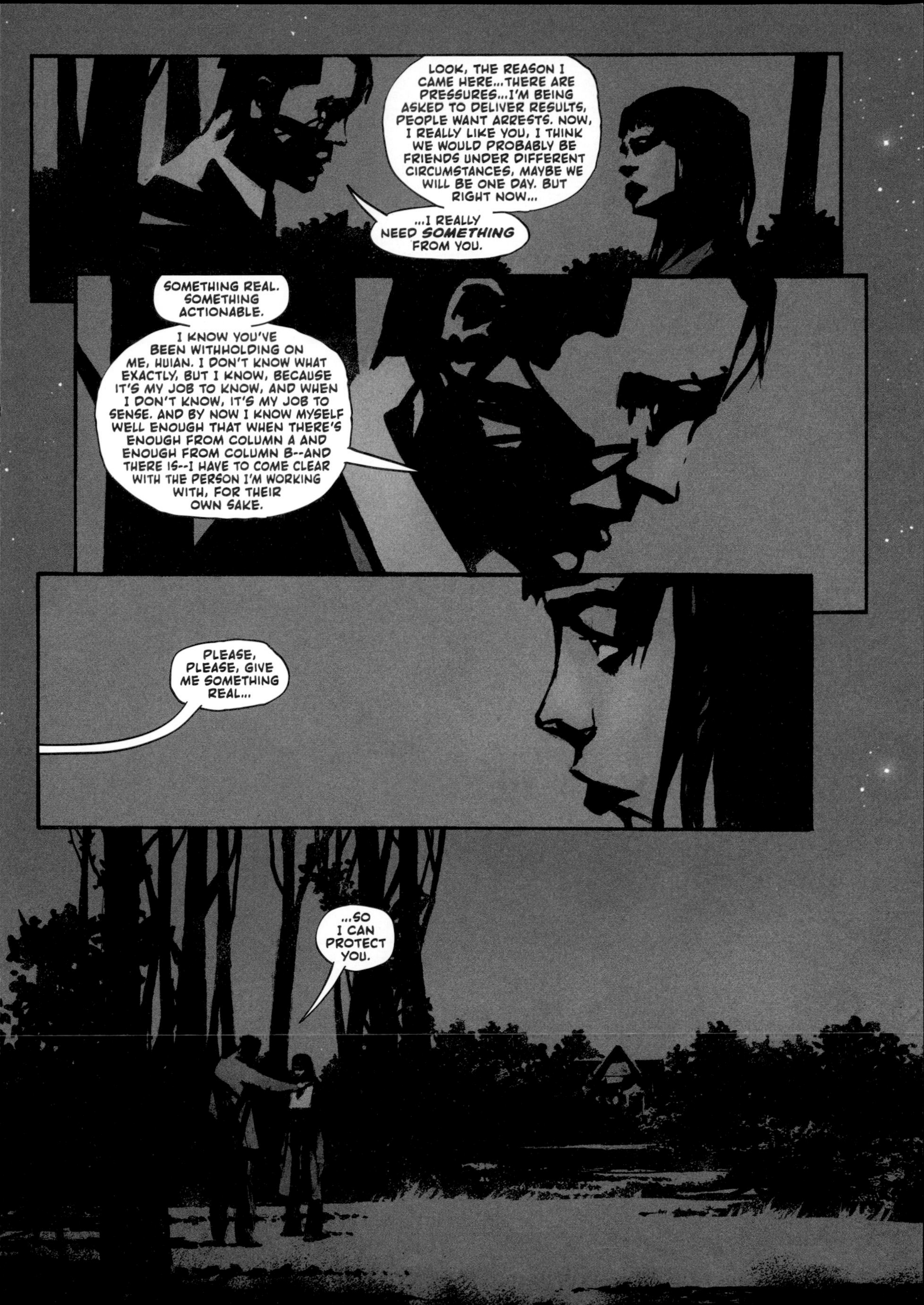
LOOK, THE REASON I CAME HERE...THERE ARE PRESSURES...I'M BEING ASKED TO DELIVER RESULTS, PEOPLE WANT ARRESTS. NOW, I REALLY LIKE YOU, I THINK WE WOULD PROBABLY BE FRIENDS UNDER DIFFERENT CIRCUMSTANCES, MAYBE WE WILL BE ONE DAY. BUT RIGHT NOW...
...I REALLY NEED *SOMETHING* FROM YOU.
SOMETHING REAL. SOMETHING ACTIONABLE.
I KNOW YOU'VE BEEN WITHHOLDING ON ME, HUIAN. I DON'T KNOW WHAT EXACTLY, BUT I KNOW, BECAUSE IT'S MY JOB TO KNOW, AND WHEN I DON'T KNOW, IT'S MY JOB TO SENSE. AND BY NOW I KNOW MYSELF WELL ENOUGH THAT WHEN THERE'S ENOUGH FROM COLUMN A AND ENOUGH FROM COLUMN B--AND THERE IS--I HAVE TO COME CLEAR WITH THE PERSON I'M WORKING WITH, FOR THEIR OWN SAKE.
PLEASE, PLEASE, GIVE ME SOMETHING REAL...
...SO I CAN PROTECT YOU.

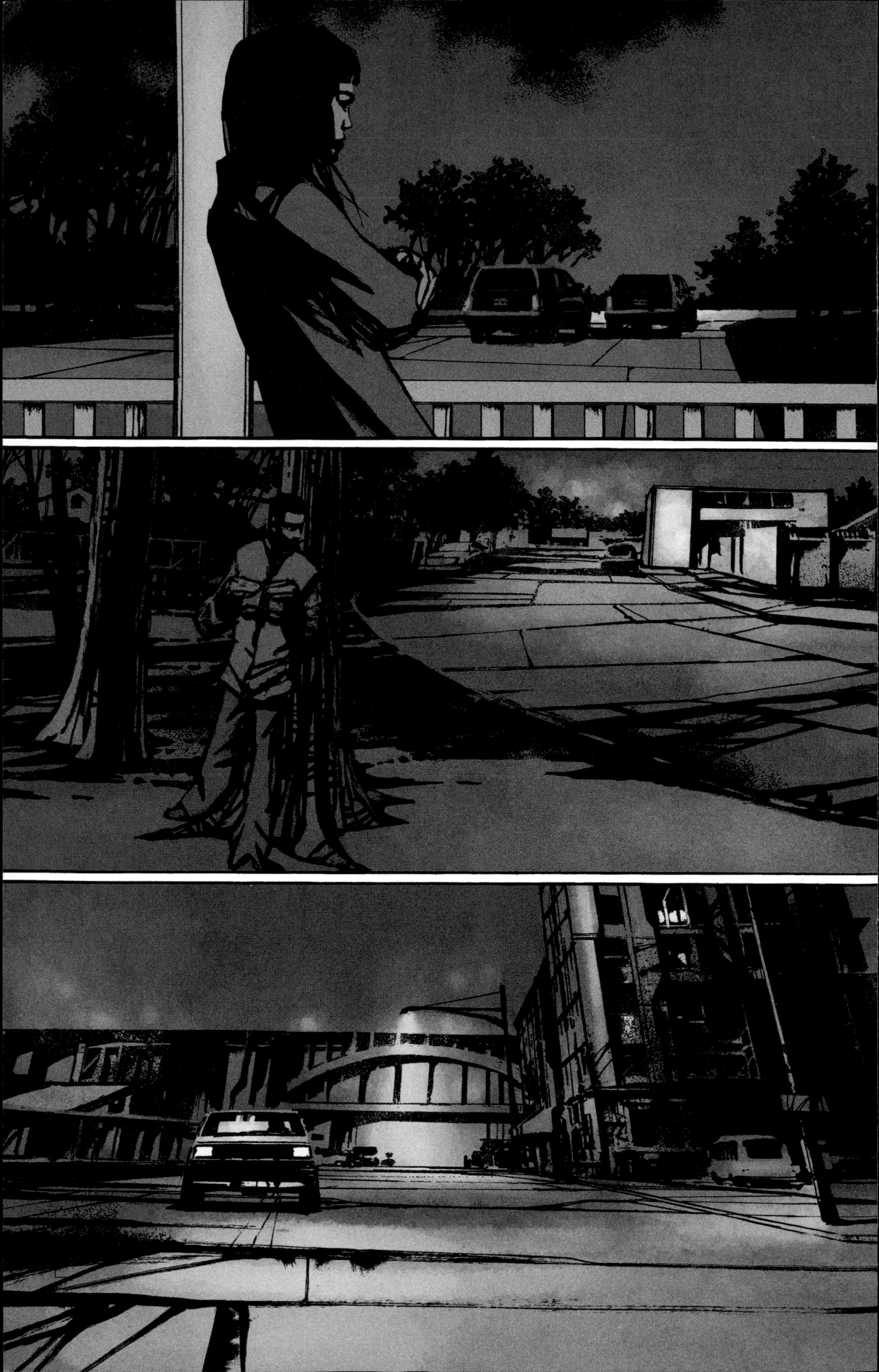

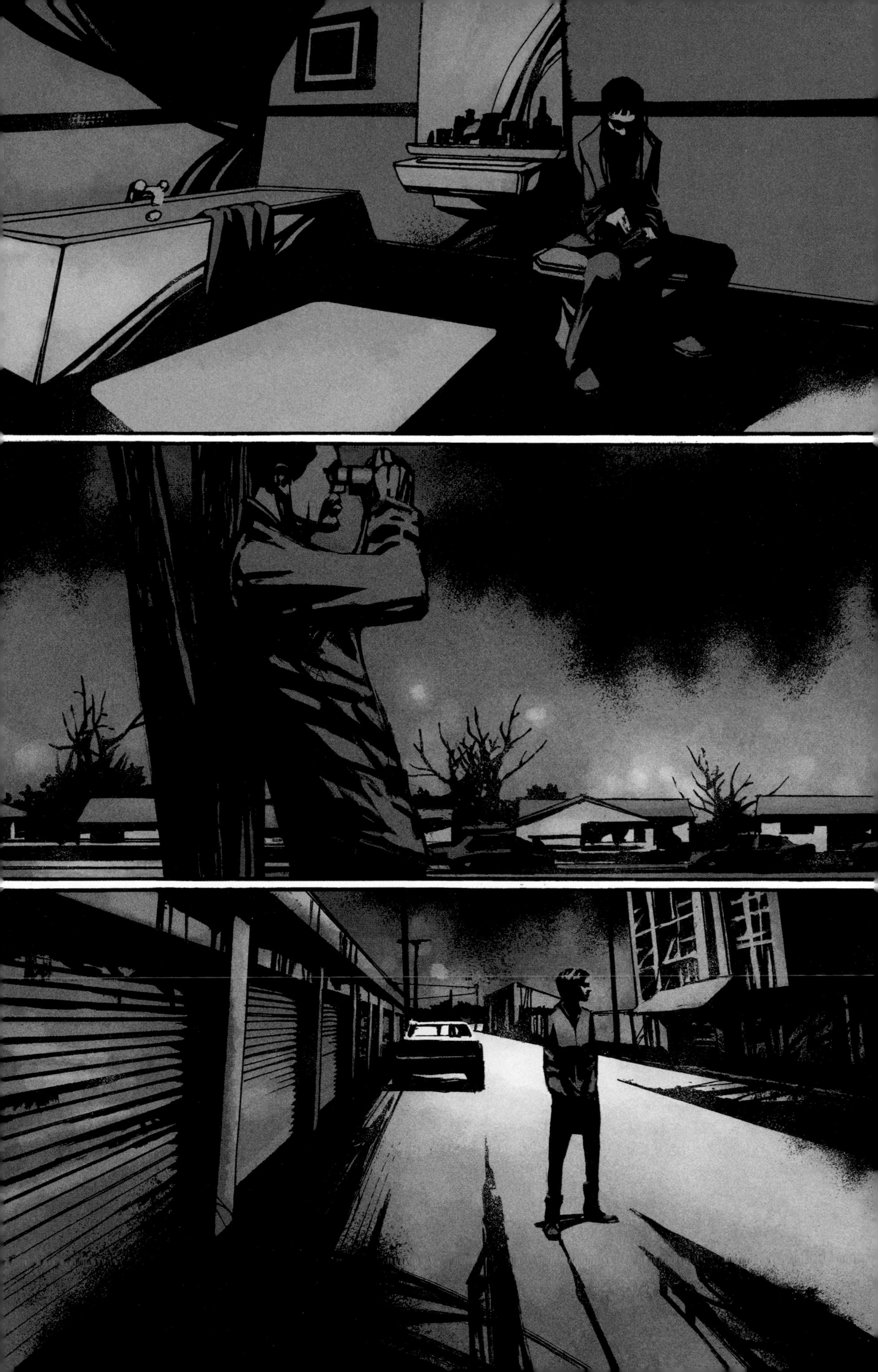

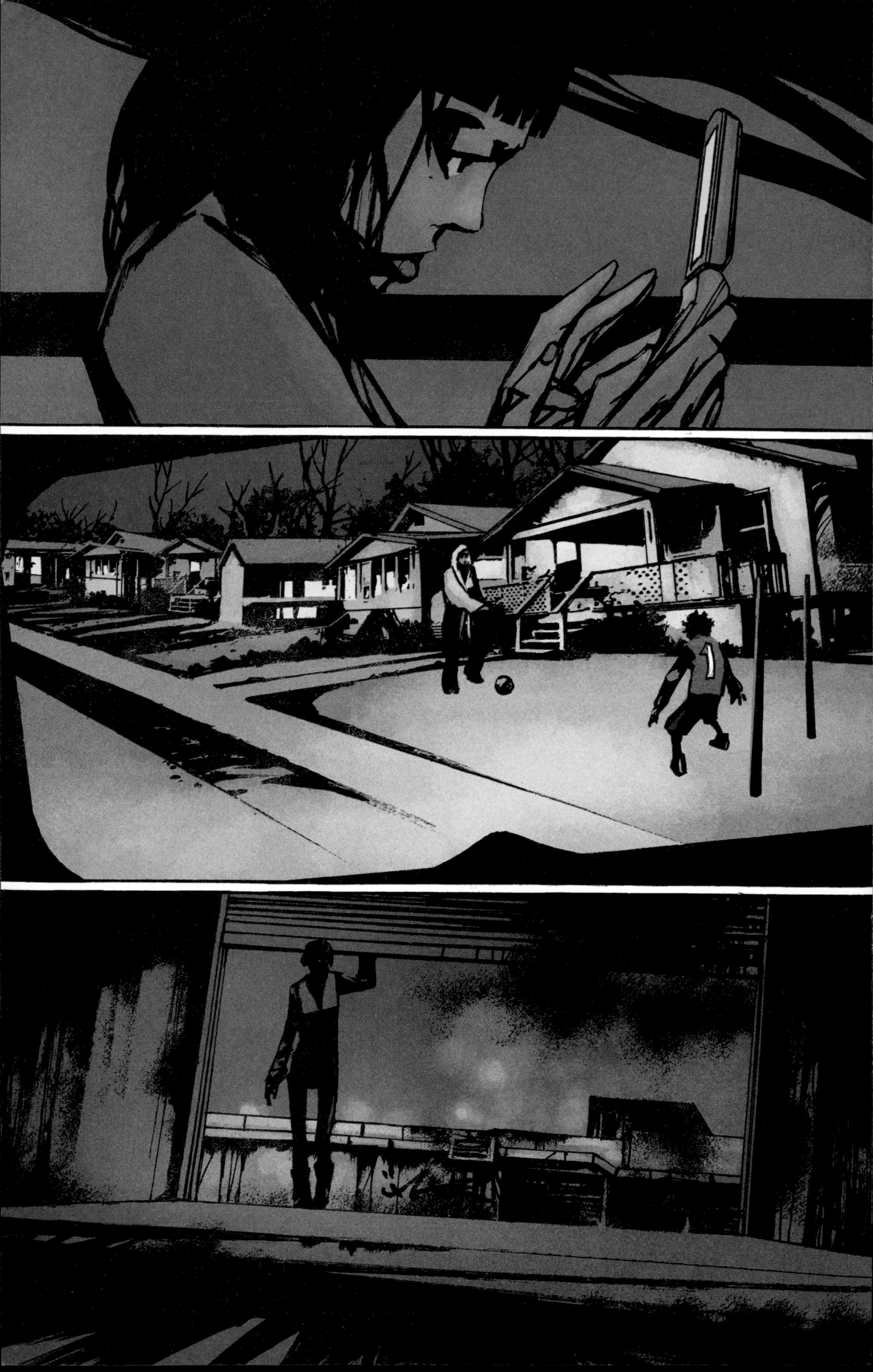

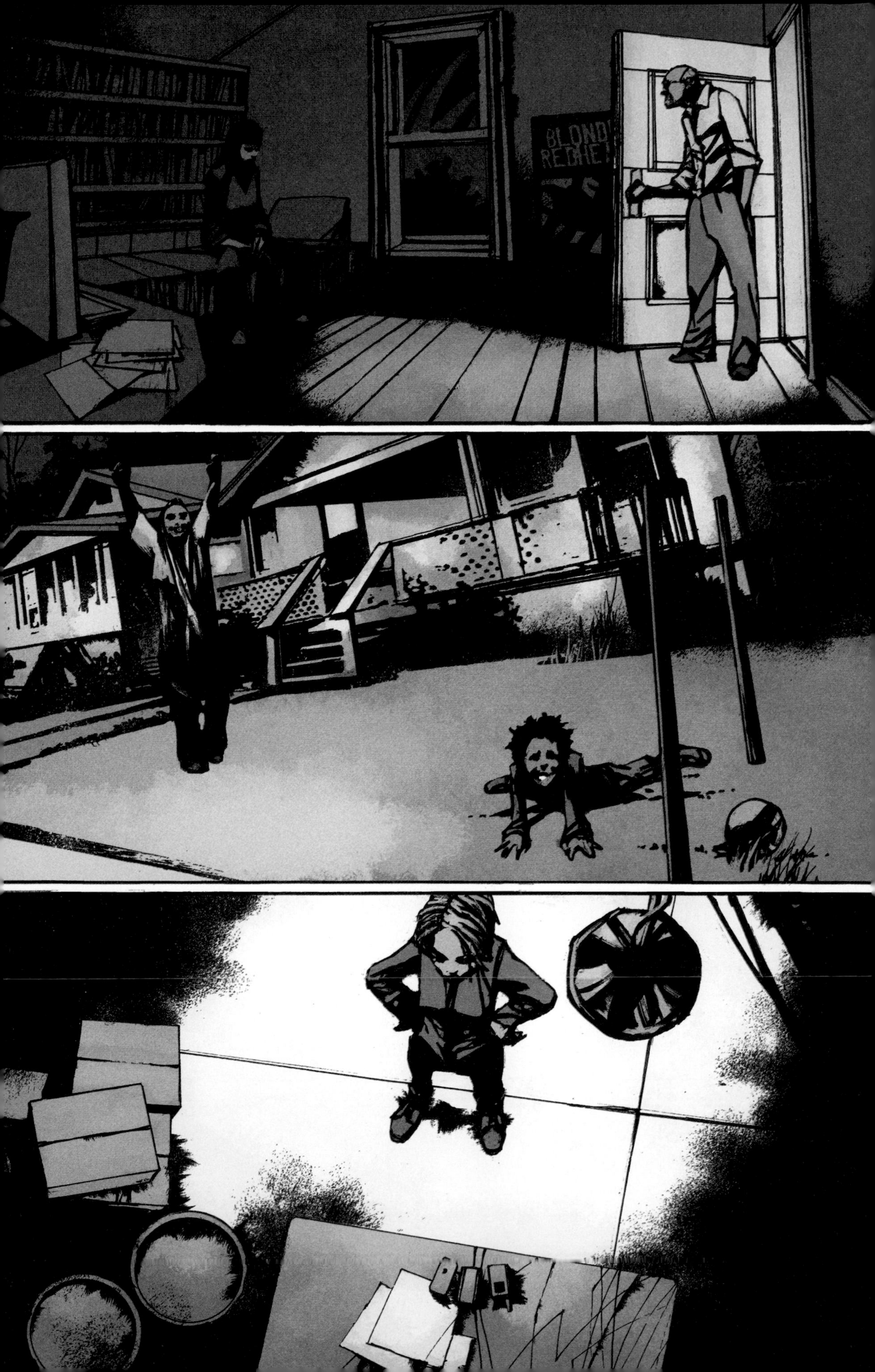
BLOND
REDHE

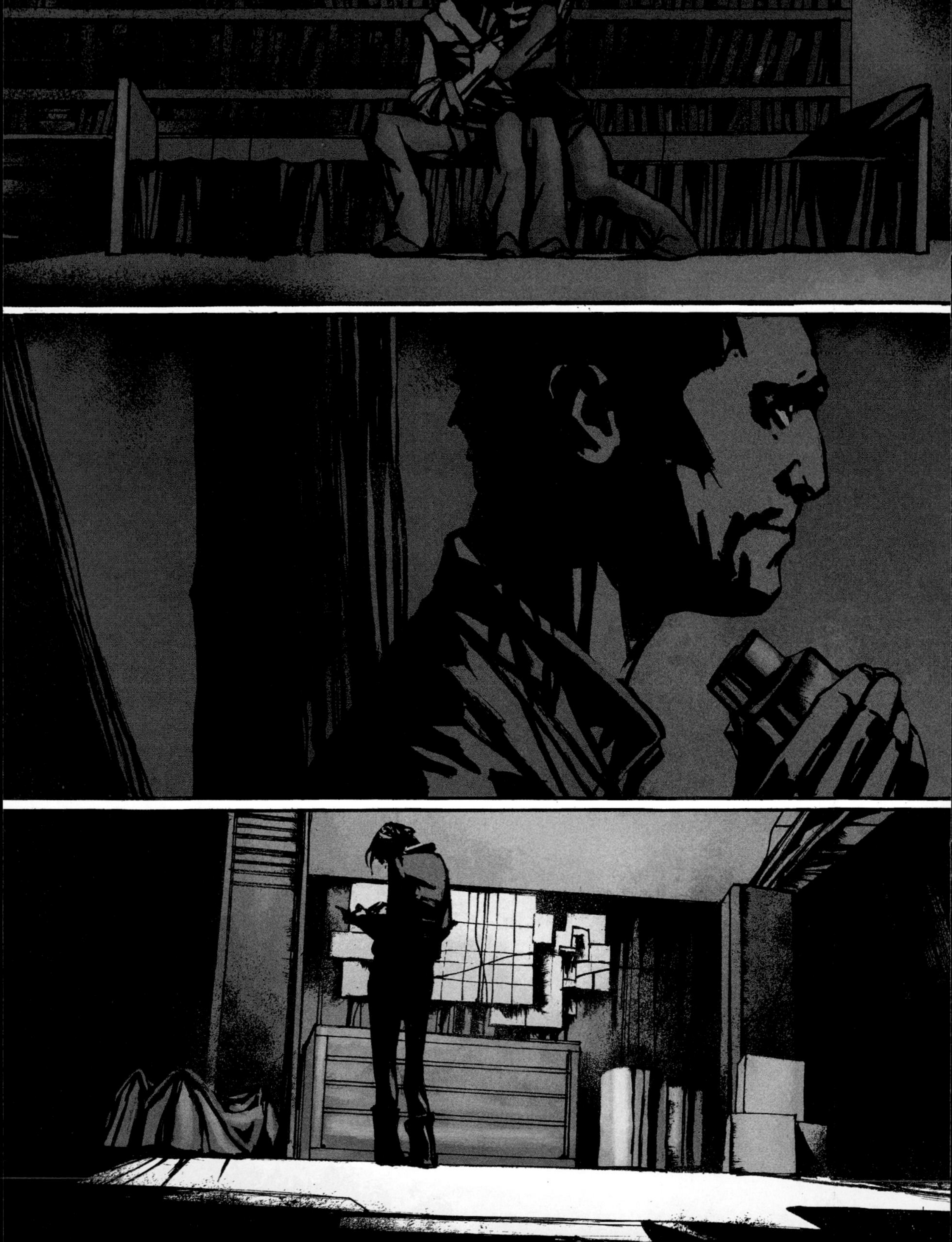

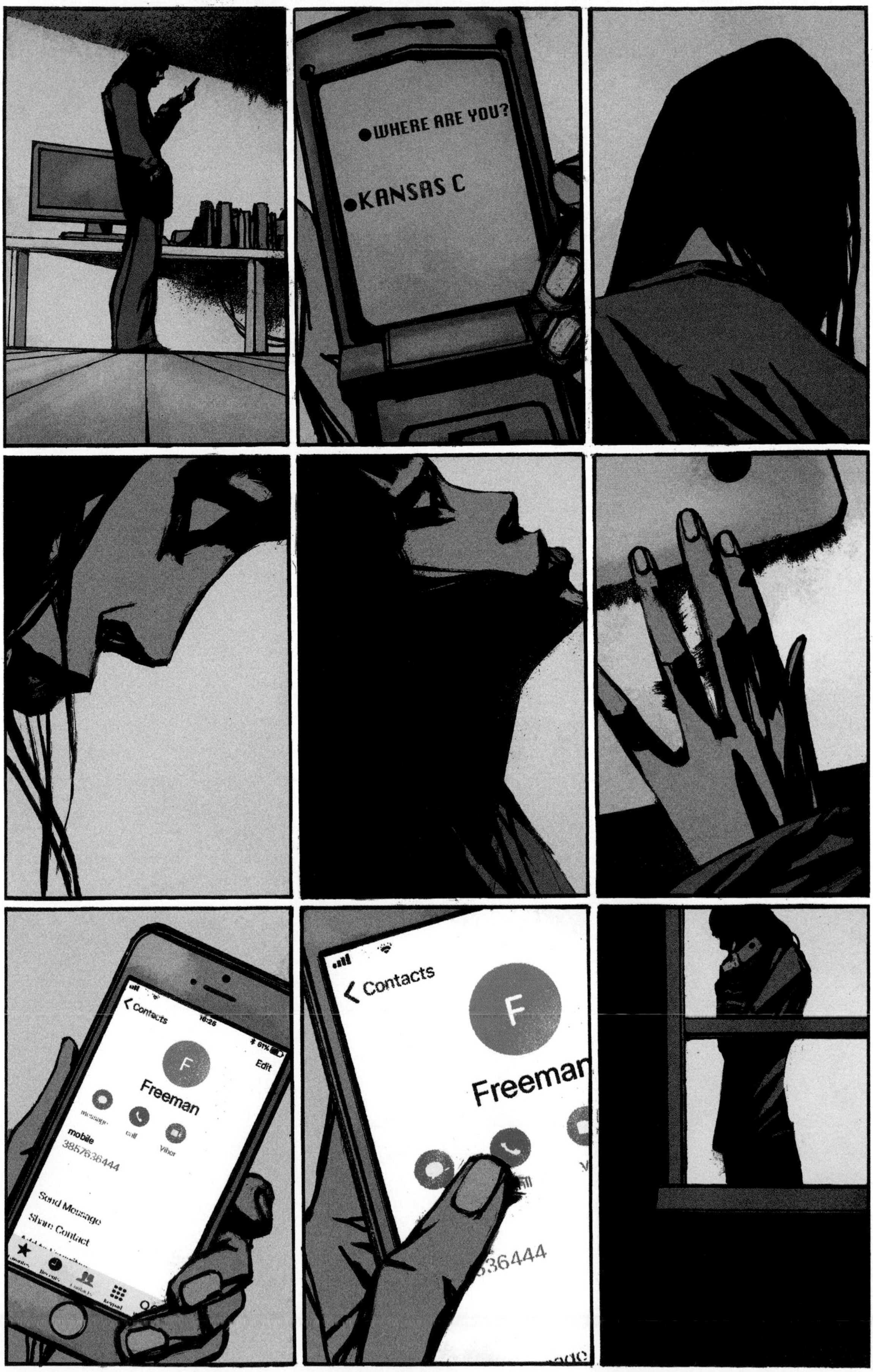
WHERE ARE YOU?
KANSAS C
Contacts
Edit
F
Freeman
message
call
Viber
mobile
3857636444
Send Message
Share Contact
Contacts
F
Freeman
36444

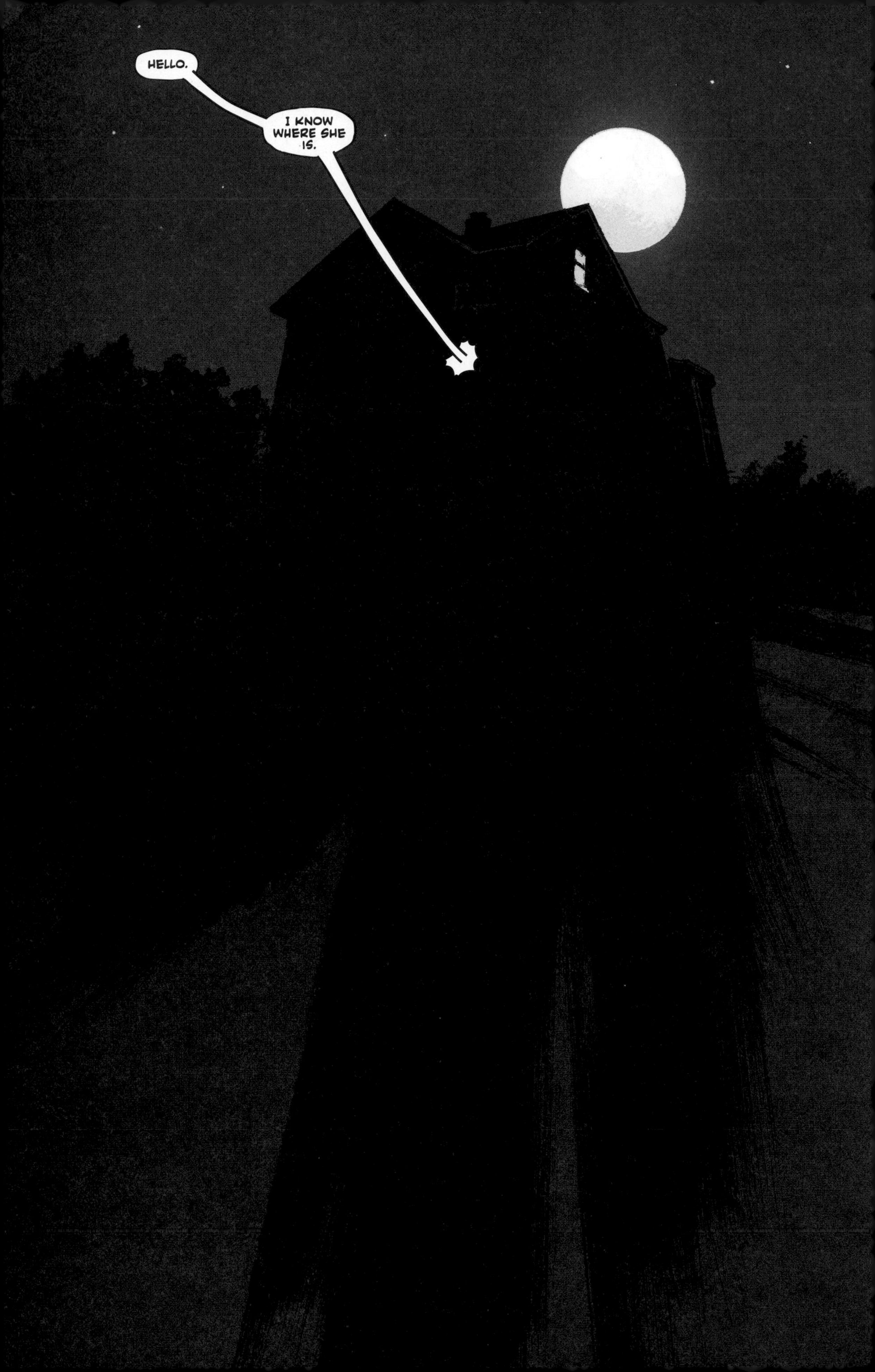
HELLO.
I KNOW WHERE SHE IS.

CHAPTER FIVE:
SURGERY

"It is natural that people do not want to be involved with us too much. There is no problem down to the smallest egotistical longing which the Gestapo cannot solve. Regarded in this way we are, if a joke is permitted, looked upon as a cross between a general maid and the dustbin of the Reich."

—Reinhard Heydrich to his officers on German Police Day (February, 1941)

"To the people and the world the uprising must assume the character of a popular revolutionary movement. To the enemy it must appear as an uprising of a few only."

—Nelson Mandela

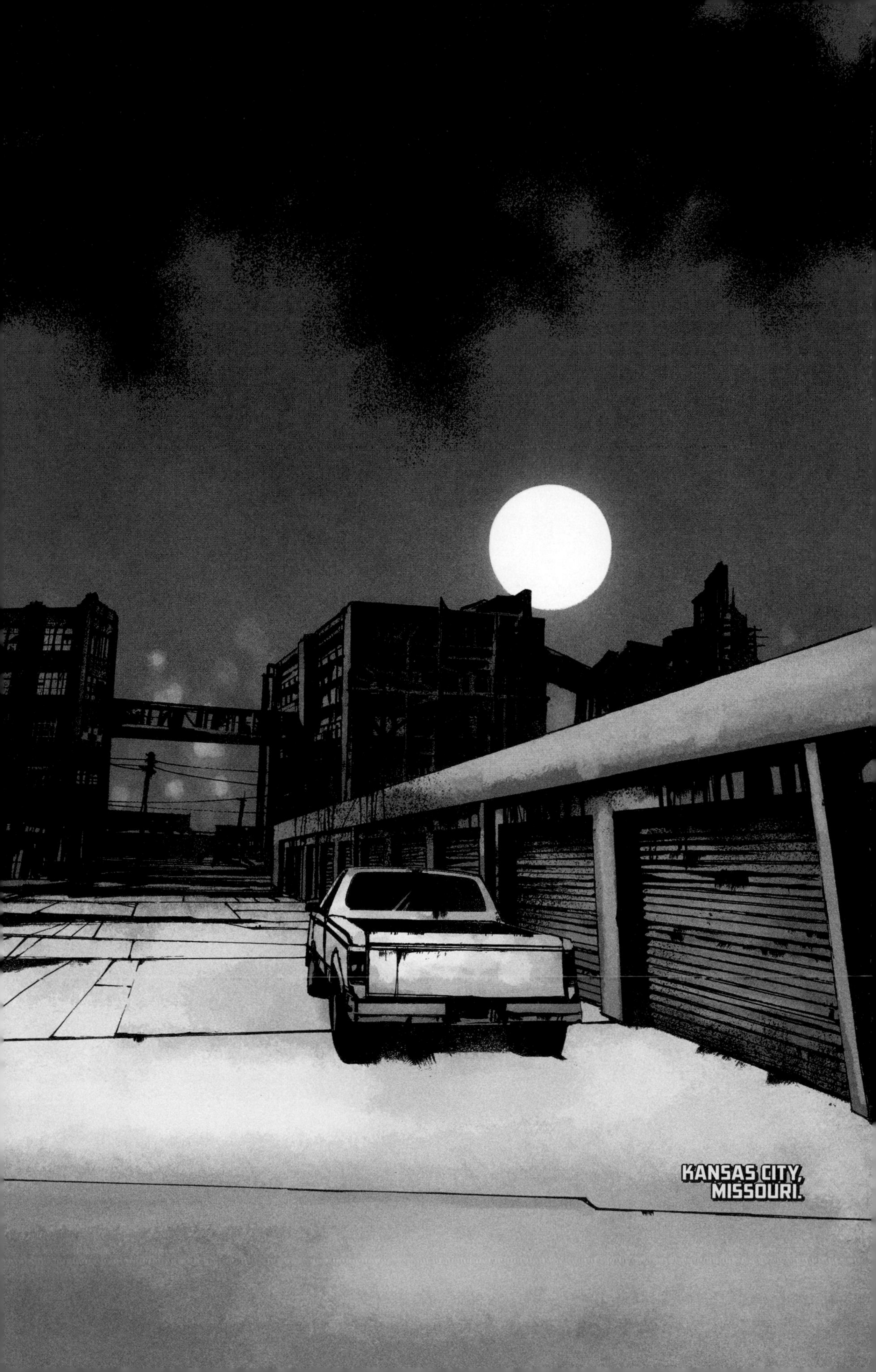
KANSAS CITY,
MISSOURI.

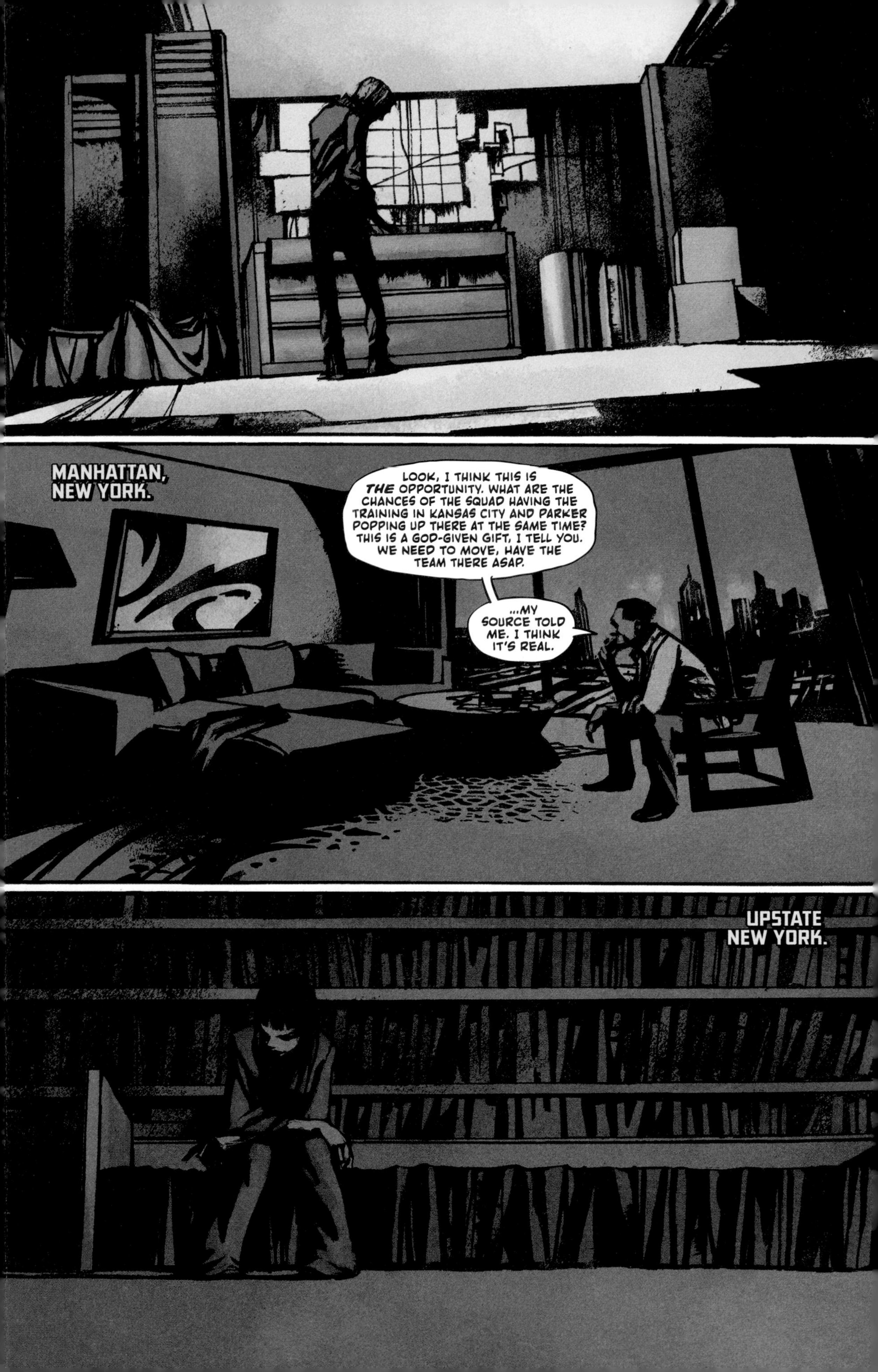

MANHATTAN, NEW YORK.
LOOK, I THINK THIS IS *THE* OPPORTUNITY. WHAT ARE THE CHANCES OF THE SQUAD HAVING THE TRAINING IN KANSAS CITY AND PARKER POPPING UP THERE AT THE SAME TIME? THIS IS A GOD-GIVEN GIFT, I TELL YOU. WE NEED TO MOVE, HAVE THE TEAM THERE ASAP.
...MY SOURCE TOLD ME. I THINK IT'S REAL.
UPSTATE NEW YORK.

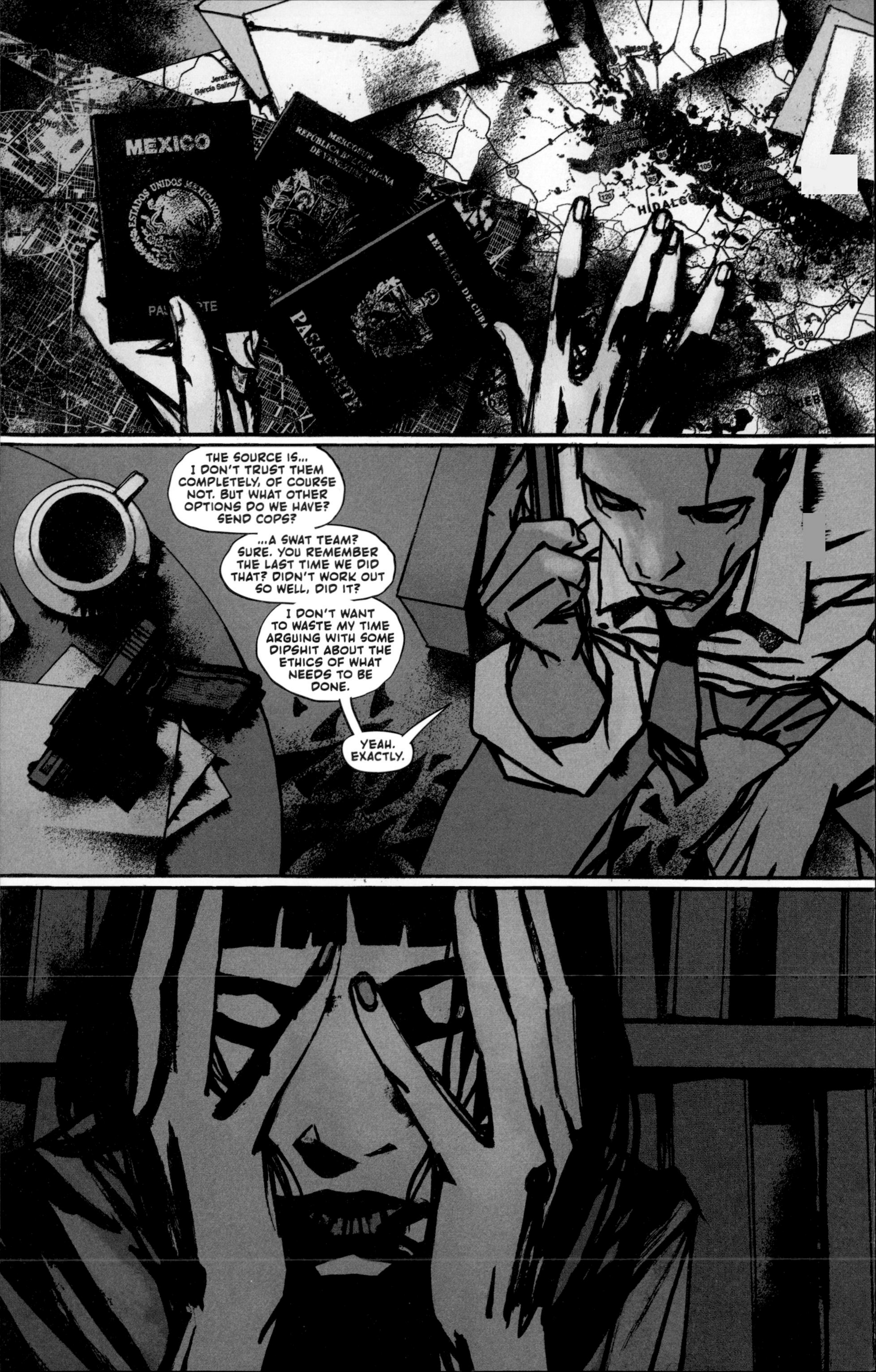
MEXICO
ESTADOS UNIDOS MEXICANOS
REPUBLICA DE CUBA
HIDALGO
THE SOURCE IS... I DON'T TRUST THEM COMPLETELY, OF COURSE NOT. BUT WHAT OTHER OPTIONS DO WE HAVE? SEND COPS?
...A SWAT TEAM? SURE. YOU REMEMBER THE LAST TIME WE DID THAT? DIDN'T WORK OUT SO WELL, DID IT?
I DON'T WANT TO WASTE MY TIME ARGUING WITH SOME DIPSHIT ABOUT THE ETHICS OF WHAT NEEDS TO BE DONE.
YEAH. EXACTLY.

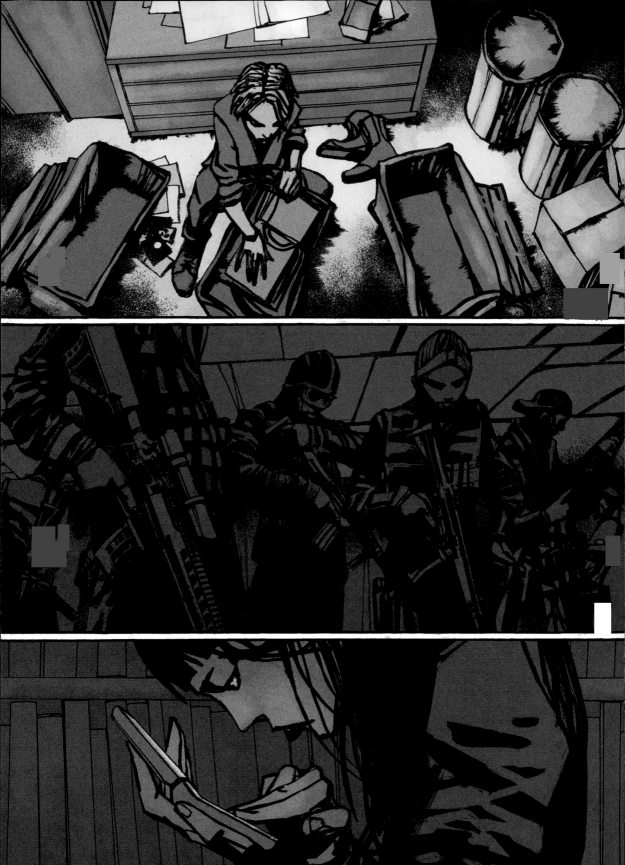

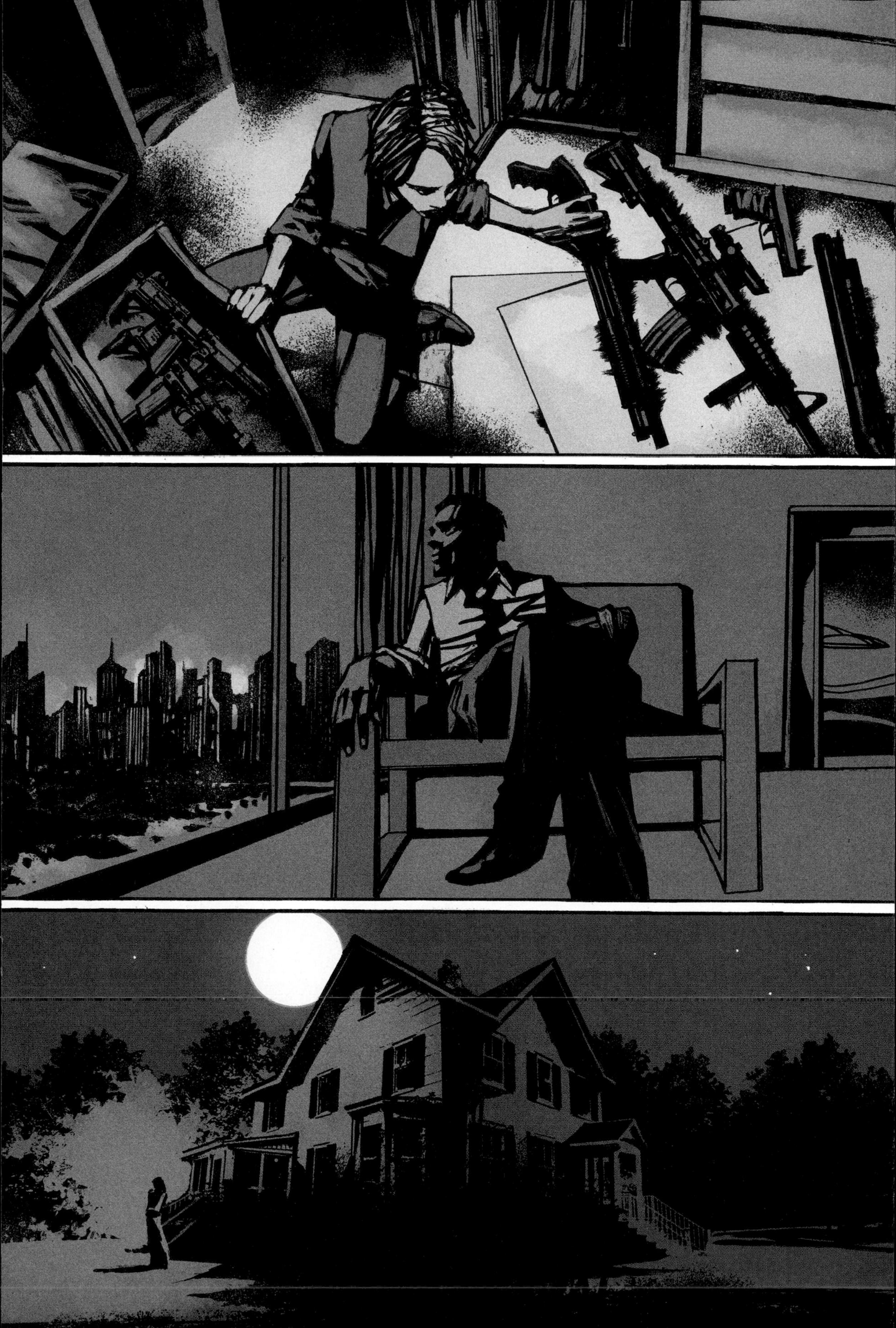

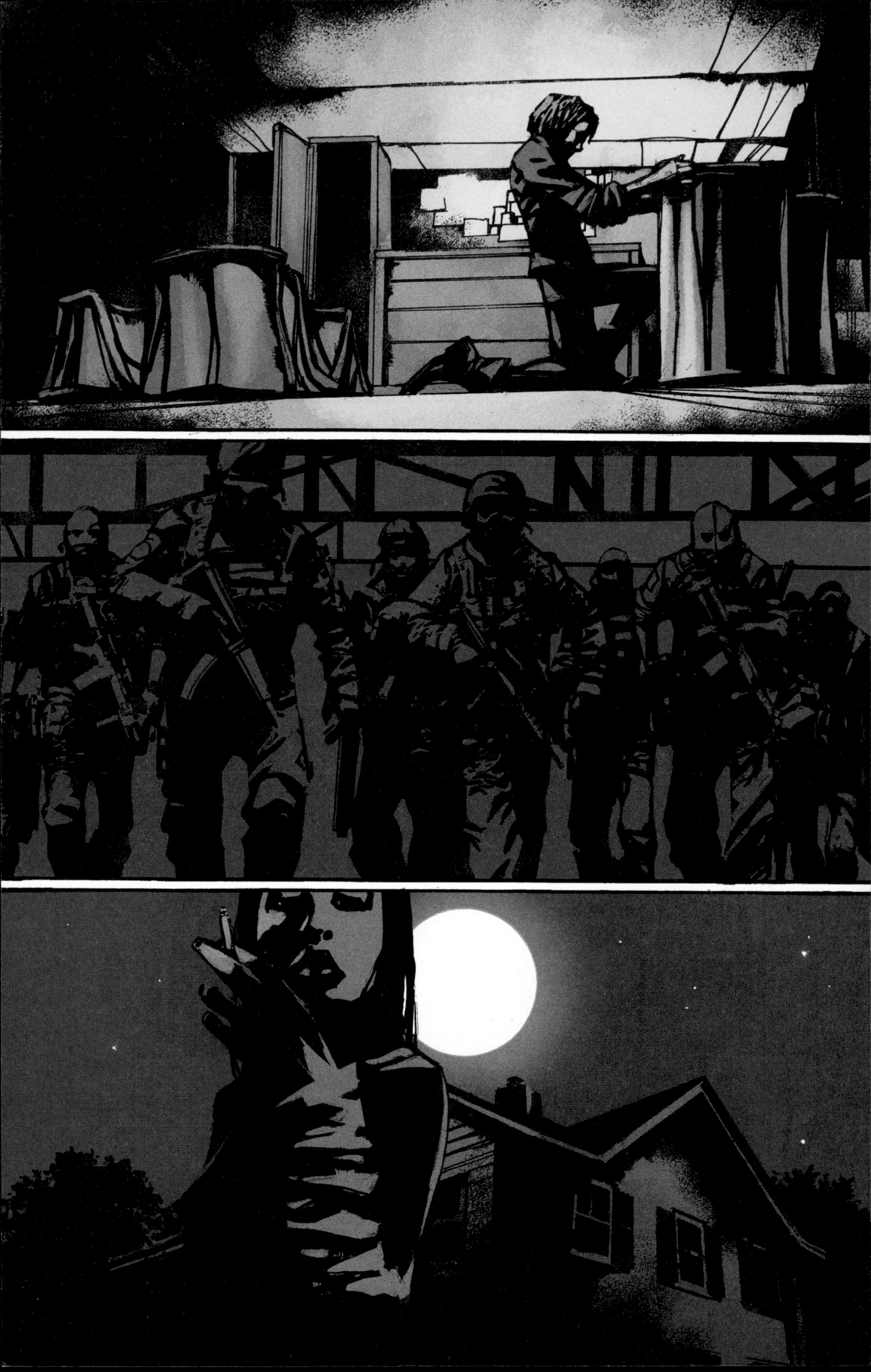

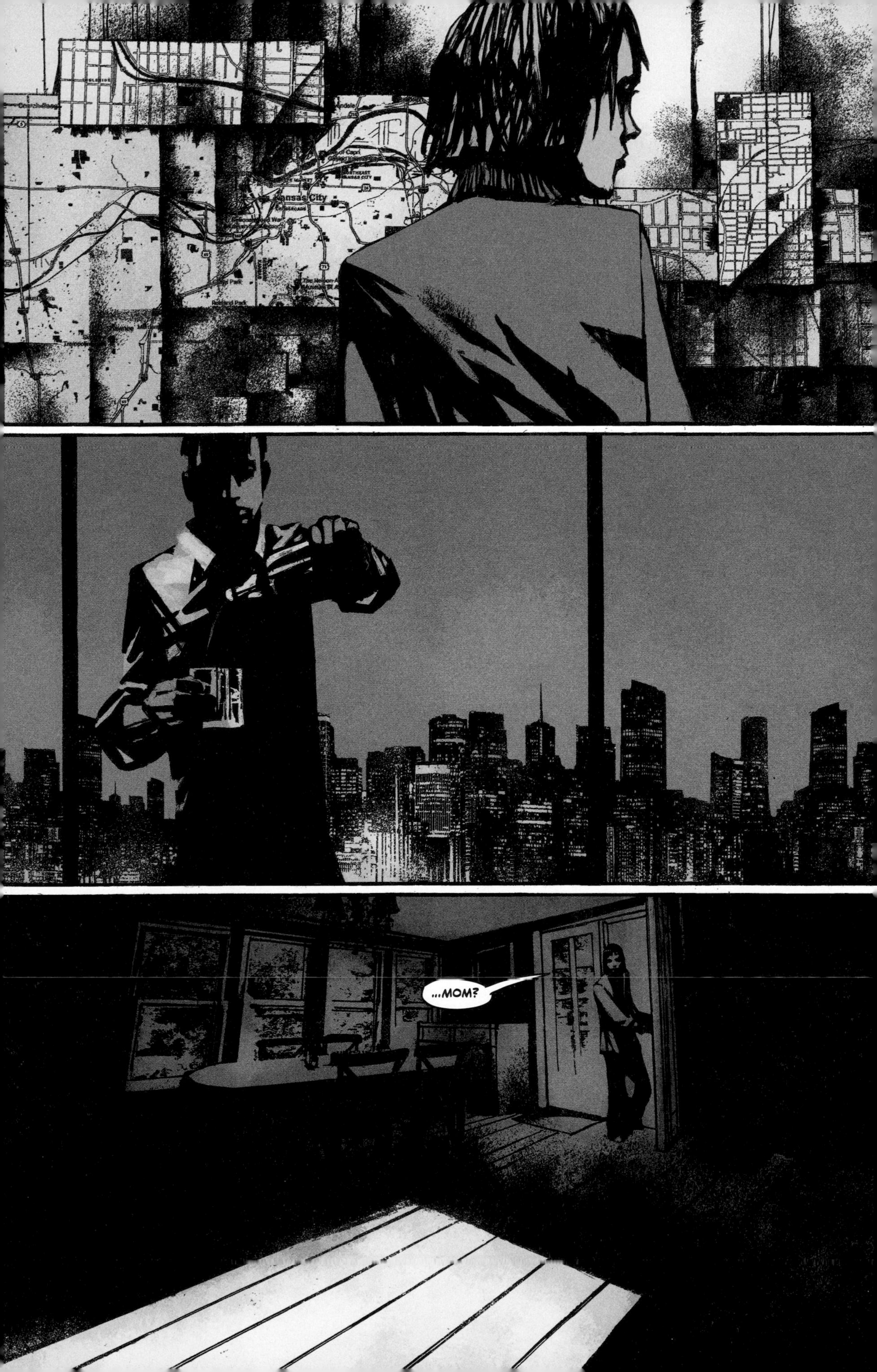
Kansas City
...MOM?

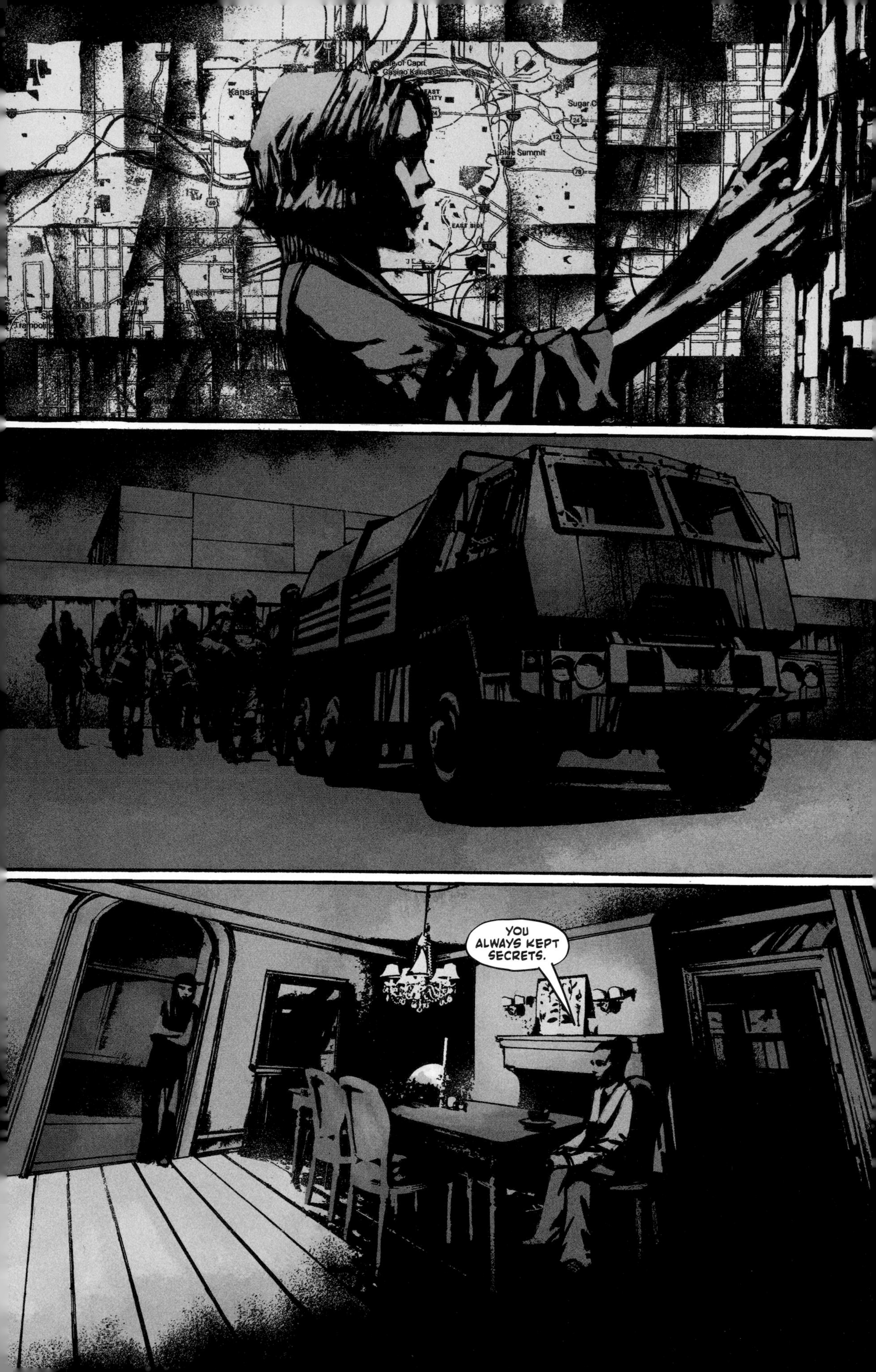
Blue Summit
EAST SIDE
YOU ALWAYS KEPT SECRETS.

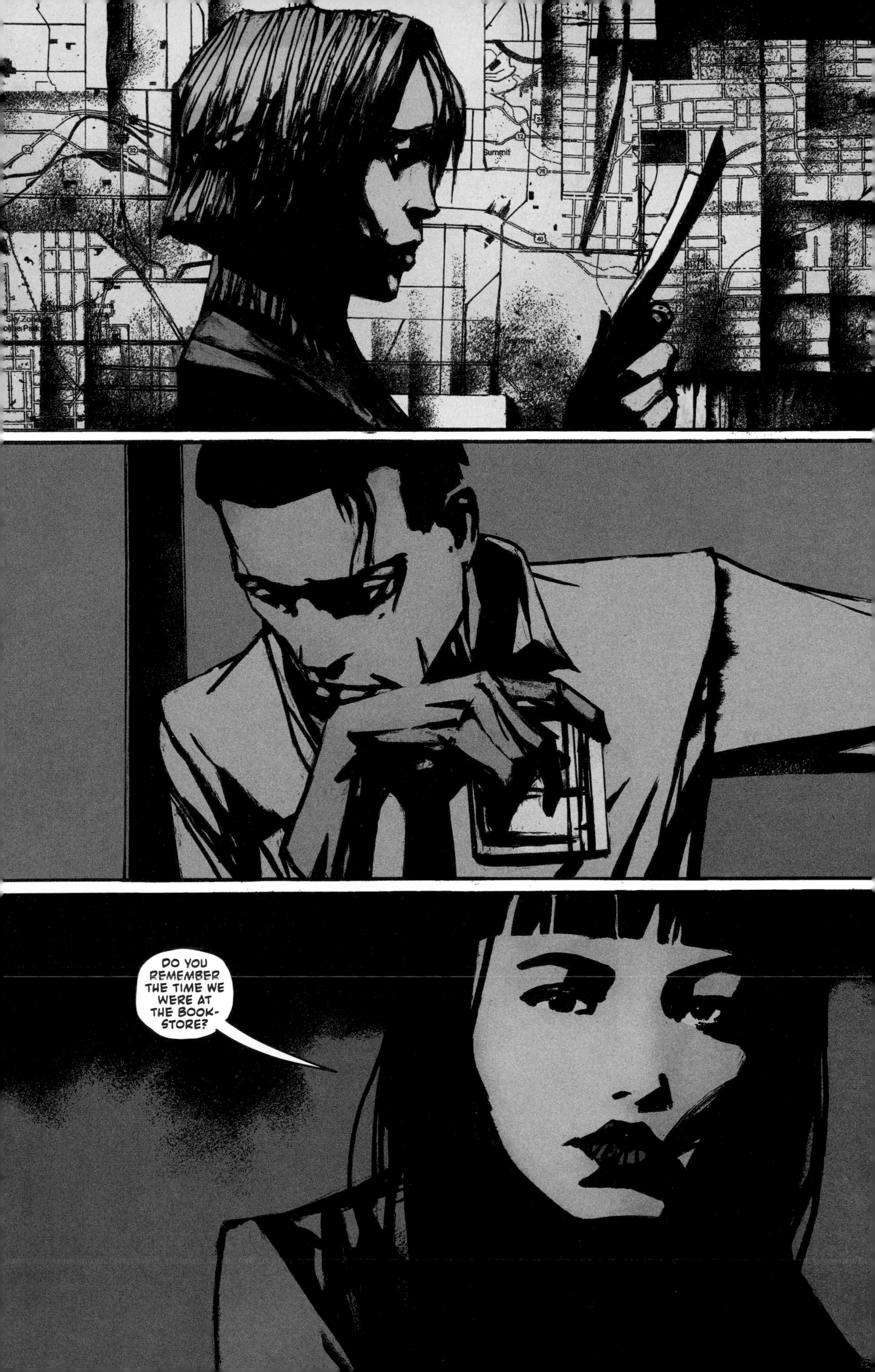
Summit
DO YOU REMEMBER THE TIME WE WERE AT THE BOOK-STORE?

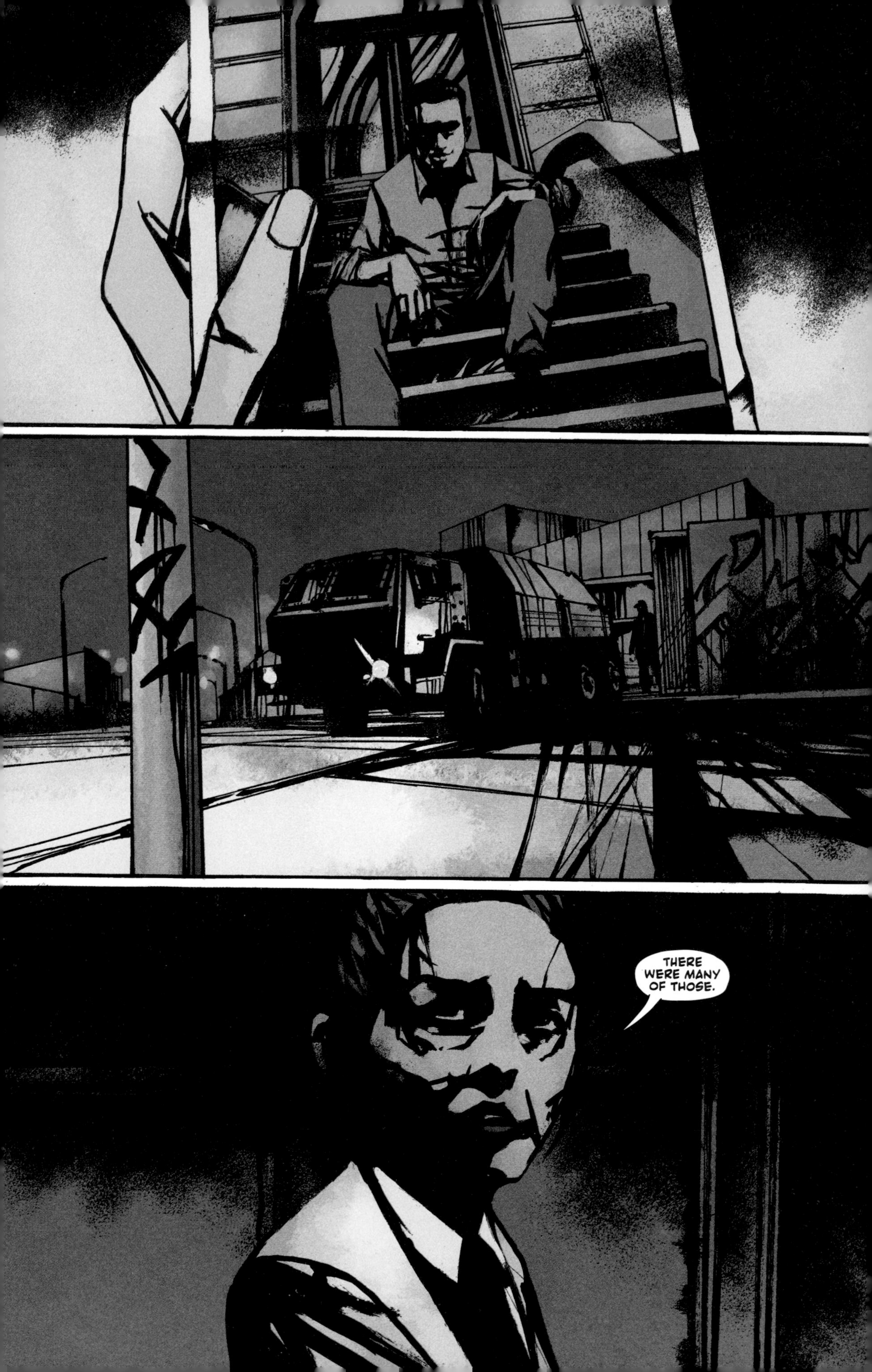
THERE WERE MANY OF THOSE.

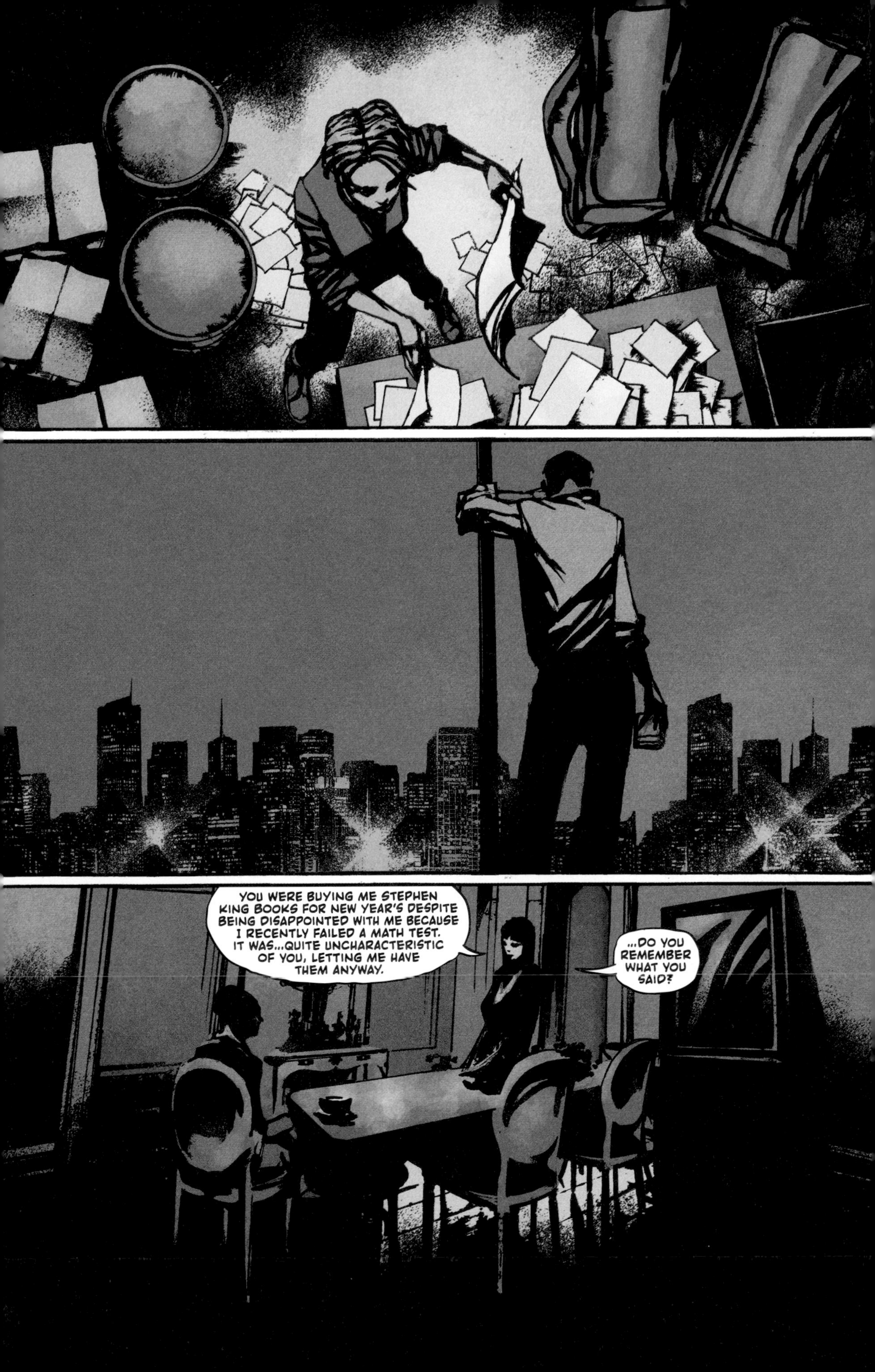
YOU WERE BUYING ME STEPHEN KING BOOKS FOR NEW YEAR'S DESPITE BEING DISAPPOINTED WITH ME BECAUSE I RECENTLY FAILED A MATH TEST. IT WAS...QUITE UNCHARACTERISTIC OF YOU, LETTING ME HAVE THEM ANYWAY.
...DO YOU REMEMBER WHAT YOU SAID?

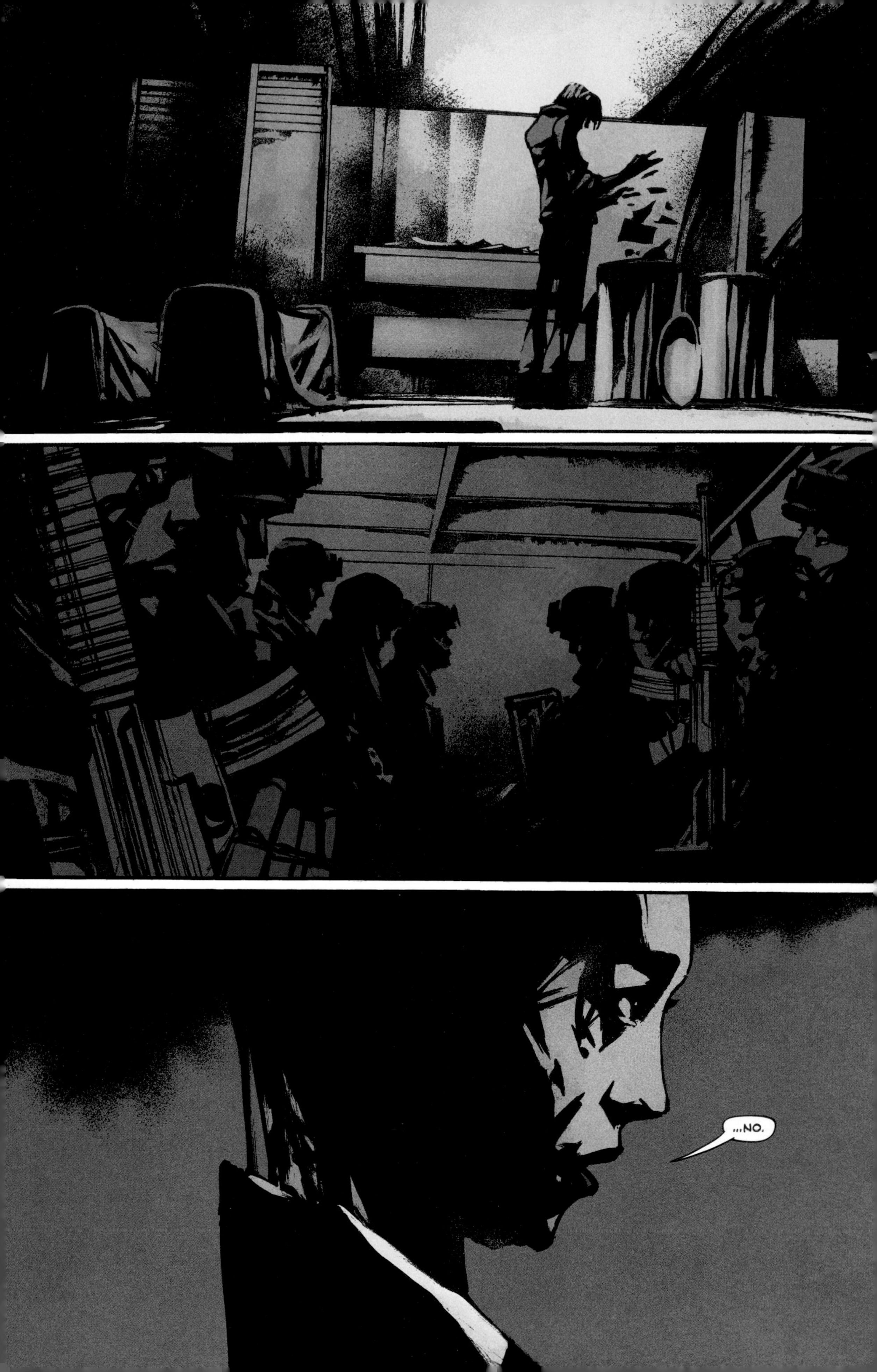
...NO.

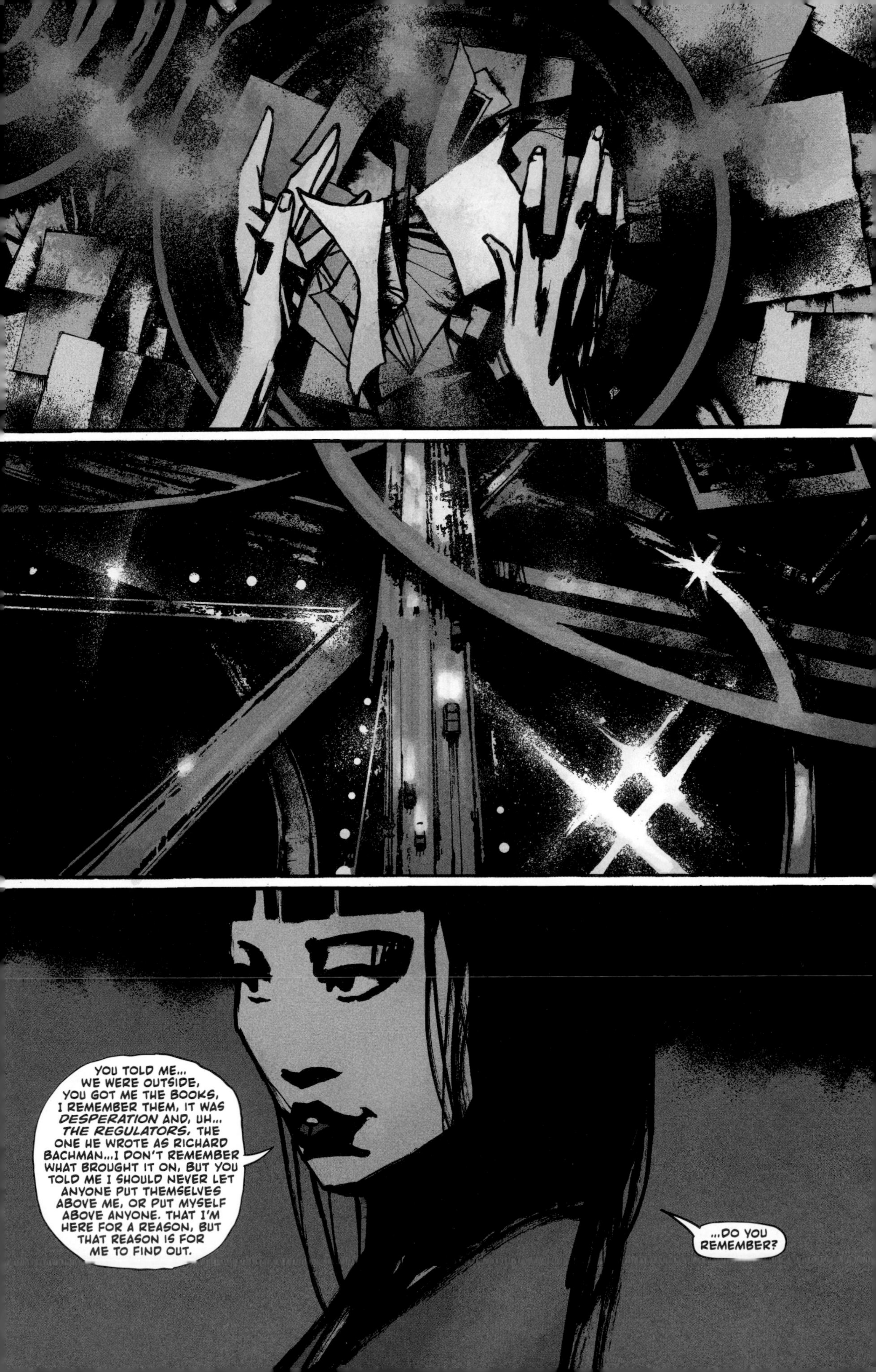
YOU TOLD ME... WE WERE OUTSIDE, YOU GOT ME THE BOOKS, I REMEMBER THEM, IT WAS *DESPERATION* AND, UH... *THE REGULATORS,* THE ONE HE WROTE AS RICHARD BACHMAN...I DON'T REMEMBER WHAT BROUGHT IT ON, BUT YOU TOLD ME I SHOULD NEVER LET ANYONE PUT THEMSELVES ABOVE ME, OR PUT MYSELF ABOVE ANYONE. THAT I'M HERE FOR A REASON, BUT THAT REASON IS FOR ME TO FIND OUT.
...DO YOU REMEMBER?

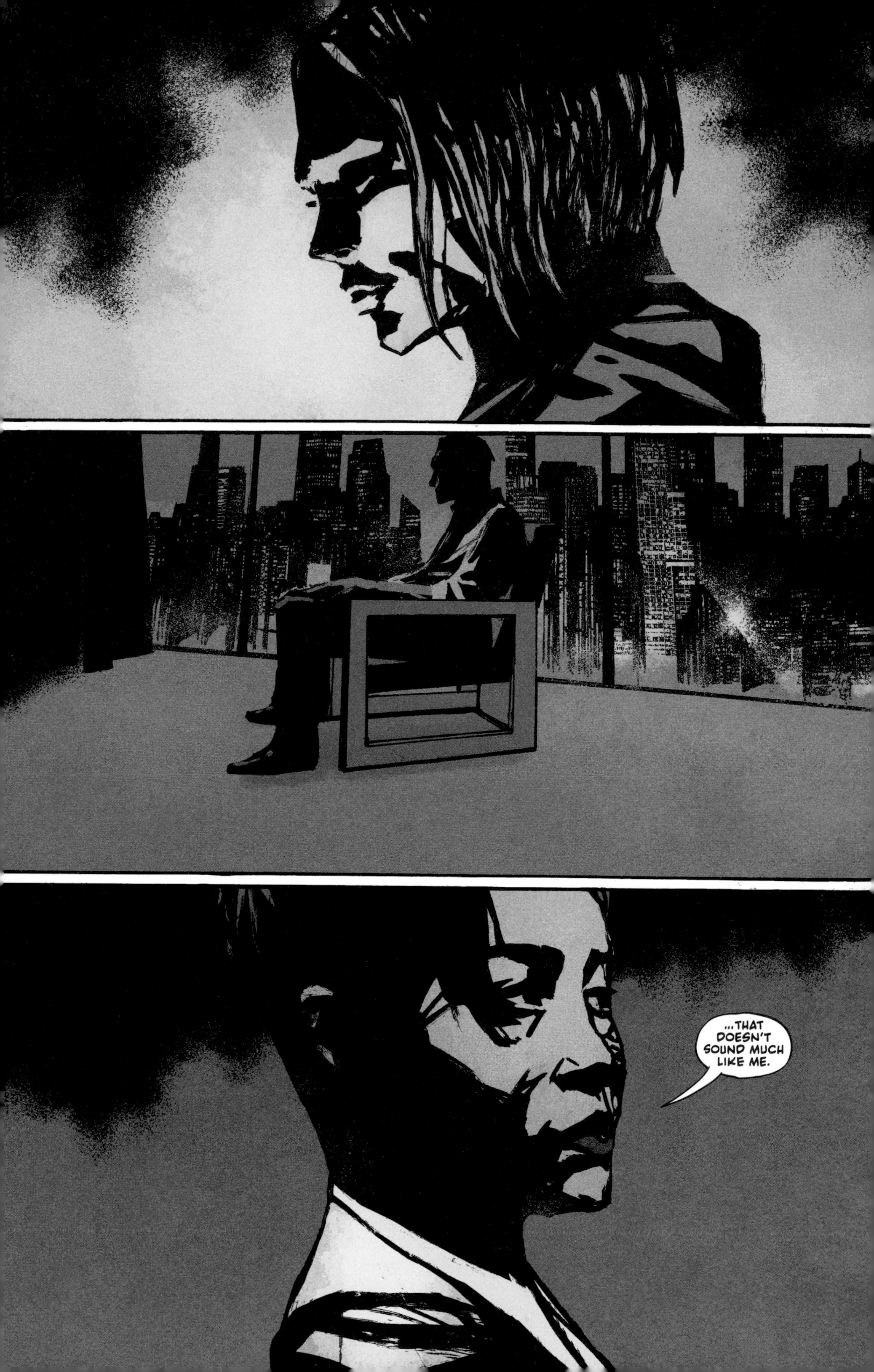
...THAT DOESN'T SOUND MUCH LIKE ME.

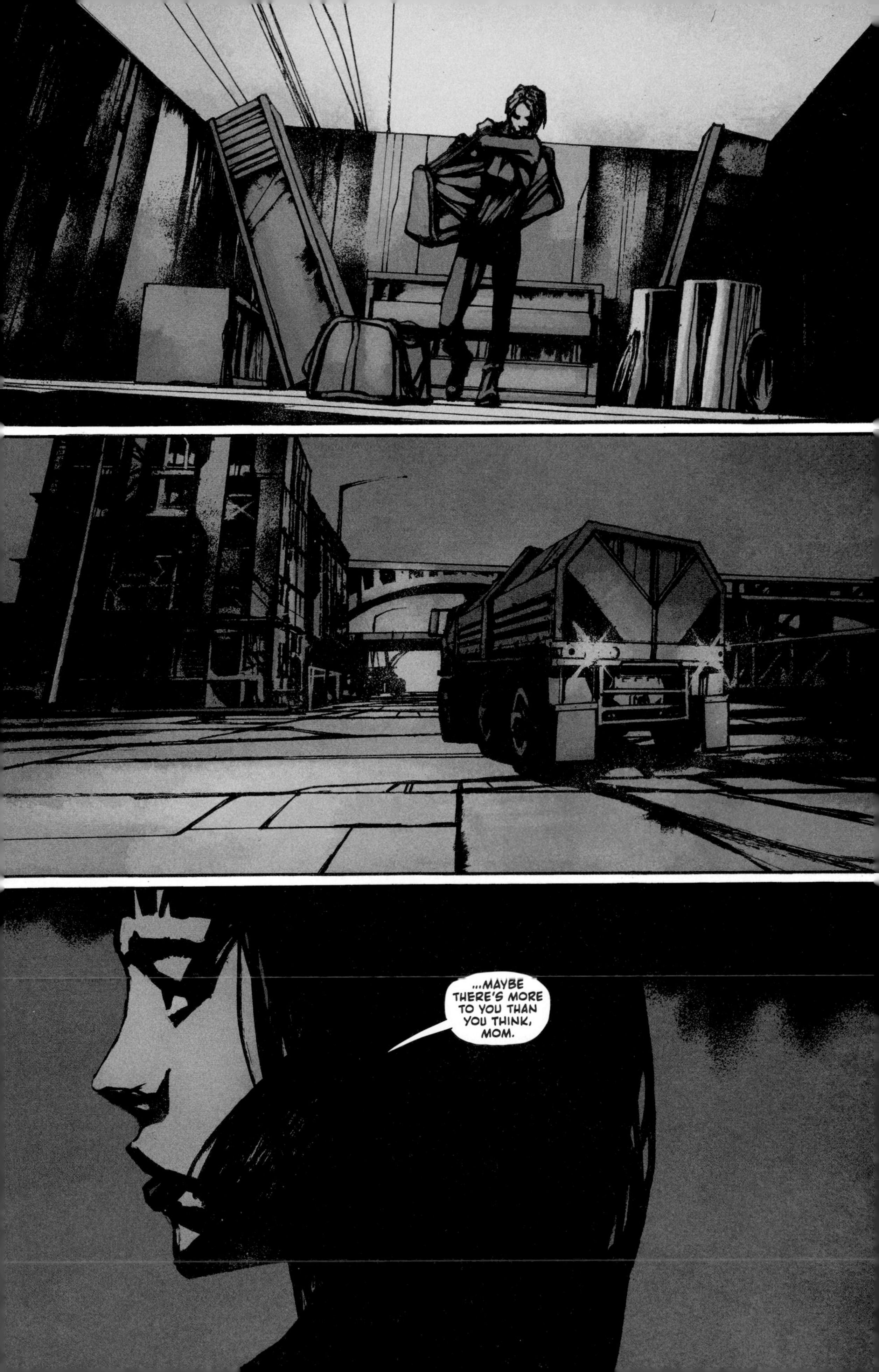
...MAYBE THERE'S MORE TO YOU THAN YOU THINK, MOM.

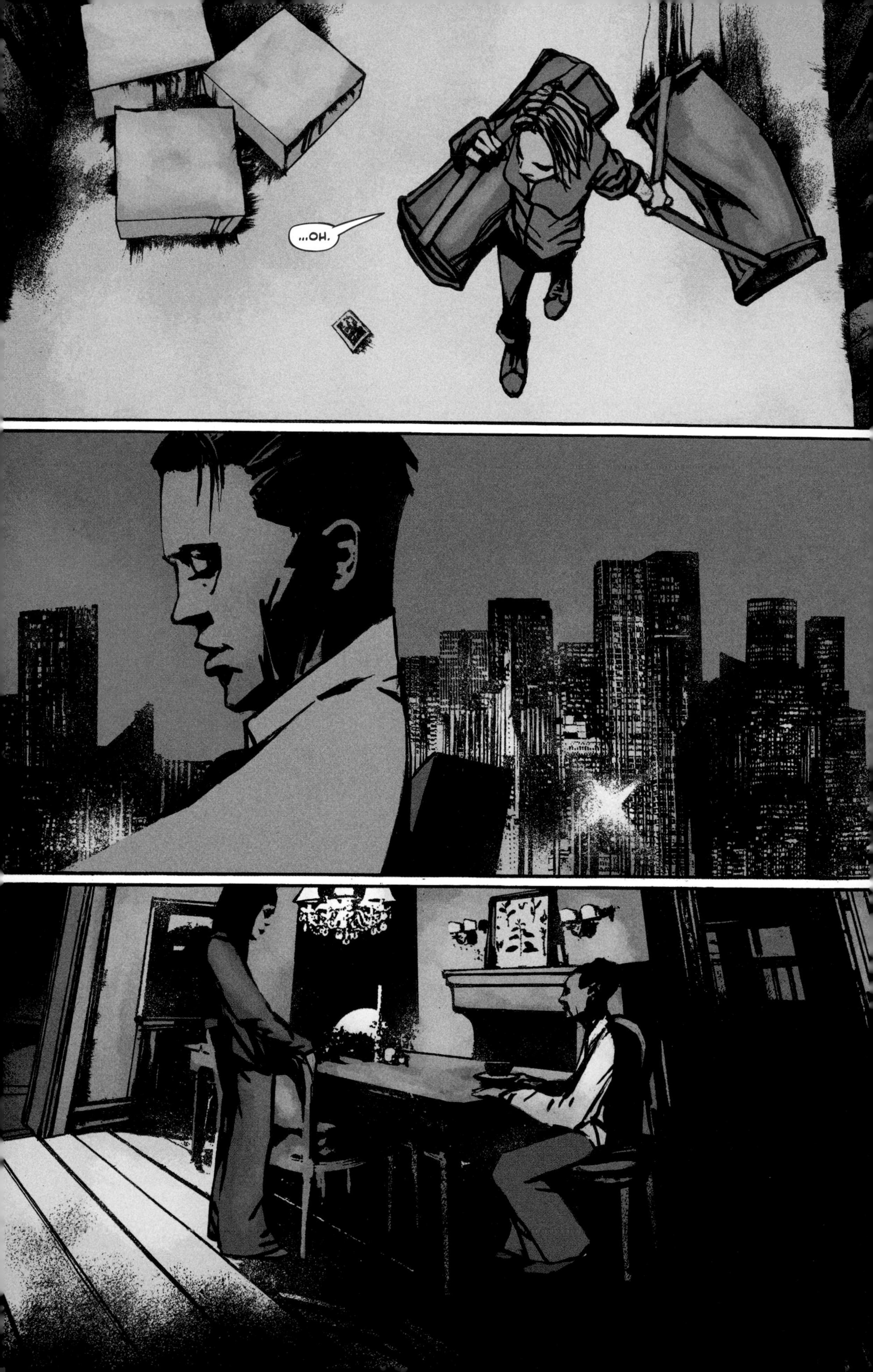
...OH.

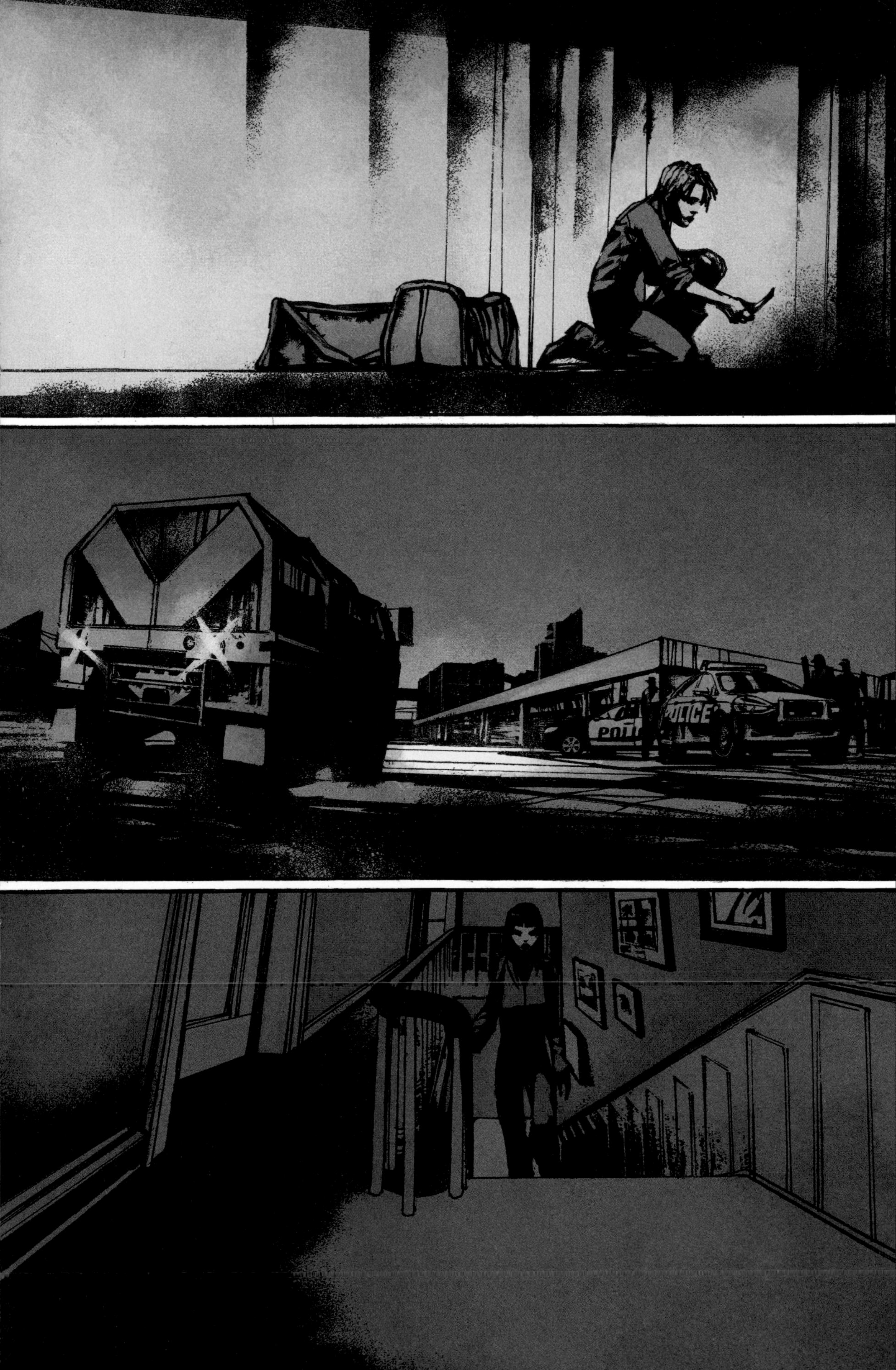
POLICE

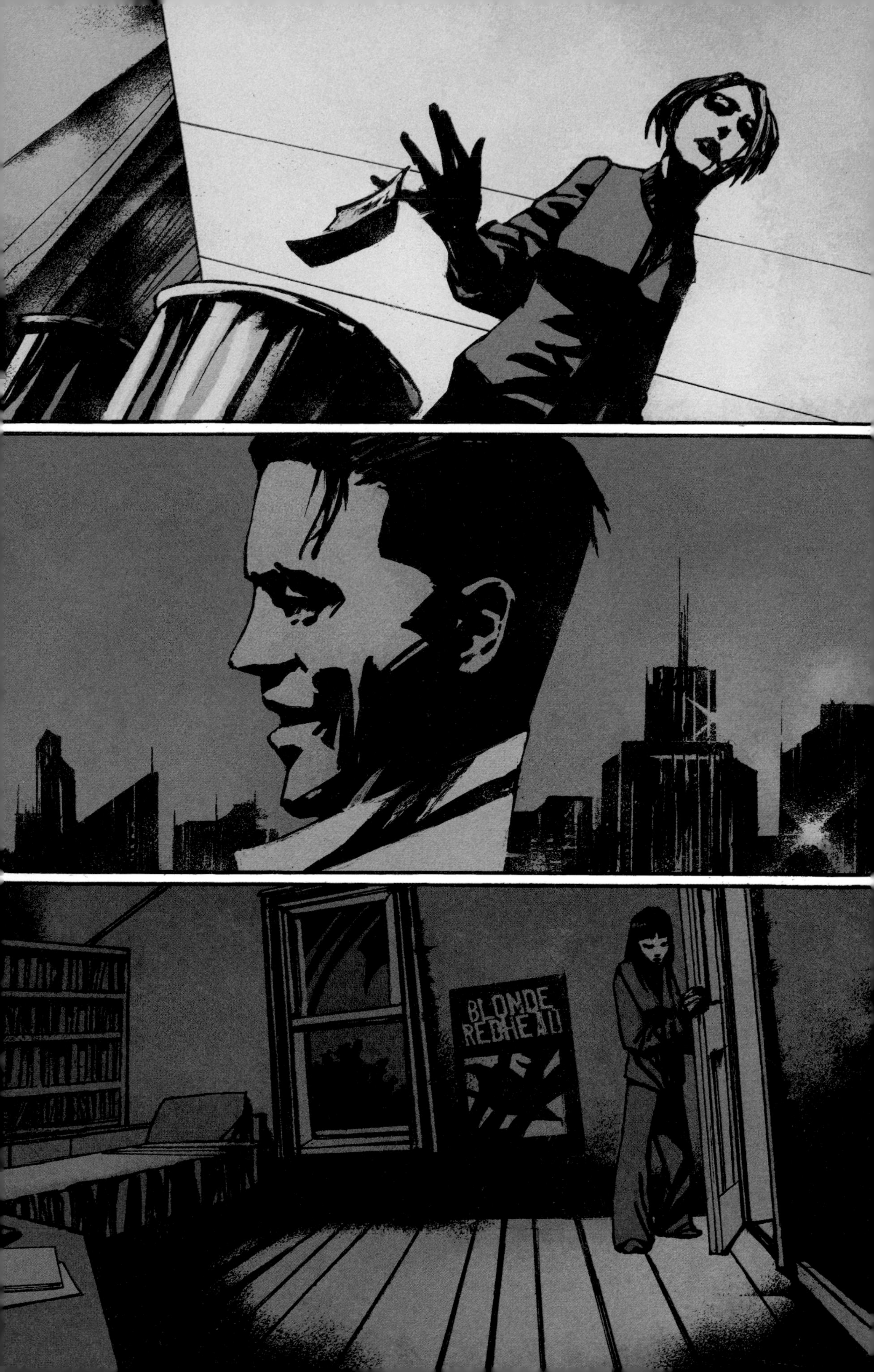
BLONDE
REDHEAD

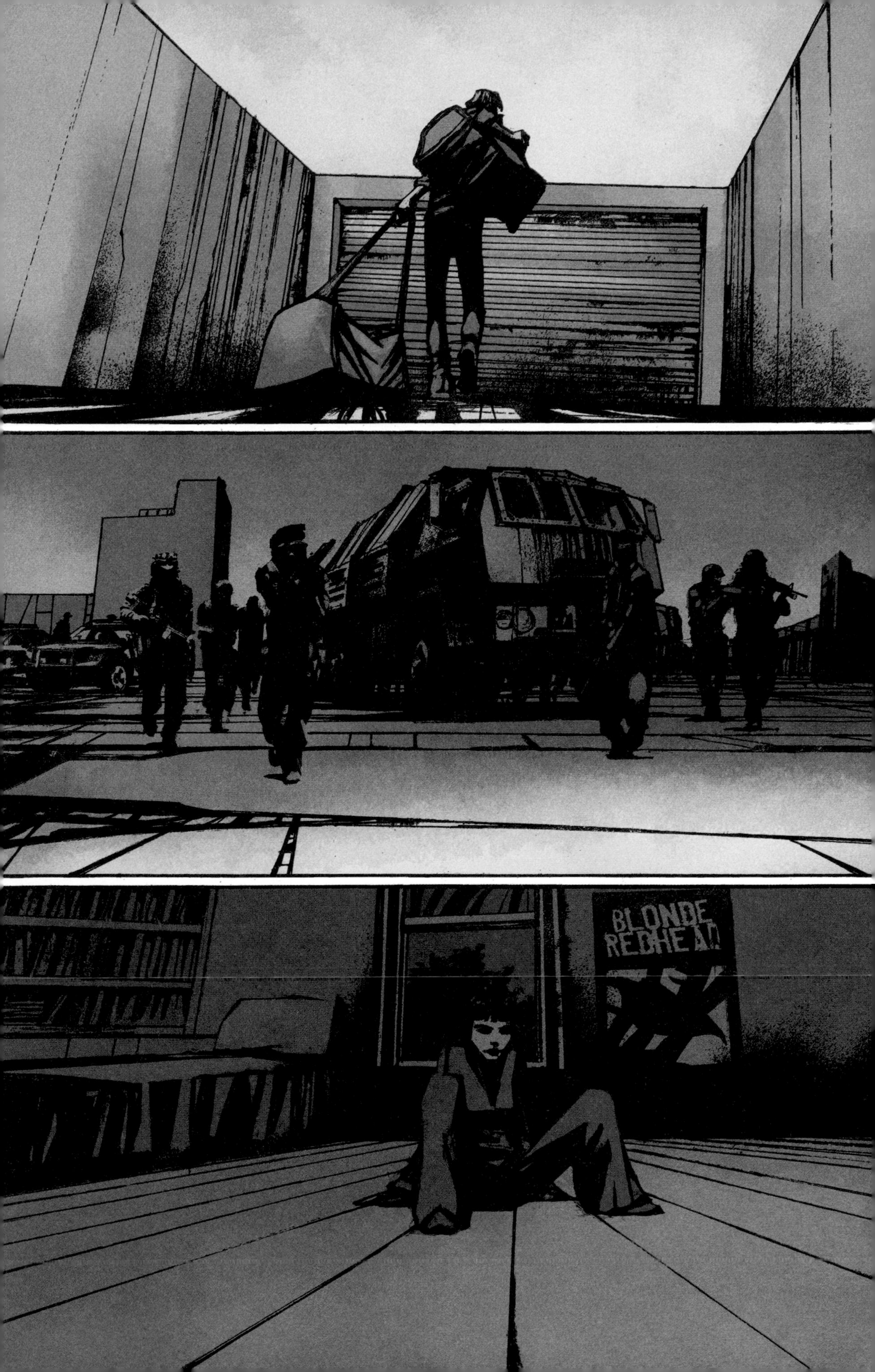
BLONDE
REDHEAD

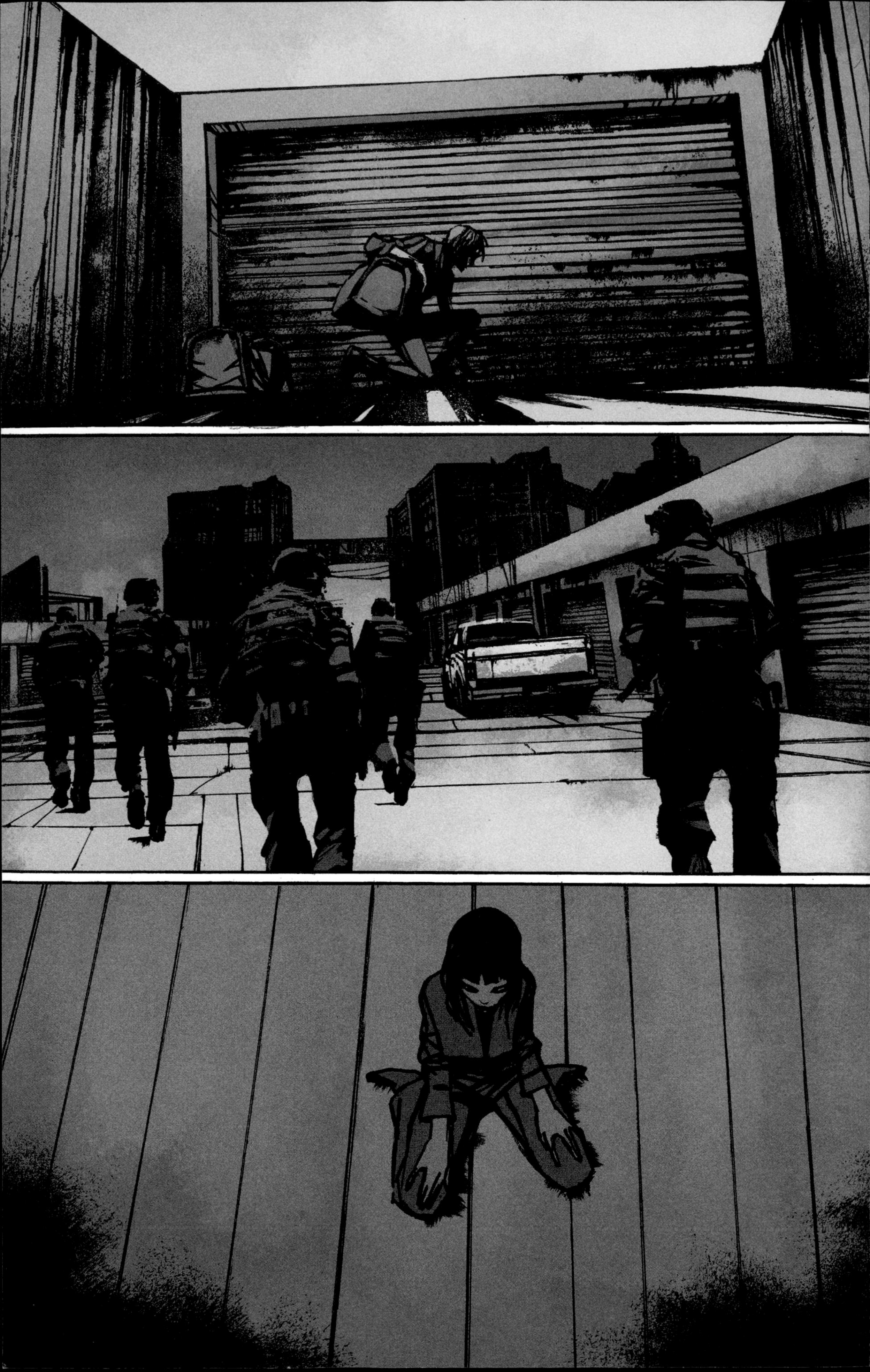

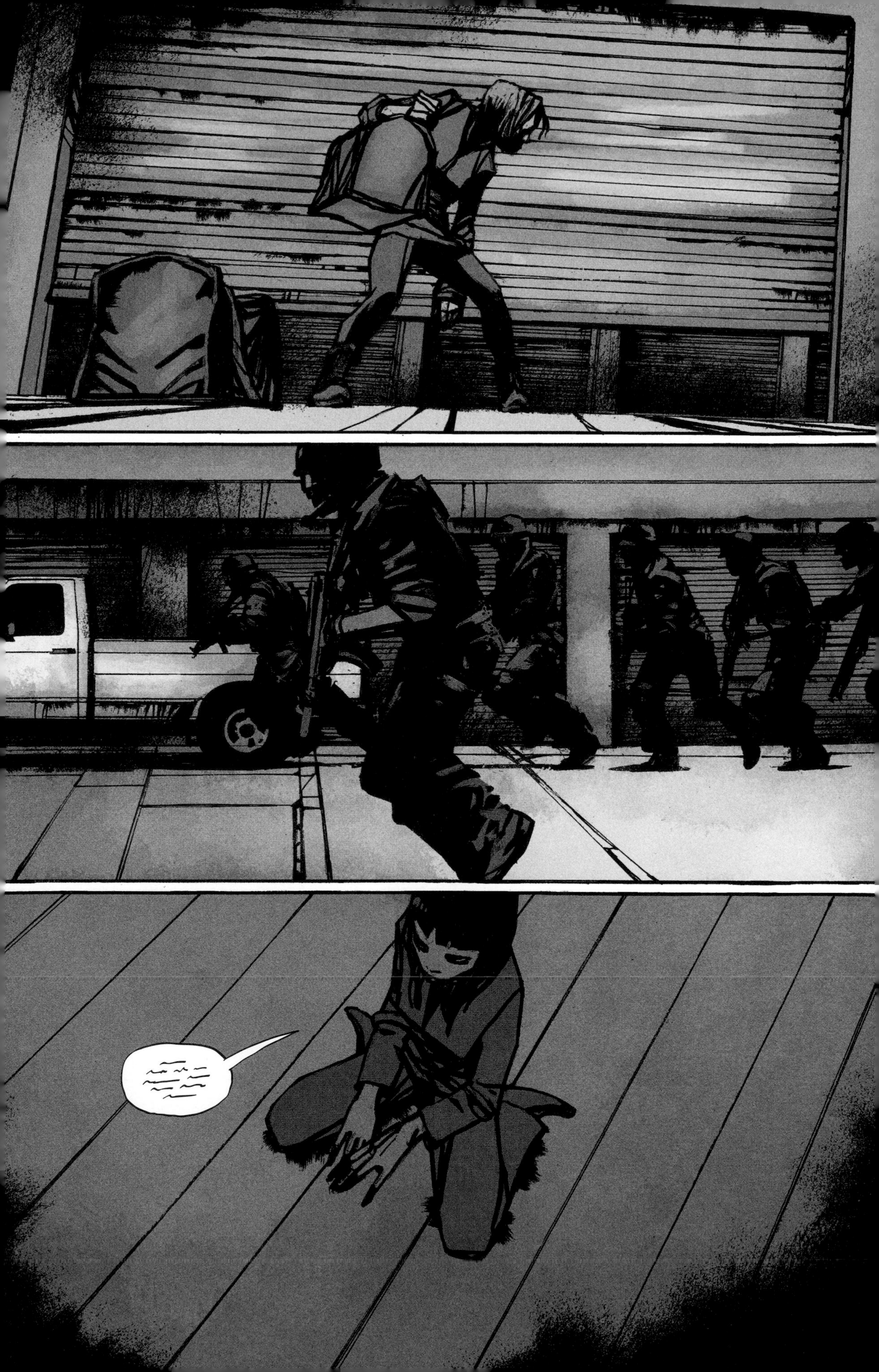

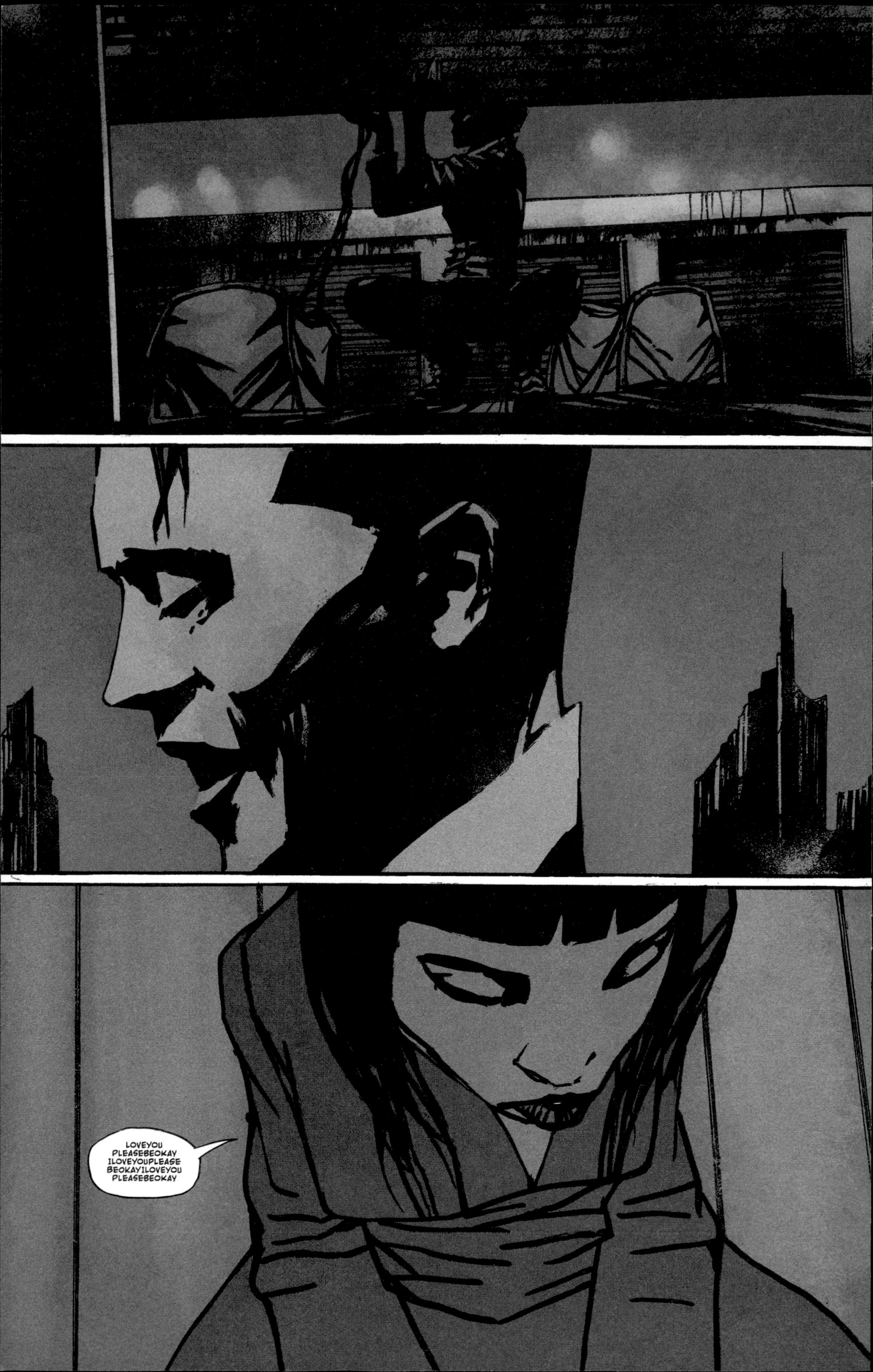
LOVEYOU
PLEASEBEOKAY
ILOVEYOUPLEASE
BEOKAYILOVEYOU
PLEASEBEOKAY

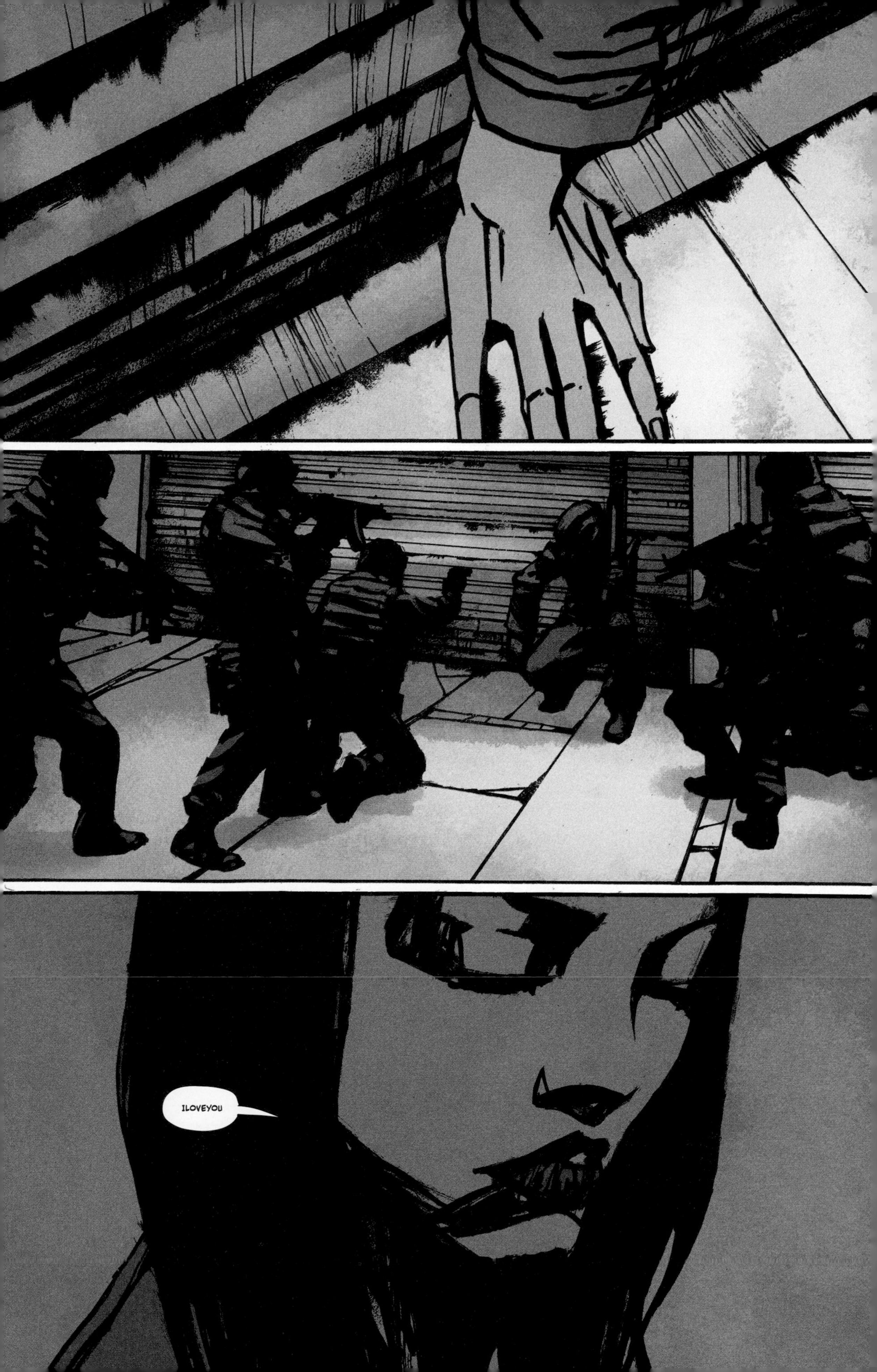
ILOVEYOU

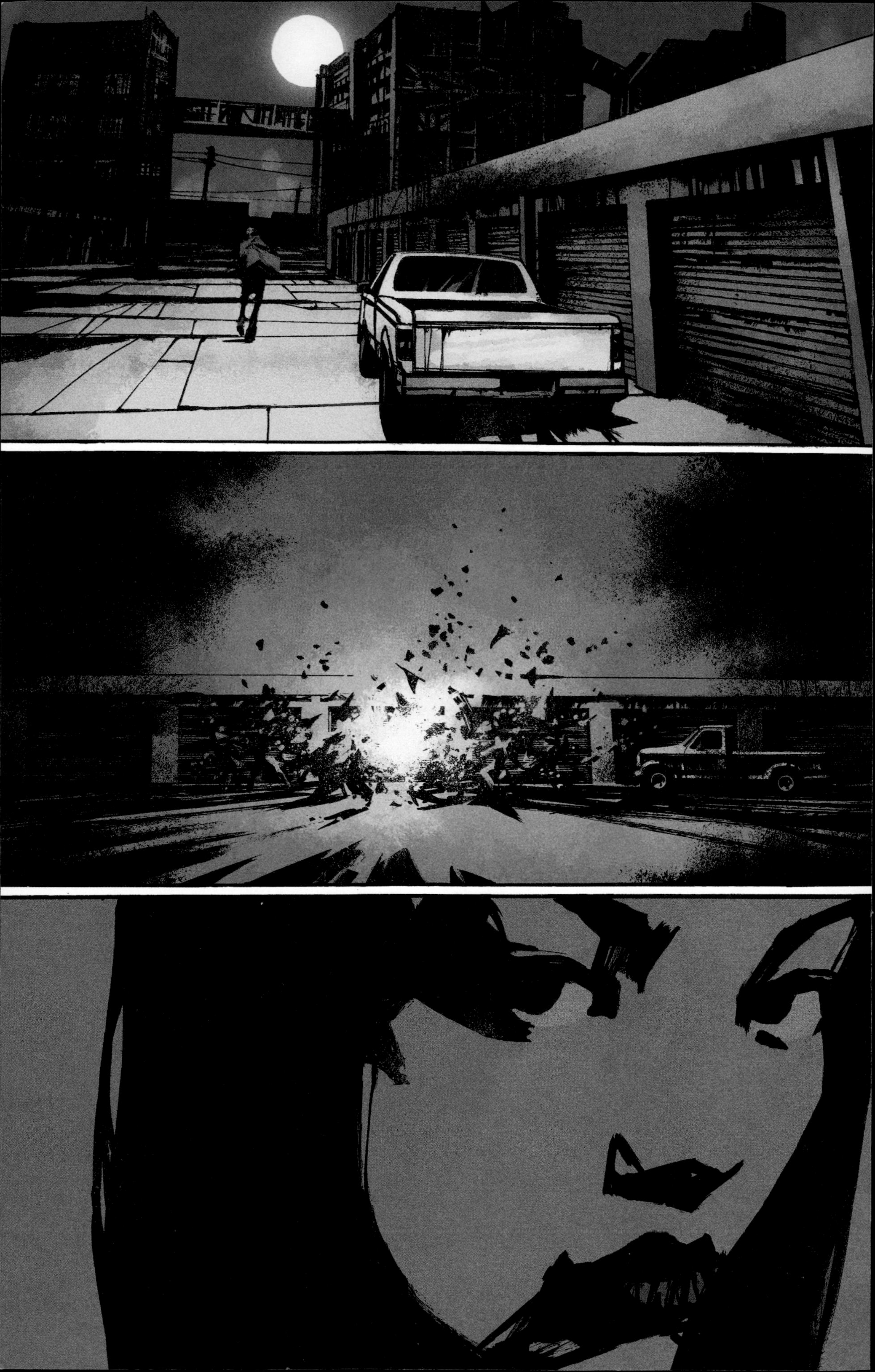

CHAPTER SIX:
ENEMIES OF THE STATE

"Does your husband know about your activities?"

"Certainly not. And neither does my child."

—Jean-Pierre Melville, "Army of Shadows"

*"Fair is foul, and foul is fair: Hover through
 the fog and filthy air"*

—William Shakespeare, "Macbeth"

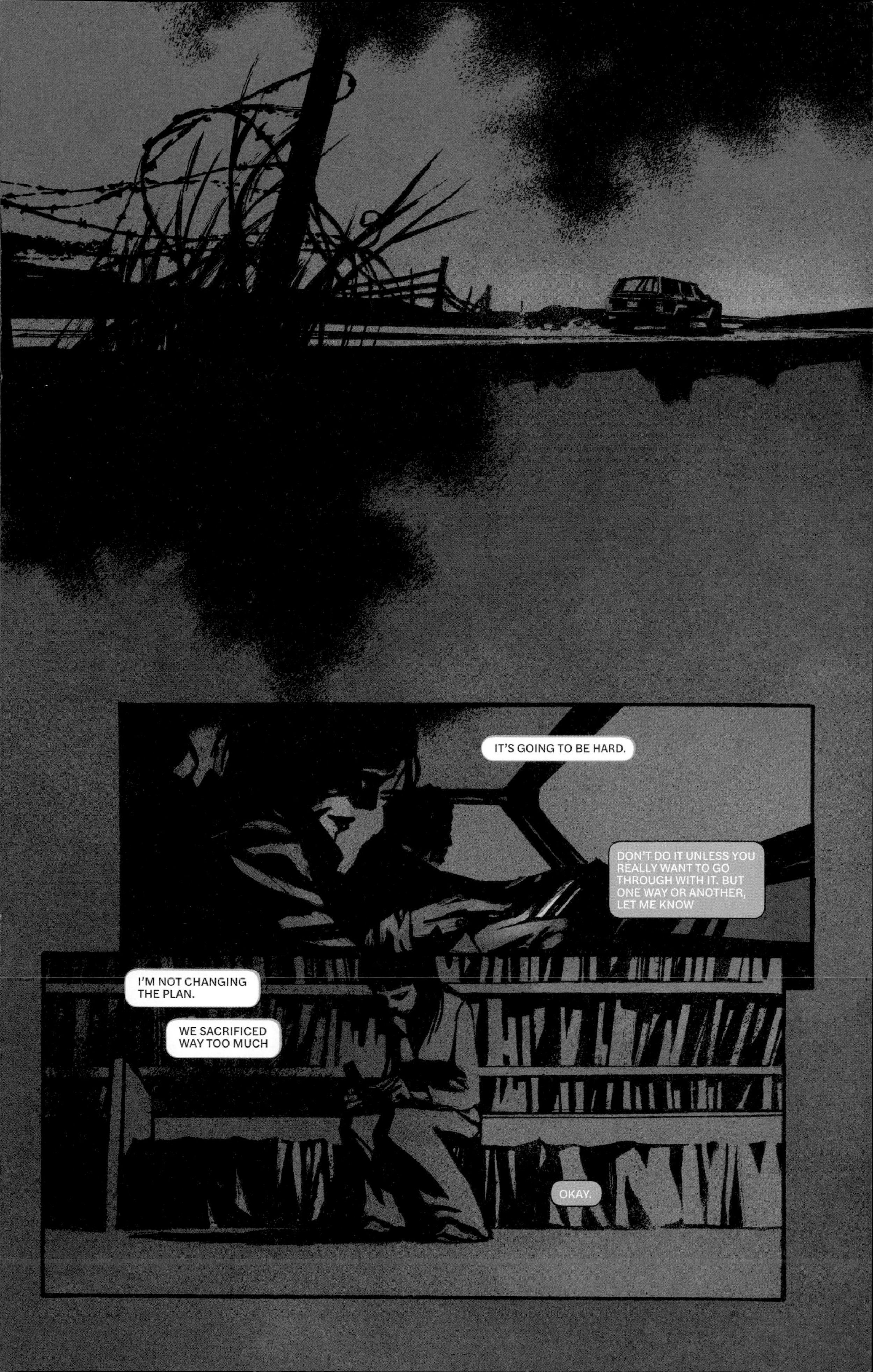
IT'S GOING TO BE HARD.
DON'T DO IT UNLESS YOU REALLY WANT TO GO THROUGH WITH IT. BUT ONE WAY OR ANOTHER, LET ME KNOW
I'M NOT CHANGING THE PLAN.
WE SACRIFICED WAY TOO MUCH
OKAY.

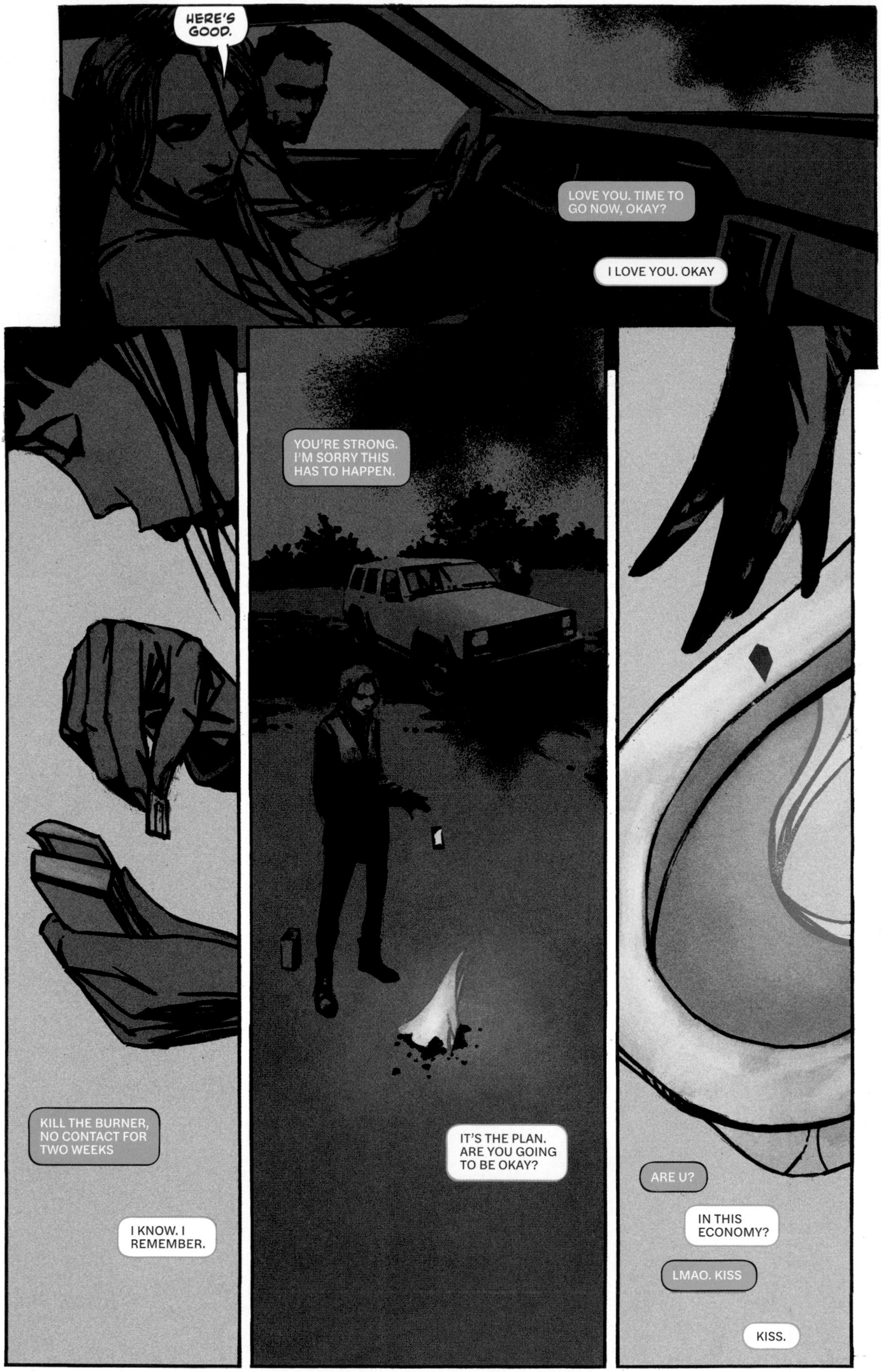
HERE'S GOOD.
LOVE YOU. TIME TO GO NOW, OKAY?
I LOVE YOU. OKAY
KILL THE BURNER, NO CONTACT FOR TWO WEEKS
I KNOW. I REMEMBER.
YOU'RE STRONG. I'M SORRY THIS HAS TO HAPPEN.
IT'S THE PLAN. ARE YOU GOING TO BE OKAY?
ARE U?
IN THIS ECONOMY?
LMAO. KISS
KISS.

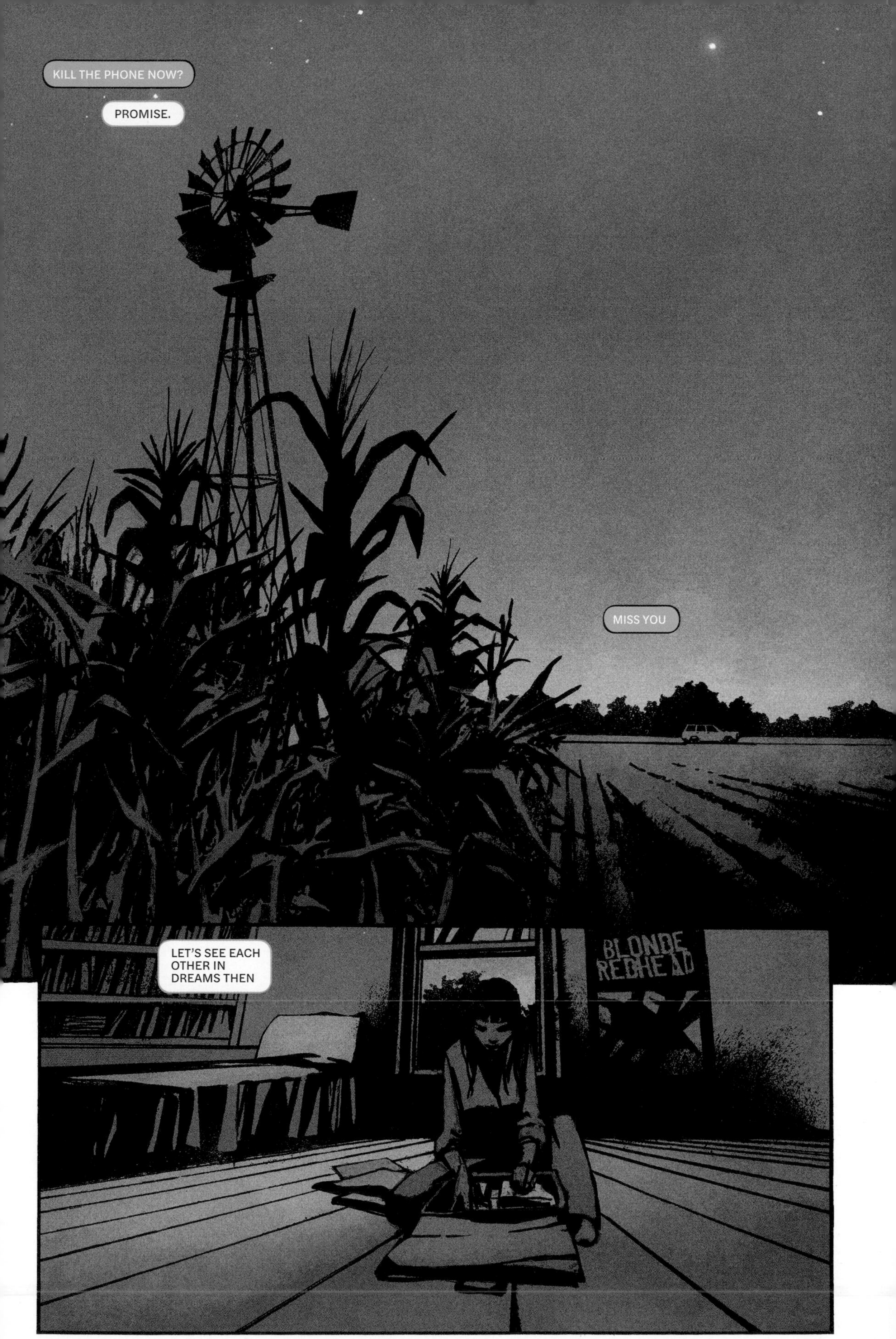
KILL THE PHONE NOW?
PROMISE.
MISS YOU
LET'S SEE EACH OTHER IN DREAMS THEN
BLONDE REDHEAD

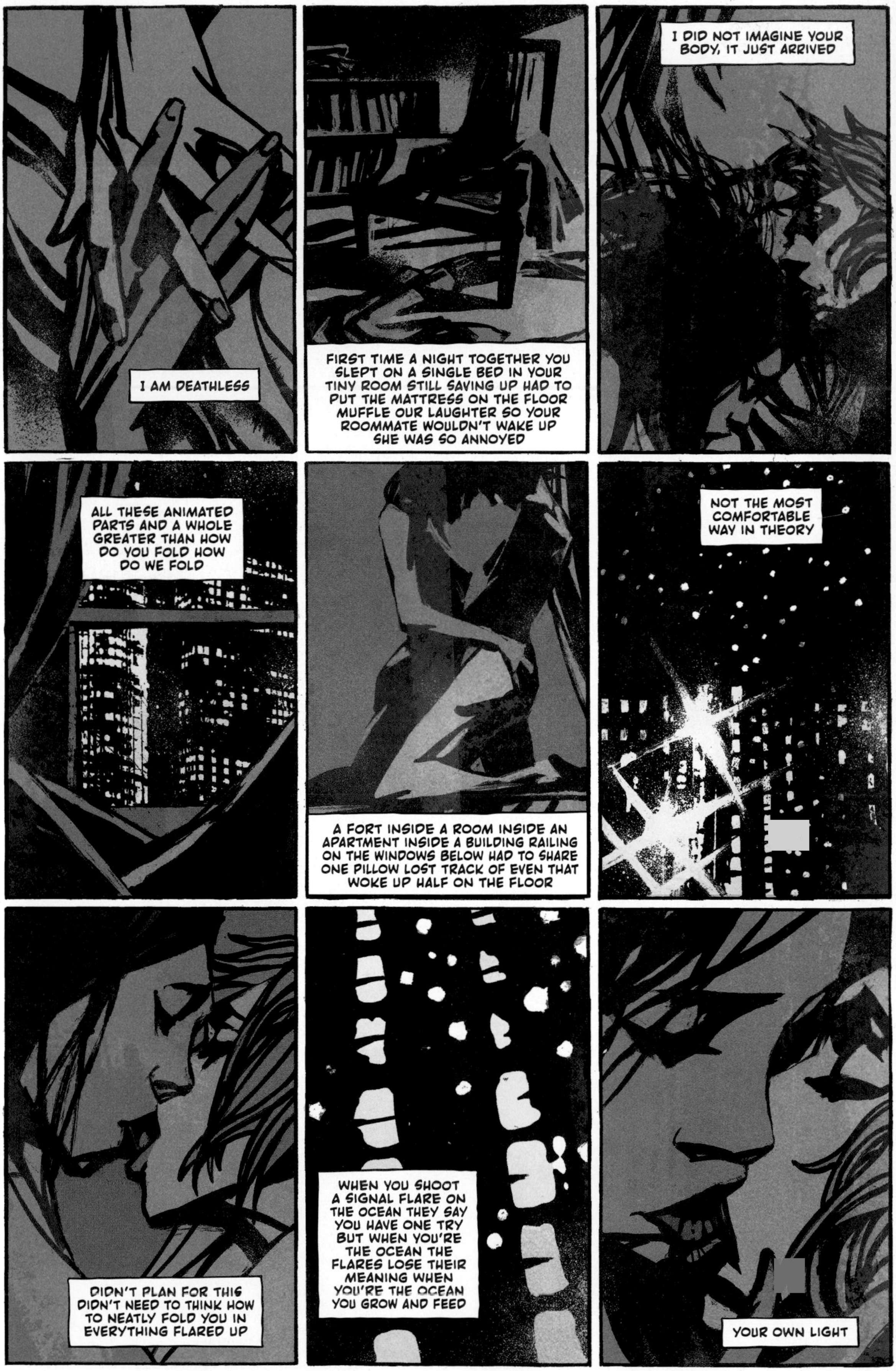
I AM DEATHLESS
FIRST TIME A NIGHT TOGETHER YOU SLEPT ON A SINGLE BED IN YOUR TINY ROOM STILL SAVING UP HAD TO PUT THE MATTRESS ON THE FLOOR MUFFLE OUR LAUGHTER SO YOUR ROOMMATE WOULDN'T WAKE UP SHE WAS SO ANNOYED
I DID NOT IMAGINE YOUR BODY, IT JUST ARRIVED
ALL THESE ANIMATED PARTS AND A WHOLE GREATER THAN HOW DO YOU FOLD HOW DO WE FOLD
A FORT INSIDE A ROOM INSIDE AN APARTMENT INSIDE A BUILDING RAILING ON THE WINDOWS BELOW HAD TO SHARE ONE PILLOW LOST TRACK OF EVEN THAT WOKE UP HALF ON THE FLOOR
NOT THE MOST COMFORTABLE WAY IN THEORY
DIDN'T PLAN FOR THIS DIDN'T NEED TO THINK HOW TO NEATLY FOLD YOU IN EVERYTHING FLARED UP
WHEN YOU SHOOT A SIGNAL FLARE ON THE OCEAN THEY SAY YOU HAVE ONE TRY BUT WHEN YOU'RE THE OCEAN THE FLARES LOSE THEIR MEANING WHEN YOU'RE THE OCEAN YOU GROW AND FEED
YOUR OWN LIGHT

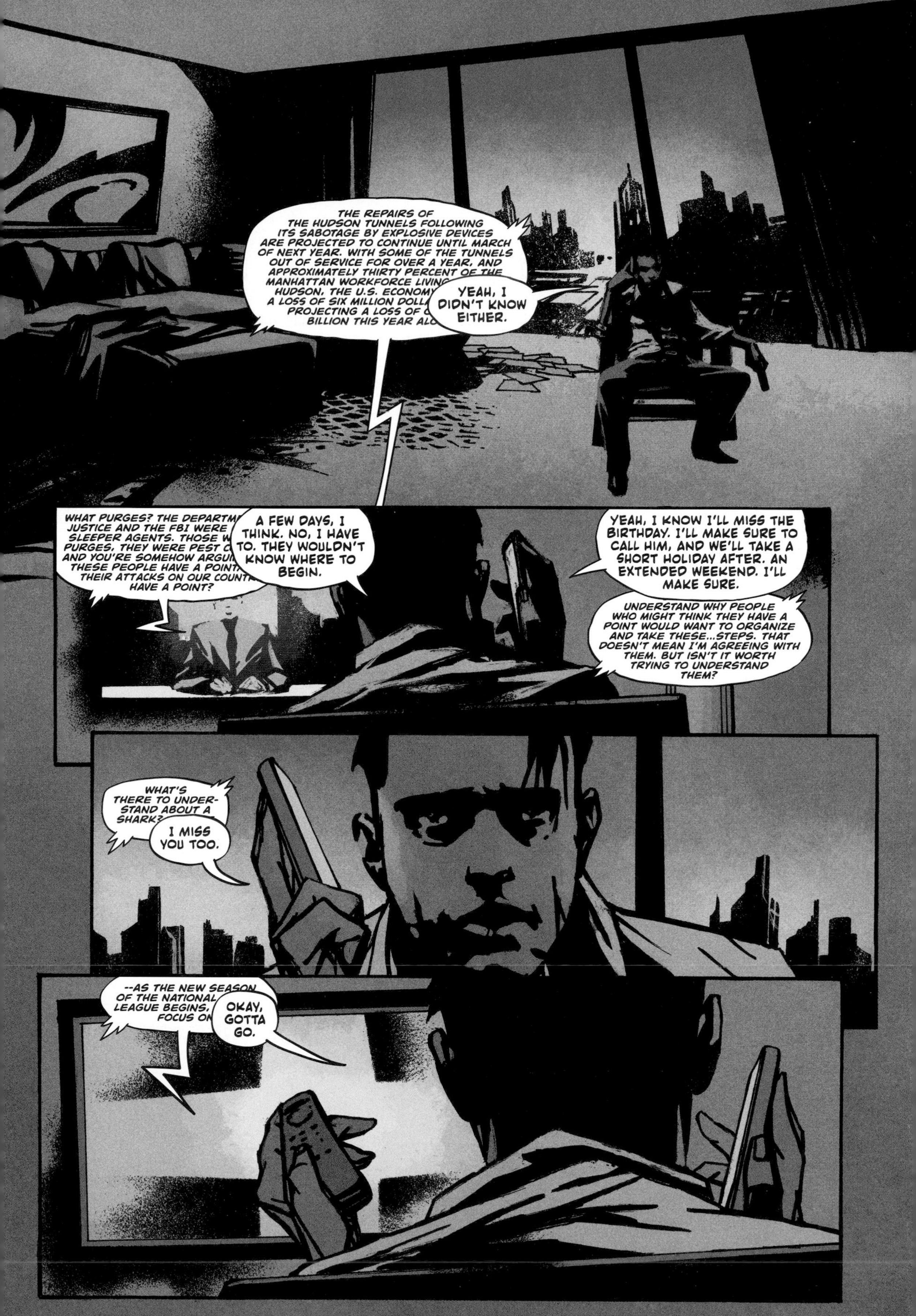
THE REPAIRS OF THE HUDSON TUNNELS FOLLOWING ITS SABOTAGE BY EXPLOSIVE DEVICES ARE PROJECTED TO CONTINUE UNTIL MARCH OF NEXT YEAR. WITH SOME OF THE TUNNELS OUT OF SERVICE FOR OVER A YEAR, AND APPROXIMATELY THIRTY PERCENT OF THE MANHATTAN WORKFORCE LIVING HUDSON, THE U.S. ECONOMY A LOSS OF SIX MILLION DOLLA PROJECTING A LOSS OF BILLION THIS YEAR ALO
YEAH, I DIDN'T KNOW EITHER.
WHAT PURGES? THE DEPARTM JUSTICE AND THE FBI WERE SLEEPER AGENTS. THOSE W PURGES, THEY WERE PEST C AND YOU'RE SOMEHOW ARGUI THESE PEOPLE HAVE A POINT THEIR ATTACKS ON OUR COUNT HAVE A POINT?
A FEW DAYS, I THINK. NO, I HAVE TO. THEY WOULDN'T KNOW WHERE TO BEGIN.
YEAH, I KNOW I'LL MISS THE BIRTHDAY. I'LL MAKE SURE TO CALL HIM, AND WE'LL TAKE A SHORT HOLIDAY AFTER. AN EXTENDED WEEKEND. I'LL MAKE SURE.
UNDERSTAND WHY PEOPLE WHO MIGHT THINK THEY HAVE A POINT WOULD WANT TO ORGANIZE AND TAKE THESE...STEPS. THAT DOESN'T MEAN I'M AGREEING WITH THEM. BUT ISN'T IT WORTH TRYING TO UNDERSTAND THEM?
WHAT'S THERE TO UNDERSTAND ABOUT A SHARK?
I MISS YOU TOO.
--AS THE NEW SEASON OF THE NATIONAL LEAGUE BEGINS, FOCUS ON
OKAY, GOTTA GO.

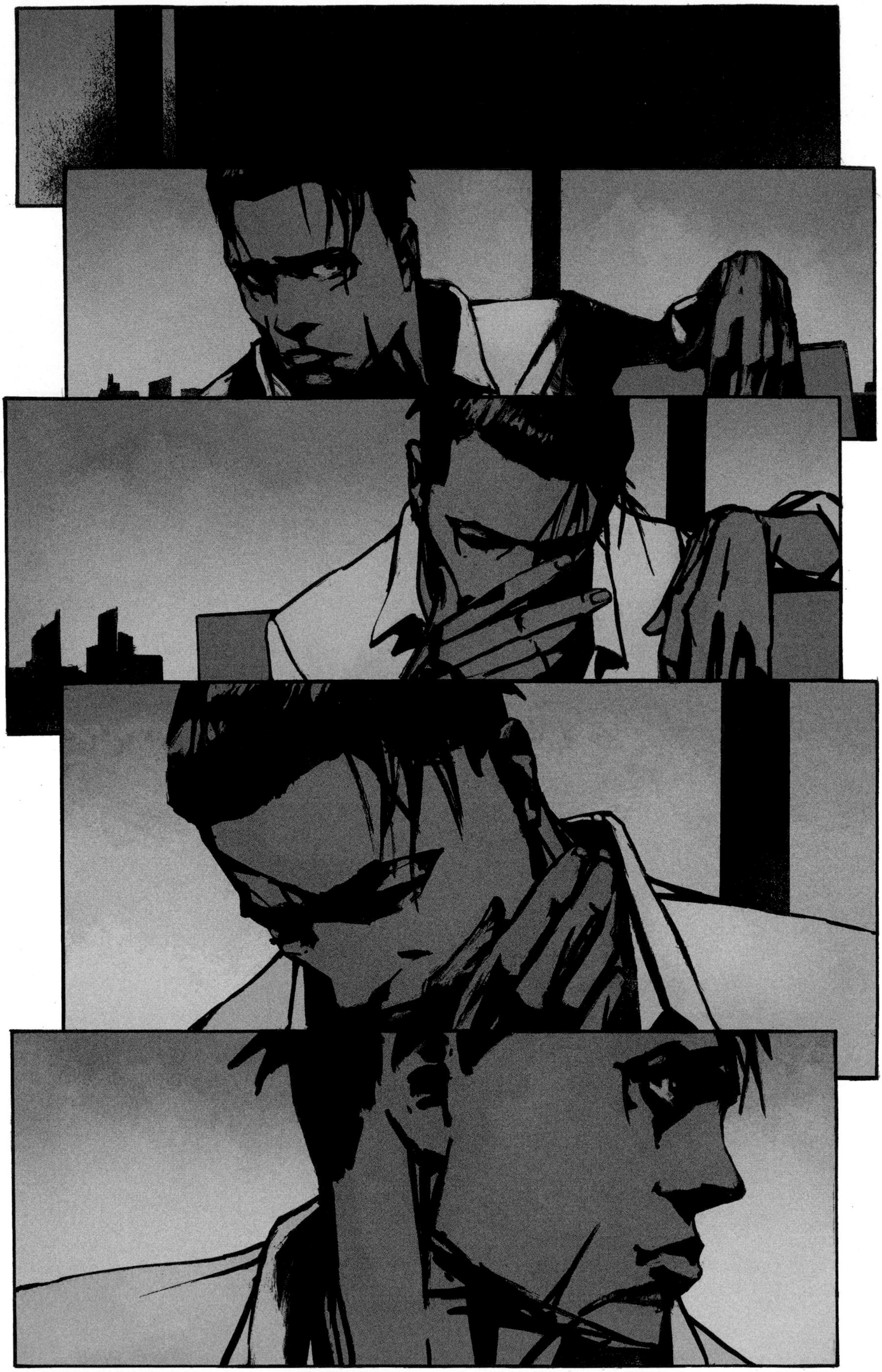

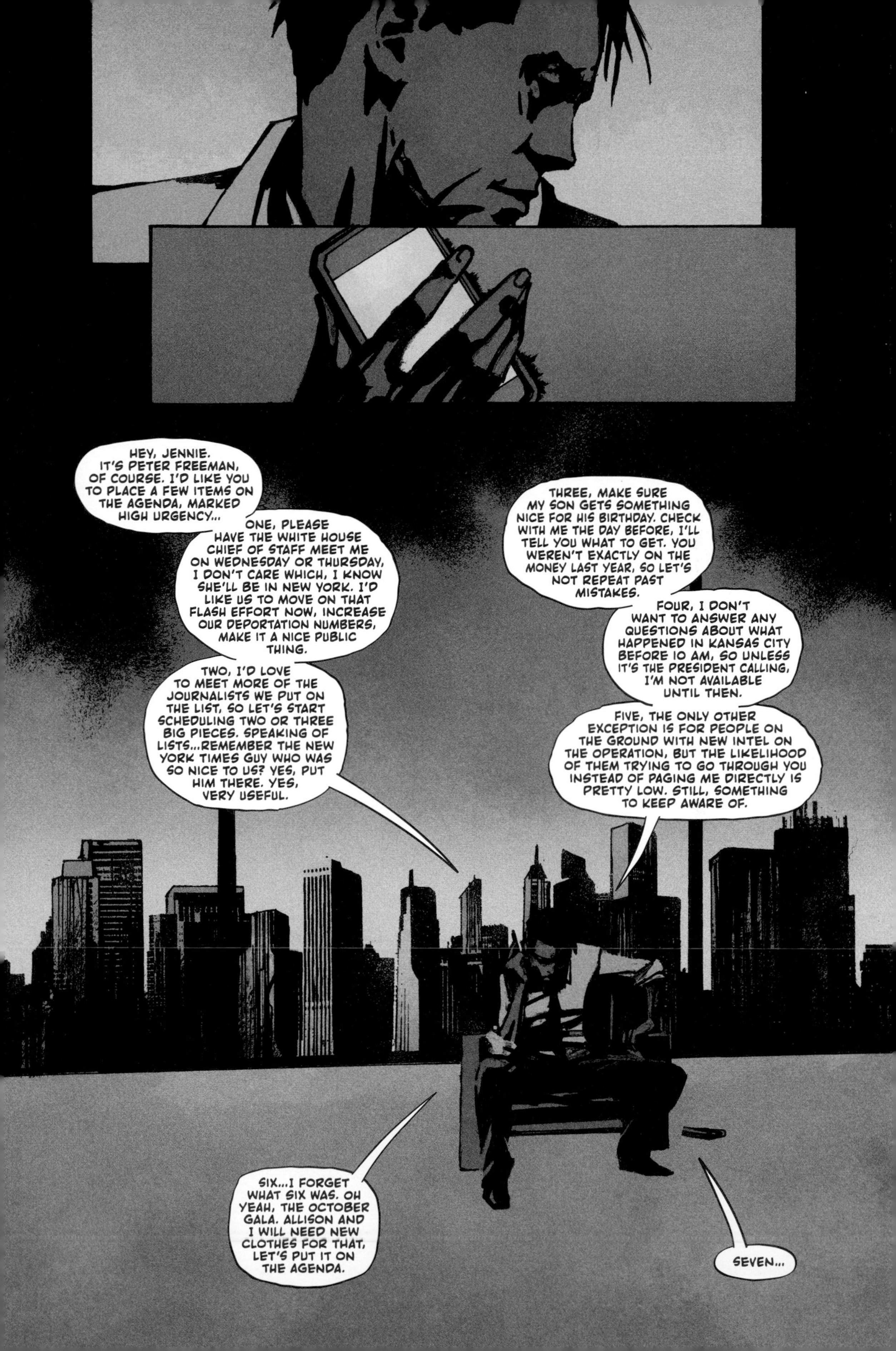
HEY, JENNIE. IT'S PETER FREEMAN, OF COURSE. I'D LIKE YOU TO PLACE A FEW ITEMS ON THE AGENDA, MARKED HIGH URGENCY...
ONE, PLEASE HAVE THE WHITE HOUSE CHIEF OF STAFF MEET ME ON WEDNESDAY OR THURSDAY, I DON'T CARE WHICH, I KNOW SHE'LL BE IN NEW YORK. I'D LIKE US TO MOVE ON THAT FLASH EFFORT NOW, INCREASE OUR DEPORTATION NUMBERS, MAKE IT A NICE PUBLIC THING.
TWO, I'D LOVE TO MEET MORE OF THE JOURNALISTS WE PUT ON THE LIST, SO LET'S START SCHEDULING TWO OR THREE BIG PIECES. SPEAKING OF LISTS...REMEMBER THE NEW YORK TIMES GUY WHO WAS SO NICE TO US? YES, PUT HIM THERE. YES, VERY USEFUL.
THREE, MAKE SURE MY SON GETS SOMETHING NICE FOR HIS BIRTHDAY. CHECK WITH ME THE DAY BEFORE, I'LL TELL YOU WHAT TO GET. YOU WEREN'T EXACTLY ON THE MONEY LAST YEAR, SO LET'S NOT REPEAT PAST MISTAKES.
FOUR, I DON'T WANT TO ANSWER ANY QUESTIONS ABOUT WHAT HAPPENED IN KANSAS CITY BEFORE 10 AM, SO UNLESS IT'S THE PRESIDENT CALLING, I'M NOT AVAILABLE UNTIL THEN.
FIVE, THE ONLY OTHER EXCEPTION IS FOR PEOPLE ON THE GROUND WITH NEW INTEL ON THE OPERATION, BUT THE LIKELIHOOD OF THEM TRYING TO GO THROUGH YOU INSTEAD OF PAGING ME DIRECTLY IS PRETTY LOW. STILL, SOMETHING TO KEEP AWARE OF.
SIX...I FORGET WHAT SIX WAS. OH YEAH, THE OCTOBER GALA. ALLISON AND I WILL NEED NEW CLOTHES FOR THAT, LET'S PUT IT ON THE AGENDA.
SEVEN...

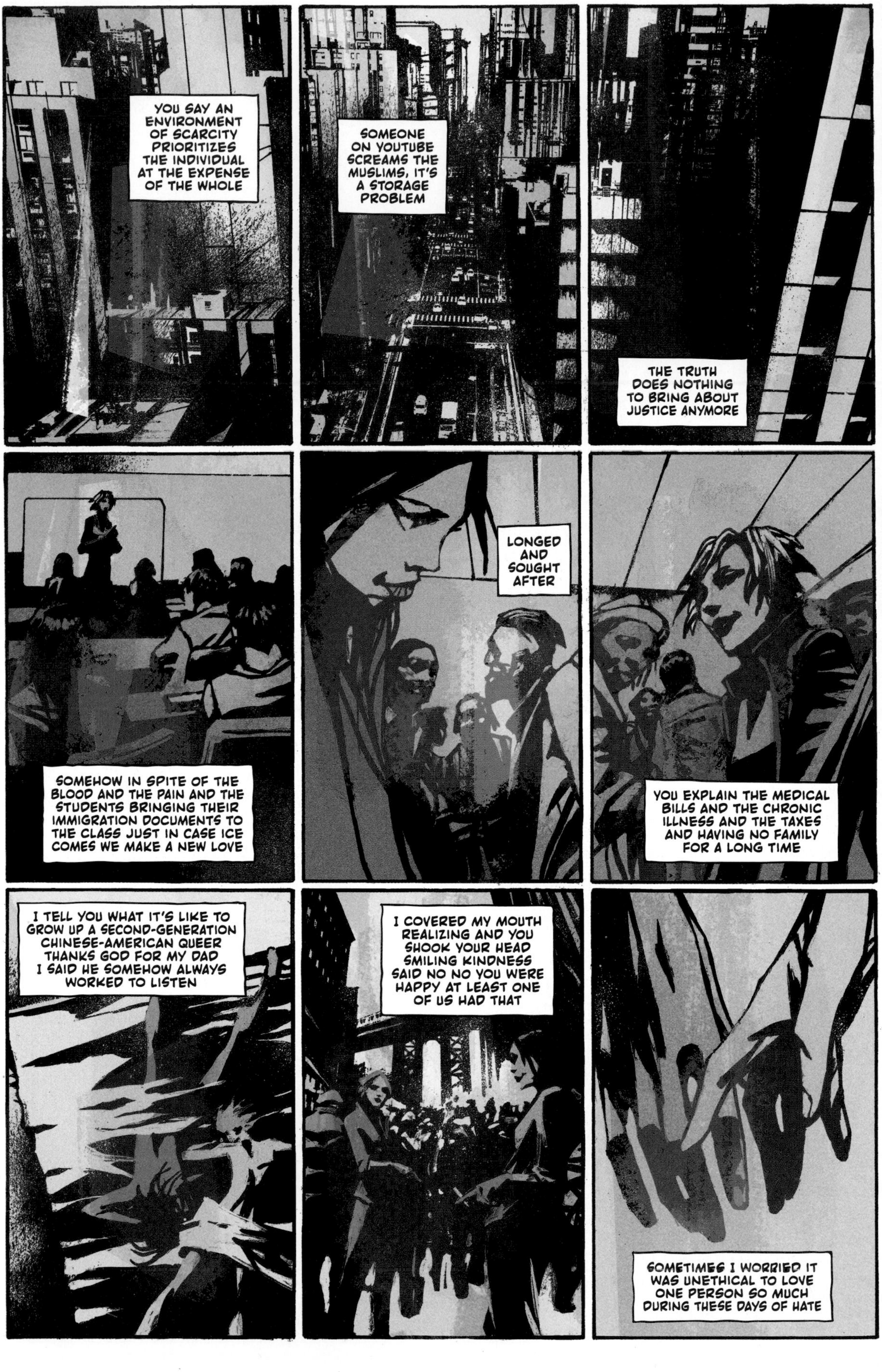
YOU SAY AN ENVIRONMENT OF SCARCITY PRIORITIZES THE INDIVIDUAL AT THE EXPENSE OF THE WHOLE
SOMEONE ON YOUTUBE SCREAMS THE MUSLIMS, IT'S A STORAGE PROBLEM
THE TRUTH DOES NOTHING TO BRING ABOUT JUSTICE ANYMORE
SOMEHOW IN SPITE OF THE BLOOD AND THE PAIN AND THE STUDENTS BRINGING THEIR IMMIGRATION DOCUMENTS TO THE CLASS JUST IN CASE ICE COMES WE MAKE A NEW LOVE
LONGED AND SOUGHT AFTER
YOU EXPLAIN THE MEDICAL BILLS AND THE CHRONIC ILLNESS AND THE TAXES AND HAVING NO FAMILY FOR A LONG TIME
I TELL YOU WHAT IT'S LIKE TO GROW UP A SECOND-GENERATION CHINESE-AMERICAN QUEER THANKS GOD FOR MY DAD I SAID HE SOMEHOW ALWAYS WORKED TO LISTEN
I COVERED MY MOUTH REALIZING AND YOU SHOOK YOUR HEAD SMILING KINDNESS SAID NO NO YOU WERE HAPPY AT LEAST ONE OF US HAD THAT
SOMETIMES I WORRIED IT WAS UNETHICAL TO LOVE ONE PERSON SO MUCH DURING THESE DAYS OF HATE

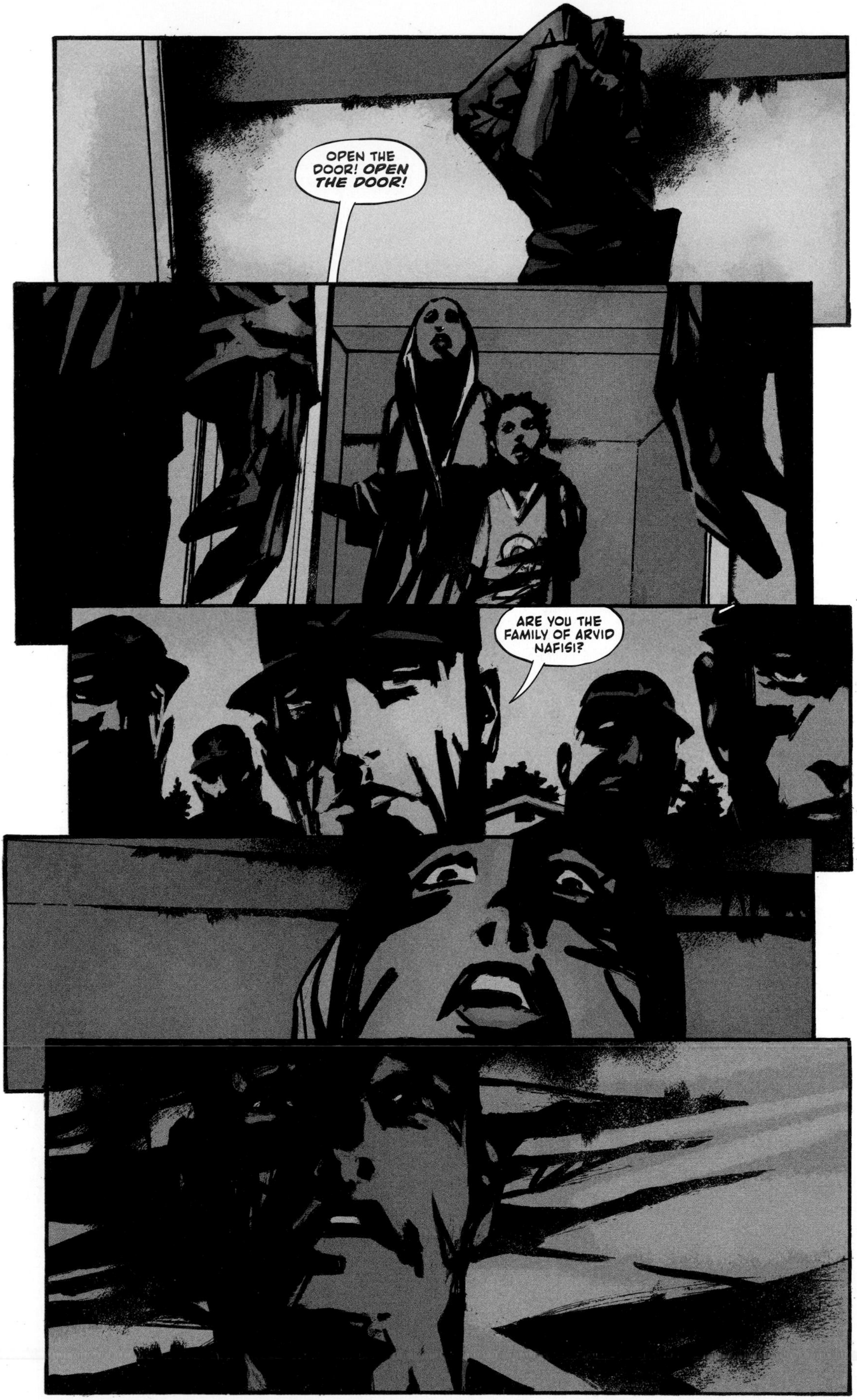
OPEN THE DOOR! OPEN THE DOOR!
ARE YOU THE FAMILY OF ARVID NAFISI?

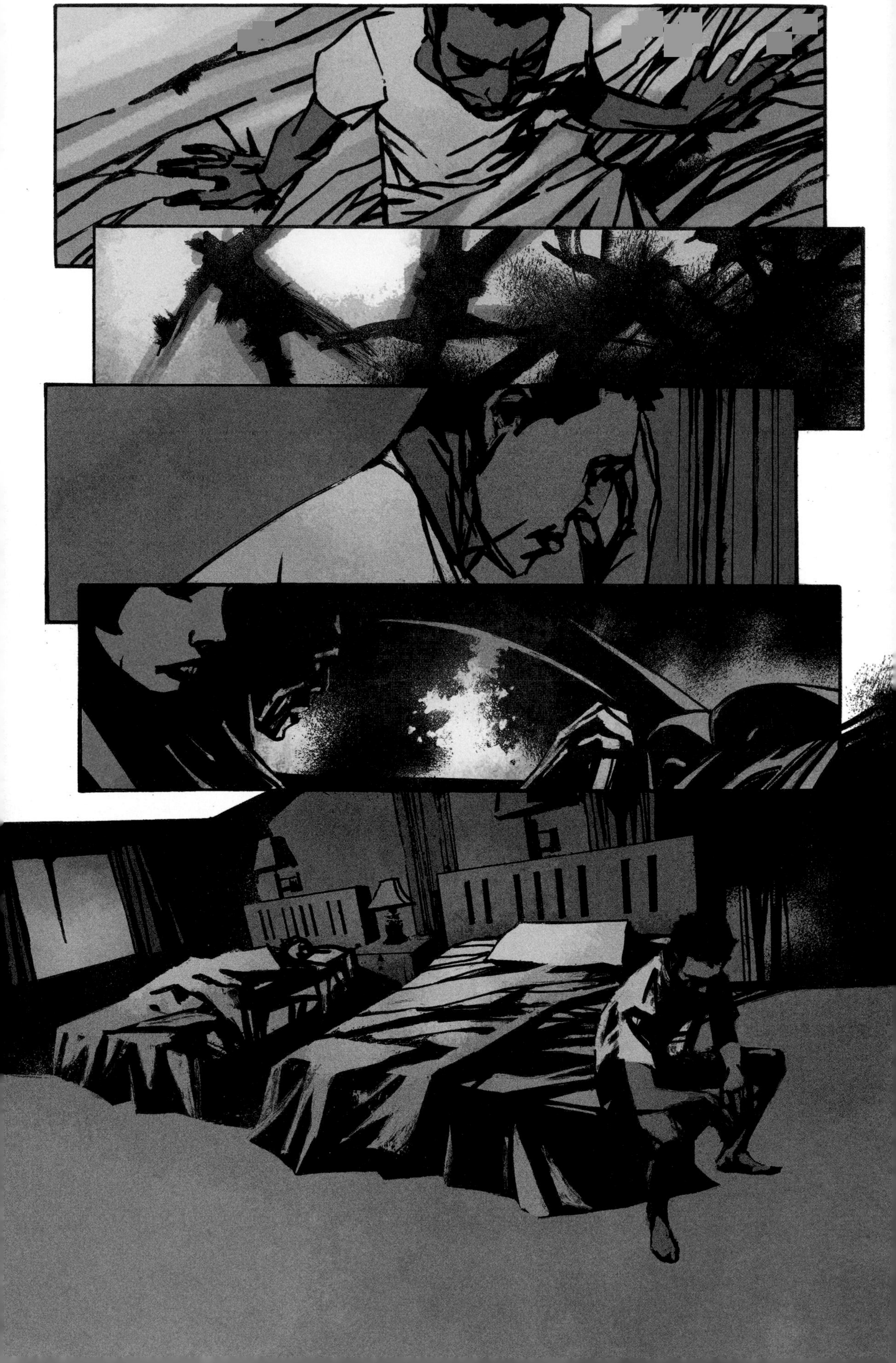

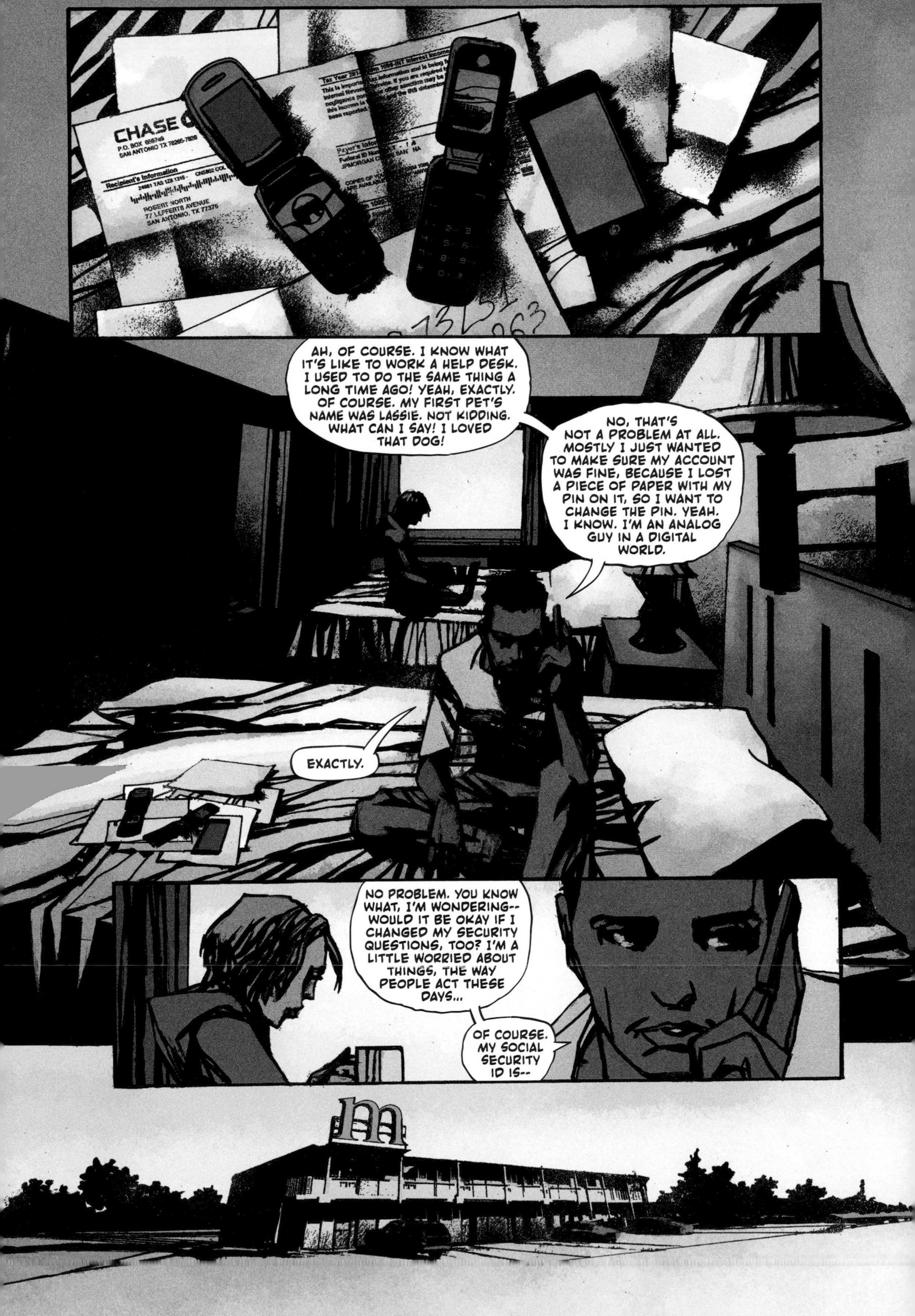
CHASE
P.O. BOX 659749
SAN ANTONIO TX 78265-7828
Recipient's Information
ROBERT NORTH
77 LEFFERTS AVENUE
SAN ANTONIO, TX 77376
AH, OF COURSE. I KNOW WHAT IT'S LIKE TO WORK A HELP DESK. I USED TO DO THE SAME THING A LONG TIME AGO! YEAH, EXACTLY. OF COURSE. MY FIRST PET'S NAME WAS LASSIE. NOT KIDDING. WHAT CAN I SAY! I LOVED THAT DOG!
NO, THAT'S NOT A PROBLEM AT ALL. MOSTLY I JUST WANTED TO MAKE SURE MY ACCOUNT WAS FINE, BECAUSE I LOST A PIECE OF PAPER WITH MY PIN ON IT, SO I WANT TO CHANGE THE PIN. YEAH. I KNOW. I'M AN ANALOG GUY IN A DIGITAL WORLD.
EXACTLY.
NO PROBLEM. YOU KNOW WHAT, I'M WONDERING-- WOULD IT BE OKAY IF I CHANGED MY SECURITY QUESTIONS, TOO? I'M A LITTLE WORRIED ABOUT THINGS, THE WAY PEOPLE ACT THESE DAYS...
OF COURSE. MY SOCIAL SECURITY ID IS--

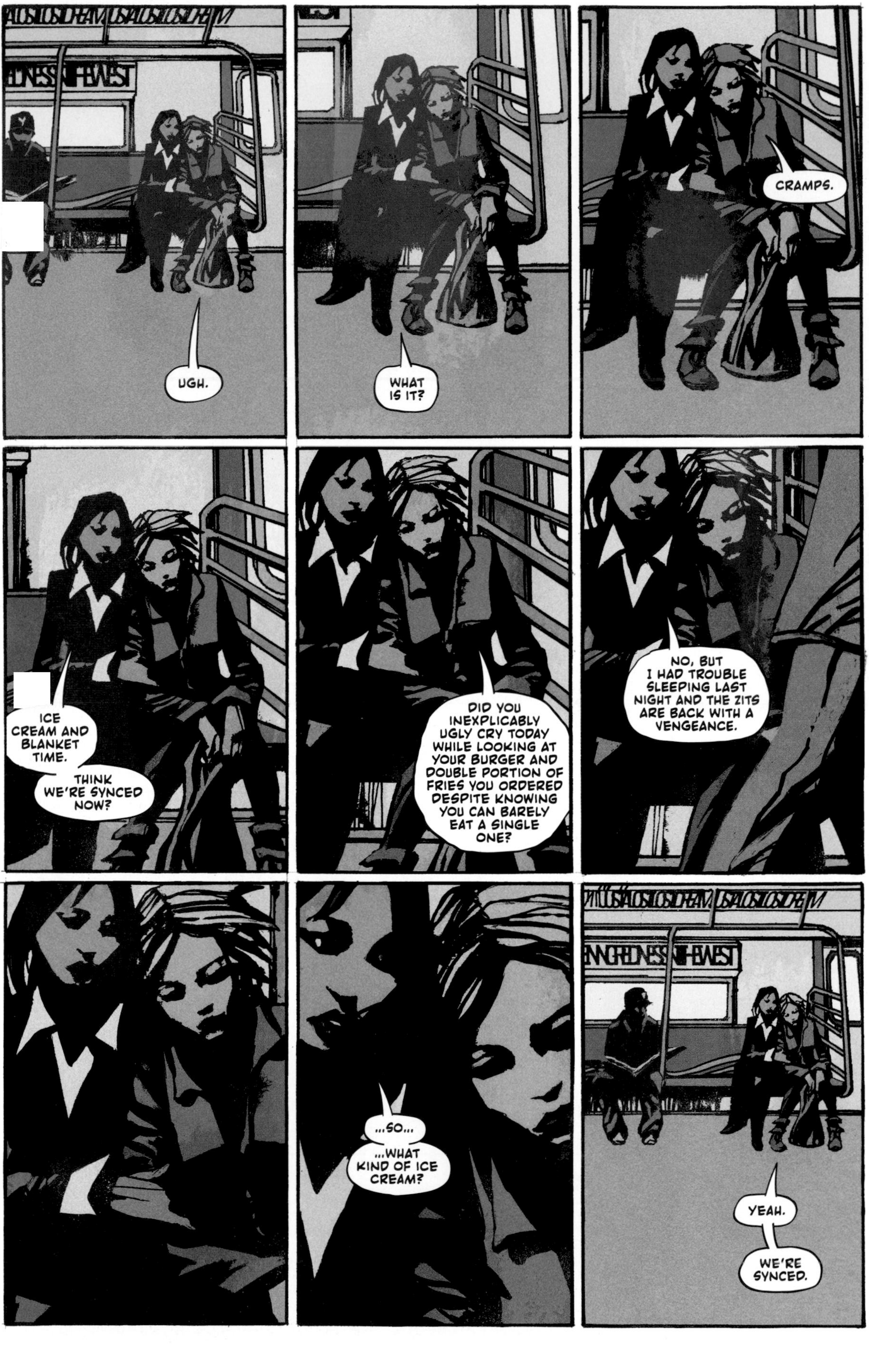
UGH.
WHAT IS IT?
CRAMPS.
ICE CREAM AND BLANKET TIME.
THINK WE'RE SYNCED NOW?
DID YOU INEXPLICABLY UGLY CRY TODAY WHILE LOOKING AT YOUR BURGER AND DOUBLE PORTION OF FRIES YOU ORDERED DESPITE KNOWING YOU CAN BARELY EAT A SINGLE ONE?
NO, BUT I HAD TROUBLE SLEEPING LAST NIGHT AND THE ZITS ARE BACK WITH A VENGEANCE.
...SO...
...WHAT KIND OF ICE CREAM?
YEAH.
WE'RE SYNCED.

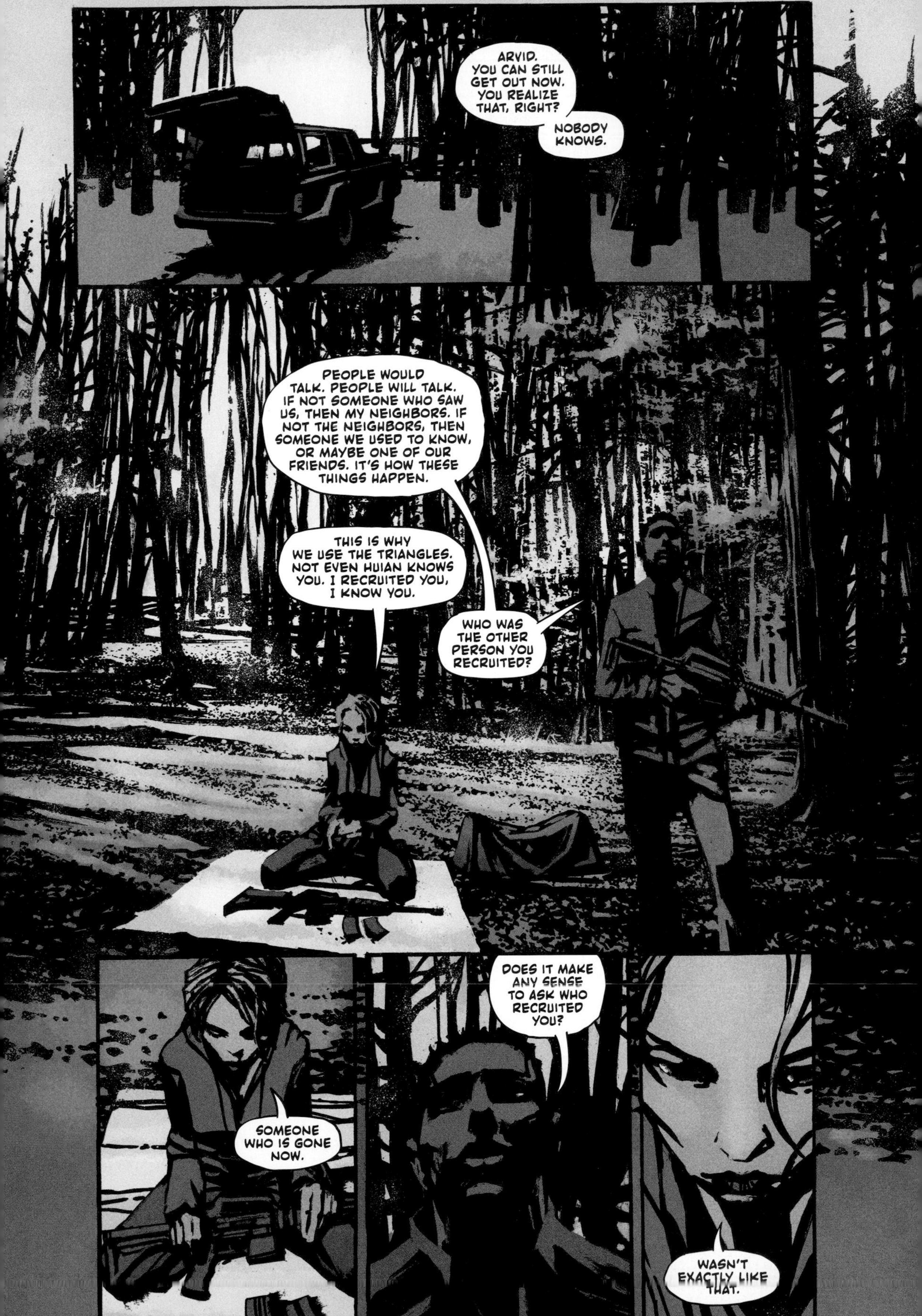
ARVID. YOU CAN STILL GET OUT NOW. YOU REALIZE THAT, RIGHT?
NOBODY KNOWS.
PEOPLE WOULD TALK. PEOPLE WILL TALK. IF NOT SOMEONE WHO SAW US, THEN MY NEIGHBORS. IF NOT THE NEIGHBORS, THEN SOMEONE WE USED TO KNOW, OR MAYBE ONE OF OUR FRIENDS. IT'S HOW THESE THINGS HAPPEN.
THIS IS WHY WE USE THE TRIANGLES. NOT EVEN HUIAN KNOWS YOU. I RECRUITED YOU, I KNOW YOU.
WHO WAS THE OTHER PERSON YOU RECRUITED?
SOMEONE WHO IS GONE NOW.
DOES IT MAKE ANY SENSE TO ASK WHO RECRUITED YOU?
WASN'T EXACTLY LIKE THAT.

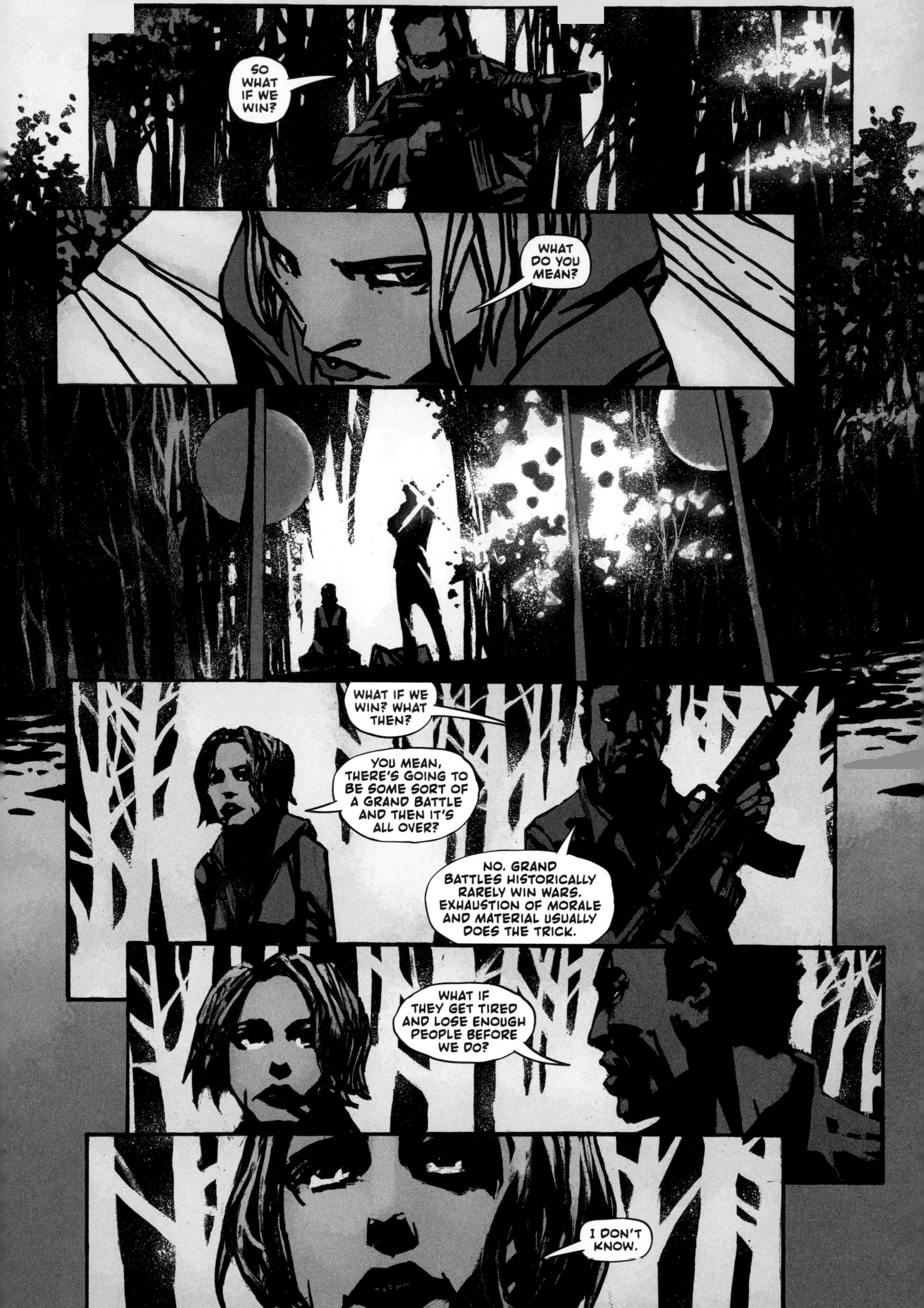
SO WHAT IF WE WIN?
WHAT DO YOU MEAN?
WHAT IF WE WIN? WHAT THEN?
YOU MEAN, THERE'S GOING TO BE SOME SORT OF A GRAND BATTLE AND THEN IT'S ALL OVER?
NO. GRAND BATTLES HISTORICALLY RARELY WIN WARS. EXHAUSTION OF MORALE AND MATERIAL USUALLY DOES THE TRICK.
WHAT IF THEY GET TIRED AND LOSE ENOUGH PEOPLE BEFORE WE DO?
I DON'T KNOW.

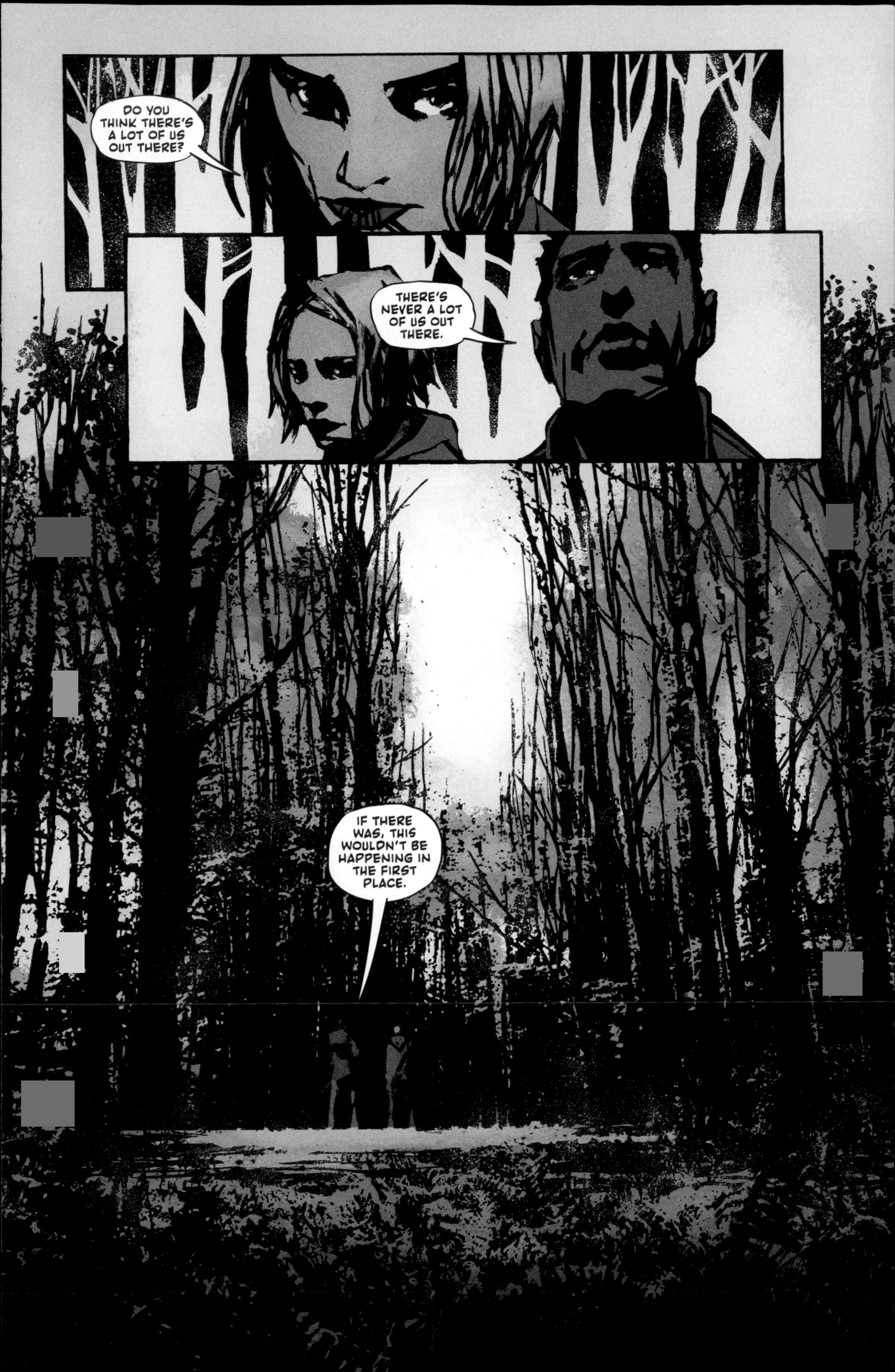
DO YOU THINK THERE'S A LOT OF US OUT THERE?
THERE'S NEVER A LOT OF US OUT THERE.
IF THERE WAS, THIS WOULDN'T BE HAPPENING IN THE FIRST PLACE.

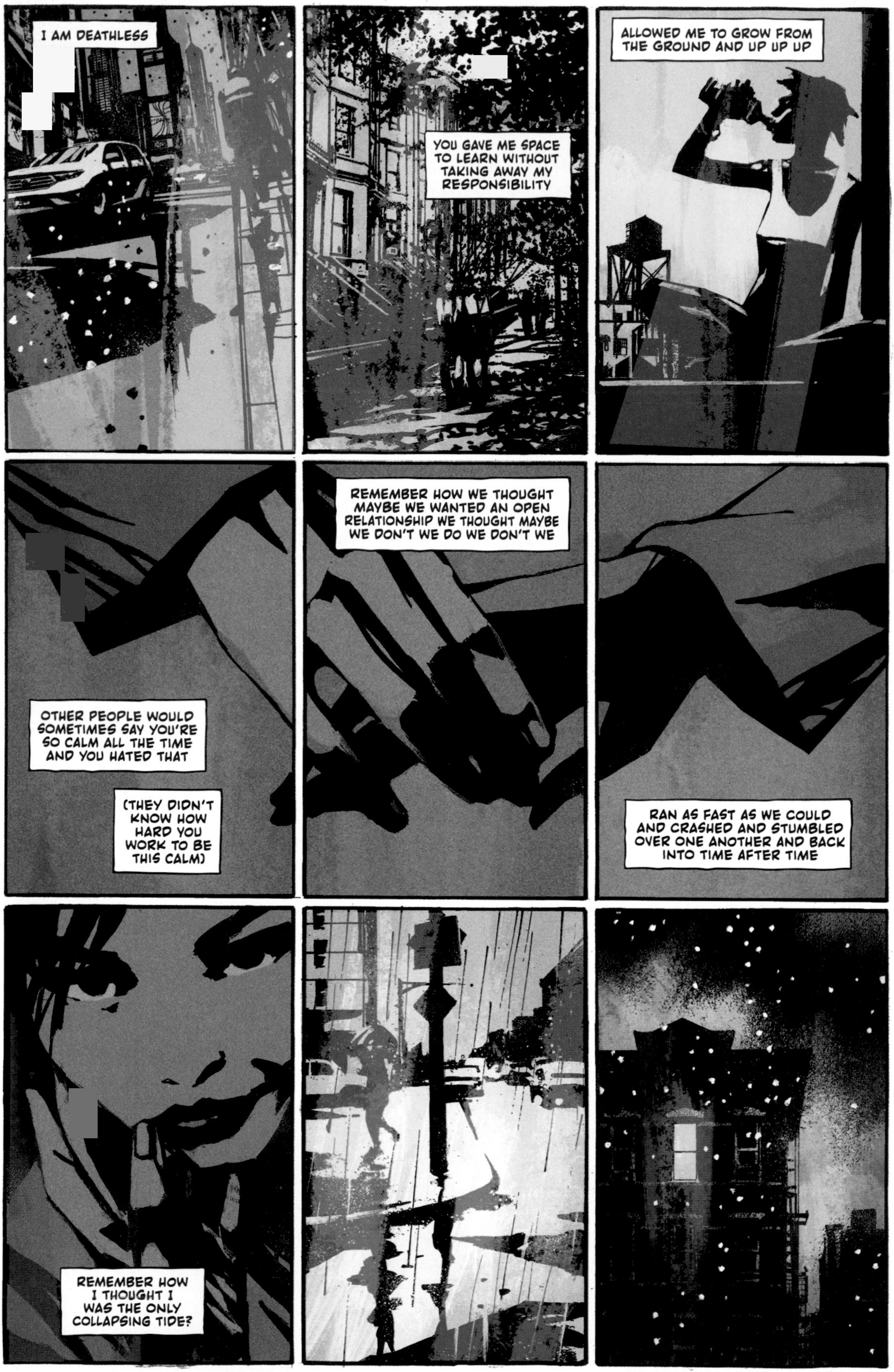
I AM DEATHLESS
YOU GAVE ME SPACE TO LEARN WITHOUT TAKING AWAY MY RESPONSIBILITY
ALLOWED ME TO GROW FROM THE GROUND AND UP UP UP
OTHER PEOPLE WOULD SOMETIMES SAY YOU'RE SO CALM ALL THE TIME AND YOU HATED THAT
(THEY DIDN'T KNOW HOW HARD YOU WORK TO BE THIS CALM)
REMEMBER HOW WE THOUGHT MAYBE WE WANTED AN OPEN RELATIONSHIP WE THOUGHT MAYBE WE DON'T WE DO WE DON'T WE
RAN AS FAST AS WE COULD AND CRASHED AND STUMBLED OVER ONE ANOTHER AND BACK INTO TIME AFTER TIME
REMEMBER HOW I THOUGHT I WAS THE ONLY COLLAPSING TIDE?

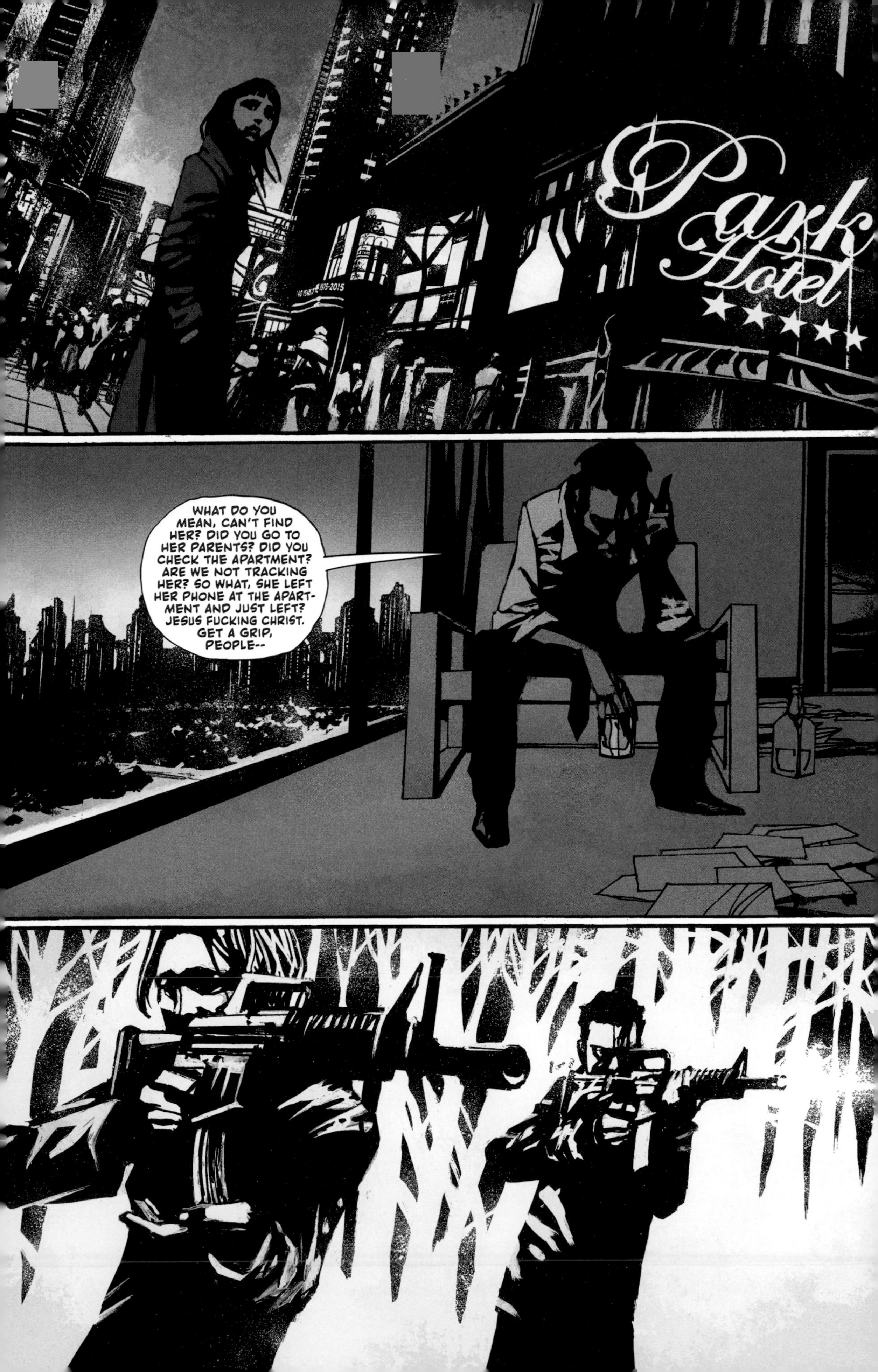
Park Hotel
WHAT DO YOU MEAN, CAN'T FIND HER? DID YOU GO TO HER PARENTS? DID YOU CHECK THE APARTMENT? ARE WE NOT TRACKING HER? SO WHAT, SHE LEFT HER PHONE AT THE APART-MENT AND JUST LEFT? JESUS FUCKING CHRIST. GET A GRIP, PEOPLE--

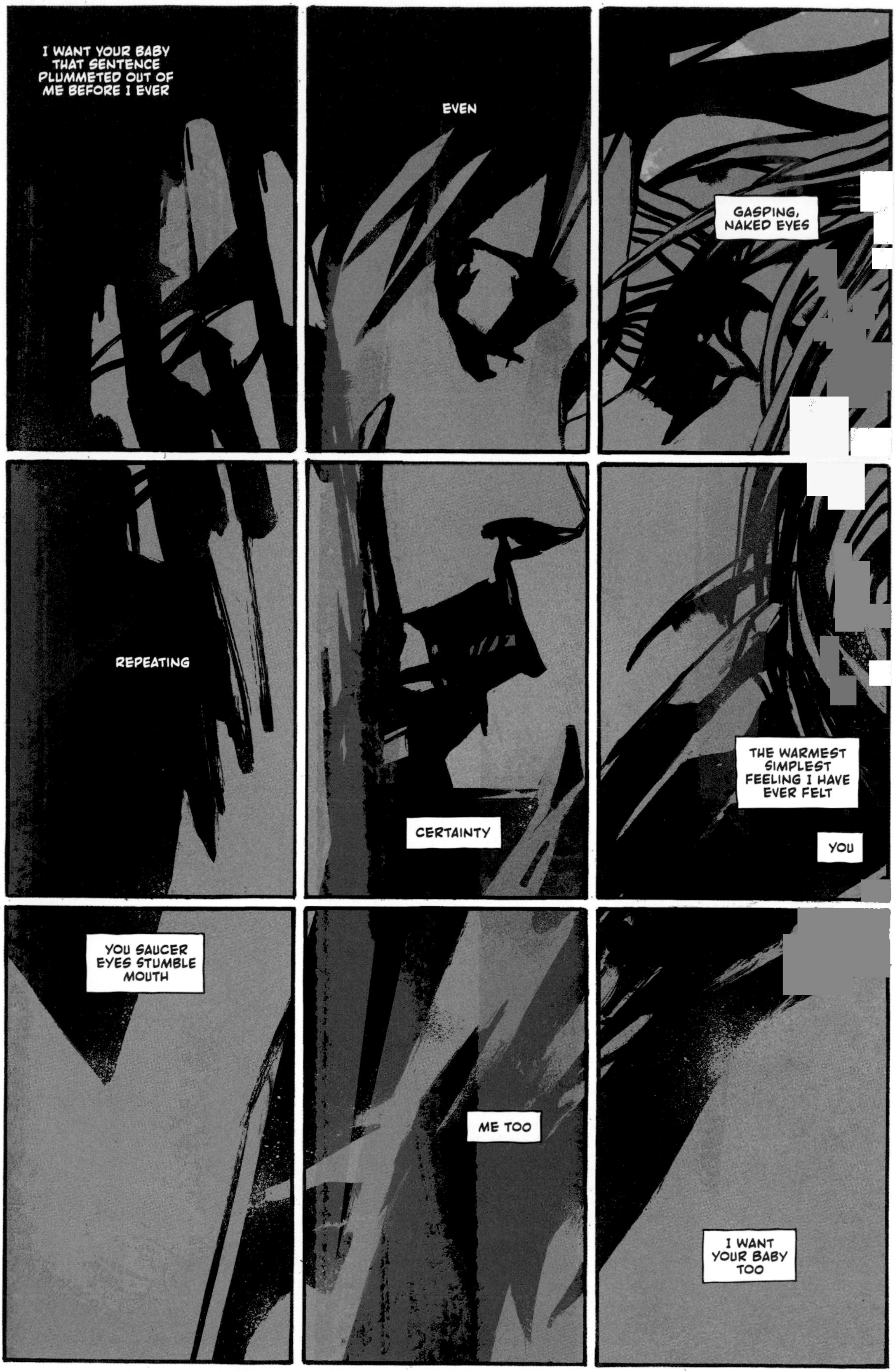

I WANT YOUR BABY THAT SENTENCE PLUMMETED OUT OF ME BEFORE I EVER
EVEN
GASPING, NAKED EYES
REPEATING
CERTAINTY
THE WARMEST SIMPLEST FEELING I HAVE EVER FELT
YOU
YOU SAUCER EYES STUMBLE MOUTH
ME TOO
I WANT YOUR BABY TOO

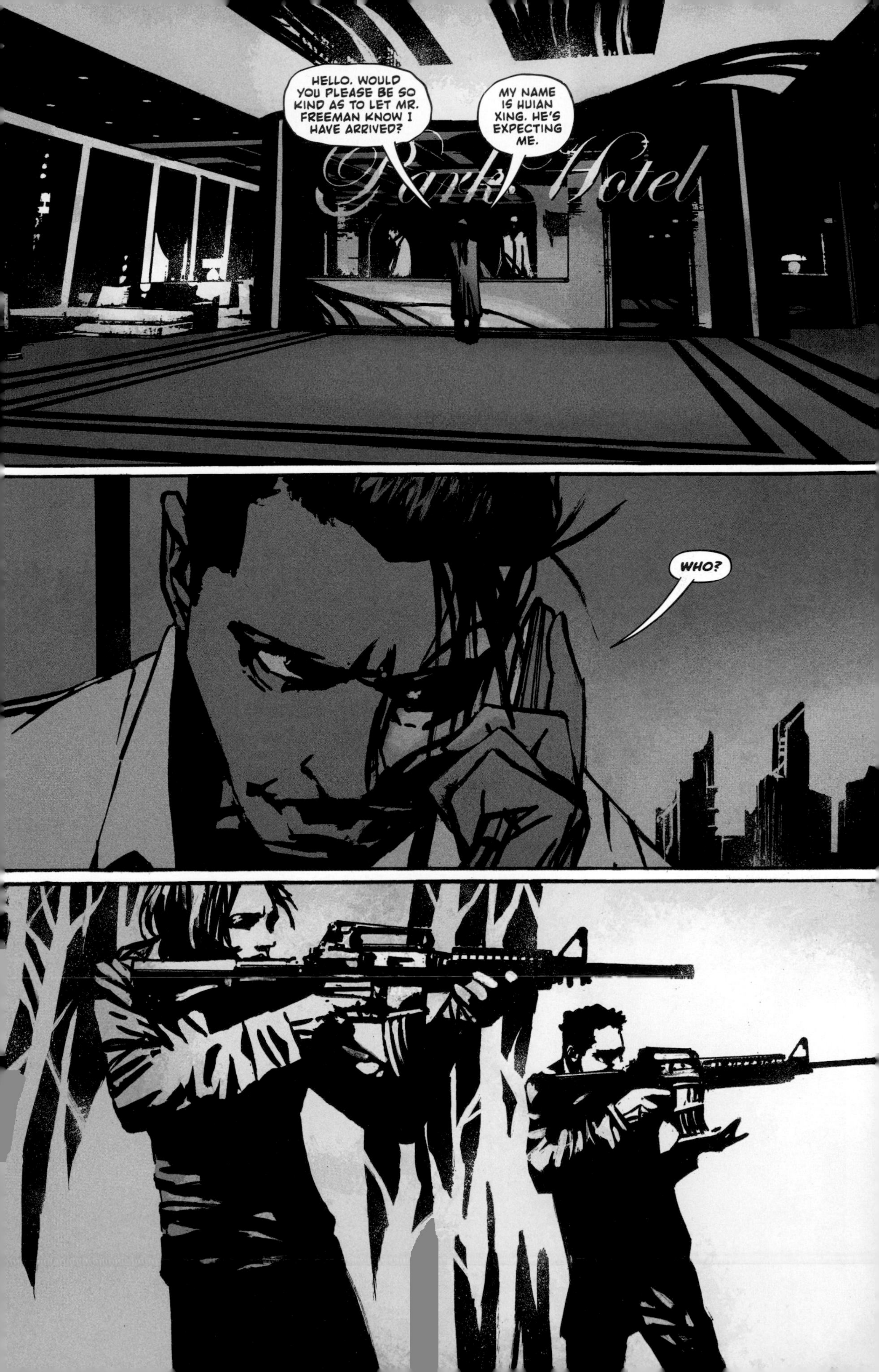
HELLO. WOULD YOU PLEASE BE SO KIND AS TO LET MR. FREEMAN KNOW I HAVE ARRIVED?
MY NAME IS HUIAN XING. HE'S EXPECTING ME.
Park Hotel
WHO?

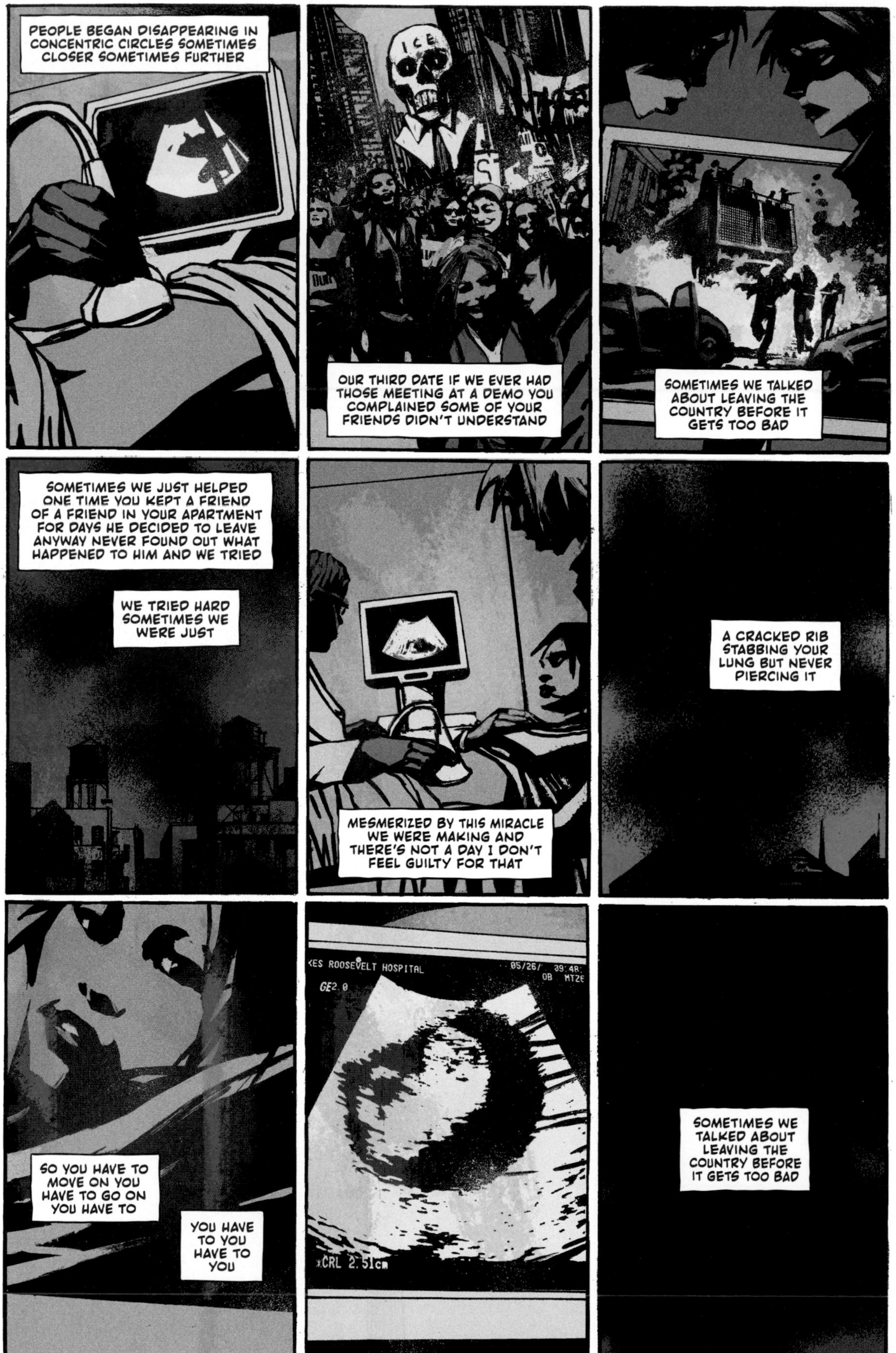
PEOPLE BEGAN DISAPPEARING IN CONCENTRIC CIRCLES SOMETIMES CLOSER SOMETIMES FURTHER
ICE
OUR THIRD DATE IF WE EVER HAD THOSE MEETING AT A DEMO YOU COMPLAINED SOME OF YOUR FRIENDS DIDN'T UNDERSTAND
SOMETIMES WE TALKED ABOUT LEAVING THE COUNTRY BEFORE IT GETS TOO BAD
SOMETIMES WE JUST HELPED ONE TIME YOU KEPT A FRIEND OF A FRIEND IN YOUR APARTMENT FOR DAYS HE DECIDED TO LEAVE ANYWAY NEVER FOUND OUT WHAT HAPPENED TO HIM AND WE TRIED
WE TRIED HARD SOMETIMES WE WERE JUST
MESMERIZED BY THIS MIRACLE WE WERE MAKING AND THERE'S NOT A DAY I DON'T FEEL GUILTY FOR THAT
A CRACKED RIB STABBING YOUR LUNG BUT NEVER PIERCING IT
SO YOU HAVE TO MOVE ON YOU HAVE TO GO ON YOU HAVE TO
YOU HAVE TO YOU HAVE TO YOU
KES ROOSEVELT HOSPITAL
05/26/ 39:4R:
OB MT26
GE2.0
CRL 2.51cm
SOMETIMES WE TALKED ABOUT LEAVING THE COUNTRY BEFORE IT GETS TOO BAD

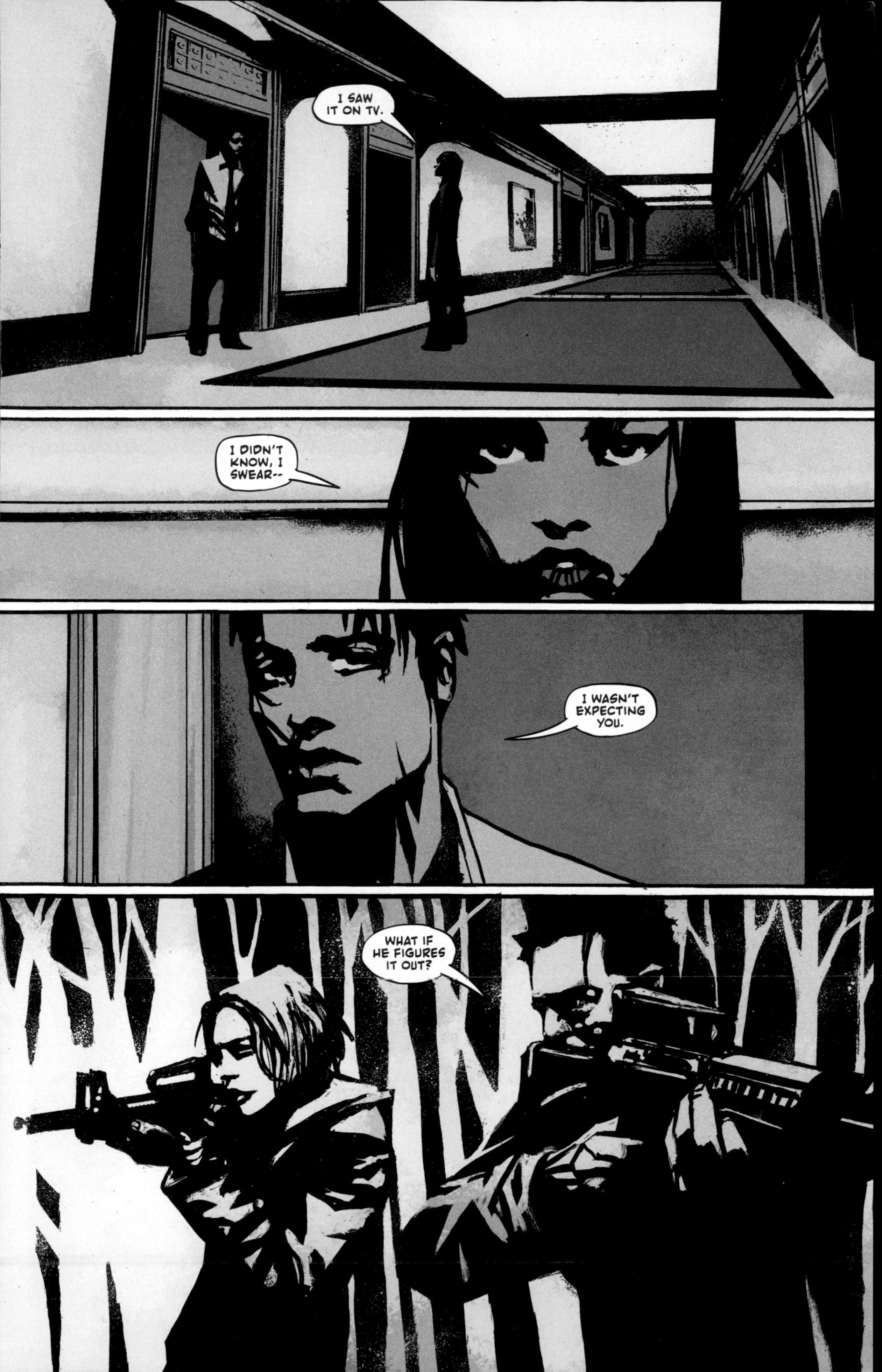

I SAW IT ON TV.
I DIDN'T KNOW, I SWEAR--
I WASN'T EXPECTING YOU.
WHAT IF HE FIGURES IT OUT?

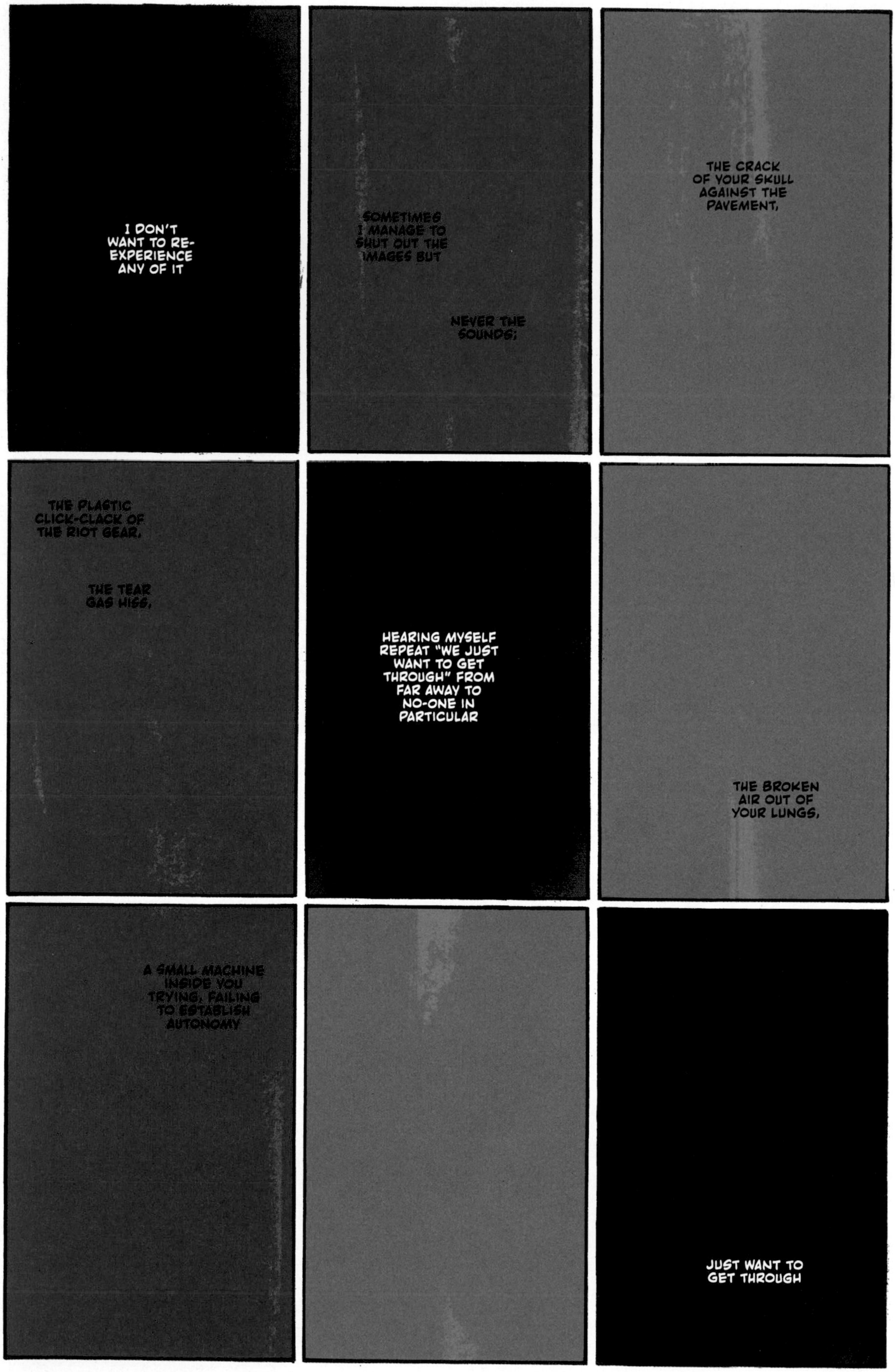
I DON'T WANT TO RE-EXPERIENCE ANY OF IT
SOMETIMES I MANAGE TO SHUT OUT THE IMAGES BUT
NEVER THE SOUNDS;
THE CRACK OF YOUR SKULL AGAINST THE PAVEMENT,
THE PLASTIC CLICK-CLACK OF THE RIOT GEAR,
THE TEAR GAS HISS,
HEARING MYSELF REPEAT "WE JUST WANT TO GET THROUGH" FROM FAR AWAY TO NO-ONE IN PARTICULAR
THE BROKEN AIR OUT OF YOUR LUNGS,
A SMALL MACHINE INSIDE YOU TRYING, FAILING TO ESTABLISH AUTONOMY
JUST WANT TO GET THROUGH

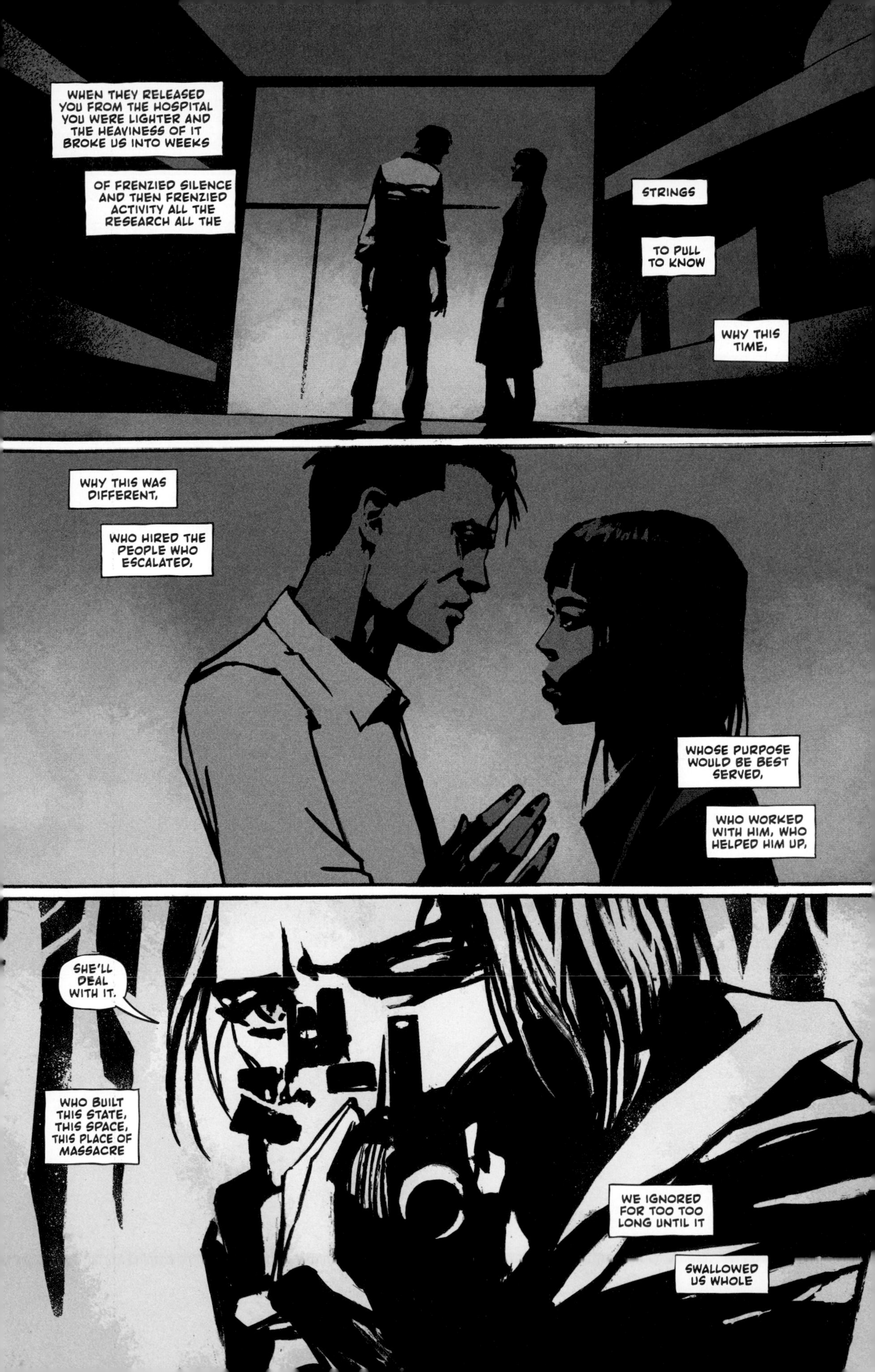

WHEN THEY RELEASED YOU FROM THE HOSPITAL YOU WERE LIGHTER AND THE HEAVINESS OF IT BROKE US INTO WEEKS
OF FRENZIED SILENCE AND THEN FRENZIED ACTIVITY ALL THE RESEARCH ALL THE
STRINGS
TO PULL TO KNOW
WHY THIS TIME,
WHY THIS WAS DIFFERENT,
WHO HIRED THE PEOPLE WHO ESCALATED,
WHOSE PURPOSE WOULD BE BEST SERVED,
WHO WORKED WITH HIM, WHO HELPED HIM UP,
SHE'LL DEAL WITH IT.
WHO BUILT THIS STATE, THIS SPACE, THIS PLACE OF MASSACRE
WE IGNORED FOR TOO TOO LONG UNTIL IT
SWALLOWED US WHOLE

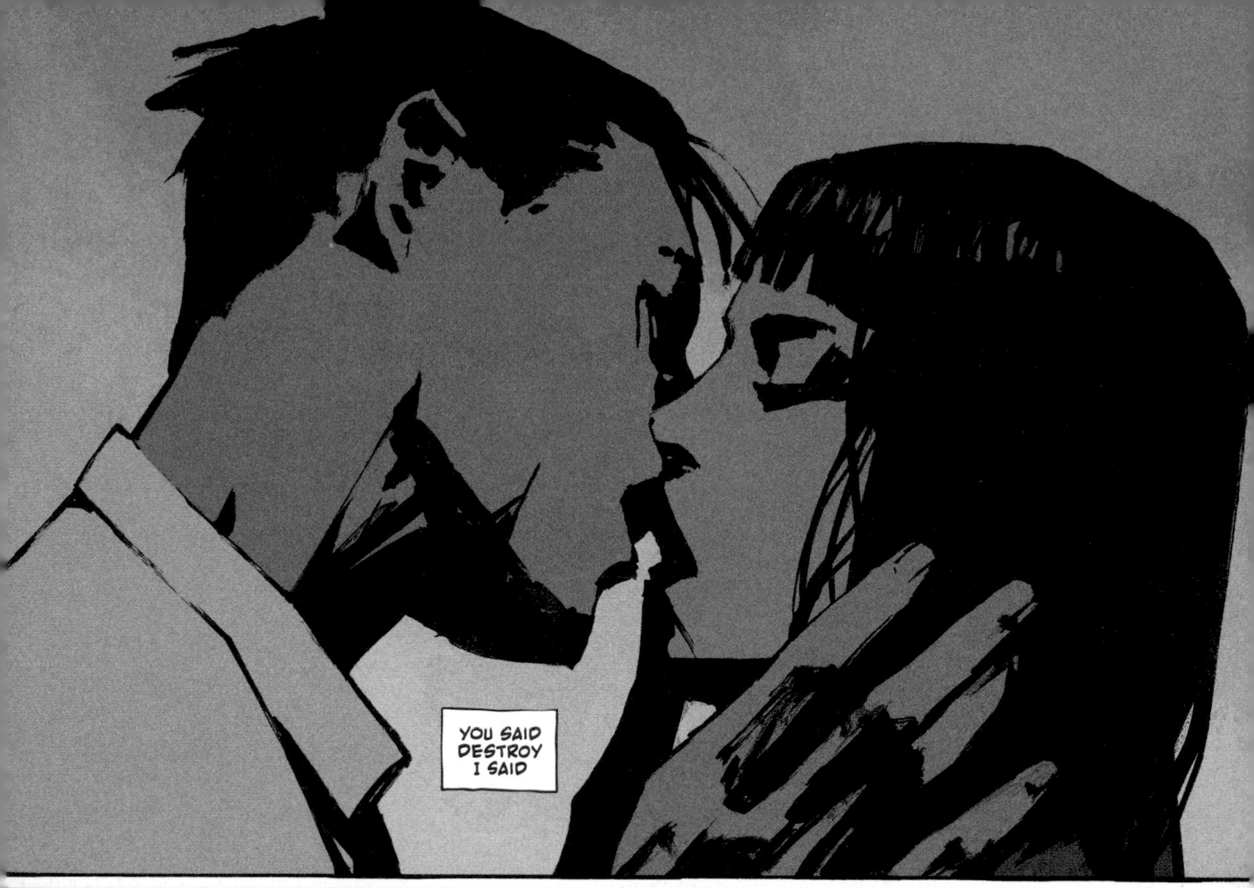
YOU SAID DESTROY I SAID

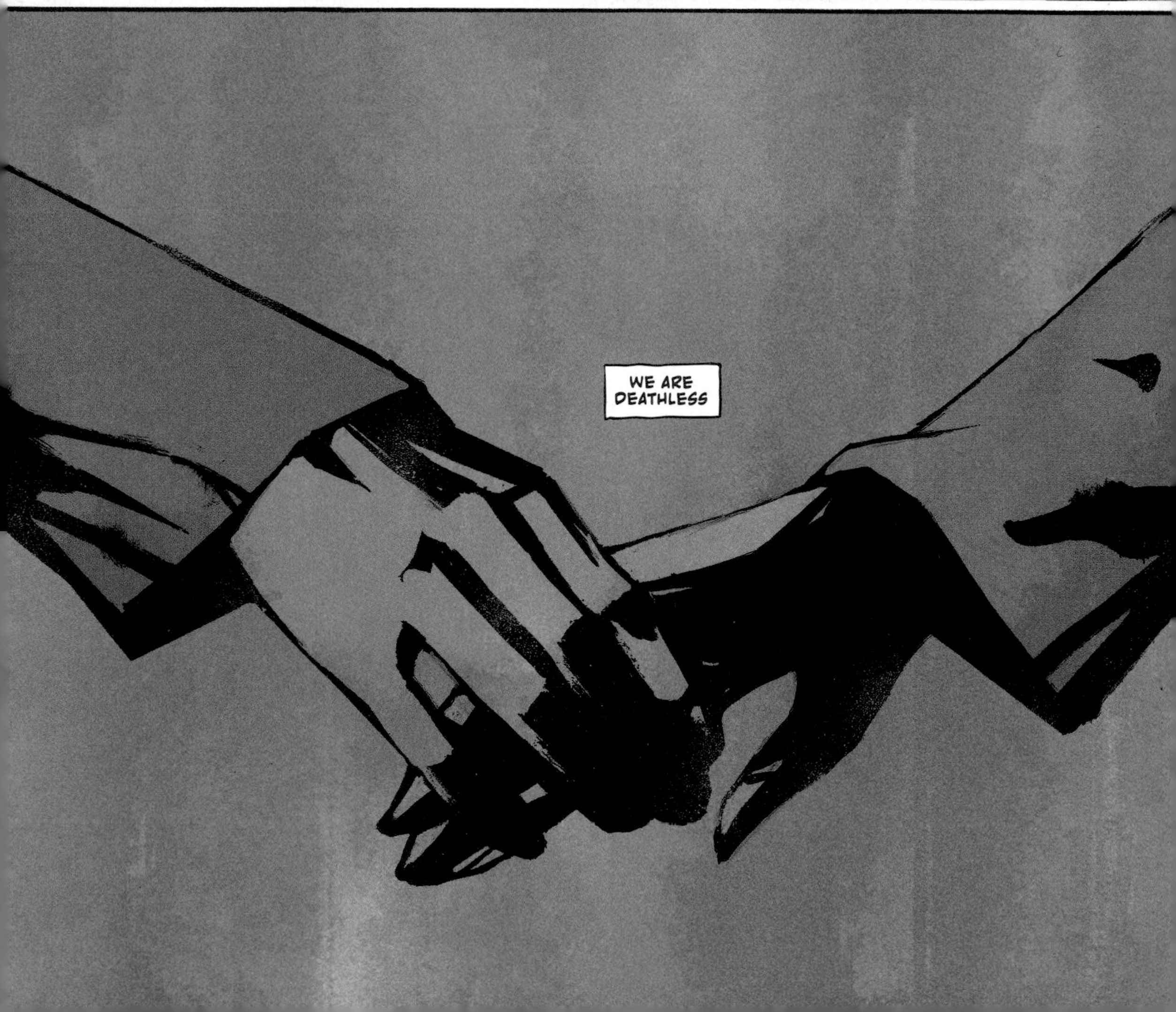
WE ARE DEATHLESS

END OF ACT ONE.

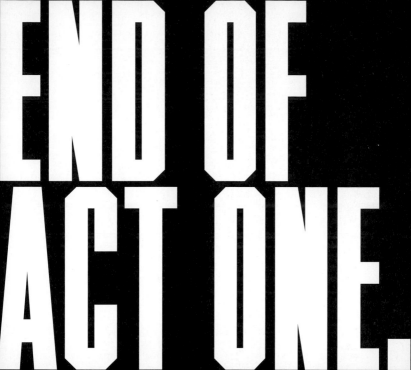

COVER GALLERY

The original cover art for Days of Hate #1–6 by series artist by Danijel Žeželj with cover design by Tom Muller.

DAYS OF HATE #1

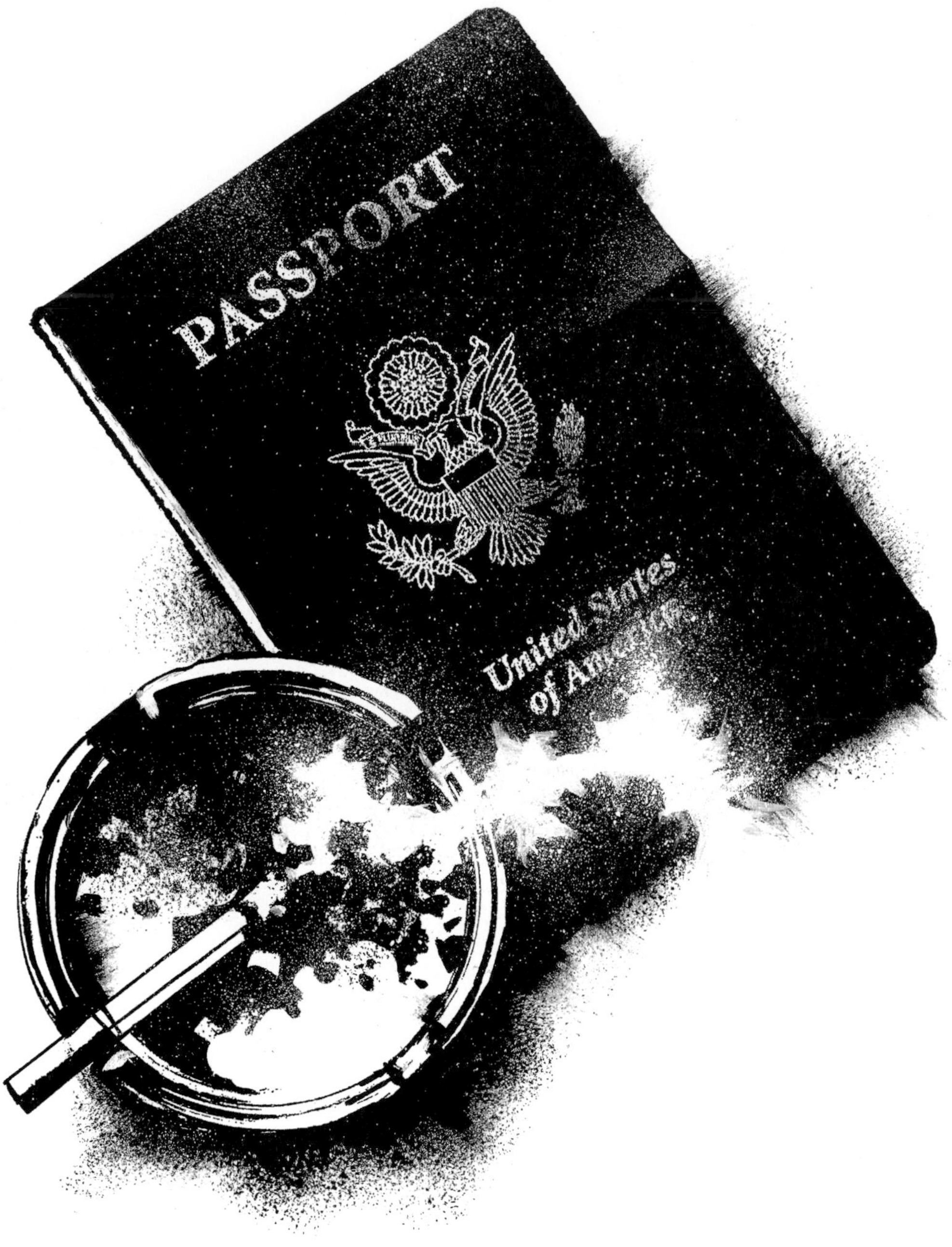
PASSPORT
United States
of America

DAYS OF HATE #2

DAYS OF HATE #3

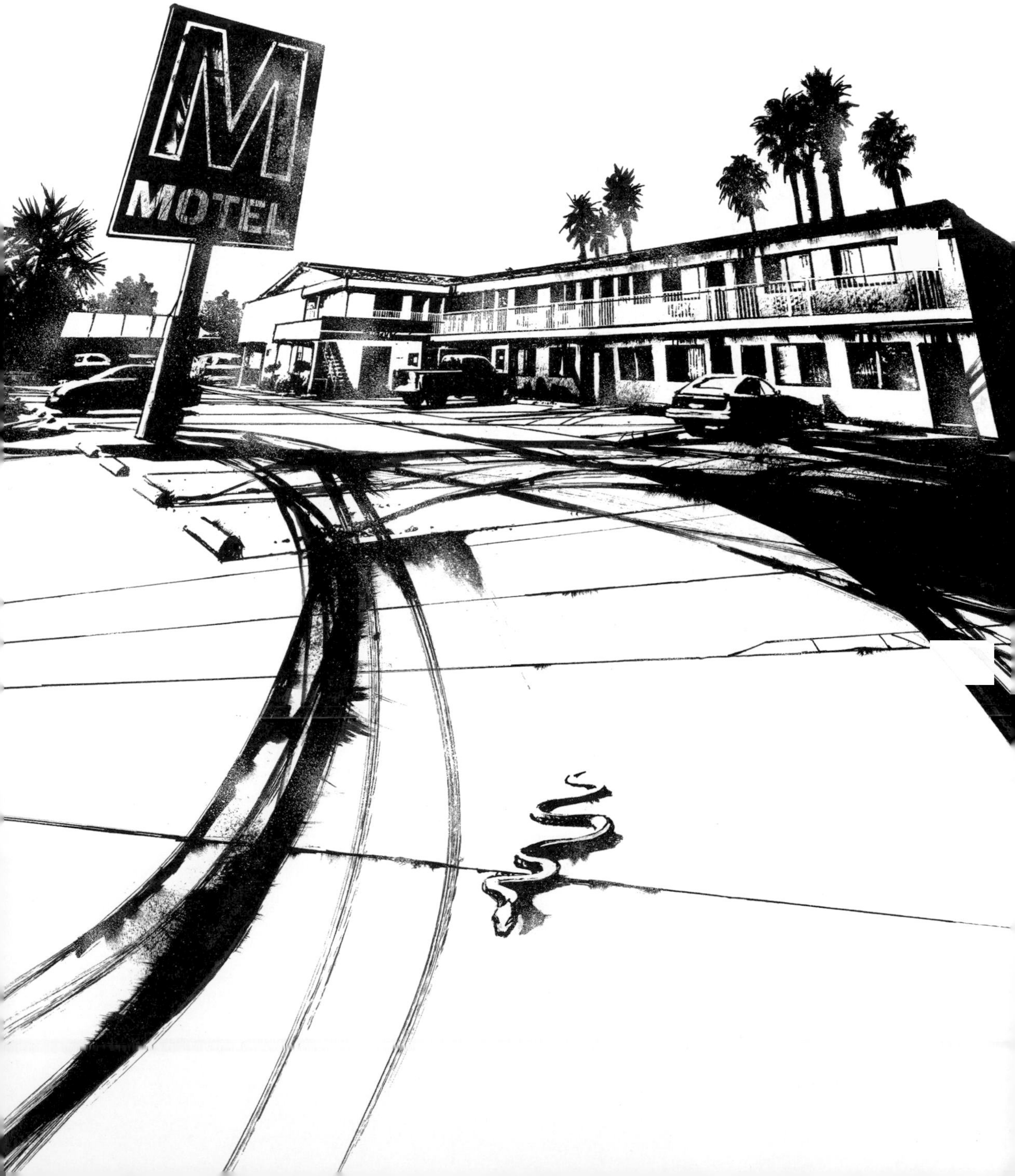
M
MOTEL

DAYS OF HATE #4

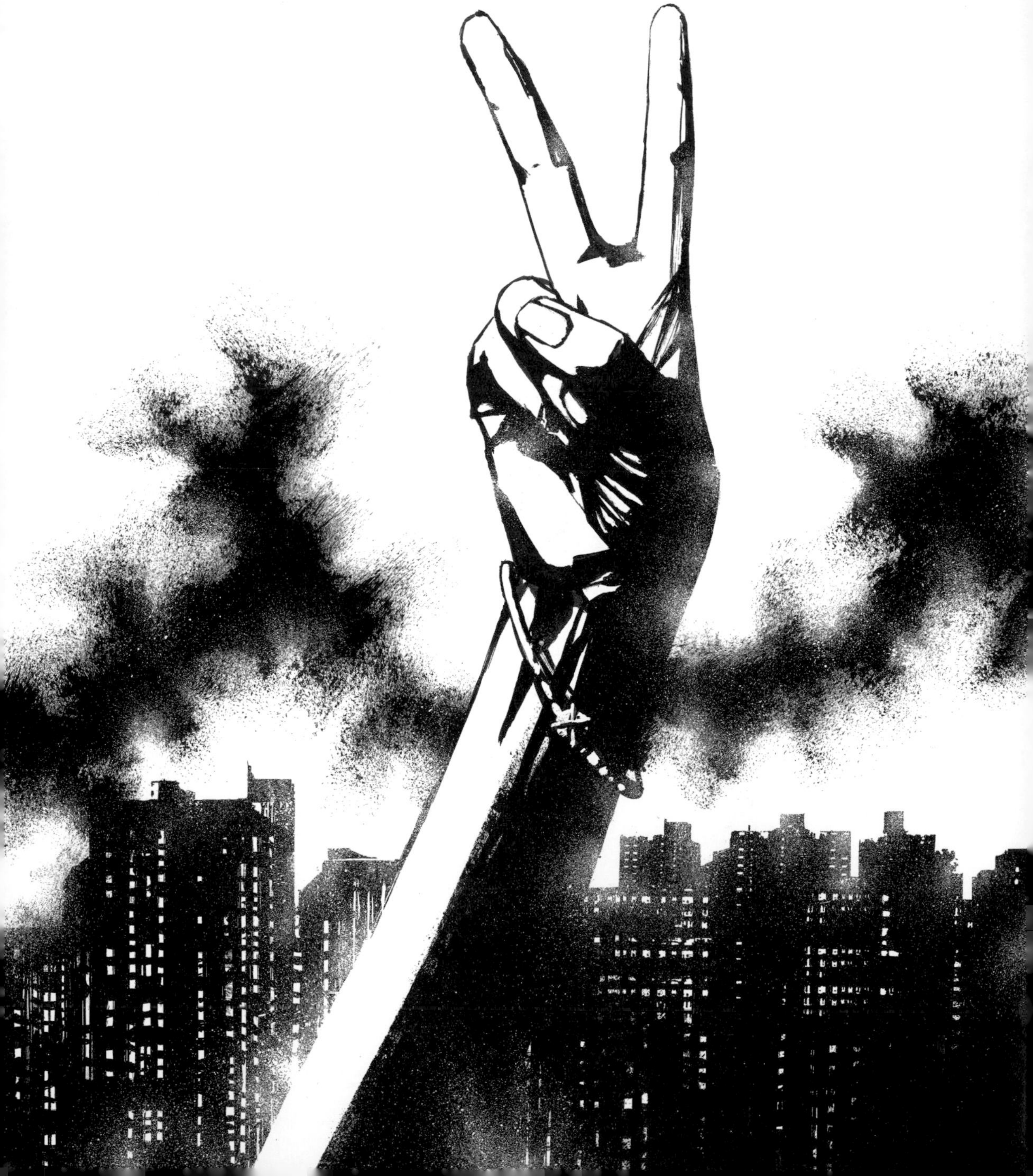

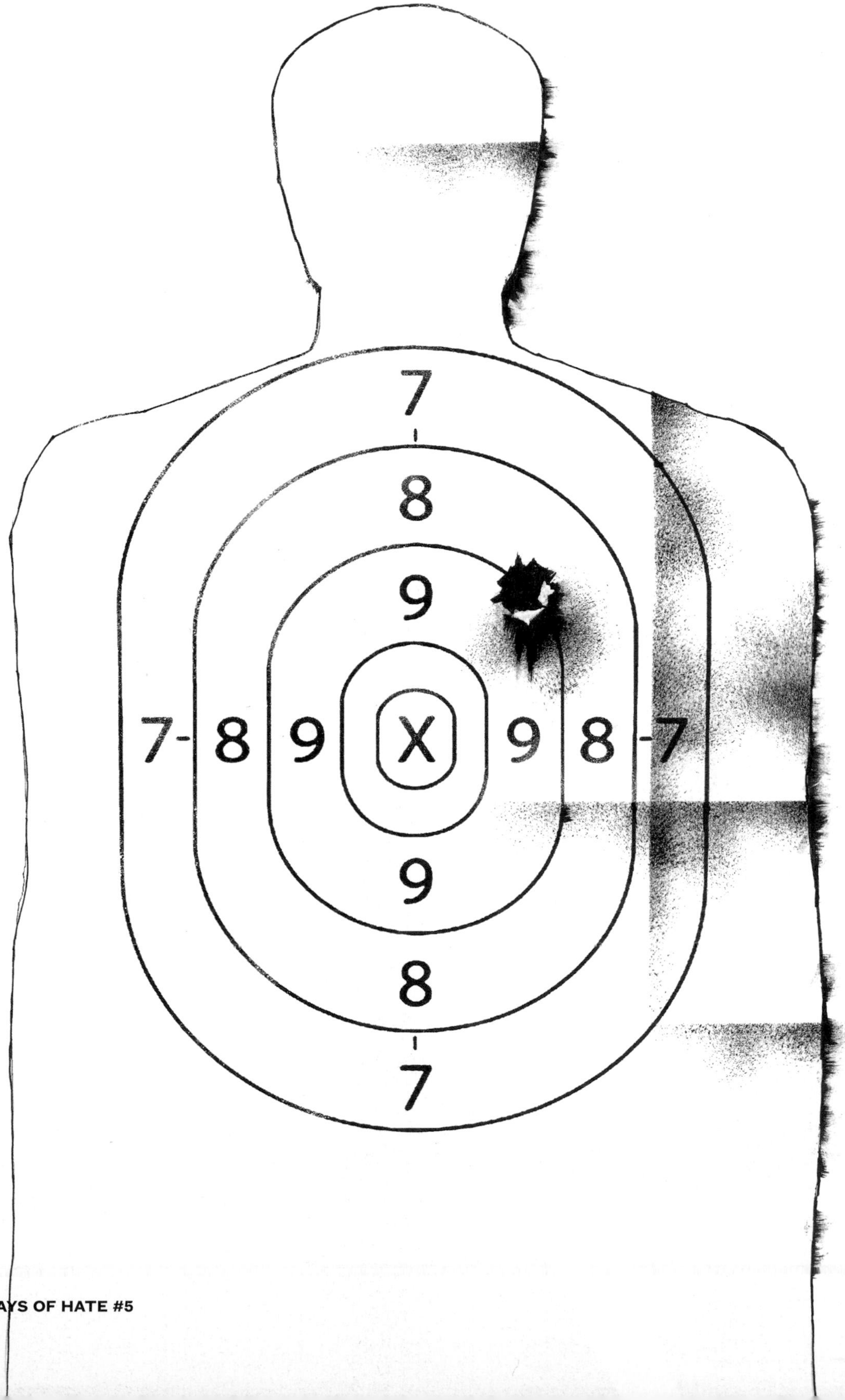
7
8
9
7 8 9 X 9 8 7
9
8
7

DAYS OF HATE #5

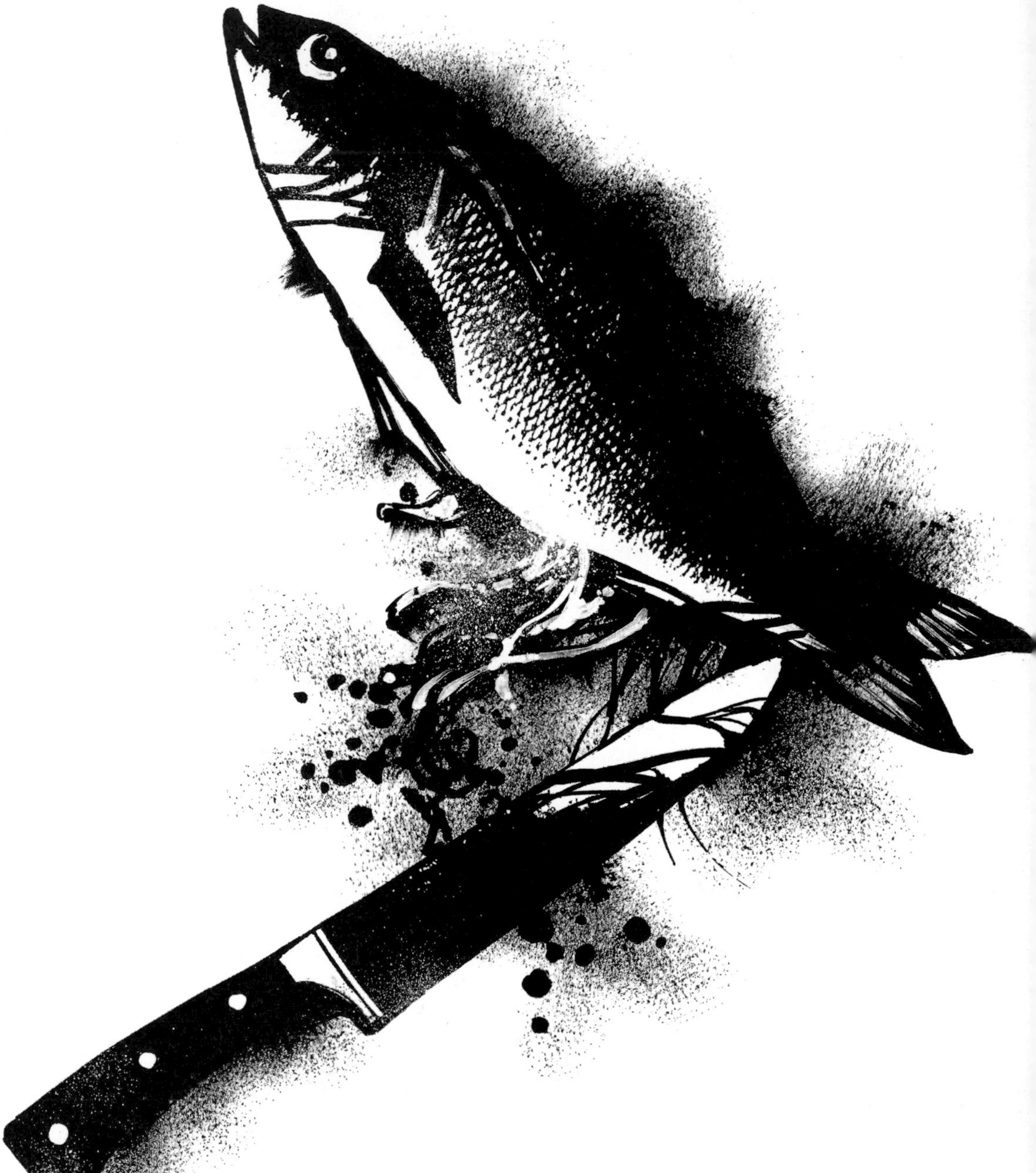

DAYS OF HATE #6

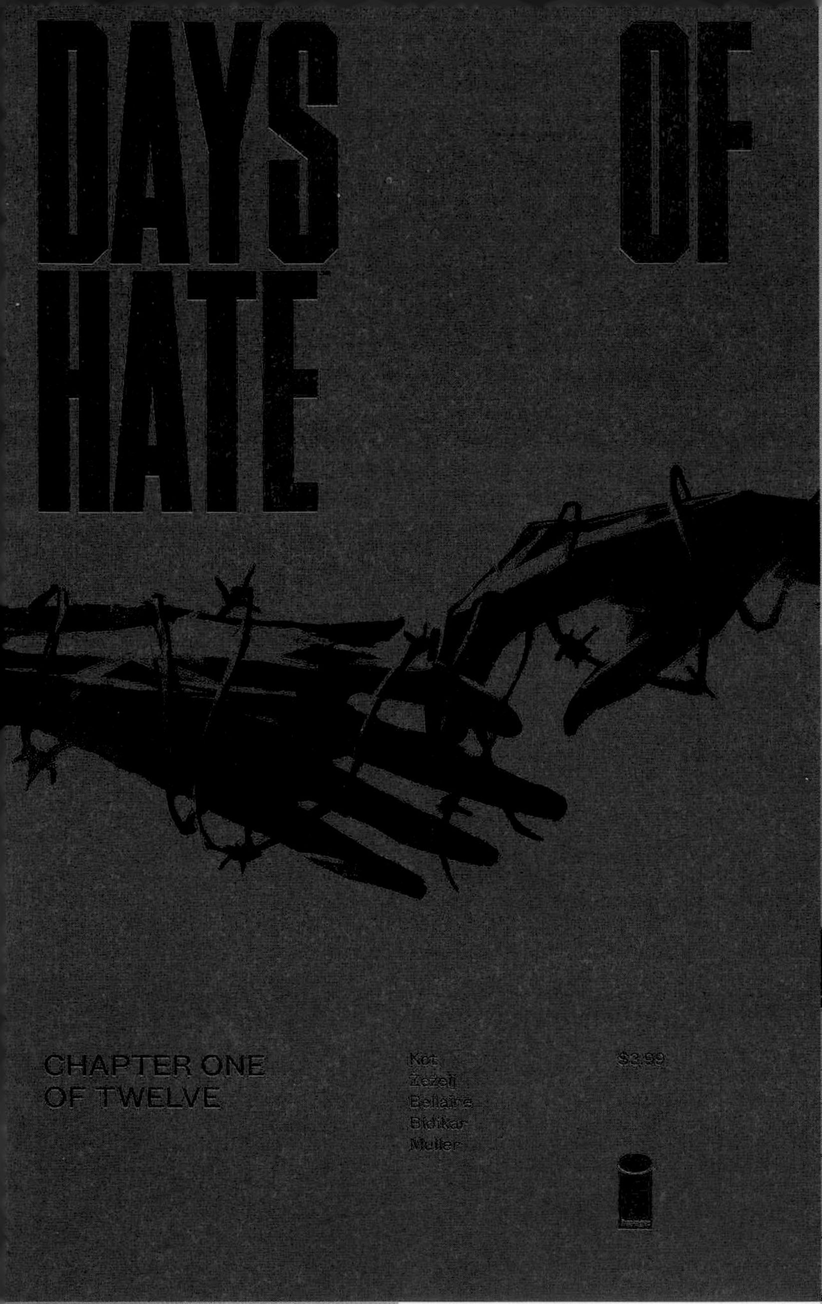
DAYS OF HATE
CHAPTER ONE OF TWELVE
Kot
Žeželj
Bellaire
Bidikar
Muller
$3.99

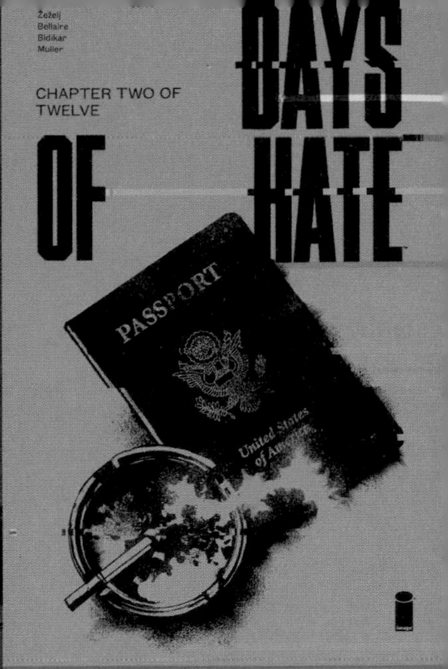
Žeželj
Bellaire
Bidikar
Muller
CHAPTER TWO OF TWELVE
DAYS OF HATE
PASSPORT
United States of America

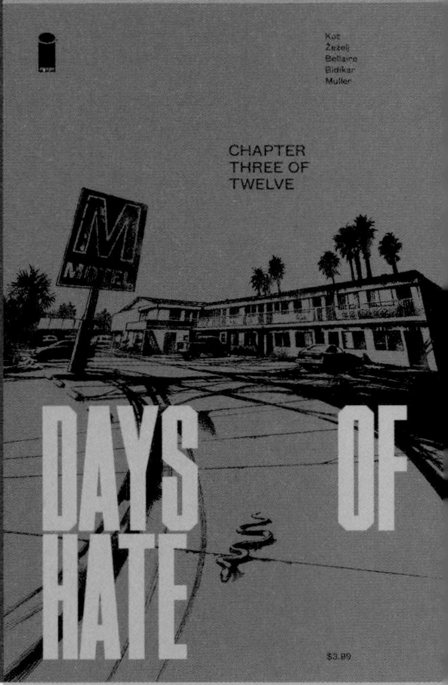
Kot
Žeželj
Bellaire
Bidikar
Muller
CHAPTER THREE OF TWELVE
DAYS OF HATE
$3.99

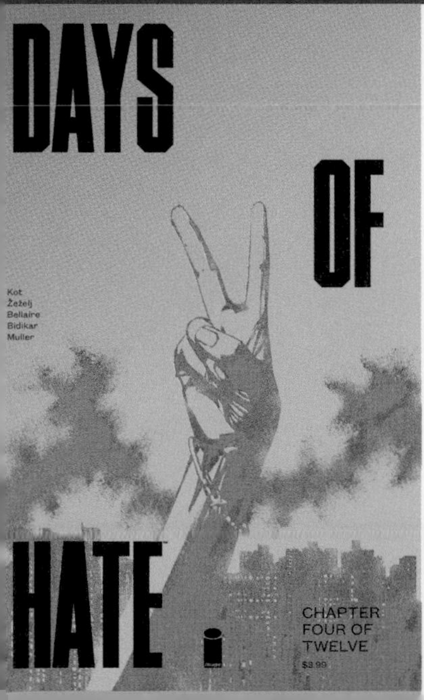
DAYS OF HATE
Kot
Žeželj
Bellaire
Bidikar
Muller
CHAPTER FOUR OF TWELVE
$3.99

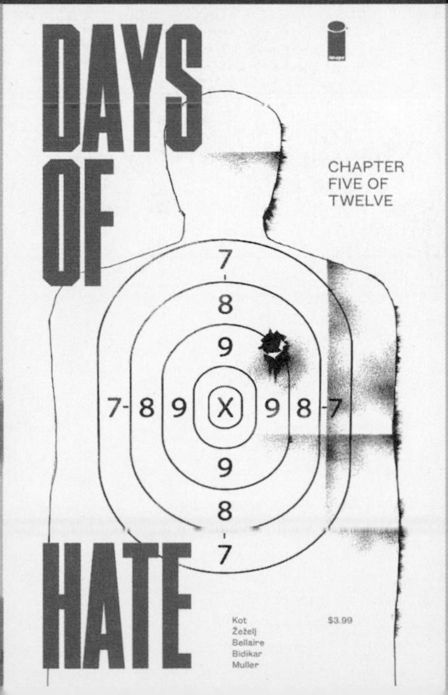
DAYS OF HATE
CHAPTER FIVE OF TWELVE
Kot
Žeželj
Bellaire
Bidikar
Muller
$3.99

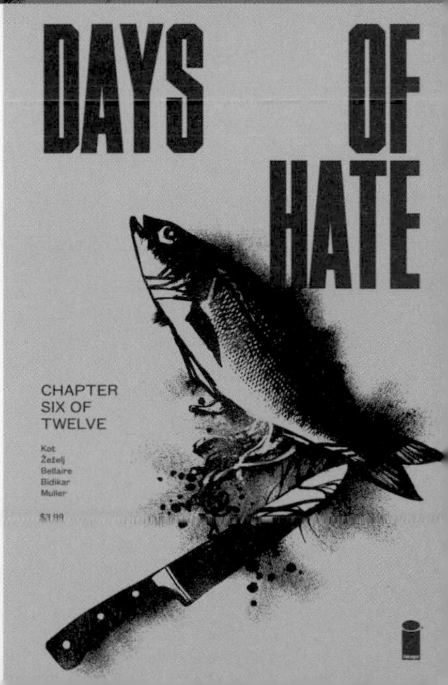
DAYS OF HATE
CHAPTER SIX OF TWELVE
Kot
Žeželj
Bellaire
Bidikar
Muller
$3.99

RECOMMENDED MEDIA:

Sara Nović
GIRL AT WAR

Manic Street Preachers
THE HOLY BIBLE

James Baldwin
NOBODY KNOWS MY NAME

Bernardo Bertolucci
THE CONFORMIST

Gaspar Noé
IRREVERSIBLE

Ocean Vuong
NIGHT SKY WITH EXIT WOUNDS

Marguerite Duras
DESTROY, SHE SAID

Tanya Hamilton
NIGHT CATCHES US

Paul Virilio
THE ADMINISTRATION OF FEAR

Nelson Mandela
CONVERSATIONS WITH MYSELF

Anne Carson
THE BEAUTY OF THE HUSBAND: A FICTIONAL ESSAY IN 29 TANGOS

Ben Frost
STEEL WOUND

Blonde Redhead
MISERY IS A BUTTERFLY

Jackie Wang
CARCERAL CAPITALISM

Asghar Farhadi
A SEPARATION

DAYS OF HATE, Act One.
First printing. July/2018.

Published by Image Comics, Inc.

Office of publication: 2701 NW Vaughn St., Suite 780, Portland, OR 97210. Copyright © 2018 Ales Kot & Danijel Žeželj. All rights reserved. Contains material originally published in single magazine form as DAYS OF HATE #1-6. "Days of Hate," its logos, and the likenesses of all characters herein are trademarks of Ales Kot & Danijel Žeželj, unless otherwise noted. "Image" and the Image Comics logos are registered trademarks of Image Comics, Inc. No part of this publication may be reproduced or transmitted, in any form or by any means (except for short excerpts for journalistic or review purposes), without the express written permission of Ales Kot & Danijel Žeželj, or Image Comics, Inc. All names, characters, events, and locales in this publication are entirely fictional. Any resemblance to actual persons (living or dead), events, or places, without satiric intent, is coincidental. Printed in the USA. For information regarding the CPSIA on this printed material call: 203-595-3636 and provide reference #RICH-801871. For international rights, contact: foreignlicensing@imagecomics.com. ISBN: 978-1-5343-0697-4.